# DANTE'S POISON

# ALSO BY LYNNE RAIMONDO

*Dante's Wood*

A MARK ANGELOTTI NOVEL

# DANTE'S POISON

## LYNNE RAIMONDO

**SEVENTH STREET BOOKS®**
AN IMPRINT OF PROMETHEUS BOOKS
59 JOHN GLENN DRIVE • AMHERST, NY 14228
www.seventhstreetbooks.com

Published 2014 by Seventh Street Books®, an imprint of Prometheus Books

Cover image of pills © Opticopia/Media Bakery
Cover image of buildings © Chuck Eckert/Media Bakery
Cover design by Jacqueline Nasso Cooke

Inquiries should be addressed to
Seventh Street Books
59 John Glenn Drive
Amherst, New York 14228
VOICE: 716–691–0133 • FAX: 716–691–0137
WWW.SEVENTHSTREETBOOKS.COM

18 17 16 15 14 • 5 4 3 2 1

Library of Congress Cataloging-in-Publication Data

Raimondo, Lynne, 1957–
    Dante's poison : a Mark Angelotti novel / by Lynne Raimondo.
        pages cm
    ISBN 978-1-61614-879-9 (pbk.)
    ISBN 978-1-61614-880-5 (ebook)
    1. Psychiatrists—Fiction. 2. Blind medical personnel—Fiction. 3. Chicago
(Ill.)—Fiction. 4. Psychological fiction. I. Title.

PS3618.A387D36 2014
813'.6—dc23

2013045364

Printed in the United States of America

*For Louise and Sandy*

*With apologies to Dorothy Sayers*

*"Tant' eran li occhi miei fissi e attenti
a disbramarsi la decenne sete,
che li altri sensi m'eran tutti spenti."*

(My eyes were fixed and so intent
to satisfy ten years of thirst,
that all my other senses were undone.)

—Dante Alighieri, *Purgatorio* XXXII
(Translated by Robert Hollander and Jean Hollander,
Doubleday, 2000)

# ONE

Melissa Singh was good at her job. In my dealings with her so far she had proved both mercilessly inquisitive and a shade less friendly than a Rottweiler. The interview was now in its second hour, and I was feeling the strain. Once I would have given my right testicle for this opportunity. Now I was having second thoughts.

"When did you first notice the symptoms?"

"Two years ago. In the fall."

"Date?"

It wasn't one I was likely to forget. "September sixth."

Melissa spoke in the clipped, efficient tones of a BBC newscaster, without a hint of her native Hindi. I figured she'd lost the accent while doing her postdoc at Cambridge. Nurse Ratched didn't square with the surname, so I'd conjured up something more Bollywood. Dark hair, kohl-lined eyes, combat boots peeking out from under her sari. Either way, I was sure she was scowling at me.

"Time?"

"In the morning, when I woke up."

She took this down, tapping rapidly on a tablet. "What were you seeing then?"

"When I looked out my left eye, there was a blurred area in the center. A scotoma, to use the technical term."

"And you'd never had a problem like it before?"

"Never."

"Yet you didn't seek help immediately."

"It didn't seem all that serious at first."

"Really?" Melissa said. I imagined an arched eyebrow and pursed, plum-colored lips. "What happened to make you change your mind?"

"Later, that evening I, uh . . . almost got into a traffic accident."

"Yes. It says in your application that you didn't notice a traffic light turning red."

"That's right."

"So that was your first red flag."

"Well, to be accurate, at the time I thought it was green."

She didn't seem to find this funny. "So the next day you went to see Dr. Turner."

I nodded and took a sip of water from the paper cup to my right. I'd been through this routine before, but always on Melissa's side of the table. I was starting to understand what it felt like to be a laboratory rat— except that rats didn't have to cough up their entire life stories. The night before, I'd listened once more to the information packet Melissa had sent me in the mail. The number of cheerily dispensed lies was breathtaking. *Before being accepted into the study, you will be asked a number of questions. These questions are not meant to intrude upon your privacy.* It depended on how you defined privacy. *Their purpose is to provide you with the information you need to make an informed choice.* Anyone who believed that should invest all their money in savings bonds.

"Doctor, are you listening?" Melissa asked impatiently.

I snapped back to attention. "Sorry. I was just remembering something I have to do today. Back at the office."

The hint was wasted on her. "I was asking about your vision at that point," she said.

"The right eye was still fine. The left was almost completely clouded over."

"Color?"

"Virtually none."

"That's an unusually rapid progression," Melissa observed.

Turner, my neuro-ophthalmologist, had thought so too. He'd acted like he couldn't wait to write me up in a journal article: "An Atypical Late Onset Case of Leber's Hereditary Optic Neuropathy (LHON)" featuring lurid color slides and a menu of nonexistent treatment options.

"All right then," Melissa continued. "It says here that Dr. Turner administered blood tests. Do you recall the results?"

"They revealed a homoplastic DNA mutation at G11778." In other words, a defective gene I'd inherited from my mother, one of several associated with a sudden shutdown of the nerves that channel information from the eye to the brain. When it strikes, which isn't always, it tends to afflict males in their twenties, though I had managed to pull off the feat at the ripe old age of forty-six.

"Did you question that finding?" Melissa asked.

"No, is there any reason I should have?"

"Only that when I spoke to him Dr. Turner thought you reacted rather strangely. According to him, you exhibited 'unnatural calm' upon hearing the results."

"I was in shock." That was true to a degree. I probably would have fainted dead away if I hadn't been busy concocting my own differential diagnosis, which assuredly did not include living out the rest of my days like Long John Silver's crewmate in *Treasure Island*.

"What did you do then?"

"I went home. To rest."

In fact, I'd gone straight to my usual watering hole, the Lucky Leprechaun, and gotten blind drunk, a warm-up I was to repeat many times over the following weeks. Luckily, the barkeep knew me well enough to sound the alarm, and my colleague, Josh Goldman, had come to collect me before I succeeded in passing out.

"Did you tell anyone about the diagnosis?"

"A friend." After I'd puked all over the interior of his new BMW 3 Series, it seemed only fair to let Josh in on the breaking story. It was the only time I'd seen him genuinely depressed.

"Is that all?"

"Well, naturally, my boss. I didn't think I'd be able to work for a while." Septimus Brennan, my department head, had listened unhappily but with the brass-tacks efficiency of a shrink in his fifth decade of practice. He wanted to hook me up immediately with a dozen specialists, but except for the obligatory second opinion, I turned down all of his proffered interventions. Too risky.

"No family members?" Melissa pressed.

"None that I'm close enough to," I said, fingers crossed.

It apparently worked. "Tell me about what was going on in your life immediately before," Melissa asked. "Were you eating and sleeping normally?"

"As normally as anyone in our line of work."

"Did you smoke?"

I shook my head.

"Drink?"

"I consider myself a social drinker."

"Were you under any stress at home or at work?"

*Remember that withholding facts from the research team can skew study results.* "Not really."

"And the next event occurred when exactly?"

"About a month later." Twenty-one days, four hours, and fifty-seven minutes later, if she really needed to know.

"What did you do in the interim?"

*What did I do?* Good question. When I wasn't drowning myself in bourbon or trashing my small apartment, I made bucket lists—*A Thousand Things to See before You Go Blind*—that I knew were pure fantasy. There were places in the world I'd always meant to travel to, but the majority were in countries where I didn't trust the medical care (despite the fact that they were home to half the residents in my hospital) or my odds of getting home in one piece when—*if*—it happened. Bike trips were out for the same reason. With my luck, the lights would go out just as I was rounding a hairpin turn in the Rockies or in the middle of rush hour on the Golden Gate Bridge. If I were going to commit suicide, I could think of many less painful ways to do it. The Art Institute was only a short walk away, but I wasn't up to viewing bucolic scenes of French country life or catching a glimpse of *The Old Guitarist*. There was only one face that I needed to remember, and I handled his photo until it was ready to fall apart.

On the few days when I could stand to think about my future, I purchased a couple of the "top-ten products for independence" touted by a local blindness organization—a talking clock, a kitchen timer with raised dots, a set of powerful magnifiers (the last being entirely wishful thinking)—that I thought might help me get through the first few weeks. I even ordered a free white cane, though when it came in the mail and I checked it out in front of a mirror, I'd gone weak at the knees and hurriedly shoved it into the back of a closet. With hindsight, there was so much more that I should have done, would curse myself later for not doing, but I was still in the throes of magical thinking. And so, when the day of reckoning finally came, I was about as ready to play in the big leagues as a boy who's just hefted his first Louisville Slugger.

I didn't crack right away. There's a novelty element to losing one of your major senses that for a while had me simply wandering around my apartment, trying on the experience like a bespoke suit and allowing me to think it just might be manageable. The slippage started a few hours later, and by nightfall, I was a flat-out wreck, hugging my knees and weeping in a corner. I'd been on my own for most of my life but *this* . . . I felt like Burgess Meredith venturing out into a postapocalyptic landscape, utterly alone and without even the solace of a good book to keep me company. If it hadn't been for the alternate reality I'd dreamed up in Turner's office, I probably would have ended it there and then.

I didn't tell any of this to Melissa, of course. Instead, I fed her some professional-sounding nonsense about loss and mourning, throwing in enough fabricated detail to make it seem like I was telling the truth. It must have succeeded, because when I was through she said, "I think we can move on now."

I breathed an enormous sigh of relief.

"I have to be frank," she continued in her prickly manner. "When you first contacted me I didn't think you'd be an appropriate candidate. Most of the success we've experienced overseas is with subjects who've only recently been diagnosed. The drug seems to work best as an early intervention, and your case is, well, rather past that."

"I know that," I said, trying not to sound too eager.

"If we include you it will be for two reasons. First, because the affected population is so small. And second, in order to test whether mild improvement is possible even in LHON sufferers who have been blind for several years. You shouldn't expect much, if anything, to come of it."

I nodded. What she was leaving out was that nearly a quarter of the subjects like me achieved enough visual acuity by the end of the trial to read a few letters off an eye chart.

This is as good a place as any to explain that what I'd ended up with, while not as bad as it could have been, was on the low end of the VI spectrum. Depending on my surroundings and the time of day, I could make out bright light and shadow, the fuzzy presence of large objects, and the occasional hint of color—the last primarily from the corner of my right eye, where I retained a sliver of peripheral vision. When forced to offer details, I told people it was like looking at the world through a sheet of wax paper. Under the circumstances, I'd consider it a victory just to be able to see an eye chart.

"And, of course, the study will be double-blind, meaning neither you nor I will know whether you are receiving the drug or a placebo."

"I can live with that," I assured her.

"Can you? For some the stress of not knowing one way or the other takes a heavy toll. And if you're in the placebo group, there could be a huge let-down at the end. I see from your application that you've been consulting a psychiatrist."

"Yes, but not because of anything having to do with this." I gestured at my eyes. "I can live with what I have. I'd just like to have a little more."

"I see." I took this to mean she wasn't convinced, so I poured on the sincerity.

"Listen, Melissa—I mean, Doctor Singh—I know you take your job seriously, and that you're concerned about all aspects of my well-being. I would be too if I were in your boots—I mean, shoes. But I'm well-adjusted to my condition and a psychiatrist besides. I'm sure I'll be able to manage the uncertainty, and if it becomes too much I'll know where to go for help."

"That's comforting," she said, as though I'd just offered her a discount on aluminum siding. "But I still have to be concerned about data loss. The manufacturer is anxious to obtain FDA approval with this trial."

I understood what she was getting at. Withdrawal from a clinical trial—either because of side effects, unpleasant study procedures, or simply because a participant doesn't feel any better—is a major headache for medical researchers. Dropouts produce biased comparisons that can drastically alter the outcome of a study or reduce its statistical significance. I assumed this was the reason for the grilling Melissa had put me through: she was trying to decide whether I had the guts to stick out the program.

"You don't have to worry about me copping out," I said. "I'll be your guinea pig for as long as you want me. If nothing else, I'd feel a responsibility to my fellow LHON sufferers—as you call them—to complete the treatment."

I was beginning to sound like a Boy Scout.

"Very well, then. I'll be meeting with the sponsors later today and should be in a position to tell you soon whether you've been accepted. Given some of the heavyweights lobbying for your inclusion"—I visualized more scowling—"I'm not anticipating a negative response. We'll have to meet again to go over informed consent, but assuming all goes according to schedule"—*shedyule*—"we should be able to commence treatment on the fifteenth."

September 15. Less than one week away.

When I left Melissa's office it was half-past noon and I hadn't eaten all day. I had an hour to spare, so I walked over to a pizza joint on Rush that serves the real stuff, not the Chicago version that comes in soggy three-inch squares and tastes like cheese curds. I was a regular, so as soon as the manager saw me he put in an order for a Margherita and steered me to a table in a corner where I could more easily stow my cane. I loosened my collar and tie, sipped at my water, and felt some of the tension ease out of me.

*I can live with what I have.* It was true up to a point. On a good day I barely gave a thought to what I was missing and had few excuses for feeling sorry for myself. I wasn't in a black hole. I could still see *something*, and my former photographic memory made up for a lot of the boredom that otherwise goes hand in hand with vision loss. Stepping off a curb no longer felt like bungee jumping in the Grand Canyon. Thanks to all the geek brains volunteering to solve my problems, I was more independent than ever. My new smartphone had apps for detecting the value of paper currency, for reading items off a menu, even for telling me when my socks were mismatched. Hell, the way the technology was headed, it wasn't crazy to think that one day I'd be behind a wheel again.

But there were also bad days. Days when I had to ransack my home to find where I'd left my keys, or been hijacked by one of the Good Samaritans lurking at crosswalks, or had to answer one too many dumb questions. ("How do you know when you're awake?") On bad days even the small frustrations—walking into a closed door, knocking over a drink—multiplied until getting out of bed the next morning seemed as pointless as scrubbing the bathroom tiles with a toothbrush or walking back and forth over hot coals. How much of this had to do with blindness, as opposed to all the other things on my plate, I couldn't tell you. But it made the possibility of even a small uptick in my fortunes all the more appealing.

Still, I wasn't naive about my state of mind. Hope is a powerful stimulant, and when the e-mail came announcing the US trial of a new drug that had shown promising results in the Netherlands, I was on the phone before I even reached the end of the subject line. To say I bullied my way into Melissa's study was putting it mildly. I called in every favor I was owed, including a major arm-twisting campaign by my boss, Sep, who played golf with half the hospital directors in the city. He wasn't wholeheartedly in favor, but couldn't say no after getting me involved in a case that had almost cost me my life. My friend Josh was even more downbeat, concerned it would undo all of the progress I'd made over the last year.

"Aren't you going to feel like shit if it doesn't work out?" he'd said to me recently on one of our Sunday forays to Jewel, the supermarket being one of the few places where I capitulated to the advantages of being guided. "You're better these days than I've seen you in a long while. You've got a great kid and an ex who's talking to you again. You have more work than you can handle, especially with all the lawyers knocking at your door. Why take a chance?" He pushed our grocery cart forward.

"You do realize that we're talking about something that might let me see again?"

"Maybe. I read the journal article put out by wooden-shoe people. The results for guys like you weren't so impressive. You want some of these apples? They're on sale for ninety-nine cents a pound."

"Sure," I said, letting him place my hand on the bin. "Anyway, a twenty-three percent success rate sounds pretty damn good to me."

"Here's a bag. Twenty-three percent made it all the way to 20/800. You'd still be taking cabs and wearing headsets at movies."

I selected a few of the fruit that didn't seem worm-eaten and popped them into the plastic. "You're really trying to talk me out of this?"

"I don't know. It's just that I remember what you were like . . . back then. Aren't you just a teensy bit worried about taking it on the chin again? You're going to be under a lot of pressure, not knowing whether the drug's doing any good, never mind whether the pills you're taking are made of sugar. If it were me, I'd be seeing all sorts of things that weren't really there."

Josh moved ahead and I followed along, hanging onto his elbow. "I'm a shrink, remember? I think I'll know it if I start hallucinating. And my expectations aren't that high."

"Forgive the look of skepticism on my face."

"C'mon, Josh. You *know* why I have to do this."

"Louis is not going to love his father any less because he can't read a newspaper."

"Yeah, but maybe he'd prefer somebody he can play ball with when he's older."

"Speaking of which, how'd the last visit go?"

I'd just returned from a weekend on the East Coast, where my son and former wife lived. It was only the third time we'd been together since he was an infant.

"I don't know. Annie's still balking about leaving us alone together. She thinks I'm not going to notice if Louis lets go of my hand and runs out into traffic. That's another reason I have to try. Maybe a change, even if it's a small one, would help win her over."

Josh couldn't argue with this and let the subject drop for the duration of the shopping trip. But I could tell he wasn't finished and had been going out of my way to avoid him ever since.

I was still thinking about our conversation when my phone played the first few bars of *The Letter*—the Box Tops version, not that I have anything against Joe Cocker—signaling an incoming text. I fished it out of the holder on my belt, slipped on my Bluetooth, and ran my finger over the glass until Weary—my nickname for the factory-supplied voiceover—chirped "Messages." I double-tapped the icon to open the program. It was Hallie Sanchez, reminding me I'd agreed to accompany her to the theater that night.

"Pick up your office 5?" it said.

I turned on the latest bit of start-up wizardry, a touch-screen program that intuited what I meant to say even if I hit all the wrong keys, and wrote: "Better say 5:30. Late start today."

A minute later Hallie texted a response. "OK but be on time—for a change. Curtain goes up at seven."

"Yes, ma'am," I thumb-typed back, before hitting Send and replacing the phone in its holder.

The server came then and slid a plate onto my table. It smelled good, and my taste buds lit up like the Fourth of July. "Careful with that, it's hot," he warned, loudly enough so you could hear him across the street. I didn't recognize the voice, so I figured he was new.

I smiled up at him and winked. "I hope so. At $14.95 a pop I'd be upset if it were cold."

He didn't respond and just stood there while I gathered up my knife and fork. When he hadn't moved off a few moments later, I lifted my head again. "Is there a problem? Don't tell me there's a fly in my soup."

"It's, uh, not soup," he said in an even louder voice. Evidently a Millennial who'd never heard of the Marx Brothers. I took pity on him. "Relax, son, I was only joking. I know it's a pizza."

He continued to hover over me. "You sure you don't need anything else?"

"No, thank you. This is more than enough for one and my drink's still full."

"What I meant was, it's not pre-cut."

By this time, I was sure every head in the restaurant was turned our way. It was becoming clear this wasn't going to be one of my good days. "All the more reason to eat it with a knife and fork," I said. To show him how it was done, I carved off a chunk and ate it.

"If you don't mind my saying so, that's amazing."

"Not as amazing as being left alone to enjoy my meal."

"No, I mean how you can do that by yourself."

"Why?" I said, my patience at an end. "Do I look like I'm two years old?"

"No."

"Or senile?"

"You shouldn't—"

"Shouldn't what?" I growled.

"Talk to me like that," he whined self-pityingly. "I was just trying to be helpful. Why do you people always have to be so bitchy?"

*You people.* Before I could stop it my hand shot up and fastened on his shirt collar. I pulled him down to my level and hissed in his ear. "Listen, pal, I'm assuming you haven't met anyone like me before. Either that or your mother didn't teach you any manners. But this isn't *Scent of a Woman* and I don't need to be babysat by a punk who only just started shaving. So why don't you get the twist out of your Hello Kitty boxers and go back to sexting your boyfriend before I rip that cute little ponytail out of your head."

The point finally sunk in. He twisted out of my grip, and took off, stage-whispering, "Asshole!" before pausing and snarling for even greater effect, "And I don't have a ponytail!"

Definitely not one of my good days.

# TWO

When I got back on the street it was nearly two and I was in a foul mood. As I was leaving, the manager had come up and offered his apologies, but it was just as much my fault as the server's. In the blind community, snark is generally looked down upon as a way of dealing with rude behavior. It just reinforces the notion that we're all miserable cripples who melt down at the slightest reminder of how bad we have it. I knew this, but cheerful acceptance of stupidity has never been one of my strong suits, even if overreacting to it inevitably causes me pangs of regret later on.

I pulled on my '69 World Series hat to shield my eyes from the sun, and set out walking south. It was a hot, late summer day, and the tourists were out in droves, gawking at the designer temples on the Mag Mile or getting fleeced in one of the horse-drawn carriages for hire by the Water Tower. Every so often a contingent of them clopped by, followed by a string of cars leaning on their horns. I tapped back and forth with my cane, idly ticking off landmarks as I went: a bicycle rack halfway up the seven hundred block of Rush, a dip in the sidewalk where it crossed the loading bay of a swank hotel.

I'd learned cane travel from a petite dictator named Cherie who'd been blind from birth but had never let that stop her. When I hired her she was working on a PhD in mathematics and teaching orientation and mobility on the side, primarily to newly blinded adults like me who thought a residential program sounded like a stint at Camp Grenada. Cherie had started me off light with a spine-tingling journey around the block, gradually ramping up the pressure over the course of months until I could go most places I wanted without puking in fright. I'd chosen a cane over a dog partly because I don't like the animals and partly out of convenience—canes don't need to be bathed or fed, and they never try to steal someone's dinner—and had even come to enjoy, in a Dora the Explorer sort of way, hiking around using a combination of sound, tactile clues, and memory for guidance. Of course, the cane drew plenty of stares, but the good news was I didn't have to see them.

At Superior, I turned left and headed east down the short block to Michigan, where I stopped at the crosswalk and listened. I usually planned my route so that I was traveling in the same direction as one-way traffic. Idling cars to my side meant the light was still red. When they started to roll I went with them, hustling ahead of slow-moving pedestrians so I wouldn't get stuck on the center island when the light changed again. The roadway was simmering in the afternoon heat, and I was relieved to get across without spearing a pile of gooey asphalt. The building I worked in was two blocks farther on, fronted by a series of rectangular tree boxes. I slid the cane tip along their bases until I reached the blast of air-conditioning coming from the door. Just before entering, I paused to check if my friend Mike, the *Streetwise* seller, was still around, but he must have sold out his stock for the day because he didn't call out his usual friendly greeting.

At the guard station inside, I stopped to register my new government ID with the security officer, a sleepy-eyed fellow named Richard who was reputed to be the building's first Kush practitioner.

"The old picture was better," he commented after perusing it. "This one makes you look like Doctor Strangelove."

"*Vielen Dank.* The guys at the Secretary of State were in a particularly surly mood this week."

"Yeah. I bet the latest clean government act is cutting down on their tips. So you're five-foot-ten?"

"Nine and a half. I fudged it some."

"And a hundred fifty?"

"That too."

"In my opinion your eyes are more hazel than green."

"Next time I'll bring you along to help me fill out the forms."

"I'd sooner spend a day having toothpicks shoved up my nails. OK, your papers are in order. Vee can let you in. But don't go sabotaging the elevators. They break down enough as it is."

"We'll meet again," I said, giving him a stiff-armed salute.

I maneuvered over to the bank on the far wall and listened impatiently to the chimes of the cars moving at a snail's pace through the floors above.

"Well, well, well. What have we here?" came a voice from behind.

I sighed inwardly. It was Graham Young, the ever-friendly and ever-present manufacturer's representative from Atria Laboratories, one of the big drug companies headquartered in the northwest suburbs. I'd known Graham B. B. (Before Blinkdom), so his looks were no mystery. He was in his late twenties, with a linebacker's build, a toothy smile, and a thick shock of auburn hair that invited comparison to Howdy Doody.

I gave him a tepid greeting.

"Just back from lunch? Or catching some rays? Can't say I blame you. Wish I had time for it myself. But you know how it is. Miles to go before I sleep."

"I didn't know you were a poetry fan."

"Yeah, love that guy. Especially the one about the road not taken in the snow. So inspirational. Can I help you with that button?"

"If I'm not mistaken, it's already lit."

"Well, now, so it is. Can't put anything by you. I always tell the other reps, watch out for that Doctor Angelotti. Sharp as a tack despite the bad peepers. How're we doing today? Keeping out of trouble?"

"Everything except the trouble that usually wants to follow me around." The elevator door opened, and I stepped aside to let the departing passengers out.

"Ha, ha, ha! You're not including me, I hope," Graham chortled. "Here, let me give you a hand."

I shook off the arm he offered and followed him in. As far as I could tell, we were the only two in the car.

"You headed up to your shop? On ten, if I remember correctly." This was an obvious charade. A day didn't go by when Graham wasn't hanging around the halls of my practice suite, pitching his wares to everyone who hadn't remembered to set the automatic lock on their door. Josh called him "Elmer" in reference to his adhesive qualities. The name I'd coined for him couldn't be printed in a newspaper.

I leaned over to push the button. "Why don't you give me your pitch while we're going up. That way we can get it over with."

"You don't mean an *elevator* pitch, do you? Ha, ha, ha!" he crowed again.

"That's exactly what I mean. I have a lot of work to get done this afternoon."

"But no patients scheduled. I checked with Yelena before driving down from Barrington." Yelena is my "assistant," the title now used in preference to the archaic and patently misogynistic term "secretary," except that assisting me in most things—including keeping Graham at bay—seemed to be outside her job description. "That's quite a gal you've got there," Graham continued. "I can tell how dedicated she is. Always picks up the phone on the first ring."

Unless it happened to be me trying to reach her. "I agree she's special. So what snake oil do you want to tell me about today?"

"Well," Graham said in a confiding tone, "I was hoping you'd have time for a little PowerPoint presentation I put together on Placeva."

Placeva was the latest iteration of a popular antidepressant that was one of Atria's biggest sellers. The drug was about to come off patent, meaning that the period when Atria could set an exorbitant price for it was nearing an end. Meaning also that Atria was in a scramble to cut off the cheaper generic competitors that would soon flood the market. Drug companies often did this by making minuscule alterations to the product in the hope of persuading the Food and Drug Administration to start the clock running again.

I said, "Let me guess. You've added a timed-release feature."

"How did you know?"

"And instead of little yellow pills, they now come in blue."

"Right again. And in an oblong tablet that's easier to swallow."

"Well, that's certainly a breakthrough."

"We think so too. And get this—our latest studies show fewer side effects than in previous versions."

"You mean no hard-ons that last for hours?"

Graham tee-heed. "You betcha. And on the flip side, almost no decrease in sexual function, which as you know is the number-one reason men stop taking their medication."

"That's good to hear. The next time I get depressed I'll know what to take."

"And if you do, uh, ever have that kind of problem, I have a Viagra substitute that might interest you. It comes in a liquid version, so you can literally pour yourself a stiff one."

It pained me to think how often he had used that one.

"That's great, Graham. I'll be sure to mention it to my urologist when I next see him."

The door to my floor finally opened and I exited, with Graham still stuck to my side.

"So can I come by your office and show you the presentation?"

"Why don't you e-mail it to me? That way I can really take my time with it."

"OK, but how about a few samples to go with?"

Free samples were the dirty little secret of the medical profession. Drug company salesmen handed them out like wampum at Plymouth Rock and for largely the same reason. Softened up this way, doctors could usually be counted on to return the favor the next time they reached for their prescription pads. I didn't normally accept them, though I occasionally broke my own rule if a patient couldn't afford a brand medication that seemed to work.

I gave Graham a baleful look. We went through the same Q&A every time he managed to corner me.

"How about some office supplies then? I have pads, pens, prescription forms . . . whatever you need."

"No thanks. I'm pretty much running a green operation these days."

"Oh, I guess that's right. Well, I guess I'll take myself off then." He continued to linger by my side. "Unless . . . I don't suppose you'd be interested in coming to one of our events? I have a really good one coming up two weekends from now at the Crystal Lake Resort. A full day of continuing education credit and all the golf you can handle."

"Thanks for the offer, but no. I'm afraid my handicap isn't what it used to be. On account of the present one, if you get my drift."

"You sure?" Graham persisted. "The food will be great and Dr. Frain will be speaking on one of the panels."

As if that was some kind of inducement. "Graham . . ." I sighed loudly.

"I know, I know. Well, thanks for the time anyway. I'll be around again in a few days to check on you."

"Don't go to any heroic measures if you can't find me," I said, finally making my escape.

I stopped by Yelena's desk to see what might be cooking, but she was apparently off on one of her afternoon intelligence-gathering missions. When I got to my office the door was shut. I turned the handle to find someone inside. "Yours truly," Josh called out from the direction of the couch. The cushion wheezed like an accordion as he heaved himself into a sitting position. I braced myself for another lecture about Melissa's study.

"Catching up on your beauty rest?" I asked, removing my jacket and hanging it on a hook behind the door, along with my cane.

"If only it were as simple as just sleeping. No, I came in here to get some reading done. And to warn you when you got back."

I stepped over to my desk and took a swipe at my in-box, which as usual had grown half a foot in my absence. "Warn me about what? Sep isn't trying to put me on the diversity committee again, is he?"

"I think he's temporarily off that scent. Nice move, by the way, getting Alison to take your place."

Alison was the newest doctor on our team and a rainbow consultant's dream: half-African American, half-Cherokee Indian, and a lesbian to boot. If she'd been the beneficiary of affirmative action it was wasted on her after graduating with honors from Johns Hopkins and landing a spot in one of the most prestigious residency programs in the country. I'd been her chief sponsor during the hiring process (not that she needed one), and she repaid the favor by rescuing me from an assignment I considered on a par with being forced to sit through endless screenings of the Jerry Lewis Telethon.

"Not that," Josh said. "You're in the soup with Jonathan again."

Jonathan Frain was another of our colleagues, a man who did for pomposity what Elvis did for rock 'n' roll. Stuffed into his white coat—the kind with his name embroidered on the pocket—he even resembled the King in his later years, though the abundant hair wasn't fooling anyone. Our relationship had started off poorly when I'd pointed out a methodological flaw in one of his research projects, and blossomed like a cold sore from there. These days we locked horns over matters ranging from the inconsequential (what brand of pods to stock in the office kitchen) to the serious (whether Graham should be barred from visiting our offices except by appointment). Josh likened our warfare to the Battle of the Somme, which didn't please me inasmuch as it implied I wasn't getting the upper hand.

"What did I do to ruffle his scales now?"

"Not sure, but I think it may have to do with that letter you sent to the *American Psychiatric Journal*."

"About the checklist for depression?"

"That's the one. I saw him marching purple-faced into Sep's office with the latest edition rolled up in his fist like he was going to swat the cat with it."

Jonathan was part of a professional committee considering changes to the Diagnostic and Statistical Manual. Then in its fourth edition, the DSM is the Julia Child cookbook of the psychiatric profession, dictating the recipes for some 297 mental disorders and therefore key to obtaining reimbursement under most insurance plans. Its revisions, every ten years or so, are as closely watched as the Super Bowl and just as hotly contested. Currently under scrutiny were the diagnostic criteria for establishing clinical depression, and, having some strong views on the subject, I'd fired off a letter to the editor criticizing the committee's latest draft.

"What's the problem? I'm not allowed to express an opinion? I thought this was a free country."

"Well, you've got to admit you used some strong language. Saying that the committee's work was an 'ill-disguised attempt to medicalize ordinary sadness, thereby stigmatizing healthy individuals and further lining the pockets of Big Pharma' might have been a tad aggressive."

I shrugged.

"As well as mentioning that several of the committee members got speaker fees for appearing at drug-company events."

"I didn't name names, did I?" I protested. "And besides, it's a clear conflict of interest."

"True, but everyone knows you were aiming a spear directly at Jonathan's tiny little heart. He's not going to take this lying down."

I considered this. "Do you think Sep will get involved?"

"Nah. As you say, you're entitled to an opinion. And you made a lot of points Sep would probably agree with if he didn't always have to be the one holding up the big tent. I'm just saying you might want to stay out of Jonathan's way for a few days."

"How am I supposed to do that?" I complained. "Wear night goggles?"

"Got me. But I'd advise you to watch out for the scent of Hugo Boss."

After Josh left I switched on my computer. Unlike some of my fellow travelers, I kept it hooked up to a monitor. It felt more natural to be sitting in front of one, even if the only thing I could see of it was a milky-white lozenge floating above my keyboard. The latter had a refreshable Braille display, a narrow strip in front with three rows of metal pins that moved up and down according to the text appearing on the screen. I could read by running my fingers over them, or by listening to a software program that spoke the words aloud. I chose one or the other depending on my mood and need for speed. At its fastest setting, the voiceover reminded me of the *Star Trek* episode (appropriately titled "Wink of an Eye") where hyper-accelerated aliens take over the *Enterprise*. But I was trained to make sense of its gibberish and usually resorted to my much-slower digits only when my ears started to ring.

When the screen came to life I moved the cursor with my arrow keys until the program told me it was over my e-mail box. I pressed Enter to open it and began to browse the subject lines, automatically deleting the spam that seemed to slip past my hospital's filter with the regularity of illegal aliens crossing the border. There were a handful of practice alerts that I moved to a special folder for reading later on, and a dozen or so urgent inquiries that I answered right away. An Alzheimer's patient had been admitted that morning complaining of chest pains, and I spoke briefly with her attending about the anti-anxiety medication she was on. I sent in a couple of prescription renewals and chatted on the phone with an Iraq War veteran I was treating for PTSD. I then set to work tackling the miscellany—departmental memos, billing questions—saving for last correspondence from the attorneys I worked with. One in particular caught my eye (so to speak), and I turned again to my phone. Rusty Halloran picked up on the second ring.

"Doctor Mid-Nite," he bellowed over the receiver. "You got my message."

"What happened to Doctor Doom?"

"I thought I ought to lighten up on you. How goes it over there in the loony bin? Knocked off any patients this week?"

"If I had, I wouldn't turn to you for advice." I was ribbing him. Rusty was one of the best trial lawyers in the city. Scrupulous to a fault, he defied all stereotypes of the fee-chasing, ethically challenged attorney and had managed to make a good living at it for close to forty years. Like me, he'd survived the rhetorical meat grinder of a Jesuit education and only took on cases he believed in, which invariably assumed the character of a holy crusade against the combined forces of Lex Luthor, the Joker, and Magneto, with Darth Vader thrown in for objectivity's sake. Needless to say, we got along famously.

"How's Deandra doing?" I asked.

Deandra Williams was a pro-bono client who'd made the head-lines after hearing voices in her head directing her to place her two-month-old infant in the barrel of a dryer at her local Soap 'n' Spin. Another patron had rescued the child before any serious injury took place, but the authorities had decided to prosecute Deandra for attempted murder anyway. It was one of the clearest cases of post-partum psychosis I'd ever encountered, and I'd been hired by Rusty to give testimony that Deandra wasn't responsible for her actions under the *McNaughton* rule. The jury apparently agreed with me because they'd brought in the lesser verdict of criminal negligence, a charge better suited to Deandra's crime of being poor, uneducated, and without access to psychiatric care. She was now serving a five-year suspended sentence.

"Much better after the free counseling you arranged for her. Last time we spoke she was working on getting her GED."

"And the child?"

"Living with his grandmother, though Deandra has high hopes of getting custody back down the road."

"That's great. Wish her well for me. So what was so urgent that it required all the exclamation points? You know the machine reads them to me one by one? Along with the emoticons—'colon right parenthesis.'"

"Not exactly a smiley face, then. I'll keep that in mind. Got a job for you if you're interested."

"Go on."

"One of your kind."

"Sight-deprived?"

"No, a head shrinker. Wife sits with Betsy on the Woman's Board. Private practice in Winnetka, specializing in adolescents. With all the New Trier students nearby he's not hurting for business." He named a name and asked me if I knew the fellow.

"Don't think so," I said.

"Good. Better that way. Anyhow, a little while back one of the tykes he was treating drove his daddy's Porsche into a hundred-year-old oak at the bottom of the Ravine. Maybe you read about it in the paper."

I hadn't, but I knew the place he was talking about. A section of Sheridan Road that snaked through one of the steep gullies carved into the glacial drift along Lake Michigan's north shore. Narrow and filled with sharp turns, it was the closest thing Chicago had to Mulholland Drive. Cyclists willing to ignore the posted ban loved it, and I'd sneaked more than one adrenaline rush there when I could still ride outdoors.

"Was he alone?"

"Apparently."

"Drinking?"

"Not according to the medical examiner. The only thing they found were traces of a prescription antidepressant, pretty standard for kids in that neck of the woods. Promising lad," he went on, "varsity swimming and an athletic scholarship to Minnesota in the fall. Police were ready to call it an accident until something that suggested suicidal thinking turned up on the boy's Facebook page."

"A note of some sort?"

"Not exactly. A link to a video on that YouTube thing. After my time, but maybe not yours. Band called Blue Öyster Cult. You remember them?"

I was afraid I did, along with their biggest hit—*Don't Fear the Reaper*. It was all over the charts when I was in my teens, and I still sometimes found myself humming the layered, haunting refrain. *We can be like they are. Come on baby . . .*

"I'm also dating myself, but sure."

"Watched the clip myself the other day. Can't say I cared for the music. But then I grew up snapping my fingers to Dave Brubeck. You can guess what this is all leading to."

"The doc's being sued for not recognizing the risk."

"Bulls-eye."

I was skeptical. "A link to a song doesn't prove much."

"True. But the parents don't want to believe their golden child just upped and killed himself. Tragedy always goes down easier when you can find someone else to blame. I'd be scrubbing floors for a living if it were otherwise."

"Still, this doesn't sound like your usual."

"It isn't. But the missus is insisting. And you know how I like an uphill battle."

"Has this ever happened to him before—a lawsuit?"

"Nope. His record's clean as a whistle."

"So why are you down on his chances?"

"Psychology. You ought to know. If the case goes to trial, the sympathy will be all with the boy's parents. The jury won't be able to ignore the fact that the patient died on the operating room table even if there wasn't a missing scalpel in his gut. It's why this kind of lawsuit usually settles—quickly and quietly. The carrier is willing to put forth a reasonable offer, but our friend won't even listen to the idea. Insists he followed professional standards, and he'll be damned if he admits to malpractice just so the boy's parents can sleep easier at night."

"So where do I fit in?"

"For now, I was hoping you could help me talk some sense into him. Sit in on an interview, take a look at the file. There'll be warts on his story—there always are. Maybe not enough to condemn him in the abstract, but enough to make him think about what a wrongful death verdict will do to his premiums."

"And if I think he's squeaky clean?"

"Then we'll take it from there. Are you game?"

I thought about it. Since I'd begun doing it, most of my expert engagements had involved the poor and relatively downtrodden. A well-off shrink in a malpractice suit wasn't an obvious candidate for my sympathy. But if the guy had never been in trouble before . . . I put myself in his shoes. Maybe he was just being defensive; maybe he really *had* done everything by the book. Either way, I knew what he was going through. I lived with the same soul-crushing doubt every waking moment. If nothing else, maybe I could help *him* sleep better at night.

"OK," I said. "But no promises about what I'll conclude."

"I wouldn't have it any other way."

We made arrangements to meet at Rusty's office in a few days' time. In the meantime, he'd send over a copy of the file. After setting down the receiver, I sat still for a moment before remembering it was late in the day and checking my watch. 5:25. If I didn't race out the door that minute, I'd be late for my date with Hallie and could look forward to a death-defying sprint through traffic to get to the Court Theater on time. I grabbed my jacket and cane from the door, turned the knob, and ran straight into . . . Jonathan.

# THREE

A few hours later, Hallie was still giving me the Sub Zero treatment over missing the first act of *Mourning Becomes Electra*.

"It's not my fault there was a Kenny Chesney concert at Soldier Field."

Hallie didn't answer.

"Or that there was a speed trap just after the Eisenhower."

She coasted her MG down a ramp.

"I said I'd pay for the ticket, didn't I?"

More silence.

Hallie and I had met the previous spring. A mentally handicapped patient of mine, Charlie Dickerson, was talked into a murder confession by the police, and not understanding what I was getting into, I volunteered to testify that he wasn't competent to waive his *Miranda* rights. If you put aside some of my youthful near-misses with the law, it was my first introduction to the criminal justice system. Under Hallie's tutelage, I'd learned all the tricks in trade of an expert witness: how to sound spontaneous despite long hours of rehearsal, when to offer information and when to shut up, and most important of all, what to do when opposing counsel has just driven a stake through the heart of your testimony. (Smile pleasantly and act as though nothing has happened.) My first cross-examination was abysmal, but it hooked me on courtroom work, and to my surprise, many lawyers found my blindness a plus. It mesmerized juries and spooked the other side, who handled me with uncommon courtesy to avoid appearing insensitive to the handicapped. I soon found myself in demand as a hired gun, which pleased my hospital's publicity department even if it fueled the resentment of colleagues like Jonathan.

Hallie was smart, funny, and direct. Based on Josh's survey, she was also wildly attractive, with the Latin coloring and ample curves I'd always found hardest to resist. She had a sweet scent that hovered between fresh figs and vanilla, and a husky contralto I could listen to for hours. And those weren't her only attractions. Her older brother, Geraldo, was born two months early during the sixties, when preemies were still treated with artificially high levels of oxygen to speed their lung development. Gerry's lungs turned out fine; his retinas didn't fare as well. Growing up with a blind sibling meant Hallie was immune to the tortured syntax and irritating over-solicitousness I'd come to expect from virtually all new acquaintances. Words like *look* and *see* didn't stick in her throat, her directions were never more than I needed, and she didn't hesitate to tell me when there was ketchup on my tie. Best of all, if she harbored any sympathy for me, she kept it to herself.

My feelings for Hallie were far from casual, but so far I'd pretended not to notice that she wanted more out of our relationship than a BFF. My therapist was disappointed. His name was Harvey, which inevitably made me think of a large, pale person with over-developed ears, when in fact (easy to tell) he was no taller than me. I'd been seeing him once a week, part of a deal I'd struck with Sep when I was in danger of losing my job. According to Harvey, healthy relationships with the opposite sex were part of my Learning To Forgive Myself program, which sounded a lot like Alcoholics Anonymous minus the abstinence and all the meetings. (Step One: admit you are powerless before your guilt. Step Two: admit you need help from a "higher power" you aren't quite sure you believe in.) Harvey thought Hallie was good for me, overriding my objection that I'd only end up driving her away. "If you're comfortable with her and she with you, that's all that matters at this point. Stop overanalyzing the situation," he said. Which was funny advice coming from another shrink.

Hallie brought the car to a stop in front of my building and yanked irascibly at the emergency brake while I attempted to get the conversation going again. "Are you still there? I'm beginning to feel like Helen Keller."

"Then you'll understand why my lips aren't moving."

*Ouch.* This was worse than I'd thought. I turned in my seat to face her, aiming for a contrite expression. "Is there anything I can do to make it up to you? I could stand on my head. Or perform a song and dance routine with my cane."

She relented a bit. "You could start by pretending you had a good time tonight."

"What do you mean? I enjoyed every minute of it."

"Nice try. You were fidgeting so much I'm surprised they didn't charge you for a new carpet square. The couple next to you kept looking over, trying to get my attention. I think they were worried you were going to start foaming at the mouth."

I squirmed under the description. I'd always been a bit loose around the knee, but the tendency had grown much worse since I lost my sight, especially when I was feeling tense. "That bad, huh? OK, I admit I found four hours of incest, adultery, murder, and suicide a little hard to stomach."

"I thought so."

"And I wasn't crazy about the ending, either."

"Why? What was wrong with it?"

"Orin's suicide. Remember the play notes you read to me while we were waiting to get in? The ones about the Greek myth the play is based on? In the Agamemnon cycle, Athena pardons Orestes so he doesn't have to spend the rest of his life being driven insane by the Furies. O'Neill should have stuck to the original."

"And given Orin a pass? He killed two people, including his mother."

"If I heard correctly, she shot herself."

She waved this off. "He did everything but pull the trigger."

"Spoken like a true ex-prosecutor."

"You'd feel the same way if you'd tried some of the people I did. Orin was a sick boy, but he deserved everything he got. I remember when we tried Donald Tesma. You'll never get me to say a monster like that shouldn't get the needle."

I was impressed. Tesma was a notorious physician-turned-serial killer who'd murdered dozens of nursing-home patients by spiking their intravenous fluid with substances that mimicked natural death. He was eventually caught, convicted, and, if I remembered right, hanged himself in prison. "You tried Tesma?"

"Not exactly. I was the junior lawyer on the team, so the only time they let me out of the library was to watch Jane's closing argument." I'd heard about Jane Barrett too. They'd met at the State's Attorney's office when Hallie was a rookie assistant and Jane was heading up the felony division. Hallie rarely gushed about anyone, but listening to her talk about Jane was like sitting through a reading from *The Lives of the Saints*. Each had since left the office—Hallie to start a white-collar practice at a big Loop firm, and Jane to head her own litigation boutique.

"You should have seen the jurors' faces," Hallie was saying. "They were weeping as hard as if Tesma had done away with their own loved ones."

"But Tesma didn't get the death penalty."

"Sadly, no. The handicapping back at the County Building was that the jury took pity on his son. The boy's mother had run off years ago and Tesma was the only family he had. Kid was sixteen at the time and wept even harder than the jurors."

"How'd the jurors get to see him? Surely he wasn't in the courtroom?"

"Not only that, but they put him on the stand during the penalty phase to plead for his father's life. I don't think I'll ever forget how he looked in the witness box."

I was horrified. "Now that's what I call criminal. The poor kid shouldn't have been within a hundred miles of that courtroom."

"Tell me about it. The defense team didn't have a choice. We were told Daddy insisted on it. Like I said, a real monster."

"Still, even without the child there, I would have voted the same way."

"I didn't know you were such a bleeding heart," she said, amused.

"I'm not. It's just that there's a growing consensus in my field that people like Tesma are born that way—without a conscience."

"That there's such a thing as a murder gene, you mean?"

"Maybe. Studies involving identical twins point strongly to an inherited component, possibly in as much as one percent of the male population. Female psychopaths are much rarer. The interesting thing is not all of them end up killers. Some who fit the diagnostic criteria end up as politicians or running big corporations. So there must be a nurture piece as well. Whatever the cause, it's clear that psychopaths don't feel empathy or remorse the way normal people do. We should be trying to cure them, not putting them to death."

Hallie laughed. "Spoken like a true psychiatrist. Next thing you know, you'll be trying to rationalize away the Nuremberg Trials. But seriously, what does that say about our justice system—about any justice system? If people aren't responsible for their crimes, doesn't the whole thing fall apart?"

"I wouldn't go that far. When we started out talking I was simply expressing the opinion that for most people the guilt from having ended another person's life is its own punishment." I was thinking not only of myself but of someone I'd put away recently, now languishing in a downstate prison. "That's my real problem with what O'Neill was saying. If you ask me, the damned *do* cry—and sometimes the hardest."

"I'm the one who should be damned for suggesting that play," Hallie said, reaching over to pat my knee in a conciliatory gesture. "I had no idea it would upset you."

"I'm not upset," I said.

"You're also a terrible liar. I'm just glad you didn't have to look at the Kabuki masks."

"Which no doubt *would* have sent me into fits."

I struggled with where to go next. We'd reached the point in the evening when it was time to say our good-byes, a parting ritual that was becoming increasingly strained. I made a show of flipping the crystal on my watch and fingering the dial. "It's late. I should let you get home."

Hallie let out a sigh.

I thought if there was ever a time when I should clear the air, this was it. "Hallie," I began.

She stopped me with a hand to my arm. "It's OK."

"No, it isn't."

"Really. You don't have to explain."

The dejection in her voice made me wince. I wanted to carry her upstairs, throw her on my bed, and screw her brains out. Instead, I went on with the speech I'd been mentally rehearsing for the better part of the evening. "Listen, I know you've been waiting for me to say something about, umm . . . us."

*There. I'd gotten started.*

I continued with mounting confidence. "And I want you to know it's got nothing to do with you."

"Of course it doesn't."

"It's me that's the problem."

She laughed bitterly. "If I had a dime for every time a guy said that to me I'd be living in Kenilworth."

I could see this wasn't coming out right.

"That's not what I meant. What I meant was—"

She stopped me again. "Anyway, it's not like I haven't been turned down before."

*I'm not turning you down*, I wanted to shout. "No, wait. You don't understand—"

She put the key back in the ignition. "Like I said, no hard feelings."

I reached over to stop her. "Please. Please just listen for a moment."

"Okaaay," Hallie said, drawing the syllables out. "I'm all ears."

Now that I finally had her full attention, I found it almost impossible to go on. My mouth had gone dry and my telltale knee was shaking. *Fuck. I was losing it already.* I swallowed hard and said, "You see, I'm not—"

Right at that moment, Providence—or maybe it was another one of my bad genies—intervened. My lips were still forming the words *what you think I am* when a cell phone started ringing in the neighborhood of the dashboard. Hallie plucked it from the jack and scanned the caller. "I'm sorry," she said, "but I have to take this." I listened while a series of low-pitched squawks came over the wire. "What?!" she said. "On what charge?... That's absurd! Hold on a sec—"

Hallie stopped and handed her handbag to me, whispering urgently. "See if there's something in here to write with." She turned her attention back to the caller. "Wait another minute while I get this down."

I fumbled open the clasp and began groping through the tissues, change, candy wrappers, and other unfathomable contents of a woman's purse until I fell upon what felt like a lipstick container. I held it out to her. "Will this do? I can't find a pen."

She yanked it from me and started writing squeakily on the driver's side window.

"Where do they have you now? Uh-huh. I'll be there first thing in the morning." She listened a few minutes more. "I know it will be hard, but try to get some sleep. We'll get this straightened out. I promise. And you know the rules. Don't talk to *anyone*."

When she rang off a few seconds later, she seemed dazed. "That's odd" was all she said.

"What is?"

"I can't believe we were talking about her only a few minutes ago."

I gave her a quizzical look.

"That was Jane. You remember, my former boss."

"Was she in some kind of accident?" I asked.

"No," Hallie said, sounding even more perplexed. "She's been picked up by the police. For murdering Rory Gallagher."

Gallagher's death was heating up to be one of the bigger news stories that month. A flamboyant, fifty-six-year-old reporter for the *Chicago Sun-Times* known for his hard drinking and headline-grabbing exposés of local government, he was almost as big a Windy City celebrity as Oprah. In Chicago, developing leads about back-room maneuvering and sleazy political deals isn't especially difficult to do—they don't call it "the

Machine" for nothing—but Gallagher had racked up a series of journalistic coups that would have been the envy of Bernstein and Woodward had they set their sights on smaller fry and made enough enemies to fill the VIP section of Soldier Field on a warm Sunday in November. So when he suddenly keeled over and dropped dead while seated at his favorite table in the Billy Goat, his press buddies were quick to look past an apparent heart attack and hint at a more sinister explanation.

According to the barkeep, who knew the regulars like the creases of his palms, Gallagher was sober but clearly not himself when he arrived at the Goat a little before 10:00 p.m. on a Friday in late August, ordering a double and careening over to join a group of cronies gathered in the famous "Wise Guys" corner. The atmosphere at the table was already grim—*Tribune* officials were hinting at yet another Chapter 11, and both the White Sox and the Cubs were trailing their divisions—but Gallagher's arrival cast an even bigger pall over the festivities. Usually the life of the party, Gallagher said nothing while he downed several drinks in succession, seemingly sunk in a vicious train of thought. Several of the table's occupants noted his pasty complexion and the strange appearance of his eyes, which darted from side to side as though he was unable to focus. One of his colleagues, a rival columnist at the *Tribune* named Orlando Brooks, was on the verge of saying, "Rory, you OK man?" when Gallagher abruptly rose, made a frantic clawing motion at his chest, and crashed to the floor, upsetting the table and half a dozen glasses of spirits as he went down. An hour later, he was pronounced dead on arrival at Chicago Kaiser.

Given his age and lifestyle, the cause of Gallagher's death was initially presumed to be a heart attack. The verdict probably would have stood there, except for the doubts of his reporter pals who, confronted with the brutal outcome of their own unhealthy habits, or else simply reverting to type, had almost immediately floated rumors of foul play, certainly a much better story than FIFTY-SOMETHING JOURNALIST FALLS VICTIM TO HIS OWN VICES. Their suspicions were vindicated when, only a few days after the funeral, an attorney for the state had shown up at the Daley Center with a sealed petition seeking exhumation of the body. The last I'd heard was that the corpse had been dug up and was awaiting analysis by the medical examiner.

"I take it the ME found something?" I said to Hallie while we were still sitting in her car.

"Yes. It was in the paper this morning. A drug used to treat mental patients—a second-generation something-or-other called Lucitrol."

"The antipsychotic?"

"Yeah, that's it. You know about it, I assume?"

"Sure." Lucitrol was another of Atria Laboratories' biggest sellers. "They're called second-generation or 'atypical' antipsychotics because they were developed to counteract some of the side effects of older medications like Haldol and Thorazine. The atypicals are controversial—no one knows yet if they're really more effective or whether they'll result in equally serious side effects over time. Was Gallagher under the care of a shrink, do you know?"

"Not so far as it's been reported."

"That's odd. Usually antipsychotics are reserved for serious mental illness, like schizophrenia or bipolar disorder. So they're saying she slipped him one?"

"That's what I'm guessing. Jane wouldn't let them question her— she knows the routine—so she couldn't tell me anything more than the bare-bones charge—first-degree murder in the death of Rory Gallagher. But how can that kind of drug be used to kill somebody?"

"Depends on the person. The kind of medication we're talking about is strongly counter-indicated for patients with, or at risk of, heart disease. Do you know what kind of shape Gallagher was in? The papers said he was a heavy drinker."

"And a pack-a-day man. He was still clinging, if barely, to his good looks, but I doubt he was competing in any marathons."

"First thing I'd do is subpoena his medical records, then. A fifty-year-old smoker with a drinking habit is a prime candidate for cardiac arrest."

"I will, but it won't help. Legally, if you feed an otherwise-innocuous substance to someone with a special propensity—a peanut allergy, say—it's the same as putting arsenic in their soup."

"I take it you'd have to know about the risk beforehand."

"That's right. If you didn't know it existed, there couldn't be *mens rea*. It would just be an accident."

"And the likelihood of him accidentally ingesting a prescription antipsychotic isn't high. But I still don't understand why the police have zeroed in on your friend."

"That's easy. The two of them have been an item for years."

I raised an eyebrow.

"Don't look at me like that. Just because a woman sleeps with a man doesn't give her a reason to kill him."

"A lot of people, women included, would disagree with you."

Hallie laughed. "OK, I get your point. But Jane's not like that. You'll see when you meet her."

"I'm going to meet her?"

"As soon as I can get her out of Cook County. I'm going to need your help."

"I'm not sure that's such a good idea," I said, thinking of the confession I'd just been on the verge of making.

"Please? You know all about these medications. What they're used for, what the warnings say. I'm going to need someone to educate me about them in a hurry. I don't think it will put much of a dent in your schedule. And I'm going to need at least one guy on the case who isn't panting after Jane's good looks."

"There are other ways of knowing when a woman is beautiful," I said resentfully.

"I know that. But I think I've guessed what you were trying to tell me a little while ago."

"You *have*?" I gulped.

"Uh-huh," Hallie said. "And it explains everything. Though I don't know why you didn't say something about it before. These days, it's nothing to be ashamed of." She sounded, I thought irritably, almost relieved. "But don't worry. If that's how you want it, your secret's safe with me. I'm just glad we can stay friends."

# FOUR

It was better that way, I told myself. At least for the time being.

After Hallie roared off, I entered my building and took the elevator up. The condominium stood just north of the Chicago River and was touted as a "luxury property" when I bought my unit. But it was the kind of cheap showpiece thrown up when times were good and developers were drowning in bank loans. Those times had changed. To the east, where yet another hotel complex had been planned, there was now a weed-infested lot. The building's slipshod construction was revealing itself too, in walls that sprouted cracks where they'd been too hastily taped and floors that rattled underfoot like an O'Hare jetport.

At nineteen I slipped my cane under my arm and walked the ten steps down the hall to my two-bedroom, unlocking the door and tossing my keys into a soup bowl on the stand just inside the door. The bowl had acquired a chipped rim in the dishwasher, and I'd been on the verge of putting it in the trash when I remembered the household organization tip I'd run across on a blind chat site. It was now the repository for all things that found their way into my pockets during the day: a fast-growing collection of change, spent cane tips, rubber bands, paper clips, charge receipts, and other junk I was too lazy to sort through when I got home. My cane joined my shoes in a heap of larger items on the floor.

I padded over to the liquor cabinet and poured myself a bourbon, mentally surveying the room. It wasn't a total man-cave—my housekeeper, Marta, attacked dust and dirt like a Navy Seal—but it wouldn't have made the pages of *Martha Stewart* either: plain white walls hung with a few fading Tour de France posters, a poly tweed sofa I'd picked up at the floor sale when Marshall Field's was being bought out by Macy's, laminate shelves sagging under the weight of the cheap thrillers I'd tried to numb myself with after the divorce. I hadn't always been this indifferent to my surroundings. Before my marriage I'd lived in a stylish prewar with custom built-ins to store all the serious reading that now sat in unopened boxes in my storage locker. It was only after my hurried exodus from the East that I discovered my inner frat boy. Now, imagining it with fresh eyes made me cringe, and I vowed to do something about it before too long.

I showered and changed into pajama bottoms and an old bathrobe, poured myself another drink, and went out on the terrace—the apartment's only decent feature—to think. A full moon hung like a dim flashlight over the Lake, and there was a bite to the air that hinted at the coming of fall. I settled into a lawn chair and put my bare feet up on the railing in spite of the chill. Urban night sounds floated up from the streets below. Glass shattering against a curb, the *bap bap bap* of a police siren on the far side of the Chicago River, a woman laughing tipsily at a companion's comment. I sipped at my drink and shivered in the breeze and counted up all the reasons I should have begged off Hallie's new case.

It wasn't that I didn't want to work with her. But the closer we got, the more unfair it seemed to let her labor under a delusion. Though I hadn't grown up in a large brood like Hallie's, I knew the code only too well. Family was everything. Nothing—not even the God you prayed to on Sundays—was as sacred as protecting your loved ones. Somewhere along the way I'd lost sight of that cultural imperative, and now, in another of the ironies that seemed to rule my life, it threatened to keep Hallie and me permanently apart.

It was raining heavily the next morning so I took the bus, a mode of transportation that had become considerably less taxing since the

Chicago Transit Authority invested in a GPS tracking system. Not everyone was a fan. The cash-strapped city fathers were always on the lookout for new ways to raise revenue—one of the more creative schemes being a sale leaseback of the Chicago Skyway, one of the main thoroughfares into the city, a few years back—and the grant of a twenty-five-year license to the system's French supplier had left citizen watchdog groups howling in protest. I, on the other hand, greatly appreciated its new audio features, which had all but eliminated my need to ask embarrassing questions of strangers. Buses now came standard with loudspeakers that announced each stop, and I had only to press a button in my shelter to know which one was pulling up. The CTA had even splurged on a special locator tone for the button, in case I couldn't be counted on to remember where it was hiding.

When I got to my office building, Mike was once again absent from his station by the door. I had a special reason for looking after his welfare, so after fruitlessly calling his name a few times, I went over to ask Richard, the security guard, if he knew what was going on.

"Nope. I haven't seen him since last week," Richard said. "You worried about him?

I nodded. For as long as I'd worked there, Mike had never missed a day of selling *Streetwise*, the newspaper put out by a local homelessness-empowerment group. Somewhere in his sixties, Mike was known to all the building's occupants for his brightly colored tie-dyed clothing and irrepressible gold-toothed smile. Living on the streets wasn't good for his health, and recently I'd noticed a rattle in his chest that wasn't there six months ago. I'd been trying to get him upstairs to be examined by one of my colleagues, but so far he'd steadfastly refused, explaining that he'd wait until the new state health exchange was up and running to see a doctor. Mike, I'd come to learn, hated all forms of charity.

"I'm worried about the old man too," Richard said. "Did you know he used to play backup for Buddy Guy?"

"No kidding. How'd he get from there to the streets?"

"The usual. Got hooked on smack and did a fiver at Dixon, where he got cornered and shanked in a fight. Messed up his fret hand so he couldn't play anymore. When he got out, Buddy offered him work doing odd jobs at Legends, but Mike was too proud to take it, and there isn't a whole lot of other work out there for ex-cons. Had a wife once, but she divorced him when he went to prison."

I was surprised. "How'd you get him to tell you all that?" I'd also learned from experience that Mike didn't like to talk about himself.

"I didn't. I recognized him on the back of an old album cover when I was at Jazz Record Mart and did some asking around at the clubs. I play blues guitar myself, and a few of the old-timers filled me in on the story. Sucks, doesn't it?"

I agreed. "Do you think any of them will know what's happened to him?"

"I doubt it, but it can't hurt to ask. Want me to make a few calls?"

"I'd really appreciate it. If he doesn't turn up soon, I don't know what I'm going to do."

"No sweat. Give me a couple of hours until I get turned loose here, and I'll see what I can find out."

"Thanks," I said. "If you do hear anything, will you call me right away?" I pulled out a business card and pen and scribbled my home phone number on the back. "Here if you can't get me on my cell. Even if it's the middle of the night, I'd rather find out that he's OK. And while we're at it, why don't you put your number in my cell, too." I handed him my card and my phone.

"You betcha," Richard said, taking them and observing that my handwriting wasn't half-bad.

"Catholic school," I said. "My knuckles are still smarting from Sister Ursula's ruler."

Before heading upstairs, I stopped at the Argo Tea franchise in the lobby for my morning caffeine jolt, listening on my phone to the baseball stats while I waited on line. The Mets appeared to be gearing up for yet another epic September fail, with series against the Nationals, Braves, and Phillies on the horizon and their star hitter in a slump after catching a mysterious disease that team doctors had first diagnosed as jungle fever. At least they got the fever part right.

I arrived at my office just in time to find Yelena exiting in a cloud of Obsession. It was one of her signatures, along with a shoe collection that would have done Imelda Marcos proud.

"'But soft, methinks, I scent the morning air,'" I said.

Yelena snorted. "Not *Hamlet* again."

"It's not cheerful enough for you? Maybe you'd prefer *King Lear*."

"Yes, if it's the part where the blind man is murdered. There's a package for you."

"Where?"

"I put it on your desk."

"Great. Would it be too much trouble to say who it's from?"

"Mr. Halloran. His assistant called to be sure it got here."

"Imagine the exertion that required. Did you open it?"

Yelena sighed loudly and followed me back in. I heard her tearing at the packet while I hung up my raincoat. "*Chyort voz'mi!*" she swore suddenly. "I just broke a nail."

"Good thing it's Monday, then," I commiserated. Yelena adhered to a strict grooming schedule that left little time for such annoyances as opening mail and answering the phone. I would have complained to her supervisor, but Josh, who shared her services with me, had advocated a Neville Chamberlain approach, pointing out that we'd never get her fired under her union contract. Monday afternoons were reserved for her bi-weekly manicure.

"What's it look like inside?"

"A letter from Mr. Halloran, saying he is enclosing some notes."

"What's with the letter?"

"The notes, of course."

"I meant are they printed or handwritten?"

I heard another disgruntled sigh.

It figured. "Too bad," I said.

Yelena pretended not to hear me.

"C'mon," I said reasonably. "You know the scanner doesn't work with handwriting. It's either transcribe them or read them to me, and you know how much you hate spending time by my side."

"True," Yelena said. "But there must be twenty pages here."

I did a quick calculation of how much time off this was worth. "I'll let you leave an hour early today."

"Make it an hour and a half and I'll see what I can do."

"OK, but you'll have to clear it with Dr. Goldman, too."

"I will, but he never says no."

"And thanks for being such a sport."

"'I must be cruel only to be kind,'" Yelena said, adding—in case I didn't get it—"Hamlet to Gertrude, Act III, Scene Four."

*Touché*, I thought, shaking my head as she waltzed out the door.

The rest of the day, my mind was only half on my work while I waited for news from Hallie. Before becoming involved in Charlie's case, I'd always thought bail was available to all those accused of a crime, the only issue being how much of their life savings they had to pony up to secure their release while the charges were pending. Not so I discovered in Illinois, where bail could be denied outright in homicide cases based on the strength of the prosecution's case. Hallie would try to broker a deal for Jane, but if the State's Attorney didn't bite, there would have to be a hearing to decide whether there was enough evidence to hold her.

Hallie didn't get back to me until almost closing hour.

"What do you know about eyewitness testimony?" she demanded as soon as I'd picked up.

"You're asking *me*?"

"Why not? There has to be a heavy psychological component."

"I've never looked into it myself, but I know there's a lot of literature on the subject."

"Good. You'll have to get up to speed on it quickly."

"Whoa," I said. "Slow down. Last time we talked I was just going to consult on some medications. Now you want me to become an authority on lineups? What's going on? Did you have the bail hearing?"

"Not yet. I asked that it be put over until Friday. It means Jane will have to spend a few more nights in the lockup, but she seems to be bearing up OK and I need the time to prepare."

I sat back and listened while she filled me in on some of the details that had been missing from our last discussion. It seemed that Jane had been doing legal work for Atria—quite a bit of it in fact—and had just won a defense verdict in a case involving Lucitrol: a wrongful death suit brought by the widow of a bipolar man who'd suffered a heart attack after starting on the medication. Jane had prevailed by shifting the blame to the state-run mental-health clinic that treated the man, arguing that its harried staff had failed to perform a full cardiac workup on the victim before writing the prescription. Not surprisingly, there were samples of Lucitrol all over Jane's office, along with reams of information about the drug's dangerous side effects.

"Well," I said, "that explains why the police might be interested in her."

"Wait," Hallie said. "There's more. Jane was with Gallagher on the night he died."

My ears pricked up. "Where?"

"At Gene and Georgetti's. I can't believe anyone still goes to that dinosaur, but it was another of Gallagher's hangouts. A couple of witnesses saw the two of them there, tying on a few, and are willing to testify that they were arguing about something."

"What does Jane say?"

"That they had a couple of drinks, and that was all."

"But the police don't believe her."

"No, and I'm not sure I do, either. I can't put my finger on it, but she's being cagey about the facts. She says she doesn't really remember much about that night. Jane has a mind like a steel trap. It's hard for me to believe she can't give me a minute-by-minute replay."

"Have you raised that with her?"

"Not in so many words. She blames it on the sleeping pill she took right after she came home. She claims it put her out almost immediately and she didn't wake until the following morning."

"That doesn't sound impossible," I said. "Short-term memory loss is common with sleeping pills, especially when taken on top of alcohol."

"Yes, but the prosecution has a witness, a woman who was out walking her dog near Gallagher's townhouse that night—right as Gallagher was being rushed from the Billy Goat to the emergency room. She'll testify that she saw Jane—or someone fitting her description—letting herself into the place. Jane denies it, but I have a bad feeling, call it an intuition if you like, that Jane was there. She admits she had a key to his place."

"The police aren't claiming Gallagher was poisoned at home, are they?"

"No."

"What's the significance then?"

"Gallagher's computer. Naturally the police thought to go through his hard drive, but when they turned it on it was wiped clean. No backup CDs or thumb drives in the home, either. To make matters worse, Jane's IT person had just ordered a disk-wiping software package for the firm. They were upgrading to new PCs, and the techie wanted to be sure there was no privileged information on the old ones before they were disposed of. She could have just downloaded the program, but she's a careful sort and went instead for the CDs, which were sitting in plain view on her desk when Jane was arrested. Jane's fingerprints weren't on them, but it's another bad fact."

"So what would be Jane's motive for getting rid of Gallagher's data?

"The prosecution's theory is that she went looking for love letters to another woman, discovered them, and destroyed the files in an act of rage. They were contacted by the woman, who'll testify that Gallagher was ready to call it quits with Jane on the night he died. They'll say that's what the two of them were fighting about at the restaurant, and that's where Jane slipped him the pill. Anyway, I can't help feeling the two things are connected—Gallagher's missing data and Jane being 'unable' to remember. Of course, if there *is* a connection, Jane's smart enough not to tell me."

"What do you mean?"

"An attorney can't ethically advance a claim they know to be false. It's why criminal lawyers go to great lengths to avoid asking their clients if they're guilty. Jane understands that better than anybody. If she's not telling me the truth, it's to protect me."

I was beginning to catch on to the problem. "Hallie, is this your roundabout way of telling me you think Jane might be guilty?"

She sighed. "I never ask that question about a client. Right now, all I have is a suspicion, and I want it to stay that way. But the whole thing worries me, along with how I'm ever going to get her out of jail. My old office decided it was a conflict for anyone there to try Jane, so I'm dealing with the bastards up in Lake County. I offered them five mil plus home detention, but they wouldn't even consider it. Bjorn's already hitting the streets—"

"Bjorn?"

"My new investigator. But it's not likely he'll find anything before the hearing. Right now, the only tangible evidence linking Jane to the crime is the eyewitness. I need to shut down her testimony fast, and I'll never be able to find a better expert in time. Will you do it?"

"If you don't think my credibility will be questioned."

"I know it's ironic, but just let them try to make something of it. And the one good thing that's happened is that the Assistant State's Attorney they're sending down to the hearing is a total newbie. He'll never know how to deal with you."

# FIVE

It's sometimes said that there are two types of psychiatrists: those who have experienced a patient's suicide, and those who will someday. Ira Levin had just joined the first and more-populous group, and he was clearly still smarting over it.

"No, I didn't write *Rosemary's Baby*," he said, giving me a jittery handshake, "and no, I didn't have reason to think Danny Carpenter was a suicide risk." Explaining the former, he told us that he'd been named after his maternal grandfather, who'd passed shortly before he was born. Under Jewish tradition, this freed up his grandfather's name for future generations and, being a fan of the book, Levin's dad couldn't resist.

"Your father must have had a sense of humor," Rusty said.

"He had to," Levin replied. "He was a pathologist for Cook County."

It was Wednesday noon, and we were gathered at Rusty's offices on Hubbard Street, in a Victorian building that once housed the Chicago Criminal Courts and was studded with history. Leopold and Loeb had been tried there, along with Shoeless Joe Jackson, and its fourth-floor pressroom had been the hangout of such literary lions as Carl Sandburg and Sherwood Anderson. This no doubt explained the building's appeal to Rusty, whose shop occupied the top floor and included, among other amenities, a mock courtroom and a half basketball court. I wondered which one got more use. Our conference room had towering windows and a table that could have accommodated the National Security Council, in addition to a groaning board of sandwiches and soft drinks. After being steered there by Rusty, I randomly picked out one of each and slid into one of the Aeron chairs arranged around the table, stowing my cane on the floor. Rusty followed me, taking the seat to my right.

"So you grew up locally?" Rusty asked Levin, who was still hovering somewhere near the door. "Please, sit down. And have something to eat."

"On the Northwest Side," Levin said, selecting some lunch items and sinking into a chair opposite us. "It's where most families like ours ended up." He launched into a brief history of the sixties and seventies in Chicago, when blockbusting was making realtors rich and the city's white population was fleeing to the suburbs. In an effort to stanch the hemorrhaging, the city council had amended the municipal code to require all of its employees to reside within its boundaries. Even without all the patronage jobs it was a clever idea, and one that had probably saved Chicago from a fate worse than death—namely, Detroit's. "My father worked for the County, so we didn't have to stay in the city, but he had a lot of friends on the police force, so we moved with them. Where we lived in Edison Park every other kid's dad was a fireman or a cop," Levin explained, "and practically everyone attended Catholic schools. I obviously couldn't, so my parents sent me to Solomon Schechter."

Rusty used this as a springboard for a series of questions about Levin's education, taking him through college at the University of Illinois and medical school at Wisconsin, where he had also done his residency. A two-year fellowship in child psychiatry at UCSF followed, after which Levin had moved back to the Chicago area. While they were talking, I removed the toothpicks from my sandwich and discovered the mystery meat inside to be turkey—not my favorite but better than one of the vegan offerings everyone now seemed compelled to offer.

"I wanted to stay in the Bay Area, but my parents were ailing, and my wife wanted to be closer to her family in Milwaukee," Levin was saying. "So we came back and settled in Glencoe. Other than the weather, I have no regrets. It's a good place to raise a family and I can actually talk to some of my patients."

The small talk seemed to have calmed him down some.

"So you do traditional therapy, then?" I asked, swallowing the last of my sandwich and wiping my face with a napkin. From what I could tell, Levin hadn't yet taken a bite of his.

"Whenever the patient—or more accurately, his or her parents—can afford it, which in that area is quite a few. It takes up eighty percent of my practice."

I was beginning to like him.

Most people visiting a psychiatrist for the first time have been conditioned to expect a concerned, nonjudgmental professional who will spend long hours ferreting out their childhood traumas while they relax on a couch in a tastefully appointed room. But advances in drug treatments, along with simple economics, have long rendered that picture obsolete. These days, the majority of psychiatrists are psychopharmacologists, doling out whatever cocktail is called for by their patients' symptoms and referring them elsewhere for counseling. A doctor can see four times as many patients an hour in a practice devoted to prescribing and monitoring medications, and while most patients do better with talk therapy, it's expensive and infrequently covered by insurance plans. I'd resisted the trend as much as I could—I hadn't gone to medical school to become a glorified pill pusher—but it was easy to see why many psychiatrists, especially those in private practice, would opt for the more lucrative alternative.

Levin, it appeared, wasn't one of them.

"And Danny's parents could afford it?" Rusty asked, apparently judging Levin loosened up enough to move on to the subject we were there for.

"Yes, at least initially. He was referred to me last winter after fainting in the middle of a swim meet. It was a big one—New Trier's first of the season against Evanston—and it cost his team the four-hundred-meter relay. Poor kid went down while he was waiting on the starting block. His pediatrician did a whole battery of tests—MRI, thyroid, etcetera—but couldn't find a physiological cause, and the boy was complaining of sleeplessness, so he sent him over to me."

"What was his age then?" I asked.

"He'd turned nineteen a few months before, in September."

"Isn't that old for a high-school senior?"

Levin laughed cynically. "You're obviously not familiar with the

Illinois school year—or North Shore parents. To enroll in kindergarten here you have to be five by September first or petition specially to get in, and that's the last thing families in the New Trier feeder schools want. Most of them 'redshirt' their kids—hold them back for as long as they can get away with, so the kid can be bigger, stronger, and smarter than the rest of their classmates. Danny had been swimming since he was three, and his father, who'd made it all the way to the Olympic trials, wanted the boy to follow in his footsteps—or, if you prefer, swim strokes."

"So the boy was under a lot of heat to succeed," Rusty said.

"Naturally, though in that respect no different than most of the kids in that pressure cooker they call a high school. Danny was also the oldest of three children. The other two were girls, so as far as the father was concerned they didn't count. It's amazing people still have these attitudes, but I see it all the time."

"What kind of business was the father in?"

"Trader at the CBOE and as overbearing and insufferable as they come."

"And the mother?"

"Homemaker. But not the usual trophy wife you find in Winnetka. Kind of mousey, actually, and planted firmly under her husband's thumb. According to Danny, the father bullied her, and I'd bet good money he abused her physically too. Anyone who thinks domestic violence is limited to the poor should spend a few days in my practice."

"Was the father abusive to the boy, too?"

"Danny didn't say so explicitly, but I guessed it was going on. I think he was frightened of what might happen to him—as well as his mother— if he ratted out his dad. It's in my notes. Have you had a chance to look at them yet?" he asked, before remembering about me. He stopped in embarrassment. "My apologies. That was insensitive of me."

Rusty came to my rescue. "Don't worry about his tender feelings," he said, clapping me on the back. "Next to Mark, the new mayor is a shrinking violet."

"And he's only missing a finger," I said.

Levin let out the barest of chuckles. "OK, OK, I get it. Nothing but gallows humor around here."

I thought I ought to explain. "I did see your notes, in a manner of speaking, before coming here." Yelena had come through with the transcription that morning. "But I was surprised you're still doing it the old-fashioned way."

"I know. I know. I should have gone paperless long before now. My staff would certainly thank me for it. But somehow I can't see myself tapping merrily away on an iPad while I'm talking to a seriously depressed patient."

"Was Danny in that category?" I asked, seeing an opening.

"Not in my opinion, though he was presenting with a number of symptoms of moderate depression—anxiety, insomnia, a falling off of interest in his usual activities—when he first came to me. I started him on Placeva and adjusted the dosage a few times until his mood stabilized. He responded to it well, and we started doing forty-five-minute sessions once a week."

It was time to get down to business.

There are about thirty thousand suicides in the United States each year, not a figure to be taken lightly yet still low enough to make suicide a comparatively rare event, as well as notoriously difficult to predict. Certainly a patient who has made several attempts before, lives alone or without supervision, and has expressed a persistent wish to die should be hospitalized. But between that extreme and someone who tests positive for ordinary depression, the possibilities abound. Even the most skilled clinician may find it hard to differentiate between benign and lethal suicidal thinking. And locking up every person who ever entertained a suicidal thought would not only stigmatize a large portion of the population but also quickly overwhelm the system.

My personal experience with suicide questionnaires (taken purely out of curiosity, you understand) should have had me running forthwith to the nearest emergency room. But despite what many might consider ample provocation, I had never seriously—or *very* seriously—considered taking my own life. For that reason I tended to doubt it when someone claimed that a psychiatrist should have seen it coming. Most experts on the subject agreed, saying the issue wasn't whether the patient's death was foreseeable—in hindsight it would always seem that way—but whether the psychiatrist had done a thorough-enough assessment of the risk factors.

I started down this road, asking Levin whether he had screened Danny for suicide risk when he first came in.

"Absolutely," Levin said. "And I wasn't concerned. For starters, he denied any suicidal intent or plan. I asked him all the standard questions: whether he had ever tried to hurt himself, whether he had ever wanted to die, whether he'd ever thought about or tried to commit suicide, etcetera, etcetera. All negative answers. I also got him to agree to a 'no harm' contract."

That much was standard and in Levin's notes. But it wasn't nearly enough, since as many as a quarter of patients deny suicidal ideation to their mental health provider, particularly when they've already made up their minds and don't want their plans interfered with. And "no harm" or "safety" contracts—where the patient signs a written agreement promising not to harm themselves—often create a false sense of security, leading practitioners to overlook other troubling signs.

"What other factors did you consider?" I asked.

"On the plus side, Danny hadn't made any previous attempts, wasn't a substance abuser, and had a strong social-support system in his swim team. He had reasonably good self-esteem and was hopeful about his future. As I mentioned, he was responding to the antidepressant and wasn't withdrawn or aggressive. Also, his activities were for the most part heavily supervised. He had a stay-at-home mom and there were no firearms in the house, nor so far as he knew a family history of suicidal behavior."

"And on the negative side?"

"He was male and over sixteen, which put him in the worst statistical grouping. As I've mentioned, his family situation was less than ideal, and he may have been physically abused by his father, although the literature suggests the last isn't all that significant."

Levin paused here, as though he had something else to add but couldn't make up his mind whether to say it.

"Anything else?" I prompted.

"Yes. Something I didn't put in my notes at Danny's request. I'm not sure I should be talking about it."

Rusty jumped in then, pointing out that we needed to know all the facts, both the good and bad. "And anything you say in this room will be covered by the attorney-client privilege."

"It's not a bad fact," Levin said. "Oh, all right, some say it is, but I didn't think so. Not in Danny's case, anyway."

I thought I knew what he was about to tell us, but I wanted to hear it from him.

"He was gay," Levin said finally, slowly and uncomfortably. "And very anxious that his parents not find out about it."

"Understandable," Rusty observed, "given the family situation you've described."

"We talked about it extensively," Levin continued. "When he first came to me, Danny was fairly sure of his sexual orientation, but hadn't acted on it yet. Over the years he'd seen enough male eye candy in the locker room to know that's what he was attracted to, but hadn't yet found the courage to come out. I didn't encourage him in that direction—I understood his concerns about his parents—but I did suggest he get in touch with a local support group for gay teens. He followed my advice, and before you know it, met someone. If I had to guess, that's what the song on Facebook—*Don't Fear the Reaper*—was about."

It made sense. The band had always said it was more about undying love than a suicide pact, and the frequent references to Romeo and Juliet, whose suicides were, if anything, unplanned, backed them up.

"So you think it was a coded message?" I said.

"Yes. I think he must have posted it as a love note to his friend, who hadn't come out yet, either. They both planned on waiting until they got to college—at least before they were discovered."

"When was that?" Rusty asked.

"It couldn't have happened at a worse time. It was toward the end

of April, right after dad had suffered a big trading loss—don't ask me
for the specifics, what I understand about options you could fit on a
postage stamp—and there was talk of needing to sell the home. Typical
McMansion by the way, on a lot barely big enough to hold the ranch
they tore down to build it. That was when the other boy's folks found
some pornographic material in his room and badgered him into a confession. They went straight to Danny's parents to complain that their
precious offspring was being 'turned' by Danny."

"How did Danny handle it?" I asked.

"As well as can be expected. Frankly, I think he was relieved to
finally have it all out in the open."

"And the parents?"

"Just what you'd expect," Levin said bitterly. "Naturally, Carpenter
senior couldn't believe that a son of his might be a 'pansy-ass,' to use
his charming term, so he needed to pass the blame, and there I was,
with a big bulls-eye on my forehead. He accused me of having tricked
Danny into exploring his otherwise-nonexistent homosexual feelings
and threatened to report me to the state board. He even had the gall
to come to my office and threaten me physically. It's one of the reasons
I have no intention of ever settling this matter. And of course, they
pulled Danny from therapy."

Danny's supposed suicide had occurred in August. "So between
late April and the accident, Danny wasn't receiving any psychiatric
care," I said, thinking that this could easily account for his wrapping a
car around a tree.

"Wrong," Levin replied. "He was on the road to recovery but still
needed my help, and I wasn't about to cut him loose mid-therapy.
He was over eighteen, so I didn't need parental consent to continue
our sessions, which I did free of charge. I also continued to write his
prescriptions."

"And this went on right up until he died?" Rusty asked.

"The last time I saw him was a week before the accident, on August
tenth. He had to be at his university early to start swim practice. I'd put
him in touch with a Twin City colleague and given him some free drug

samples to tide him over until he could begin therapy again. It was an emotional parting, but not a sad one. He seemed so excited about going away and starting a new life, one where he'd finally have the freedom to be himself." Levin's voice had grown thick. He stopped and blew loudly into a handkerchief. "Honestly, if I'd had any idea, I would never . . ."

I realized with a jolt of sympathy that he had begun to weep.

"So what do you think?" Rusty asked me. It had taken some minutes for Levin to recover, and when another half hour of questioning had failed to add anything to our inventory of facts, Rusty had let the psychiatrist go, telling him not to worry, we'd get the case straightened out without much trouble. But beneath the gung-ho demeanor, I could tell Rusty was concerned.

"Based on what we know right now, I'd say he's pretty clean. I'm not happy that he left the boy's homosexuality out of his notes—or about his excuse. Since Danny was over eighteen, his parents could be denied access to his medical records, so why the worry? But I suppose if my young patient begged me, I might have taken my chances and done the same thing. The trouble is we now only have Levin's word for it."

Rusty agreed it wasn't a helpful fact. "Plus the parents' attorney will surely try to make it sound like he was hiding something. Does the fact of the boy's sexual orientation matter from a medical point of view?"

I shrugged. "It's definitely another risk factor. There's a lot of evidence that LGBT adolescents attempt suicide at a much higher rate than their peers, especially when they're facing stiff disapproval at home. It adds to the mix, but it doesn't tip the balance one way or the other. The trouble is, these situations are always so nuanced."

Rusty sighed. "I expected as much. Well, we'll work with what we have. The biggest problem will be getting him to relax enough to testify on his own behalf. You couldn't see it, but he had a face on like he'd just eaten a sour cherry the whole time, especially when we were talking about Carpenter senior. That's not going to go over well with a jury. And he barely took a bite of his sandwich."

"Ugh," I said. "I thought so. It's typical of physicians accused of malpractice to experience extreme stress: they usually blame themselves more than they blame the party suing them. There's even a name for it—Medical Malpractice Stress Syndrome. If you can, try to get him into therapy. I can give you some names."

"Please do," Rusty said. "And I'll do my damnedest to get him to agree. I'd hate to see the poor fellow wrap his own car around a tree."

# SIX

When I got back to my office, there was an e-mail waiting for me from Melissa. I wasn't sure I could control the shaking of my hand long enough to tap it open, so instead I went over and flopped on my couch, taking belly breaths to slow my heart rate. All it did was remind me of long-ago Lamaze classes, which resurrected the reason I'd volunteered for this insanity in the first place.

I thought once more about my conversation with Josh. How exactly *would* I feel if nothing happened? And was I really doing it for Louis's sake? Now three and a half, my son seemed remarkably unfazed by my blindness. Like most small children, he hadn't yet been conditioned to think that disability was strange or scary, and appeared to accept me as if all fathers came that way. The situation would probably change as he grew older, but weren't all adolescents embarrassed by their parents' shortcomings? And according to the library I'd collected on the subject, sighted children were no worse off for the experience of having a blind parent. If anything, it made them into more tolerant, well-rounded human beings.

Annie, of course, was an entirely different story, but given our history she had every reason to be suspicious of my parenting skills. And therein lay the crux of the problem. How much of my eagerness to be a test subject came down to the one thing I could never fix or make better? Was healing myself physically just a way of paving over the guilt that had stalked me like a velociraptor since the day our first son died? No matter what way you looked at it, I was responsible, if not for causing the infection that killed Jack, than for not diagnosing it in time.

Harvey, my therapist, thought I should go easier on myself. "In its early stages, meningitis easily passes for the common cold. Any doctor could have made the same mistake." But, of course, I hadn't been just any doctor, and my excuse for being gone that night made my neglect all the more unforgivable. Harvey's therapeutic ministrations to one side, there was no way to put a positive spin on a man who had cheated on his wife multiple times and then failed to save his child because he was miles away in another woman's arms. Some might say I'd been justly punished for my sins, but I couldn't go there either. Josh was right about me. Despite my desire to move ahead, I still hadn't come close to anything like acceptance—of either my shameful past or my mortifying present. At best, I was hanging on from day to day like a survivor of the *Titanic* clinging to a scrap of flotsam. Was I really prepared to gamble my shaky equilibrium on the slim chance that I could score a letter or two on a Snellen chart?

After several more rounds of internal wrangling, I decided to declare the match a draw. Where was it written I had to *like* being a gimp? No one in their right mind would turn down the opportunity I was being offered. Even if it didn't pan out, at least I could tell myself I'd tried. And if it turned out to be nothing but false hope—if I really *was* destined to be a cripple for the rest of my life—then there would be plenty of time to deal with it. Later.

I rose from the couch, crossed the room, and nearly dislocated my index finger driving it into the Enter key.

Afterwards I needed a drink, but I didn't think Josh would find Melissa's e-mail a cause for celebration, so I set out for the Double L on my own. Still feeling a bit unsteady, I thought I could use extra help getting there, so when I got downstairs I put my Bluetooth in my ear and opened my phone's GPS app. Unlike the ones you're probably familiar with, mine was essentially a talking map. It didn't just tell me where I was, it gave me detailed information about my surroundings. I could move my finger around a virtual compass on the screen and be informed of what was ahead of and behind me, right down to numbered addresses, street names, and points of interest, like restaurants, stores, and professional buildings. I could also "save" favorite destinations whose proximity would then be relayed to me as I moved along.

A few blocks on, my phone told me I was thirty, then twenty, then ten yards from the Double L.

The Double L, aka the Lucky Leprechaun, is my favorite drinking establishment, a dive that probably saw its last paint job when Mike Ditka was a tight end for the Bears. Fly-spotted photos of dead celebrities fill its walls, and Christmas lights wink above the bar in all seasons. Adding to the period charm, the beverage menu studiously avoids anything that might be mistaken for a premium brand. On the plus side, the drinks are cheap, and except for the hospital employees who pour in after the day shift, the place is never heavily populated.

I stopped in front of the door, shifted my cane to a pencil grip, and held it out while I pushed my way in. The barkeep on duty was Hallie's cousin, Jesus.

"*Hola, mi Freddy,*" he called out cheerfully. "Empty barstool at your two o'clock."

I gleaned there were few other customers, which meant that Jesus would be eager to chat. I searched out the seat he'd indicated and asked for a double, adding, "I'll pay for the good stuff, if you have it." Jesus kept a bottle of twenty-year-old Maker's Mark not on offer to the general public in a cabinet under the bar.

"Yeah? Something to celebrate?" he asked meaningfully.

"You could call it that."

He reached over and clapped me on the shoulder. "That's *fantastico*, bro. I was wondering when it was going to happen. 'Course Jackie will be all pissed off, but that's her problem."

"Jackie?"

"My aunt, Jacinta. She and Hallie are only a year apart and they're as tight as tortillas." Jesus finished pouring and pushed a tumbler across the bar.

"And what would Jackie have to be pissed about?" I asked without thinking, picking up the glass and putting it to my lips.

"Well, don't let on that I told you, but Jackie's decided she doesn't like you."

"Like me?" I repeated quizzically. "She's never even met me."

"Yeah, but ever since she broke up with her ex, she's had this thing against divorced dudes. Thinks they're all liars and cheats."

I almost spit out the mouthful of bourbon I was on the point of swallowing. "Wait a minute. Back up here. Who says I'm divorced?"

"Hallie. At least that's what I overheard her say at my nephew Ramon's First Communion party. Jackie was pretty worked up over it. '*Orralay*, girl,' she was telling Hallie, 'why are you going within ten feet of him?'" Jesus paused as if maybe he'd spoken out of school. "You are, aren't you? Divorced, I mean. Hallie's sources are usually pretty accurate."

I should have anticipated something like this. "Which sources?" I asked shakily.

Jesus leaned over the bar and said in a conspiratorial tone, "You know, prosecutors and their friends on the force, here and across state lines. It's a professional courtesy they extend to one another. Call it an unofficial background check. Hallie won't go anywhere with a guy until she's vetted him. Makes sense. If you're a gal, you don't want to find yourself alone with some *pinchero* whose ex has got a court order against him."

I was starting to feel ill. "And what did this 'unofficial' background check reveal about me?"

"I don't know the particulars, but Hallie said that except for the decree you were clear. And current on your support payments."

*So Hallie knew about Louis too?* I downed the rest of my drink in one swallow. All this time I'd been worrying how to come clean with her and . . . I wasn't sure whether to laugh hysterically or run outside and throw myself under a speeding truck. What must she think of me, keeping Louis a secret all this time? Of course, the fact that I'd been married and had a child was only part of it. And the not-so-debatable part. "You better give me another shot," I said, pushing my glass forward.

"Sure," Jesus said, taking the glass and pouring again. "But why all the *nervios*? It's not like it's any big deal. Shit, a guy your age? If you hadn't been hooked up with somebody before, Hallie'd probably think you were gay."

I almost spit out another mouthful. I needed to put an end to this conversation in a hurry. "Listen, Jesus, I think we're operating under a misconception. I like your cousin, really I do. She's a very fine lady. But there's nothing happening between us." Or ever would be, I thought dispiritedly.

"Really? *De pinga!*" He sounded genuinely disappointed. "I'm sorry, man. It's just that when you came in here smiling and looking all lighthearted for a change, I assumed it was because you were getting laid. . . . Anyway, I'm sorry for Hallie, too. I always thought you two would make a great couple."

"I'm sure there are a lot of other men out there who would make her happy," I said.

"I dunno about that," Jesus replied. "Though I guess this clears the way for Bjorn."

"The investigator she's using?"

"Yeah, that's the one. Have you met him?"

No, but I might as well know the worst. "Uh-uh. What can you tell me?"

Jesus was always forthcoming with the minutest details. "Comes from African American royalty. Youngest kid of the Reverend Aloysius Dixon and his Swedish wife, Ingrid. Dixon's got one of the biggest congregations on the South Side, rakes in enough dough every week to float a bond issue. Family's got connections all over the place, which is probably why baby Bjorn decided to go into private investigation. Mostly he does big corporate cases—cybercrime and stuff like that—but he met Hallie at a party and offered her his personal attention, if you know what I mean."

"You seen him?"

"Only on the news when he was busting that hacker who shut down ComEd in July. Paper-bag complexion, eyes the color of an Alaskan Husky. He'd look at home in a Calvin Klein ad if that tells you anything."

It did, and a lot more than I wanted to know.

The next morning, Mike was still missing when I made a brief stop at my office before heading over for my new medication. I called the *Streetwise* offices to see if anyone had seen him, but the staff member I spoke to said he hadn't picked up his paper stock in over a week. They were mildly worried and had called around to several homeless shelters to see if he'd shown up, but without luck. I wasn't surprised. Mike disliked the shelters, which were usually miserably crowded, and only used them when the mercury dipped into the single digits.

It took most of the day to get my pills. I first had to take off my clothes, step on a scale, open my mouth and say "aaaah," get strapped to a blood-pressure cuff, pee in a jar, give a blood sample, and be generally poked, prodded, and manhandled until I was at last deemed an acceptable specimen and not on the verge of death. Then it was on to yet more eye tests. Ophthalmology residents waved various objects before my face, my fundus—the medical term for the back of the eye—was dilated and photographed, a perimetrist mapped my visual field, electrodes were placed on my eyes to test their responsiveness to light. All of these things had been done to me many times before, and on far less sunny occasions, but the routine was still well past its expiration date. By late afternoon, when I was sitting down with a nurse practitioner to go over my instructions, I was feeling as strung out as Malcolm McDowell after a session of the Ludovico technique.

The nurse, whose name was Abby, wanted to be sure I understood what a placebo was.

"Sure. They're like the 'ones that mother gives you,'" I said, dredging up the old lyric from *Surrealistic Pillow*.

Abby was perplexed. "Huh?"

"They don't do anything at all."

"I still don't get it," Abby said.

Was there anyone in the younger generation I could communicate with? "You've really never heard of Jefferson Airplane?" I asked.

"Are they like Virgin Air or something? And I don't understand what planes have to do with my question."

"It's not important," I sighed.

I explained what a placebo was and answered her further questions as patiently as I could until it was finally time for her to hand over the goods—a small bottle with a tamper-proof cap that Abby told me was filled with a four-week supply. I was to take the tablets inside three times a day, preferably with meals, starting first thing tomorrow. I was to return for a check-up and a new bottle when I'd used up the contents. I was to contact the team immediately if I experienced any of the following: headache; stomach upset; rash; itching or swelling (especially of the face, tongue, or throat); fainting; dizziness; trouble breathing; fast or irregular heartbeat; ringing of the ears; nausea; difficulty standing, walking, or getting up; confusion; inability to concentrate; nervousness; changes in urine; drowsiness; increased sweating; hallucinations; or seizures.

At least I didn't have to worry about sudden loss of or changes in vision.

Melissa came in then to shake my hand and wish me luck.

"If there is going to be an improvement, you should start noticing something in the next few weeks. In the meantime, try not to think too much about it. There's some evidence that the therapeutic effect is weakened when the patient is anxious or under stress. Enjoy all your normal activities and get plenty of rest."

I pledged that I would.

"And doctor?" she said, as I was pocketing the bottle and picking up my cane to leave.

"Yes?"

"Don't let me down."

# SEVEN

The next day, a Friday, found me in one of Boris's town cars, going over my notes for Jane's bond hearing.

Boris was Yelena's ex, a taciturn man who runs an independent limousine service. Perhaps out of lingering affection, or more likely so that she wouldn't be cheated out of support payments, Yelena still managed his books and appointments, another diversion from her secretarial duties though one I didn't mind because it meant I always had a ride when I needed one. Cabs were cheaper, but their drivers weren't always trustworthy—either about taking the least circuitous route or returning the correct amount of change—and I never had to fear what health hazards might be lurking in Boris's upholstery. He'd picked me up at 1:00 p.m. sharp, and we'd cruised down the Drive before turning onto the Stevenson Expressway and proceeding a few miles on to the exit at California. We were now parked on a side street, waiting for Hallie to call from the courthouse several blocks away. It was a warm September day, but Boris had all the windows up and the doors firmly locked, not trusting the neighborhood.

I was then six hours into my drug trial.

I'd tumbled out of bed at daylight after a mostly sleep-tossed night before heading for my kitchen and boiling some water, which I used to make tea and packet of instant oatmeal. I wasn't hungry, but with Abby's admonition about meals still fresh in my mind, I forced myself to clean the bowl and the dried-out—and hopefully mold-free—remnants of a container of blueberries. Then it was on to a slice of toast and orange juice. As I was finishing up, I remembered something I should have done earlier and went back to my bedroom for my phone, which was charged up and ready to go on the nightstand. I brought the phone back to the kitchen, turned on all the lights to get the clearest possible picture, and using another one of my blink apps snapped a photo of the pill bottle with its label facing the camera. Bypassing the Internet search feature, I gave the photo a moniker—White Rabbit— and stored it in the app's database of images. Later, if I had trouble distinguishing the bottle from something else that felt similar, all I had to do was point the camera at it and the app would sing out its name.

With these preparations behind me, I figured it was time for lift-off. The tamper-proof cap gave me some trouble, but I eventually guessed that I was supposed to push down on the top while simultaneously twisting it to the right. There was the obligatory wad of cotton inside, which I had to pick out in clumps before the bottle would yield its treasure. With the contents finally freed, I turned the bottle over and shook one into my palm, holding it there a few minutes like a Communion wafer. Then I popped it into my mouth like I was Michael Jordan putting one over the rim and washed it down with a swallow of the tea. As it slid down my throat, I said a little prayer that I was getting the real thing. One pill makes you larger, and one pill makes you small.

I knew better than to expect anything so soon, but it was hard to temper a sense of excitement as I bided my time in Boris's car. On top of that, I was experiencing my usual pre-court jitters, similar to being a Christian anticipating a pride of hungry lions before opening ceremonies at the Colosseum. Hallie said that preparing for trial was like rolling every anxious moment in your life into one. I could tell her a thing or two about anxious moments, but I understood what she meant. Even old court hands told me they always experienced a case of the butterflies before an important hearing—or did if they were any good. It was only when a lawyer was too stupid or lazy to care that he could walk through a courthouse door and not feel like he was wearing a neon "Hit Me" sign on his forehead.

In the town car, my phone played the opening bars of *Rikki Don't Lose That Number*, and I scrambled to answer it. It was Hallie, informing me that we'd be up in an hour's time. She sounded as pumped up as I was. "I'm going to try to get a few minutes with Jane in the lockup, so

I may not be in the courtroom when you get there," she said. "Just sit someplace where I can find you."

Like I had a prayer of vanishing into the crowd.

"Time to get moving," I told Boris.

The Cook County Circuit Courthouse, known to Chicagoans as "Twenty-Sixth and Cal," processes some 28,000 criminal cases annually. Given the sea of humanity that passes through its portals each day, it couldn't be more unhappily located. Tucked away in a remote corner of the Southwest Side, miles away from anything resembling a business district or even a fast-food outlet, it has been the butt of jokes ever since it opened on April Fool's Day in 1929. Local lore has it that the site of the courthouse was dictated by Anton Cermak, the father of the Chicago Machine, who wanted it on his turf as a cottage industry for his ward organization. Whatever the reason, it had never done anything to boost the surrounding real estate, and jurors unfortunate enough to be summoned to its blighted precincts were advised by the Sheriff's office to bring plenty of quarters for the vending machines if they didn't want to go hungry all day. Visitors to the courthouse often remarked on the imposing reliefs carved aside its seventh-story windows, symbolizing law, liberty, justice, truth, might, love, and wisdom. The only thing not represented was the American Way.

Boris dropped me off in front, and I scraped across a concrete walk to a short flight of shallow steps, divided into six sections by iron railings. I took one of the sections in the center and then angled toward the hydraulic *whoosh* of the heavy brass doors another ten yards off. Once inside, I prepared myself for a long wait: the line to get past the metal detector usually resembled the entrance to a Wal-Mart just before opening hour on Black Friday. Amazingly, it took only fifteen minutes to get to the head of the queue. Equally astounding, when my cane set off the alarm (as it always did) the guards did not insist on a full-body pat down. "Doesn't look like a Ruger," one of them said in apparent seriousness as they nudged me roughly ahead.

I took the elevator to the fifth floor. Normally, bond hearings took place in one of the airless lower-floor rooms called the "fishbowl" because of the bulletproof glass partitions separating visitors from the proceedings. But because the prosecution intended to put on evidence, the clerk had assigned us to the judge who would eventually try the case: one Eugene Cudahay, known in legal circles by such nicknames as "Cuddles," "Cudgel," and "Conundrum." According to Hallie, none of the names did justice to his reputation as a meticulous jurist with no bias in favor of either the prosecution or the defense, which was probably the reason he had one of the highest case backlogs in the county. This was good news for Jane but probably meant we had a long afternoon ahead of us.

I asked a passerby for help locating the correct courtroom and stepped through the door. I tried to pick out Hallie's voice above the din inside—Jane's hearing had evidently aroused the customary fascination with celebrities accused of a major crime—but apparently she was still in the lockup. This presented me with a dilemma: should I remain hovering by the entrance or inch my way up the center aisle in search of a seat? I was saved from thinking too hard about it by a friendly voice calling my name. "Angelotti, get over here—by the jury box."

It was Tom Klutsky, the *Sun-Times* reporter who covered legal affairs. I headed over in his direction, narrowly avoiding several outstretched limbs along the way. Klutsky exited the box and met me halfway. He shook my hand and offered me a beefy elbow before guiding me up the steps and past multiple other body parts to a place in the front row, where members of the fourth estate often sat when there was no jury present.

Klutsky had befriended me the previous spring, partly out of kindness but also to sell me on giving him a story. For a reporter, he wasn't a bad sort, and I'd eventually agreed to be the subject of one of his features in exchange for a hefty donation to a low-vision foundation and his solemn promise not to overdramatize the situation. Klutsky had managed to keep half of the bargain. In his telling, I was practically the Lou Gehrig of blindness, bravely coping with a turn of fortune that would have felled many a less-noble soul. At least he didn't quote me as saying I was the luckiest man on the face of the earth.

"So to what do we owe the pleasure of your company?" Klutsky asked in his nasally Chicago accent when we were settled in.

I filled him in on the particulars.

"That's a hoot," he said when I was finished. "You'll have fun with the ASA. He looks like he just got out of nursery school. I watched him try a case up in Lake County last month. You remember the one where the guy cut up his wife and used her to angle for bass in Fox Lake? He might have gotten away with it if he hadn't forgotten to get a fishing license."

I did remember. The story had appeared under Klutsky's byline and the headline WADSWORTH MAN ON THE HOOK FOR MURDERING WIFE. "What's his name?" I asked.

"The prosecutor? Adam Frost. Though he doesn't live up to it. He looked like he was going to lose his lunch while he was publishing photos of the remains to the jury. The husband had a cooler full of them, all neatly separated into gallon freezer bags. Frost's uncle is the head of the Waukegan Democratic Organization, which is probably the only reason he got the job. The kid has all the killer instincts of an earthworm. He won't give you any trouble."

I hoped not.

"You know the lady we're here for?" Klutsky asked, switching topics.

"Never met or seen her."

"Too bad. Beautiful woman. Think Katharine Hepburn with the same DAR pedigree. Brooks here can give you the scoop." Brooks, it turned out, was the columnist for the *Tribune* who'd been drinking with Rory Gallagher on the night he died and had done a freelance article about Jane for the *Chicago Bar Journal* not long ago.

"Do you want the Cliff Notes or the full-blown?" Brooks asked when we'd been introduced.

"Cliff Notes to begin," I said.

"Oldest daughter of three. Father was classics professor at the University of Chicago. Mother a curator at the Oriental Institute. Family home in Kenwood. Valedictorian of her high-school class at the Lab

School. *Summa cum laude* from Princeton. *Harvard Law Review.* Artist, too. Does some kind of glass sculpture."

"Nice résumé," I said. "Does she have a personality to go with it?"

Brooks leaned in and lowered his voice confidingly. "Well, that's the thing. Though you couldn't tell it from the interview—I mean, the woman could charm the pants off the Reverend Billy Graham—she has a reputation as a real ice princess. Only comes alive in front of a jury. And lots of enemies at the State's Attorney's. Matter of fact, I couldn't find any of her old colleagues who liked her. Too much on her high horse and not shy about ripping into associates when they screwed up. I had to go easy on her in the article—some of the stories I heard painted her as a real Medusa—but the general feeling was you didn't ever want to cross her."

I was surprised. "That's not what I heard. I was under the impression she was some kind of latter-day Joan of Arc."

"Who, as you'll recall, also got burned at the stake," Brooks said.

"Is that what you think this murder charge is about?" I asked him. "A witch hunt?"

"All I know is, nobody shed any tears when she upped and quit the office a few years back," Brooks answered. "And they were all as tight-mouthed as clams about the reason."

# EIGHT

I was about to ask Klutsky and Brooks more questions when Hallie showed up, bringing a tall, fragrant individual whom she introduced to all around as Bjorn Dixon. He gave me his hand, and I observed he was the pinky ring type, in addition to the flowery cologne type.

"Cheers," Bjorn drawled, sounding like Melissa Singh's long-lost cousin. "Glad we're finally having this meet-up."

"Balliol or All Souls?" I couldn't stop myself from asking.

"Neither," he laughed. "But it goes over well with the ladies. Here's my card," he said, reaching out and slipping one into the breast pocket of my jacket. He paused to finger the material like I was a store manne-quin. "Nice suit."

"Thanks," I said, brushing his hand off. "I'll be sure to tell my Savile Row man that you liked it."

I turned my attention to Hallie. "Where do you want me?"

"At counsel table. And we'd better get over there now. Bjorn, I'm afraid you'll have to stay here, unless you can find room in the spectator section."

"No worries," Bjorn said. "I've always preferred dress circle to stalls."

"Where did you pick him up?" I hissed in Hallie's ear while she walked me over. "He sounds like a cross between Prince Charles and Simon Cowell."

"I like it. And why do you care? Unless you're planning on dating him, too?"

I was about to say something foolish when the clerk bellowed, "All rise! The Circuit Court of Cook County, the Honorable Eugene Cudahay presiding, is now in session."

Hallie and I hastened to take up our positions at counsel table. The judge ascended the dais, and Jane was brought in from the lockup behind the bench.

I'm not a believer in premonitions, at least in the mystical sense. Too often they seem like *post hoc* explanations for unfortunate events, a way to avoid the terrifying proposition that we really *are* alone in a cruel and random universe. But I do believe the subconscious "sees" more than our waking minds, and that somewhere in the primitive regions of the brain a switch gets turned on when we feel danger coming. If so, a siren had begun to wail in my head the moment Jane entered the room. Before I'd even heard her voice or pressed her flesh—in other words before I had a clue to go on besides the matinee-idol descriptions I'd been given—I knew this woman was trouble.

She crossed the room with a deputy sheriff and sat down to Hallie's left. I had the distinct impression her eyes were on me the whole time. Though I could have been entirely wrong, she seemed fixated on me—and not in a promising way.

After the case name and number were called and the state had presented its verified petition in support of a no-bail order, Judge Cudahay admonished counsel to keep the hearing short and to the point. "This is a bond hearing, not a reading from the Megillah." Everyone in the room dutifully laughed. "The only issue before me is whether bail should be denied or set, and if so, in what amount. In other words, I expect to be home in time for an early dinner."

"Certainly, Your Honor," ASA Frost piped up. "We'll be as succinct as possible."

"Get to it then," Cudahay advised him.

Everything I'd heard about Frost was right: he was greener than the grass over a septic tank.

He led off by calling a "life and death" witness, Andrew Urquhart, Gallagher's nephew and only living relative. I'd learned from Hallie, who loved to talk trial strategy, that the prosecution always called "life and death" witnesses in murder trials to establish the self-evident fact of the victim's demise. Hearing from a close relative—preferably one who will break down, sob, and have to be carried out of the courtroom after being reminded of their loved one's tragic end—puts a face on the victim and helps get the jury invested in the proceedings. There was no jury today, but Frost no doubt wanted to lead with a splash.

It turned out to be more like a trickle.

Urquhart was sworn and stated his name for the record. He affirmed that he was the only child of Gallagher's sole sibling, a sister who had died with her husband in 1972 on United Flight 553, notorious for having crashed into a row of bungalows while attempting to land at Midway Airport. Urquhart was five at the time, and being without close relatives on his father's side, had been taken in by Gallagher's aging parents. At that point, Gallagher was already in college, but he treated the younger boy like the little brother he'd never had. When Gallagher's parents also passed in the eighties, the journalist paid for Urquhart's schooling and footed the start-up costs for the chain of electronics stores he now owned, scattered around the southwest suburbs. "He was like a second father to me," Urquhart said, with a catch in his throat that sounded as genuine as paste jewelry.

The sob story did not impress Judge Cudahay. "Counsel, what is the purpose of calling this witness?" he demanded of Frost.

"I, uh . . . was hoping to establish that the victim was, ahem, dead and properly identified."

"I'm sure the defense would be willing to stipulate to that fact, isn't that right, Ms. Sanchez?"

Hallie rose quickly beside me. "We most certainly would, Your Honor."

"Then I'm sure we won't be needing any more of Mr. Urquhart's testimony today, will we, Mr. Frost?"

"Well, if the court isn't interested . . ." Frost sputtered. Cudahay must have glared at him because Frost's next words were "I mean, sure."

"The witness is excused, then."

Hallie sat back down, and though she didn't say anything—outwardly gloating over opposing counsel's missteps was a no-no—I could tell she thought we were off to a good start.

Frost then read into the record the sworn statement of Gallagher's cardiologist, Dr. Catherine Climpson, who recounted that she had administered a stress test and an EKG on Gallagher the year before, after the deceased had been referred to her complaining of shortness of breath. The results were both abnormal and alarming. Climpson had advised an immediate change in diet and lifestyle to little avail. When Gallagher next visited her six months later, he was showing all the signs of advanced coronary artery disease, but except for a course of statins, was following none of her health recommendations. In accordance with her professional responsibilities, Climpson had kept the results of her examinations confidential but could not, of course, say with whom Gallagher may have shared them.

Frost's next witness was the medical examiner, Dr. James Lubbock. The examination was painful, proceeding in fits and starts and filled with leading questions, but except for a single hearsay objection—when Frost tried to elicit the reason for the exhumation request—Hallie was quiet, probably having surmised that she'd earn more points with the judge by letting Frost crater on his own. It ended with Lubbock's opinion that Gallagher had died of cardiac arrest, in all likelihood brought on by his ingestion of the prescription antipsychotic Lucitrol.

It was then Hallie's turn to cross-examine. She got up and walked over to the witness box. When judges permitted it, Hallie liked to get as close to a potentially hostile witness as possible.

"Dr. Lubbock, I understand that no autopsy was performed on Mr. Gallagher's body immediately after his death. Is that common?"

Lubbock answered, "Due to staffing shortages, our current policy is not to perform an autopsy on persons known to have suffered from heart or lung disease, or to have abused drugs or alcohol."

"And did Mr. Gallagher fit one or both of those criteria?"

"The former, certainly."

"What about the latter?"

"I'm not sure I'm in a position to say," Lubbock tried.

"Come now, doctor. Surely you examined his liver?"

Though clearly loath to admit it, Lubbock conceded that the deceased's liver showed signs of early-stage cirrhosis.

"Going back to your current policy on autopsies, are there any exceptions?"

"Yes, if the family specifically requests it."

"But no such request was made here?"

"Apparently not."

"So his corpse was not examined by your office until almost two weeks after his death."

"That is correct," Lubbock answered.

"After the body had been embalmed by an undertaker."

Lubbock was again forced to agree.

"And been buried in the ground for nearly eight days."

"Yes."

"At that point, am I correct in assuming that substantial decomposition had taken place?"

"Yes, although the rate of decomposition was slowed somewhat by the embalming procedure."

"Am I also correct in assuming that embalming can interfere with toxicology samples?"

"Yes, that's true."

"And that decomposition would also affect the quality of the samples taken?"

"That is also correct."

"For example, content that may have been present in the decedent's stomach?"

"Yes, decomposition usually begins in the stomach and intestinal passages."

"Were you able, then, to draw any inferences about when the decedent took the drug you say killed him?"

Lubbock paused here as though he wished he didn't have to answer. "Not from the stomach contents. But given the amount present in blood and liver samples, we believe it was ingested in the thirty-six-hour period prior to his death."

"Thirty-six hours," Hallie repeated for emphasis. "So you cannot say whether he took the drug just before he suffered a heart attack?"

"No."

"Or earlier on the same day."

"No."

"Or even a full day before he died."

"That's right," Lubbock conceded in a pained voice.

Having inflicted this damage, Hallie wisely didn't challenge Lubbock's claim that Lucitrol was the immediate cause of Gallagher's heart attack. "No further questions," she said, returning to her seat. I scribbled "nice job!" on the legal pad in front of her. Hallie wrote something on the pad too and passed it to Jane, who added a comment and silently passed it back. Naturally, I felt irked to be left out of the conversation.

Frost's next witnesses were patrons of Gene & Georgetti's, who could attest to overhearing Jane and Gallagher arguing heatedly on the evening of August 26, mere hours before he died. First, a Mr. and Mrs. John Dwyer, suburbanites from Gurnee, who had dined at the restaurant on their way to an 8:00 p.m. performance of *Les Misérables* at the Oriental Theater and were just finishing up their $24.95 Filet Florentine when the fracas began. Neither one of the couple could say what it had been about, though Mrs. Dwyer was certain she had overheard the defendant hissing, "You won't get away with it!" and the name "Lucy" repeated several times. The disturbance was sufficient to cause Mr. Dwyer severe indigestion, which had all but destroyed his enjoyment of the meal. "If you ask me, I deserve a refund."

Next, Walter Lasorda (no relation to Tommy), the bartender, who had watched in amusement as Jane stood and dumped the remains of a carafe of house red over Gallagher's head before strolling over to the valet station and requesting her car. "She looked damned pleased with herself," Lasorda chuckled. "And I was enjoying it too. Gallagher never tipped any more than a dime." Last, the waiter, Vincent Iglesias, who had rushed over to provide a towel to Gallagher, who seemed nonplussed and was still munching contentedly on his fried calamari appetizer notwithstanding the Chianti Classico now trickling down onto the floor beside him. "Hormones," Gallagher had remarked to Iglesias as the latter was mopping up the mess and laying out fresh table linen.

Since she hadn't yet interviewed these witnesses, Hallie did almost no cross-examination—on cross, she'd explained to me many times, you almost never ask a question for which you don't already know the answer—simply eliciting the facts that Gallagher and Jane had been together at the table the whole time, that Gallagher had himself left the restaurant around 8:30 p.m., and that after being bused from the table, the glass Gallagher had been drinking from had joined hundreds of other indistinguishable containers in the restaurant's industrial-grade dishwashers.

Frost proceeded to read into the record the statement of Beverly Van Wagner, age sixty-seven, a retired Chicago public-school teacher and widow, who a little before 9:00 p.m. that same evening had taken time out from *Storage Wars* to walk Snoopy, her Bichon Havanese, just in time to observe a tall, redheaded woman entering Gallagher's town-home on the fourteen hundred block of South Federal. Despite the woman's attempt to hide behind sunglasses and a scarf, Van Wagner claimed to have gotten a good look at her because Snoopy had chosen that precise moment to stop and sniff at a lamppost on the adjoining parkway and thereafter decided the time was ripe to empty his bowels. Being of an advanced age and constipated from stealing a chocolate bar earlier in the day, Snoopy had required a long time to complete his business, thereby giving Mrs. Van Wagner plenty of time to observe Gallagher's clandestine visitor. The woman removed a set of keys from her overcoat and, glancing around once or twice—"like she was afraid of being noticed"—let herself in. After reading of Gallagher's death in the newspaper and volunteering her information to the authori-ties, Van Wagner had been asked to participate in a lineup at the police station and had easily picked out Jane from among the photographs she was shown. According to Frost, Van Wagner was unable to appear in court that morning because of an urgent, last-minute call to babysit her grandchildren in Fort Myers, a thousand miles away. I didn't believe it for a minute.

Next, we heard from the police detective, Garrett Yanowski, who took the courtroom through his search of Jane's office and the discovery of the Lucitrol samples and disc-wiping software, as well as his inspection of Gallagher's townhome. On Yanowski's cross Hallie violated her own rule, hoping to get more information out of him than could be gleaned from the bare-bones police report.

"Detective, when you were searching the deceased's home, was there any indication that my client was present there on the night in question?"

"What do you mean by 'indication'?" Yanowski asked, playing dumb.

"Well, for example, I assume you dusted the location for fingerprints. Did you find any belonging to Ms. Barrett?"

"A few. Mostly in and around the bedroom." There were scattered titters across the courtroom.

"Quiet," Judge Cudahay growled.

"I take it you cannot tell us when those fingerprints were left."

"That's right."

"Were there any fingerprints belonging to Ms. Barrett in or around the deceased's computer station?"

Yanowski allowed as there were none. "Though she may have been wearing gloves."

Hallie asked that the last response be stricken from the record as nonresponsive, and Judge Cudahay so instructed the court reporter.

Hallie next proceeded to the questions we had worked on together. "Detective, will you describe for us the procedure that the police used during Mrs. Van Wagner's purported identification of my client?"

"Sure. What would you like to know?" Yanowski asked, going out of his way to make this difficult.

"Well, let's start with who conducted the lineup. Was it you personally?"

"Certainly. I was the principal investigating officer."

"Precisely," Hallie commented for emphasis. "And at that point had you already made up your mind to arrest my client?"

"I wouldn't say 'made up my mind,' but yes, she was our chief suspect."

"Have you ever heard the term 'filler' when used in connection with a police lineup?"

"Sure."

"Will you explain to the court what a 'filler' is?"

"A filler is a person whose physical characteristics match the verbal description given by the eyewitness. In a photo lineup it is typical to display photographs of six or more fillers in addition to that of the suspect."

"How many fillers did you use in the photo lineup in which Mrs. Van Wagner claimed to have identified my client?"

"We used a total of ten."

Hallie then asked Yanowski to explain the two common types of lineups: simultaneous and sequential. In a simultaneous lineup, as the name implies, an eyewitness is shown all of the photographs at the same time. In a sequential lineup, the photographs are displayed one by one.

Yanowski had used the first type, which was good for us.

Hallie's last questions to Yanowski were also predicated on some ideas I'd given her.

"Detective, going back to your search of Mr. Gallagher's residence, is it fair to assume that you collected all medications, prescription or otherwise, that could be found on the premises?"

"Of course. We know how to do our job," Yanowski puffed.

"How many such medications did you find?"

"Quite a few. Upward of twenty different prescription bottles, most of which had expired."

"And none of which could be identified as Lucitrol?"

"That is correct."

"Did you test the contents to be certain, or simply rely on the labeling?"

Yanowski was caught short. "We, uh . . . didn't do any testing."

"Were there any medications in unmarked containers?"

"A few," Yanowski admitted.

"Did you test the contents of those containers to rule out the possibility that they contained Lucitrol?"

"No, because it wasn't necessary." Yanowski said, finally catching on to where this was headed. "He wasn't under the care of a psychiatrist."

"That you know of," Hallie said.

"What's that supposed to mean?" Yanowski demanded.

Hallie reminded him that she was the one asking the questions. "But since you're curious, Detective, let me explain the purpose of my questions. During your exhaustive investigation into Mr. Gallagher's death, did it ever cross your mind that the deceased may have taken steps to hide a mental-health problem so that it could not be discovered by others—such as by seeing a psychiatrist in secret?"

Yanowski allowed he had not.

"Or that he may have obtained a prescription for the drug from a nonpsychiatrist provider?"

"Can that happen?" Judge Cudahay interposed.

Hallie was ready with an answer. "Yes, Your Honor, it can." She returned to counsel table, removed a document from her briefcase, and crossed the room to tender it to the court. "If the court wishes, it can take judicial notice of a recent study by the Pritzker School of Medicine, finding that the number of office visits where individuals are prescribed antidepressants with no accompanying psychiatric diagnosis ranges from twenty to fifty percent. Lucitrol is a much stronger medication, but it can be prescribed by any doctor."

Hallie then proceeded to her last set of questions. "Detective Yanowski, were you aware that, according to its financial statements, Atria's sales of Lucitrol last year accounted for more than three billion in net revenue for the company?"

Yanowski wasn't.

"Or that a standard one-hundred-milligram prescription costs on average seventy-five dollars per month?"

"I didn't do a price check, if that's what you're asking," Yanowski replied testily.

"Does that suggest to you that quite a large number of individuals have, or are currently taking the medication?"

"I guess it does."

"Some percentage of which live in the Chicago area?"

"I suppose so," Yanowski answered.

Hallie didn't need to point out that any one of them might have been responsible for feeding the drug to Gallagher.

"One last question, Detective," Hallie said. "Given your last several answers, are you in any position to say that the Lucitrol ingested by the deceased could only have come from my client?"

Yanowski was forced to admit he could not.

Hallie announced that she had no further questions and Yanowski was excused.

Frost's instincts weren't all bad, since he saved what should have been his best witness for last: a Ms. Lucille Sparks, Gallagher's twenty-eight-year-old fiancée, who Hallie told me later walked into court wearing a rock the size of a hen's egg. I didn't need to know much else about her looks because, in addition to working part-time as a coat-checker at the Union League Club, Sparks (her stage name) had a much-coveted spot on the Chicago "Luvabulls," a troupe of cheerleaders who strutted and tossed their Charlie's Angels manes to the music of Britney Spears and Lady Gaga during Bulls game breaks at the United Center. According to the Luvabulls' press kit, they were chosen each year in a contest focused on talent and athletic ability, though everyone in the city knew the real requirement was looking hot enough to sizzle a steak in a push-up bra, hot pants, and high-heeled boots. Hallie hated them with a passion, and even more so after various sports leagues banned appearances by Chief Illiniwek—the one-time mascot of her beloved Fighting Illini—for perpetuating negative stereotypes of Native Americans. "What about negative stereotypes of women?" she demanded to know. I wisely agreed with her whenever the subject came up.

I figured Hallie was going to warm to Sparks like ice circulating in Lake Michigan.

On direct, Sparks was appropriately histrionic. She and Gallagher had been "like a hundred percent in love." Their hot and heavy affair began the year before his death, when Gallagher had "come on to" Sparks while dropping off his trench coat on his way to a lunchtime meeting of the International Press Club. A few nights later, he wined and dined her at an Italian restaurant on Taylor Street, in Sparks's reenactment as tender a courtship scene as the one in which Tramp wooed Lady over a spaghetti dinner at Tony's. "I knew, like, right away, he was the one." Sparks was a little miffed that Gallagher didn't break up with Jane right away, but as Gallagher explained to her, the two had been lovers for a long time. "She was, you know, kinda getting up there and he didn't want her to feel bad about losing out to a younger girl like me. I mean, it would have been so unfair to just, like, dump her." The relationship had proceeded in this fashion until Gallagher gave Sparks the ring—bought, she pointed out with pride, at a pre-Labor Day sale at Kay's—at which point Sparks felt secure enough about Gallagher's affections to demand that Jane be given her marching orders. According to Sparks, the big break-up was to occur on the night "her Rory" was taken from her.

Hallie rose and objected that no foundation had been laid for such a statement, and the objection was sustained.

"How do you know that the victim, uh, intended to terminate his relationship with the defendant that evening?" Frost prompted, trying to get the crucial piece of information into the record.

"Because he told me so. While we were in bed that morning at my place. Right after we finished hooking up. Rory was always so horny in the morning," she confided. Judge Cudahay coughed, and Sparks apparently remembered where she was. "Sorry about that. I didn't mean no offense. Well, anyhow, like I was saying, he reached over and patted me on the you-know-what and said, 'Lucy, I think it's time you got everything you deserve.'"

"And what did you take that to mean?"

Hallie shot up again like an arrow. "Objection. The witness's interpretation of the deceased's statement is hearsay."

Judge Cudahay agreed. "Sustained."

This wasn't working out the way Frost intended. He tried once again to regain his footing. "Was that all your fiancé said?"

"Well, no," Sparks said meditatively. "We talked about our schedules for the day, you know, what we were planning and all, and when Rory would be able to come round again. It wasn't going to be until Saturday because I had work and a game that night and he was supposed to be meeting with her." I guessed she was pointing at Jane.

"Go on," Frost urged. "Did he say what the meeting was about?"

"Just that he was looking forward to it. Something about her not being able to stop it."

An ambiguous piece of testimony if ever there was one.

"Were those his precise words?"

"Maybe. I don't remember exactly. I mean, it was early and I wasn't really awake yet."

"Is there anything else you can tell us about the meeting between your fiancé and the defendant?" Frost asked, beginning to sound desperate.

"Why? I mean, it was so obvious. He was going to break up with her. Like, what else could he have been planning?"

Hallie asked that the witness's last comments be stricken from the record as speculative and nonresponsive, and it was so ordered.

Frustrated, Frost was reduced to near-hysteria. "On the day he died, did your fiancé indicate to you specifically, by his words or in any other verbal manner, his intention to break off a relationship with the defendant that evening or at any other time?"

Hallie was up again. "Objection. Leading."

I might have added incomprehensible.

Judge Cudahay sustained the objection, whereupon a defeated Frost ceded the floor to Hallie.

"Miss Sparks, you testified that you were with Mr. Gallagher the morning of August twenty-sixth. Was that the last time you saw him?"

"Yes," Sparks sniffled, resuming her distraught manner.

"Did you share breakfast together?"

"Yeah. I mean, Rory ate some eggs I scrambled for him. I made us some coffee, too."

"Were the two of you together when you made the eggs and coffee?"

"I think . . . I think he must have been in the shower while I was cooking because he complained that the eggs were cold when he sat down."

"Did you eat some of the eggs, too?"

"No. I'm a vegan."

"And after breakfast, the two of you parted?"

"Yeah. He kissed me at the door to my building. I didn't know then it would be for the last time." She sniffled again.

"Did you communicate with the deceased at any time later in the day?"

"No, he said he was going to be busy. Rory didn't like it when I interrupted him at work."

"So no phone calls or texts during the day?"

"No."

"What about later in the evening, after work or when you weren't performing? Did you make any attempt to reach him then?"

Sparks must have just shaken her head, because Hallie had to remind her to speak so the court reporter could get it down.

"I didn't do anything like that."

"So let me get this straight," Hallie said, going in for the kill. "You expected that Mr. Gallagher would be meeting with my client that night, is that right?"

Sparks agreed.

"To discuss something of some importance to them both, correct?"

"Yes."

"But you made no effort to contact him afterward?"

"I guess that's right."

"Or to find out how the meeting went?"

Sparks once again agreed.

"So as you sit here today, you have no idea what your fiancé said to Ms. Barrett that night or she to him, isn't that right?"

"I suppose so," Sparks let out in a near whisper.

"Or even what the upshot of their meeting was."

"But I *know*—" Sparks began to protest.

"Yes," Hallie cut her off. "We've all heard what you think you know. No further questions."

# NINE

Hallie called only one witness. Me.

Putting Jane on the stand was too risky, and since Hallie didn't yet have a theory of the case, much less any evidence to back one up, her best chance of securing bond was to cast doubt on the State's one eyewitness, who, being conveniently absent, was unavailable for cross-examination. Hallie and I had decided in advance not to attack Mrs. Van Wagner's statement directly. After all, neither of us was in a position to know what the old woman saw, and beating up on public pensioners, even in the State of Illinois, might be considered bad form. Instead, my job was to trot out enough of the psychiatric research on eyewitness identifications to raise a specter of doubt about the identity of the woman who had been seen entering Gallagher's home that night.

Hallie touched my sleeve to let me know it was time and said, "The defense calls Dante Marco Angelotti, MD."

Bracing myself for what was to come, I rose, took my cane from my lap, and shook it out. Normally, when I had to walk any distance I used a rigid cane with a sturdy metal tip, but it was noisy and about as easy to store as a fishing rod, so I sometimes opted for "cane lite," a folding model with a nylon marshmallow that could be glided along the floor like a ball bearing. The elastic cord running through it brought back some uncomfortable memories, but it was better suited for locations where I didn't want to be seen waving a stick around like a drunken samurai. I held the cane out vertically and pushed it ahead of me in a little figure-eight motion until it met the steps leading to the witness box, pulled it up a few inches so it would graze the top of the risers, and climbed up. I performed a reverse maneuver at the top, planting the cane on the floor next to the chair and sliding my hand down its length to ascertain the seat height. All of this took several minutes to accomplish in a room otherwise quiet enough to pick out the scuttle of a cockroach.

The first order of business was my credentials. While lay witnesses are sometimes permitted to share their conclusions, more often a witness who offers an opinion—a so-called expert—must be shown to have some scientific, technical, or other specialized knowledge to back it up. In lawyer speak, this is referred to as "qualifying" the expert and is decided as a preliminary matter by the court. An expert witness doesn't have to have a PhD—depending on the type of case, expert status could be awarded to a bricklayer—and the standard for deciding the issue is simply whether the testimony would be "helpful" to the judge or jury trying the case. Consequently, it didn't matter that I hadn't personally studied eyewitness identifications, so long as my background gave some assurance I wasn't pulling my opinion out of thin air. Courts are also wary of hired guns spouting "junk science," so my testimony had to be grounded in research that was considered valid by a significant swathe of the scientific community.

"I take it you're not here to offer your own view of what the witness saw that night," Judge Cudahay said in amusement when Hallie had finished running down my résumé.

"I think we can agree that my qualifications in that area would be suspect," I quipped back to muffled chuckles.

"All right then," he told Hallie. "You can proceed. But keep him honest. I know a con job when I *see* it," he said to more laughter.

Hallie began with a series of questions that allowed me to explain that nationwide, eyewitness identifications played a part in as many as seventy-five percent of convictions later overturned because of DNA evidence. "What this tells us is that even the most well-intentioned witness can identify the wrong person," I explained. "These cases have caused behavioral scientists and criminal-justice professionals to take a closer look"—I stopped and smiled impishly—"at the techniques for obtaining eyewitness identifications, in particular the common practice of asking witnesses to pick out a suspect from a live or photographic lineup."

"When you say, 'closer look' what do you mean exactly?" Hallie asked, continuing the play-acting.

"I was referring to studies performed either in controlled laboratory settings or in the field that investigate which lineup procedures result in the fewest mistaken identifications. Generally speaking, researchers have focused on two areas: who administers the lineup and how it is performed—that is, simultaneously or sequentially."

"With regard to the first area, what have these studies found?"

"Well, as you might expect, when the investigating officer himself conducts the lineup, as Detective Yanowski did here, there's a significant risk that he will provide subtle verbal and nonverbal clues that lead the witness to identify the suspect the police already have in their sights. For example, when the witness is lingering over a particular photo, a statement along the lines of 'take your time and make sure you look at all the photos' can lead the witness away from a filler and toward the administrator's desired choice."

"Are you saying that the police do this on purpose?"

"It doesn't have to be on purpose. It can be, and probably most often is, completely inadvertent. But it has led researchers to conclude that the best practice—and I'm not joking when I use this term—is a double-blind procedure in which neither the lineup administrator nor the witness knows the suspect's identity. The studies I've cited also conclude that the rate of mistaken identifications goes down significantly when the lineup is conducted sequentially rather than simultaneously."

"Have these studies offered a reason why?"

"Again, it gets back to human nature. In a simultaneous lineup, witnesses tend to use 'relative judgment'—that is, they compare lineup photos to each other, increasing the risk that they will choose whoever looks the most like the person they remember. Sequential lineups require witnesses to use what's called 'absolute judgment,' comparing each individual they see to their actual recollection of the suspect. In laboratory studies, using a double-blind, sequential technique results in identifications twice as reliable as those obtained from the lineup procedure Detective Yanowski used here."

"Are there any other factors that cause you concern about the lineup procedures used by Detective Yanowski?"

"Well, it's not a concern about the lineup, but the research we've been talking about also suggests that when the lineup doesn't contain the actual perpetrator, young children and the elderly make mistaken identifications at a much higher rate than other witnesses."

Hallie then moved in for the wrap-up we had planned. "Just to be clear on this, are you saying that Mrs. Van Wagner was lying when she identified Jane Barrett as the woman she saw entering the deceased's home on the evening of August twenty-sixth?"

"Absolutely not. All I am saying is that, because of the way the lineup was conducted and due to Mrs. Van Wagner's age, there is a statistically significant chance, perhaps as high as twenty percent, that she mistook Ms. Barrett for the woman she believes she saw that night."

"Thank you, Doctor," Hallie said primly and sat down.

I actually felt sorry for Frost when he rose to conduct my cross-examination. He took several steps in my direction before deciding to keep a safe distance and returning to the safety of the lectern, where he ruffled some papers a good two minutes before proceeding.

"Um, Doctor, these studies you mentioned. Did you, uh, conduct any of them yourself?"

"No. As you might guess, I'm not very handy with photographs. Though, now that you mention it, it could be the ultimate double-blind—or if you like, triple-blind—procedure." I smiled to let him know I wasn't being serious.

Frost giggled nervously. "Ah, yes. Yes, I guess it could be. Um, so . . . how many of them are there? Studies, that is."

"Several dozen," I answered. "All conducted in the last several years." Frost had given me an opening to go on, but I didn't want the judge to think I was taking advantage of the situation. And I was feeling sorry for Frost, who was plainly discombobulated by me.

"And, uh, have there been any contrary findings?"

"A few," I admitted. "But none without flaws in their methodology that have led most researchers to question their results."

"So, uh, did any of these last studies involve a double . . . I mean, a double . . ." He stopped, unable to get the word past his lips.

"Blind?" I offered, to help him out.

"Yes, yes," Frost agreed. "Double-bbblind," he sputtered at last, sounding on the verge of tears.

"Is that a question, Counsel?" Judge Cudahay interjected, more out of kindness than impatience. "Because the afternoon is getting old."

"No. I, uh . . . I have no further questions," Frost sighed abjectly, before retreating from the lectern like a dog that's just been kicked.

"Redirect?" the judge asked Hallie.

"None, Your Honor."

"Good," the judge said. "The witness is excused. And thank you, Doctor Angelotti, for that very *enlightening* testimony," he said, clearly impressed with his own wit.

"Don't look so pleased with yourself," Hallie whispered in my ear as I reclaimed my spot next to her. "We still have our work cut out for us."

After all the hoopla that preceded them, the closing arguments were remarkably short.

Frost structured his around the tired old saw of "means, motive, and opportunity." Jane had the means to murder Gallagher because of her ready access to a large quantity of Lucitrol, which she hadn't even attempted to hide when the police showed up. Yes, it was true that the drug could be obtained by almost anyone, but it was highly suspicious that Gallagher had been poisoned in this manner immediately following Jane's victory in a civil case hinging upon Lucitrol's fatal propensities for persons with a preexisting heart condition. Jane knew about Gallagher's health issues because the two of them had been intimate for years—a fact the defense did not deny. As a former prosecutor she also would have been aware of the medical examiner's policy on autopsies, which she must have calculated would permit her crime to go undetected. What Jane hadn't counted on was the exhumation of the body, which, "like a footprint left at the scene of the crime," created a trail leading directly back to her heinous deed.

In Frost's view, motive too was simple. It was the oldest one in history: a middle-aged woman's rage at being rejected by her lover of many years in favor of a much younger rival. Regardless of what Gallagher had told Jane that night, several witnesses could attest to the fact that he and the defendant had been arguing, and that she had physically assaulted Gallagher before stomping off to lick her wounds. Her plainly overheard words—"you won't get away with it"—supported the prosecution's theory that Gallagher had followed through on his intention to break off their relationship, as did the repetition of the name "Lucy," which could only have referred to Gallagher's fiancée and the soon-to-be-completed nuptials. The defendant's ire upon being dumped in favor of a more youthful bride had found further expression in the vindictive destruction of Gallagher's records, carried out by Jane later that night and confirmed by the statement of an eyewitness, a retired public servant whose integrity was above reproach.

Last was opportunity, which came down to the fact that Jane had shared drinks with Gallagher that same night and could easily have slipped the pill into the carafe the two were sharing while Gallagher was distracted or not paying attention. Frost reminded the court that a drug like Lucitrol would have no ill effect on a healthy subject like Jane, even while it worked its insidious damage on her lover. In Frost's view, Jane had come up with an ingenious murder plan using a substance that both could consume in full view of others but that would be poisonous only to Gallagher. Indeed, it was probable that the defendant had chosen a public place to carry out the offense precisely for that reason, and had intentionally dumped the contents of the carafe over Gallagher's head to ensure that the evidence would never be discovered. Frost finished with a flourish, pointing out that only a former prosecutor would have been capable of planning what was nearly the perfect crime.

I had to give Frost credit. Though I wanted to think otherwise for Hallie's sake, this last set of conjectures had started me down the path of wondering whether Jane might really be guilty. Granted, the alleged motive for the murder seemed silly—it was hard to believe that such an accomplished woman would regard a two-bit showgirl as any kind of rival—and the theory depended on Jane having decided in advance to poison her lover, or she would not have come to the restaurant that night already armed with the Lucitrol that killed him.

But if Frost was right about what had taken place, the scheme was virtually foolproof. It would require a razor-sharp intelligence to devise it, and I had no doubt that the mysterious presence seated only a few feet from me—a woman who, though reportedly cold and haughty in ordinary life, could turn on the charisma required to bring a jury to tears—would have had the stage presence to carry it off. Viewed from one angle, the theatrical emptying of the carafe over Gallagher's head undercut Frost's theory, since a Jane bent on murdering her lover would have no reason to call further attention to their clash. But if she hadn't been sure how quickly the Lucitrol would take effect, the ploy had been brilliant, guaranteeing that the critical evidence would be mopped up long before Gallagher crashed to the ground in death.

Whoever had murdered Gallagher had counted on his demise looking exactly like what it initially appeared to be: the sudden heart attack of a man well known for his excesses in food, nicotine, and drink. If so, the poison had been selected carefully and with precisely that guise in mind. Who else besides Jane would have been familiar with the drug's black-box warnings? And who else besides her would have known that the medical examiner was unlikely to perform an autopsy? I was sure there were others who fit both descriptions, but it was all too neat, including the fact that whoever had fed the Lucitrol to Gallagher would almost certainly have gotten away with it but for the request to dig up the body. Which raised another question: exactly who or what had led to that request? And what was in Gallagher's computer files that so urgently needed to be disposed of, by Jane or someone else? I made a mental note to raise all these questions with Hallie.

Hallie, meanwhile, had risen to take the stage and was busily ticking off all the reasons why the prosecution's case fell far short of the proof needed to justify a no-bail order. "I needn't remind the court that the object of bail is to ensure the defendant's appearance at trial, and that under both our federal and state constitutions my client must be presumed innocent until proven otherwise. It is only when the prosecution has presented overwhelming evidence of guilt—in the words of the statute, that 'the proof of guilt is evident and the presumption great'—that bail may be denied. The State hasn't come close to meeting this standard. All of its arguments are pure speculation. There isn't a single piece of evidence linking Ms. Barrett to this purported crime.

"The State's surmise that my client must have poisoned the deceased is built on two utterly flimsy foundations. First, that Ms. Barrett had access to samples of Lucitrol in connection with her defense of its manufacturer, Atria, in a recent civil matter. As we have shown, however, thousands, if not tens of thousands of persons in the Chicago area also have access to the drug through their own prescriptions or those of a close relative. The State did not bother to test other medications collected from Mr. Gallagher's apartment to see if he himself may have been taking the drug, and Detective Yanowski frankly admitted he could not prove that my client supplied the Lucitrol ingested by the deceased. Further, Dr. Lubbock was unable to say exactly when the alleged poisoning took place—I say alleged, since Mr. Gallagher may have taken the drug himself—except that it occurred sometime within the thirty-six hours preceding Mr. Gallagher's death, hardly a basis for theorizing that it was given to him on the night of August twenty-sixth.

"The State's only other evidence is the statement of a purported eyewitness who very conveniently was unavailable to be brought before the court so that her recollection could be tested. The court has heard the testimony of Dr. Angelotti explaining how the flawed lineup procedures used by the police might easily have resulted in a false identification. Further, even if the court were willing to assume that Ms. Barrett visited the deceased's home on the evening in question—which she may very well have done simply to collect items that belonged to her—there is no evidence that it was she who destroyed his computer records. The State surmises that my client was on a rampage to erase evidence of the deceased's involvement with another woman but is unable to produce a shred of proof that Ms. Barrett knew, or even cared, about Mr. Gallagher's engagement to Ms. Sparks, or that she had any other cause for concern about what was in his files. In short, the State's second foundation for accusing my client of murder is as riddled with holes as the first.

"I might also remind the court, since the State has seen fit not to address the matter, that my client has none of the attributes of a flight risk. Ms. Barrett is a leading member of the local bar with a spotless record, a respected officer of the court with a busy law practice and numerous clients who have the right to be represented by the counsel of their choice while the State neglects its responsibility to seek out the real culprit in Mr. Gallagher's murder—if in fact he was murdered at all. Ms. Barrett will agree to surrender her passport and to seek the court's permission before leaving the jurisdiction should traveling across state lines be required in service to her clients. The State cannot reasonably ask for more. Accordingly, we respectfully request that the court deny the State's petition for a no-bail order and set bond in an appropriate amount, certainly not to exceed one million dollars."

Whereupon Hallie thanked the court for its indulgence and sat down.

Frost got up and made a halfhearted plea for electronic monitoring, but Judge Cudahay cut him off. "I've heard enough. Bond is set at one million, the defendant to appear in court on October tenth for arraignment and at such times thereafter as the court shall direct. The State's petition for a no-bail order is *denied*."

We'd won. But I couldn't help wondering if we'd live to regret it.

# TEN

There were enough handshakes all around to resemble a Fortune 500 board meeting. Bjorn came up behind me and clapped me on the shoulder and said "Jolly good show" and all kidding aside would I put him on to my tailor, and Hallie turned to me after hugging Jane and said I had "cleaned Frost's clock," a lawyer idiom I'd been told came from a moldy casebook they were all required to commit to memory during their first year of law school. Then I found myself being pushed toward the Mata Hari who had caused all this commotion, who appeared to top my height by several inches and said, in a voice as deep as Hallie's but without the endearing tomboyish lilt, "Thank you" and then: "Are you always able to do that?"

I wasn't sure what to make of the question. "You mean open my mouth?"

"No," Jane said, sounding amused. "I'm sure you do that quite often and not always wisely."

"What makes you say that?" I replied, thinking about putting out my hand but deciding against it. The last thing I wanted to do in front of this woman was appear to be groping. "Do I look reckless?" I added, trying to sound light.

"Oh, far from it. But a former bad boy if I had to guess."

I thought about saying at least I hadn't played Lucrezia Borgia to my boyfriend but stopped myself. I was supposed to be on her side, after all. And what the hell did she mean by *former*?

Jane, meanwhile, had searched out my hand and enclosed it in fingers that felt like something Michelangelo might have sculpted during breaks from painting the Sistine Chapel. She pulled it toward her and rotated the wrist so that my palm was face-up. "Mmm-hmm," she murmured thoughtfully. "Definitely a bad boy."

"What is this, a palm reading?" I asked sarcastically.

"As a matter of fact, yes. Chirology is a hobby of mine. At a glance, I'd say you've been prey to some serious misfortune."

"It doesn't take a crystal ball to figure that out," I said, yanking my hand back. It seemed to be my day for being pawed at by strangers. "Do you have any other brilliant insights to share?"

"Your heart line is interesting, too. High up and filled with breaks and crosses. Not to mention a very clear triangle on the Mount of Venus."

My curiosity got the better of me. "What does that mean?"

"It means I shall look forward to knowing you better."

Not if I could help it.

Meanwhile, the deputy who was to escort her back to the Cook County Jail for processing had come up and was apparently signaling it was time to go. "Yes, officer," she said in her regal way. "I'm ready to go with you." She sounded as unconcerned as if she were being led off for a spa treatment. "It's been a pleasure," she said, giving me a finger tap on the cheek like I was a naughty child. I felt like I'd just been held down and strip-searched in the middle of Daley Plaza.

Immediately after, Hallie was back at my side. "I'm sorry I can't give you a lift. It's going to take hours to get her checked out. And I have to arrange for payment. They don't take credit cards downstairs."

"Doesn't the bail bondsman do that?"

"Uh-uh. Illinois is one of the few states that doesn't have them. The good news is, she'll only have to put up ten percent, which will be chump change for her. Can you get back downtown all right? I can ask Bjorn to take you in the Land Rover."

I'd sooner accept a lift from Ted Bundy. "No thanks," I said. "I'm sure it would be a frightfully good time, but it might make me late for my appointment with Professor Higgins."

"What's gotten into you today?" Hallie rebuked. "You're acting like someone who didn't get everything he asked for on his Christmas list. We won, didn't we?"

This wasn't the time or place to raise all of my misgivings, but I couldn't help sharing one worry. "About that, are you positive of every-thing you said back there? If I were in Jane's shoes I'd be sorely tempted to fly off to some island nation that isn't party to an extradition treaty."

"Not Jane," Hallie pooh-poohed. "She's married to her job and always has been. I can't see her happy spending the rest of her life sitting on a beach drinking rum and Cokes. Which is why we have to get this thing resolved—and quickly. Jane's clients aren't going to stay loyal for very long with a murder charge hanging over her head."

"If you ask me, she doesn't seem all that concerned about what might happen to her."

"That's just a front for your buddies in the press box. Anyway, I've really got to get going. Thanks again for what you did today. And please promise me you won't take public transportation. I'd hate to see you winding up in the hospital with a cracked skull."

At least she still had a glimmer of affection for me.

"Don't worry. If I can't find a cab I can always call paratransit."

"Don't do that," Hallie said with a chuckle. "The world might come to an end."

As it turned out, there was no need to risk life and limb walking the ten blocks to the Pink Line. Just as I was leaving the courthouse I heard my name being called. The voice belonged to Bill O'Leary, the Chicago police detective who'd led the investigation in Charlie Dickerson's case. We'd since shared drinks and an occasional outing to Comiskey Park, where O'Leary had season tickets. I say "Comiskey Park" instead of Cellular Field because as far as O'Leary was concerned, the renaming of the newer stadium was tantamount to the desecration of a cathedral. Being originally from Bridgeport, O'Leary took his White Sox as seriously as the pope takes deviations from Church dogma, so we tended to share games in conversational silence while I followed Ed Farmer's play-by-play on my phone.

"You're not going where I think you're going," O'Leary remarked dryly as he came up.

"Why? Is there an element of danger involved? I thought you guys were out there ensuring that the streets were safe for law-abiding citizens."

"If you could see them, you'd know how my eyes were rolling. Have I not impressed upon you sufficiently the odds of being deprived of your wallet—or worse—if you roam around certain areas on foot?"

"Yeah, well. Why don't you tell that to the guys who decided to build a courthouse on the outer edges of Timbuktu."

"I'll thank you to remember the vital role patronage jobs play in our local economy. Can I interest you in a ride in my chariot instead? We can take the scenic route."

"Sure," I said. "If you're going my way, I'll take an armor-plated vehicle over an exposed 'L' car any day. And there's something I want to talk to you about."

On the way back to the Loop in O'Leary's car I explained what it was.

"You've got to be kidding," O'Leary said when I was through. "You want to file a missing person report on a homeless man?"

"Mike's a person and he's missing," I pointed out. "Can I do it even if we're not related?"

O'Leary thought about this. "You can if you're familiar with his ordinary schedule and activities, though it's not going to get much play unless you can point to some unusual circumstances surrounding the so-called disappearance. You probably aren't aware of it, but the statistic is that someone in Chicago disappears every thirty minutes. I can report him for you, but the missing-person unit has its hands full just searching for folks with fixed abodes. Do you know what he looks like?"

I pulled up a mental picture from my warehouse of stored faces. "African American, around five-eleven, maybe a hundred and eighty pounds. Lighter-skinned. Wears dreadlocks—or used to, anyway—and has a gold-plated left incisor."

"Well, that will certainly help him stand out among the city's homeless population," O'Leary said, rounding a corner in a squeal of brakes. "Where does he usually hang out?"

"I'm not sure exactly. I know he moves around a lot. In the summer, by the mouth of the river. But now that the nights are getting chilly, he's probably moved over to lower Wacker Drive. I may be able to get a photo from the newspaper he works for. I think they did a profile on him a few months back."

"E-mail it to me then. I'll get it into Clearpath—that's the neighborhood community-policing database—and ask a few of the guys I know in the First District to keep an eye out for him. But don't expect anything too soon. And stop worrying. Chances are he's just sleeping off a bender and will turn up in a day or two."

I didn't think so, but there was no sense in arguing with O'Leary about it.

The following few days passed uneventfully.

I dutifully took my pills three times a day with meals, and even worked up the energy to cook a few dishes on my own. On Saturday, I caught up with my journal reading and rewarded myself with a long afternoon walk along the Lake. It was a balmy Indian summer day with no hint of the cold fronts that would soon start barreling down from Canada, apart from the geese of the same name honking overhead en route to wherever it was they spent the winter. (There always seemed to be enough of them around leaving greasy piles for my shoes in all seasons.) Every so often I lifted my sunglasses to see if I could catch a glimpse of something concrete, but it was always the same pea soup. I reminded myself for about the thousandth time to be patient.

That night, I took in a Batman movie at the AMC outlet on Grand, and on Sunday morning, I joined a spin class at my health club. I'd started taking the class after deciding it wasn't healthy to be spending all of my exercise hours alone in my apartment and convincing a doubtful instructor that I could not only mount a bike with my eyes closed but out-pedal just about everyone in the class. That day's soundtrack drew heavily on the sixties, and we finished up with a heart-pounding, four-minute sprint to the ever-intensifying beat of *Sympathy for the Devil*, leaving me at the end satisfyingly winded and with thigh muscles begging for mercy. I spent another half-hour in the weight room, topped off the workout with a steam shower, and arrived home, scrubbed and sore, just in time for my weekly Skype session with Louis.

The idea, surprisingly, had been my ex-wife's. While my person was still pretty much anathema to her, I gave Annie credit for wanting Louis and me to build a relationship of sorts. Skyping didn't do much for me, but it allowed Louis to "show" me his nursery-school output and other things he was excited about, and kept my face in the forefront of his mind. I would have eagerly hopped a plane every weekend to be with him, but I was afraid of pushing my luck—under the divorce decree I had almost no visitation rights to speak of—or overwhelming Louis with my company. It seemed better to take things slowly, letting our intimacy develop gradually and making the best of extreme-distance parenting.

This week's offerings were several finger paintings, a Lego truck Louis had built by himself, and a new Snow White coloring book. Annie had taken him to see a digitalized and restored version of the Disney film, and he seemed quite taken by the story, chatting away happily about the "bad queen" and the beautiful princess and all the funny little dwarves.

"Which one was your favorite?" I asked.

"I liked the baby one because he couldn't get the soap and then he ate it and he burped and bubbles came out of his mouth," Louis said in a rush that ended in a mirthful giggle. "Soap tastes bad," he added in a more serious vein.

"Yes it does. And so do rotten apples," I said.

"Uh-huh," he agreed. "Mom says I can't have any apples on Halloween. I'm going to be a prince and have a sword. But I'm not going to kiss any girls, even if they're asleep. Why didn't the queen like Snow White?"

I thought about how to answer this. How do you explain poisonous envy to a three-year-old? "Well, probably because when the queen was young she was very beautiful, just like Snow White, and as she got older she wasn't as pretty anymore."

"And that made her sad?"

"That's right. And angry. Sometimes when we're sad or angry we try to get rid of the thing that's making us feel that way so we don't have to think about it anymore."

"Like taking out the garbage?"

"Ri-ight," I said slowly. The analogy wasn't perfect, but it was always startling to me how easily small children picked up on psychological nuance. "So you don't like kissing girls?" I teased.

"No, it's nasty. Except for mom. I like kissing mom, but not too much. Did you like kissing your mom?"

Another hard question. "I'm afraid I was a little like Snow White. My mom died when I was very young—even younger than you are now."

"That's sad, too," Louis said with the utmost gravity.

"It is, but it was OK. My father took good care of me and loved me very much." Too much, if you wanted to know the truth, but it wasn't something I ever planned on telling Louis.

"Like you love me?" were his next words.

"Yes, Louis," I said, trying not to tear up. "Like I love you."

# ELEVEN

On Monday morning, Mike was still gone, and again on Tuesday. True to his word, Richard had asked around, but no one had seen Mike for days, and when I called *Streetwise* again they had all but given up on his coming back. "It happens sometimes," the staffer said. "They wander off or get sick, and you never hear from them again. On the other hand, winter is coming. Maybe your friend decided to head south for the cold months. A lot of them do."

I didn't buy that Mike would have taken an extended vacation without saying good-bye, and as far as I knew, the paper was his only livelihood. I phoned O'Leary several times to find out if there were any leads, but so far there were none. "Have patience," O'Leary said, "though I know that's like asking a dog to give up its bone. And if you're right about his being ill, chances are good he'll show up in an emergency room somewhere."

Which was hardly reassuring.

By the close of business on Tuesday when Hallie called to update me on Jane's case, I was nearly frantic with worry about my homeless friend.

"Bjorn's done it again," she said dreamily when I picked up.

"What? Led his cricket team to victory?"

She ignored this. "Come through with the goods. Guess who stood to gain the most from Gallagher's death?"

"His undertaker?"

"No. I was talking about estate planning. Bjorn gave me the full rundown last night over dinner at Alinea. He checked the probate court records, and it turns out the nephew gets everything."

I didn't want to know how they had ended up at one of Chicago's chicest restaurants on a weeknight. "It doesn't take an Einstein to figure that out," I said spitefully. "From what came out at the hearing, Urquhart was Gallagher's only living relative."

"You're right," Hallie said. "But get this. Bjorn did a credit check on Urquhart's business, and it's in trouble. His receivables are financed to the hilt, and he's behind on his bank loans. And they're building a new Best Buy down the road from his main sales outlet. Urquhart hired a lawyer to try to stop it before the local planning board—as if anyone does urban planning in the south suburbs—and they turned him down flat. Bjorn figures it's only a matter of time before Urquhart has to file for bankruptcy."

"How much is in the estate?"

"It's not clear yet. They'll have to liquidate some of Gallagher's stock holdings and put the townhome on the market, but we're talking at least a million, not counting life insurance. Which is the other juicy bit Bjorn dug up. The policy had a double-indemnity clause."

I couldn't remember any of the details from the old Fred Mac-Murray movie, so I was forced to seek an explanation.

"It's a provision in the policy that says the insurance company has to pay double if the policyholder dies accidentally instead of by natural causes. Gallagher's ordinary benefit was $750,000, so we're talking quite a chunk of change. 'Accidentally' includes being the victim of a homicide."

This was interesting, but I needed to ask her a favor.

"Isn't he the guy who saved your life last spring?" Hallie asked when I was through with my petition.

"That's the one. And I can't stand the thought that he's alone and sick out there without me lifting a finger about it."

"You did something. You talked to the police."

"I doubt he's anywhere near the top of their priority list, even with O'Leary's influence. I don't think I can sleep another night worrying about him, and I know Mike would be moving mountains to find me if our positions were reversed. Will you come? We can make a date out of it."

Hallie laughed. "You have an amusing concept of what constitutes a date. But why not? I've been sitting in an office all day. I could use the fresh air. But only if you promise to make time for dinner afterward. There's something else I want to run by you about Jane's case. Something I just thought of this afternoon."

A little while later found me waiting for Hallie where we'd arranged to meet, in Millennium Park next to the Cloud Gate, a giant, polished steel sculpture shaped like a lima bean and nicknamed—you guessed it—the Bean. Tourists never seemed to tire of its funhouse reflections, and as usual, the surrounding plaza was host to a big crowd of people snapping pictures and knocking at the artwork's hollow sides. I listened to the commotion from a park bench nearby, thinking about what I had planned for the evening and hoping it would turn up a sign of Mike.

Hallie arrived on schedule just before six. "Don't tell me you're thinking of taking to the streets, too," she said, referring to the mountain of plastic bags by my feet. It looks like you've brought everything but a Bunsen burner."

On my way over to the park I'd stopped by a Walgreens and bought out its entire supply of candy bars, tube socks, batteries, Wet Ones, and other small items I thought might come in handy for someone living without a roof over their head, along with a flashlight for Hallie and a roll of masking tape.

"It's the old Boy Scout in me. You know, be prepared."

"I'm surprised they let you into the Boy Scouts. Don't they have a rule about being cheerful?"

"They allowed me to get by on thrifty, reverent, and clean. I thought care packages might earn us some goodwill. Here, what do you think of these?"

I showed her the eight-by-twelve flyers I'd bribed Yelena into making for me by offering her yet another afternoon off. It included a physical description, Mike's picture from the *Streetwise* website, my contact information, and the offer of a hundred-dollar reward for any information leading to his whereabouts.

Hallie agreed that the likeness was good and asked which way I wanted to go.

"I thought we'd start on Lower Randolph and head west from there."

Hallie took half the bags, and I took the other. They were heavy and flapped back and forth while I swung my cane, making for slow progress as we hiked through the Pritzker Pavilion and onto the BP Bridge, another steel-plated attraction that rose like a serpent's tail over Columbus Drive.

"Stop and rest for a minute?" I said to Hallie when we reached the bridge's pinnacle, which offered magnificent views of the Lake and the entire length of Grant Park.

"I won't say no to that," Hallie replied, panting a bit from the exertion.

We unloaded our booty and leaned over the railing into the soft wind. The setting sun warmed the side of my face and sent sparkles into the corner of my right eye, where my vision was strongest. I knew better than to think it signaled an improvement. My eyes were still photosensitive, and sometimes painfully so. But in the waning light of day it was a pleasant sensation, and with Hallie so close by, sent a trill of contentment down my spine. Now if we could just find Mike . . .

I asked if the trees were turning color yet.

"A little," Hallie said. "Some splashes of gold and orange. And there's a maple over there that will be fully red in a week." She sighed and added wistfully, "It's beautiful out here tonight."

"That it certainly is," I agreed without a trace of irony.

Resuming our mission, we descended the bridge and began journeying along the subterranean passages that led to Lower Wacker, familiar to non-Chicagoans as the place where Jake and Elwood incapacitated two-thirds of the Chicago police force, and to natives as the "Emerald City," a reference to the era when it was lit by garish green lights. Even in a car, it's not for the faint of heart. Filled with short entrance ramps, blind turns, and trucks going the unofficial minimum of seventy, it's always an accident waiting to happen. The first time I'd ventured down there in my old Toyota—which I still hadn't worked up the resolve to sell—had left me mopping the sweat from my brow and vowing thereafter to stick to the clogged avenues overhead. But if you were without a place of your own, it offered shelter from rain and snow, the warmth of skyscraper heating vents, and relative peace. Apart from the occasional halfhearted sweep, the authorities were by and large content to leave its occupants to themselves, underground and out of the sight of tourists and conventioneers.

We trudged all the way to Congress Parkway and back, through a pungent atmosphere of exhaust fumes, rotting foodstuffs, and body odor, taking care not to come up by surprise on the bundles stretched out along the walks or hidden away in one of the myriad nooks and crannies created by the massive concrete supports of the roadway overhead. There were easily hundreds of makeshift homes. Some of them were remarkably clean and well organized, with designated areas for eating, washing, and sleeping. In others, we had to pick our way through mounds of trash and haphazardly placed bedrolls. Despite the grinding poverty and poor lighting, I felt no sense of menace. Almost everyone who wasn't sleeping soundly responded politely, and even with friendliness, to our inquiries. Judging by their speech and topics of conversation, the majority were mentally ill or elderly, though I was shocked several times to hear the voices of children above the constant din of traffic. There were also veterans aplenty, some of whom amusingly asked if I'd lost my sight in combat, along with the usual sad complement of drunks begging for change.

We handed out supplies to all who would take them and taped flyers on walls wherever the layers of grime permitted it, but it was always the same story—at least from those lucid enough to tell it. Yes, many people knew Mike, who, though he mostly kept to himself, was regarded as a courteous brother who shared food and cigarettes and did not wake his neighbors with unnecessary fits of loud cursing and screaming. No, nobody knew where he was staying these days. Yes, he hadn't been seen around in several weeks. No, he hadn't told anyone he was going away or where he might have been headed. Some of our informants offered the possibility he had simply cleared out for the winter; others that he had permanently relocated to the more hospitable climes of Miami or LA. If you had the coin and were fit to travel, you'd have to be a right crazy motherfucker to stay in Chicago during cold season.

"I'm sorry," Hallie said with genuine sympathy when we'd retraced our steps back to Columbus and were standing at the foot of the stairway leading up to ground level. "Try not to assume the worst."

I responded by balling up my share of the now-empty shopping bags and flinging them into the street, not the most environmentally friendly gesture, but a good way to vent some of my frustration.

She reached down and squeezed my hand. "Stop worrying. He'll turn up. I'm sure of it."

I bit my lip and nodded. I wanted to keep going, but we'd been at it for nearly two hours and night was setting in.

"Are you still up for something to eat?" Hallie asked.

I wasn't at all hungry, but I'd promised. And maybe the evening didn't have to be a complete waste. "What would you say to picking something up and bringing it back to my place? We're only a few blocks away, and I'd . . . I'd like to continue the conversation we were having just before Jane was arrested."

"Really? You're inviting me over? I was beginning to wonder what you were hiding up there. I will if you promise there aren't any dead babies in the closet."

I marveled at how close she had come to hitting the nail on the head. "Great, but you have to swear not to make fun of my skills as a decorator—"

Right then I detected footsteps coming toward us at a light jog. My heart lifted. Could it be someone with information to share about Mike? I listened in hope as the footfalls drew nearer, beginning to pound the pavement. As the runner came up I half-turned in anticipation, just in time to hear Hallie hiss, "You!" in what sounded like shocked surprise. Then something weighty cracked my skull and the lights went out.

# TWELVE

I awoke to stars. No, a meteor shower. I hadn't seen anything like it in a while, so at first I just lay back, enjoying the show. Until the meteors flew off and were sucked into a deep, black well. With the spectacle gone, I became aware of a throbbing at the back of my skull and a buzzing in my ears. An alarm clock was going off somewhere, disturbing my well-deserved rest. I covered my ears and tried to get back to sleep, but the damn thing wouldn't stop ringing. All right, all right, I said. I'll get up in a minute. Just as soon as this headache goes away.

"Probably concussed," I heard someone say from what seemed like a great distance.

"Sir, can you hear me?" Slowly, I became aware of a latex paw on my cheek, rotating it this way and that.

Of course I can, I said. Just let me sleep a little longer.

Someone else placed an evil-smelling thing under my nose. I had a momentary jolt of awareness, which only convinced me I should go back to sleep. But I couldn't because of the alarm, which was growing louder and louder. *Will somebody please turn that fucking thing off?*

"Good. He's coming around," came another voice. Male, like the first.

I opened my eyes to stabbing pain in the vicinity of my left temporal lobe.

"Eyes wide open now," said the first voice. "Let's get a light on them."

I tried to protest, but my jaws were stuck together with Silly Putty.

"Something funny going on there."

The light jabbed at my pupils like a tattoo needle. I made another effort to get my lips moving. "Mmmm, mmmm."

"Relax, sir. Don't try to speak just yet. Hold them open for me a bit longer, please. That's it. Thank you." He sat back in evident surprise. "Shit, Brian, I don't think this guy can see!"

A genius.

"Maybe we should get something on them right away," Brian said, sounding worried. "It doesn't look like an acid attack, but who knows?"

"Nooo," I managed to slur, trying to shake my head and succeeding only in making the pain over my ear worse. "Always li' that." My voice sounded like I was choking on wet sand.

"Don't worry, sir. We'll have you bandaged up and on your way to the ER in a jiffy."

"I don' need—" I said, forcing my shoulders up to further ice picks in my skull.

It was only then that I connected the dots.

In the near distance someone was shouting. "Come on! Come on! Get her into the van! Let's move it, people! Radio ahead and notify them we have a blunt trauma to the head with possible cerebral edema. Patient is in shock and barely responsive. Tell the ER to get a neurosurgeon scrubbed and ready. She's going to need all the help we can give her!"

Hallie? *HALLIE?*

Oh, no. Please God, no.

O'Leary was polite but unconvinced.

"I talked to the boys about it. The place where you got whomped has seen a lot of recent muggings."

I shook my head. "How many muggers do you know who come armed with big clubs? And Hallie knew who our attacker was, I'm sure of it."

We were sitting side by side on the couch in my office, where I'd gone to get cleaned up after spending a sleepless night outside the hospital surgery unit. Compared to Hallie, I'd gotten off light. When they dropped me off at the emergency room, the doctor on duty was Tim, the same resident who'd performed triage on me the last time I was set upon by an unidentifiable assailant. Tim made a crack about auditioning for the Boris Karloff role in *The Mummy*—in the end I hadn't succeeded in talking the EMT guys out of wrapping yards of gauze around my head—but dropped the gaiety when he saw the look on my face. He cut away the blindfold and sent me upstairs for an MRI before stitching me up and writing me a prescription for painkillers. He also wanted to hold me for observation, but I told him he'd have to chain me to a bed if he wanted to keep me there.

"What's your rush?" Tim asked. "She's still in surgery. I just checked for you. You might as well stay here where the beds are comfortable."

"I know, but I have to make some phone calls. Speaking of which, do you see my cell anywhere around here?"

Tim handed me a plastic bag with my personal belongings. My cane wasn't among them, but I was relieved to find the bottle with my pills. I remembered that I hadn't fulfilled my quota for the day and asked Tim for some water.

"Are you sure you shouldn't be sticking around? I mean, you took quite a blow to the head," he said, handing me a paper cup.

"There was nothing on the scan, right? And I'm not dizzy anymore." My head still felt like it had been used to sink pilings, but the discomfort paled in comparison to the recriminations I was heaping on myself. I swallowed the pill and angrily crumpled the cup into a ball.

"True," Tim said. "But you know the symptoms of a concussion can be delayed for hours or even days. You should be getting rest."

I shook my head. "I'm not resting until I know Hallie's OK."

"All right, but do me a favor. You know the signs, so watch out for them. Excessive sleepiness, for one. And disorientation. You start experiencing the slightest bit of confusion, I want you on the phone to me or 911 immediately. No stalling."

I was feeling too wretched to argue with him.

"And Mark?" Tim said.

"Yes?"

"We've got to stop meeting like this."

Responding to my frantic messages, O'Leary had gone to view the crime scene at first light, before swinging around a little before 7:00 a.m. to where I was waiting in my office. He brought a bottle of Jameson's and two steaming cups of coffee, into which he poured each of us a shot. I accepted it with gratitude, even though a drink wasn't the smartest idea for someone in my condition.

"How's the girl doing, anyway?" O'Leary asked.

"Still in critical condition. Her surgeon thought the procedure went well, but it will be a while before they know more. They've put her in an induced coma."

Post-op, I hadn't even tried to see her. I knew physical contact would be forbidden, and my imagination was more than enough to supply an image of her lying in an ICU bed, deathly pale and swathed in bandages, with a wall of beeping machines keeping track of her vital signs. Then, too, there was the risk of running into someone from her family.

"How long will they keep her that way?"

I remembered the surgeon's words, calculated to soothe while not pinning him down to anything. "It depends on how quickly the swelling goes down. If it starts to recede, they may cut back a bit on the coma to see how she's doing. Even then, it's doubtful she'll remember much." As reported by her doctor, Hallie had taken most of the hit on the lower back of her head, near the area of the brain that processes memory.

"Which means she won't be able to identify the assailant for some time, if at all," O'Leary said thoughtfully. "Was she awake at all before the surgery, do you know?"

"Only briefly. Her doctor said she was muttering something about being ill and needing to use an app, of all things, plus some numbers. It may have just been confusion, but it could mean that her phone holds some kind of clue."

"That's not going to get us very far. Her handbag wasn't found anywhere on the scene. Which, if you don't mind my pointing it out, strongly suggests robbery as a motive."

"Then why didn't he take my wallet, too?"

"Lack of time, no doubt. When you're in a hurry it's a lot easier to grab a woman's purse than to sift through a fellow's pants pockets, especially when he's lying on his back on the ground. Tell me one more time what you heard."

I went through the whole story again.

"What do you think hit you?"

"Not sure, but it came from a few feet off. A baseball bat, maybe."

"And the footsteps—male or female?"

"I don't know. It could have been a man or a very tall woman, I wasn't paying close attention. All I know is that the shoes didn't make much noise and that he or she was moving quickly. I assume there weren't any footprints."

"On a city sidewalk? You assume correctly." O'Leary sighed. "That's the trouble with this kind of incident. Unless we can get a description from the victim there's almost nothing to go on. They're putting a GPS trace on your friend's phone, but unless the perp has the brains of a termite he's either removed the SIM card or thrown the thing in the river."

I'd figured as much, and it only made things worse. Not only hadn't I been able to protect Hallie, I couldn't even give the police a lead on who had done this to her. "So that's it then, there's nothing else you can do?"

"I didn't say that," O'Leary said. "Just that we may have to go at it from a different angle."

My expression must have revealed my state of mind.

O'Leary put his hand on my shoulder. "You're sweet on this girl, aren't you?"

I nodded glumly. "Some."

"All right, I'll see what I can do. But only if you'll promise to get some sleep. And I hope I don't need to remind you once more of the obvious."

"That I'm the biggest jackass who ever walked the face of the planet?"

"I was planning on deferring that observation until you were feeling better. But since you bring it up, do something smart for a change. Remember you're a civilian. And for the love of Jesus, don't go walking down any more dark alleys."

By the time O'Leary left, I was close to collapse. Even in a cab I didn't think I was in any shape to get home, so I locked my office door and curled up on the couch under an old overcoat. I was out as soon as my cheek touched the cushion. When I woke again, it was past noon and my bladder was sending out urgent distress signals. I staggered out into the hallway and to the men's room, stopping on the way back at Yelena's desk.

"I canceled all your appointments for you," she said.

"That was considerate of you," I said, meaning it for a change. "How did you . . . ?"

"I found you when I unlocked the door to bring in the mail. You were really out of it, so I asked Dr. Goldman what to do. He said we should wake you up if you slept more than a few hours. Your things are here."

While I was waiting to talk to Hallie's surgeon, I'd called Josh from a pay phone in the hospital, asking him to stop by my apartment and pick up a clean shirt and my folding cane in case I didn't make it home that night. Yelena handed the bundle to me.

"Where is Dr. Goldman now?"

"He's with a patient. I'll buzz him when he's through and tell him you're up. Can I get you anything to drink?" Yelena asked.

I wondered what had prompted this outpouring of solicitude from her. "Some water. And if you would, a bite from the cafeteria." I hadn't eaten in more than twenty-four hours, and my empty stomach was doing cartwheels under my rib cage. I would have liked a shower too, but it could wait. Hallie's surgeon had promised to call me midday with an update. "Are there any messages for me?"

"Just this. Danielle found it lying on the reception desk when she came back from lunch. It doesn't say who it's from." She handed me a letter-sized envelope. "Would you like me to read it to you?"

If this kept up much longer we'd be announcing our engagement. "You're in a swell mood today," I said, handing the envelope back. "Is there something I'm missing out on?"

"It's a secret," Yelena said, almost purring. "I promised I wouldn't tell you until it's been announced."

"OK, then. What's behind Door Number Two?"

Yelena removed the envelope's contents and shook out a sheet of paper. "This is weird," she said immediately.

"What is?"

"It's like something you read about in spy novels—letters from the newspaper all cut up and pasted together."

"Go on," I said, thinking it was just an office prank. "What's it say?"

Yelena began reading:


TWO PLUS TWO USUALLY EQUALS FOUR.
IF YOU WANT TO KNOW WHO BRAINED YOUR GIRLFRIEND,
THINK BACK TO WHAT SHE DID THIS WEEK.
BUT SSSSHH! DON'T TELL THE POLICE.
IF YOU DO, WORSE THINGS COULD BE AROUND THE CORNER.

# THIRTEEN

"Who do you think sent it?" Josh said.

"I haven't a clue." We were in our suite's coffee room, where I was fortifying myself with chicken soup and crackers. "But someone out there isn't too happy about us getting Jane released."

"So you think they went after Hallie to get her off the case?"

"Possibly. But why? It's not like Jane can't afford another lawyer. And there are plenty of them out there who'd be thrilled to take on such a high-profile matter." I picked up one of the crackers and nibbled on the end. It tasted like sawdust, and I put it back on the wrapper.

Josh said, "Here, pass those to me. If you're not going to enjoy your food you might as well give it to someone who will. So what's your theory then?"

"For one thing, whoever wrote that note knows something about Gallagher's death that no one else does. Something they're anxious to see unearthed, if you'll excuse the poor pun."

"Fair enough. But then why haven't they just come forward and told the police?"

"That's the part I don't get. Unless the note writer has some reason to fear being identified."

"Or is in fact the murderer," Josh said, munching. "The note could be a taunt—come and get me if you can—like the ones sent by the Zodiac killer or the Unabomber. Has it occurred to you there could be a psychopath at work here?"

I forced myself to take another spoonful of the soup. "It's certainly a possibility. But there haven't been any other poisonings like Gallagher's reported in the press. Usually serial killers don't limit themselves to one victim."

"True. But Gallagher's death wouldn't have been discovered except for the exhumation order. For all you know, the killer's already knocked off dozens of folks and is getting frustrated that no one's noticed."

"Then why pick a substance that's so hard to identify? Even the Tylenol killer was smart enough to use cyanide, which can be smelled on the victim's lips. Excuse me a sec." It was time for another of my pills. I went over to the water dispenser and poured myself a cup, downing the tablet before returning to my seat.

"How's that going, by the way?" Josh asked, full of concern. "You notice any changes?"

I shook my head. "But Melissa said it would take time for the drug to build up in my system."

"Didn't she also say you should be getting plenty of rest?"

"Hey, I didn't ask to get bludgeoned into unconsciousness, did I?"

"Which raises another point. You shouldn't be by yourself for the next twenty-four hours. Why don't you spend the night at my place? Debbie can make up the spare room, and I can drive you back here in the morning. In the meantime, the police can start tearing that note apart."

My face must have betrayed my intentions.

"Don't tell me," Josh groaned. "You're planning on keeping this to yourself."

"I have to. I can't run the risk of anything else happening to Hallie."

"She's in the ICU, man. What could possibly happen to her there?"

"I don't know. But after last night I'm not taking any chances. Besides, how seriously are the police going to take it anyway? They already think they have Gallagher's killer. If I know them, they'll say the note's just a prank."

"So that's it, then?" Josh said in exasperation. "You're going to go out there and play Daredevil again? God help me for saying this, but you're a forty-eight-year-old desk jockey who can't see past his nose, is probably concussed, and doesn't weigh much more than your average long-distance runner, none of which is likely to present a material challenge to the next thug who comes after you with a club—or, heaven forbid, a gun."

"Don't worry," I reassured him. "Present appearances to the contrary, I'm not that stupid. I know I need help, and I have someone in mind for it."

"So you'll take this to O'Leary?"

"No, but how would you feel about James Bond?"

When I left Josh, the back of my head was throbbing again, but after checking in with Hallie's surgeon—there was no change—I forced myself downstairs and into a cab, stopping only long enough to look up an address and make a photocopy of the note. I put the original inside an old textbook from my shelf, stuck the book inside a manila envelope, and placed both at the back of a drawer full of files, which I then locked with a key. The key went across the room, underneath a flowerpot on the windowsill with a cast iron plant that had long since died. I'd selected it because the variety was supposed to be impervious to neglect, but even the hardiest species needs to be watered from time to time.

Twenty minutes later, the cab dropped me off on West Randolph Street at the offices of Jane Barrett and Associates, LLP. Her ground-floor suite was guarded by a male receptionist of indeterminate age who lifted my business card from my fingers as though it were carrying a nasty strain of bird flu. Ms. Barrett, he informed me in a highborn tone, did not entertain visitors without an appointment.

"Does that policy extend to matters of life and death?" I inquired.

"All of Ms. Barrett's cases are matters of life and death," he sniffed. "Especially to her valued clients."

"How do you know I'm not one of them?"

He didn't reply right away, apparently looking me up and down. I'd changed into the clean shirt Josh had brought me, but was still in the suit I'd been wearing the night before, which, if not spattered with blood, was undoubtedly filthy. That along with the wad of bandage above my ear apparently disqualified me from Ms. Barrett's exalted attention. "I'm afraid Ms. Barrett does not involve herself in plaintiffs' work, let alone charity cases," he said. "Now if you'll excuse me . . ." I heard him turn back to his keyboard.

I considered my options. Raining down blows on him with my cane might satisfy a certain primitive urge but was likely to succeed only in my being arrested and forcibly removed. Instead, I stepped away from his desk, extracted my phone from its holder, and pretended to enter a telephone number. I held it up to my ear and waited a second or two before commencing a loud soliloquy. "Hello? Is this the Disability Advocate at the Attorney General's office? . . . Yes, thank you, I can hold. . . . Yes, hello? I'm calling to lodge a complaint against a licensed member of the bar. You see, I'm blind and I came here to . . . that's right, she won't even speak to me. Yes, I'm at her office now. Oh, you say I should be calling the Attorney Registration and Disciplinary Committee hotline? Right. If you'll just give me that number. . . ."

A few minutes later, I was in a private elevator going up to the building's penthouse, where Jane apparently kept her living quarters so as to be instantly available to clients—at least those wise enough to have called ahead. The car ride took all of thirty seconds, whereupon I was deposited in a small anteroom whose carpeting molded itself to my shoes like a Tempur-Pedic mattress. From my tactile inspection the door a few yards ahead had probably wiped out an entire grove of ancient oaks.

I located the bell at its side and rang. Nothing happened. After a while I put my ear to the door, listening for some indication of life inside, but there was none. I rang again, holding my finger to the button for a full minute in the hope of getting someone's attention. At last a set of footsteps approached. With a click of the latch the mammoth door swung inward. I caught the scent of a rich, exotic perfume I couldn't identify, along with something I would have sworn was glue.

"Doctor, how delightful of you to come," Jane said.

"That's not the way your winged monkey downstairs put it," I said.

"Yes, Gregory is sometimes overzealous in the performance of his duties. But you can hardly blame him. As you might imagine, we've been overrun with curiosity seekers recently. Please accept my apologies for his behavior. And for the delay in coming to the door. I was lighting some logs in the outdoor fireplace when you rang." It sounded as phony as one of Graham Young's drug sales pitches.

"Are you going to let me in?"

"Certainly," Jane said. "I was merely wondering how best to help you."

"Just tell me where to go and I'll be fine."

I followed her instructions to a sofa in the center of a spacious, sunlit room. A door was open somewhere beyond it, bringing the marine odor of the nearby river and the sweet scent of wood smoke. I collapsed my cane and settled myself down on a silk-covered sofa no bigger than a houseboat. I hoped I wouldn't soil it with my clothes. On second thought, maybe I did.

"Would you like some tea?" Jane asked. "I order it specially from Mariage Frères in Paris. I'm particularly fond of their Eros infusion. And perhaps some *macarons* to go with it? I just picked them up at Vanille this morning."

"Never mind that," I said testily. "Have you heard what happened to Hallie?"

"Yes," she replied. "A colleague called with the news this morning. Poor darling. And by the appearance of things, poor you. You look like you're still in shock. And shivering. I can shut the door to the terrace if it's too cold. Why don't you just get comfortable and I'll bring that tea. Unless you'd prefer something stronger . . ."

"Look," I said. "I didn't come here for *petit fours*. I need to ask you some questions."

"But you are my guest and I insist upon it. Now relax and I'll get us some refreshments."

I decided I wasn't in any position to argue. Jane moved off to what sounded like an open kitchen area and began bustling around while I sat back and listened. The couch was soft and I must have dozed off briefly because the next thing I knew she was perched beside me holding a steaming towel. From the smell, there was also something strong and aromatic brewing nearby.

"Here," she said. "You still have dried blood on your face." She moved in closer. I was too taken aback to do anything but sit still while she dabbed at my cheek and chin. "There. That's much better." The warmth was soothing, and I admit it felt good to be nursed.

She removed the towel and sat back within inches of me, not saying anything. This close, her perfume was stronger and I could detect her low, rhythmic breathing. Once again I had the unnerving sense I was being examined under a microscope by a patient and disinterested scientist. I couldn't remove her gaze by returning it, which only intensified my feeling of being on the wrong end of a powerful lens. And there was something else too about her silent and unhurried inspection. If I didn't know better, I'd think I was being sized up for something. I shifted in my seat to put more distance between us.

"How much can you see?" were her next, abrupt words.

"That's none of your business."

"Of course. How rude of me. But if we're going to become close you'll have to get used to it. I always want to know everything about my new friends. But you do see something, yes?"

"My real friends know better than to ask questions like that. Can we talk about Hallie now?"

"In a bit. But first you must satisfy my curiosity about something."

She rose then and walked briskly across the room, opening a drawer and shutting it again. She returned and put a pack of cards in my hands. "Do you know what these are?"

"Don't tell me you're going to show off one of your card tricks."

"No, but I'd like to finish what we started in court. Mix them up and pick one out."

I sighed. But it didn't appear that I had a choice, so I did what she asked, shuffling the deck several times before removing a card from the middle and running it Carnac the Magnificent style across my forehead. "Two minutes," I said, returning the rest of the deck to her.

"I beg your pardon?"

"That's the answer to the question of how long I'm going to remain politely sitting here before my patience is gone."

She laughed again. "I don't think so. Since I appear to be holding all the cards—in more ways than one. Do you know anything about the Tarot?"

"Not a thing."

"Well, there are two types of cards. The Minor Arcana, which roughly corresponds to an ordinary deck of playing cards, and the Major Arcana, which depicts characters and scenes of deeper meaning and significance. The one you're holding comes from the Major Arcana and is called the Hanged Man. It shows a man hanging upside down from a tree. One of his legs is tied to a branch, and the other is free, though bent downward at the knee. The man has a halo of light around his head, and his face is serene, as though he were calm and patiently awaiting something."

"And that tells you what?" I asked. "That I'm in line to become the next Jesus Christ?"

"No, although untimely death is one possible interpretation. More often, though, the Hanged Man is a sign of an individual at a cross-roads—suspended between the past and the future, if you will—who must let go of a treasured hope before he can move on. He'll remain hanging there until he accepts that what he so desperately desires is unattainable."

My thoughts immediately flashed to the bottle of pills in my pocket. Could there be some truth to this gimmickry? Or was she giving me a clue I was supposed to figure out? I shook my head. "That's very interesting, but how do I know this hanging man, or whatever you call him, is on the card I picked—I could be holding any one in the deck."

"I'm afraid you'll have to take my word for it. Now, let's drink our tea and get down to business. Cream and sugar?" I nodded yes while she continued. "You said you had some questions for me. What do you want to know?"

"You could start with what you were lying to Hallie about," I said, taking the cup from her and briefly wondering whether I would survive the first sip. I tried it anyway. The tea was remarkably good and instantly made my head feel better.

"What makes you say I've been lying?" Jane asked, seeming not in the least offended by the question.

"A feeling of Hallie's—she called it an instinct—that you weren't telling her the truth. And that you were there that night, in Gallagher's townhouse. Were you?"

"I don't know that I should answer that. And how is it important? I assume you're here because Hallie was mugged. Surely you don't believe there's a connection to my case?"

I considered telling her about the strange note but decided against it. "Let's just say I don't think it was a random street incident."

"Why? Did Hallie say something to indicate the contrary?"

I shook my head. "She was only awake long enough to say she was sick and needed to get to a phone. But she knew who it was, I'm sure of it."

"And that leads you to believe the attack is related to her representing me? Interesting. But not entirely fanciful. I have a number of enemies, some of whom, no doubt, would view my release from prison as unfortunate. Still, it would be foolish to think my defense could not go forward without Hallie. As talented as she is, there are dozens of attorneys in the city who could take her place."

"I'll grant you that, but if there is a connection, I'd like to know what it is, starting with an explanation of what you've been holding back."

She studied me again in silence. I wondered if she would be any easier to read if I could see her. Somehow I doubted it.

Her next remark surprised me. "How much do you know about the rules of evidence?"

"About as much as I know about the Code of Hammurabi."

"Well, let's see if I can make this simple. You've heard the term 'hearsay,' I presume?"

"Sure. Isn't it like rumor or innuendo?"

"That's the ordinary definition. But in the law it has a much more technical meaning, stemming from the nature of our adversary system. The system places great weight on witnesses being under oath when they testify, as well as physically present in the courtroom. It's thought that direct observation of their testimony is of the utmost importance, both so that the jury can judge its credibility, and also so that the witness's version of events can be tested through cross-examination. Are you with me so far?"

I nodded, though I hadn't a clue where this was headed.

"The corollary is that the system generally frowns on the introduction of statements made outside the courthouse, whose truth or falsity the jury has no practical means of assessing. That's the legal definition of hearsay: an out-of-court statement offered in evidence to prove the truth of its contents. An easier way to think about it is testimony that quotes somebody else."

"So you're saying hearsay is claiming to know a fact you only heard about?" It wasn't all that different from my feeble layman's understanding.

"Close enough. The classic example is when Tom testifies, 'I know Dick murdered Aunt Sally because Harry told me so.' What Tom heard Harry say is clearly hearsay and won't be allowed into evidence unless Harry is subject to the court's jurisdiction and willing to repeat his statement under oath. Only Harry can testify about what he knows."

"Go on," I said, thinking this couldn't be all there was.

"There are, however, exceptions, the most common of which are admissions against interest. If Tom testifies, 'I know Dick murdered Aunt Sally because Dick told me so,' Tom will be allowed to repeat Dick's words on the theory that Dick wouldn't confess to a crime he didn't commit. It doesn't have to be a formal confession to qualify. Nearly any statement that flies against the speaker's self-interest will do. So now you'll understand why I'm unable to help you," she finished cryptically.

My forbearance, such as it was, had reached the breaking point. "I'm sure all of this is of intense interest to legal scholars, but I don't see what it has to do with my question."

"You really don't?" she said in a pitying tone, like I was a promising student who'd just earned a failing grade in her class.

I grimaced in annoyance. "Just answer this. Were you lying to Hallie about not being at Gallagher's place that night?"

"I see I shall have to spell it out for you. The trouble is, if I had gone to Rory's house that night—hypothetically speaking, of course—and I were to tell you so, it would qualify as one of the admissions we've just been talking about."

"Meaning?"

"Meaning that you could be subpoenaed and forced to divulge everything I said under oath."

"I still don't get it," I said, more out of spite than genuine confusion.

"Too bad. I gave you more intellectual credit than that. But you are obviously not at your best at the moment. Think about it some more—after you've gotten a good night's sleep—and you'll have your answer."

I was thoroughly sick of whatever game we were playing. "And that's all you're willing to tell me?" I said harshly. "While your friend is lying in the hospital in a coma?" I searched for the saucer for my cup and put it down, rattling the china.

Jane reached out and put her hand on mine. "Don't be upset. I'm sure Hallie will come out of it soon."

"And if she doesn't?"

"Then, regrettably, I shall be forced to hire another lawyer."

# FOURTEEN

"What a bloody mash-up," Bjorn was saying. "I'm as done in over it as you are."

I was in his office, located in a modest low-rise on Stony Island. Boris had dropped me off there at 9:00 a.m. and provided a quick snapshot of the building, which stood in the shadow of the Reverend Dixon's People United in Freedom church. Based on Boris's description, the latter was a lofty structure not far in appearance from the Hagia Sophia. "I prefer to remain close to my roots," Bjorn explained when I expressed surprise at the non-Loop address. I wondered if his roots included a peerage or two. Or a great-great-great-grandfather present at the signing of the Magna Carta.

"And my father gives me a break on the rent," Bjorn said. "If it gives you any peace of mind, I've arranged for round-the-clock security outside Hallie's room. My lads will make sure the wanker who did this doesn't get within a hundred feet of the door."

"That's not a hundred percent reassuring," I said. "I know hospitals. You'd be surprised at how easy it is to get past the front desk. Or pretend to be someone you're not."

"They have a list of everyone who's authorized to go in and out. I made sure you were on it, by the way."

"That was sporting of you," I said.

"Don't mention it," Bjorn said. "It's small beer compared to what you've been through. If you don't mind my saying so, you look a fright."

I was sure he was right. I'd hardly slept an hour the night before, and between the bags under my eyes and the bandage on my head I could probably pass for an extra in *Night of the Living Dead*.

"And I know Hallie would want it that way," he continued. "The girl is positively bonkers over you. In a purely platonic way, of course."

Of course. "Have you and your lads developed any leads?" I asked.

"On Hallie's attacker?"

"Or Gallagher's killer."

Bjorn considered this. "So you think the two incidents are connected?" he said from his place on the opposite side of a broad desk. The shades of the window behind it were up, giving me a sense of his height, which would have been at home on a point guard for the Bulls. Outside the building's thin walls, there was a continuous grumble of cars headed for the Skyway. "I'm hard on that theory myself, though it seems right barmy. By the way, do you mind if I smoke? It's another reason I keep my office down here, where the bobbies are too busy to enforce the building code."

"Yes, I think they're related. Take a look at what came across my desk yesterday." I removed the photocopy of the pasted-together note from my pocket and tossed it onto the desk.

Bjorn lit his cigarette with the flick of a lighter and perused what I'd given him. "Somebody's been playing with scissors," he remarked before too long.

"Either that or reading too much Agatha Christie."

"It does seem a bit old-fashioned."

"So what does that say to you?"

"The author was trying to make a statement?"

"That too, but I think there's more to it. Tell me something. In our computer age, how hard is it to trace a document back to the machine it was printed on?"

"Not that hard actually. Forensic scientists have come up with several ways to do it, using quality defects like banding—excess lines caused by successive passes of the printer head—or by analyzing toners. There are enough anomalies among different makes and models to allow for a statistical analysis that can pretty accurately say where a document came from."

I'd figured as much. "So if you wanted to be sure something couldn't be traced back to you, you wouldn't just dash it off on your word processor."

Bjorn sucked in a big lungful of his cigarette and blew it out again. "Well, it depends. Very few people have that kind of sophisticated knowledge about forensic techniques."

"Who besides you, for example?"

"Well, just about anyone in law enforcement—police departments, Homeland Security, the FBI, etcetera—but also anyone who routinely works with legal documents. It used to be that a witness could just deny authorship of a 'smoking gun' and feel fairly certain of not being caught out unless it contained their signature. Nowadays, all the big law firms hire e-discovery consultants when the origin of a document is in dispute. In fact, we were just hired to do that kind of analysis for—" He stopped short. "Bollocks."

Bollocks was right.

"Are you thinking the same thing I am?" Bjorn asked, blowing some more smoke my way.

"That Jane was the sender? I wasn't sure until a minute ago, but now I'm positive."

"But why would she do that?"

"I don't know. Hallie must have shared her concerns with you. Jane's been hiding something about Gallagher's murder from day one. And whatever it is, we're not going to get it out of her." I told him about my visit to Jane's penthouse the day before. Sometime between stumbling out of her spider's lair and waking up this morning, I'd settled on the meaning of her last remarks. "So not only is she not going to tell us what she knows, but she'll deny being at Gallagher's townhouse that night."

"Do you think it means . . . ?" Bjorn said, trailing off unhappily.

"That she's guilty? At this point, it's anybody's guess."

He sighed loudly. "Because if she is, it puts me in a sticky wicket. I can't very well run around trying to put my own client away."

"It's still an open question whether she poisoned Gallagher. I don't think you need to resign—yet."

"But if Jane is guilty, why the note? She must have known it would get our attention."

"Exactly. For whatever reason, she wanted to be sure we'd make the connection. After all, apart from the timing—which even I could concede was sheer coincidence—there's nothing obvious linking the attack on Hallie and me to what happened at Jane's hearing. There must be something we're supposed to find out—without her majesty's help."

"So what do we do now?"

"We keep on looking for someone besides your esteemed client who had a reason to want Gallagher out of the way. Which brings me back to my original question. What have you found out so far?"

"Not much, I'm afraid. I assume Hallie told you about the nephew, Urquhart. He certainly had enough motive, but it'll be hell proving he actually slipped the pill to Gallagher. That's the trouble with poisonings—the killer can be miles away when the victim dies. I've got someone tailing him, but I'm not confident it will turn anything up."

"And that's only half of it. If I understood what Hallie told me about accidental-death insurance, Urquhart doesn't make much sense as our man."

"Why do you say that?"

"Think about it. Urquhart stood to gain twice as much insurance if Gallagher's death was a homicide. If that's the case, why choose a poison that would make it look like his uncle died of natural causes?"

"To divert suspicion from himself?"

"OK, but then why didn't he ask for an immediate autopsy? The ME said they'll do one if the family requests it. If it hadn't been for the exhumation, Gallagher's body would still be moldering in its grave and no one would be the wiser."

"You've got me there," Bjorn said thoughtfully.

"And that's another thing. We've got to find out what prompted the exhumation request."

"All right," Bjorn said, scribbling this down on a pad. "Anything else?"

"Gallagher's movements that night. There are two hours unaccounted for between the time he left Gene and Georgetti's and when he showed up at the Billy Goat. It can't hurt to know where he went.

His cardiologist is another thing to follow up on. With all the privacy regulations in place, it's not easy for a casual bystander to find out if someone has a heart condition, but who besides Jane and the nephew knew? And while you're doing all this running around, why not pay a social call on Gallagher's fiancée, the cheerleader? If I had to guess, there's a lot more to that story than meets the eye."

In the cab going back uptown, I realized my stomach was empty again, so I had the cabbie drop me off at a greasy spoon around the corner before trudging wearily back to my office, stopping first at Richard's station before heading upstairs. Upon taking stock of my appearance, he respectfully inquired whether I'd been in a bar brawl.

"More like a trip down the wrong blind alley." I told him what had happened.

"Sweet Jesus," he said. "I wish you'd asked me along."

"Me too," I said, regretting once more that I'd brought Hallie with me. "Can you do me another favor?"

"So long as it doesn't involve eating what's in that bag."

"I'm going to be tied up for a while trying to find out who did this to us. It would take a little of the weight off my mind to know someone was still looking for Mike. Will you do it?"

"No problem, but only in return for something."

"And that would be?" I asked.

"You promising to get some shut-eye. The circles under your eyes are as deep as the mayor's campaign chest."

"I'll try, but sleep isn't at the forefront of my priorities right now."

Richard's voice dropped to a whisper. "If you're interested, I have something that might help in that department."

"Thanks," I said. "But I've grown attached to my license. And my days are already surreal enough as it is."

Back at my desk I called to ascertain that Hallie was still in a stable condition before washing down another one of my pills and forcing myself through a grilled cheese sandwich that might have been two boards stuck together with glue. I e-mailed Tom Klutsky and set up an appointment with him after he got off work. I then went about arranging some days off. Sep had gotten wind of what happened and readily agreed that I should take it easy for a while. Josh said he'd cover my patients, and Yelena—still mysteriously effervescent—volunteered to screen my e-mails. Harvey's receptionist accepted my excuse of a last-minute vacation. This housekeeping out of the way, I still had a few free hours before I was due to meet Klutsky, so I sat down at my computer to find out what else I could learn about Gallagher.

Not surprisingly, Gallagher was well represented on the Internet. My first search turned up more than ten thousand hits. Someone with nothing else to occupy their time had supplied a biography on *Wikipedia*, so I started there, scrolling through the text with my earphones while I typed notes into my phone.

Rory Sean Gallagher had been born in Peoria in 1956, the son of an insurance salesman and a homemaker. He attended the University of Missouri as an undergraduate and had gone on to obtain a master's degree in journalism at Medill before joining the *Sun-Times* as a cub reporter in the early eighties. His rise there was as meteoric as they come, starting with a story that exposed massive corruption in (where else?) the state contracting authority that eventually led to federal convictions on bribery charges of nearly every high-ranking staffer in the governor's office and eventually the chief executive himself.

From there, Gallagher became a reliable chronicler of every social ill the Land of Lincoln could offer, gleefully uncovering the misdeeds of crooked judges, Outfit mobsters, AWOL patronage workers, and fabricated voters in his syndicated column "The Sinful City." In 1990, he was one of the first journalists to break the story of sexual abuse by Catholic priests in the Chicago Archdiocese, and in 1994, he won the Pulitzer Prize for his coverage of gang violence in the Cabrini Green Housing Project.

And so on, until about ten years ago, when the tidal wave of scandalous exposés abruptly ceased. From that point on, Gallagher appeared content to rest on his laurels, increasingly turning out stories that were little more than thinly disguised gossip. Like many a former *enfant terrible*, infatuated with his own image but no longer willing to do the hard work that garnered his success, Gallagher had grown complacent. Slowly but surely, his readership fell off. And just as surely, the lawsuits began rolling in. An heiress falsely accused of neglecting her aged, Alzheimer's-afflicted father quietly settled with the *Sun-Times* for an undisclosed sum. A community organization successfully sued for retraction of a column claiming that its funding was being used to advise low-income clients on how to game the tax system. Meanwhile, Gallagher's extravagant lifestyle had itself become fodder for the gossip columnists, culminating in a racy piece in *The Reader* the year before captioned ALL THE *SUN-TIMES'* MEN: THE SAD DEMISE OF RORY GALLAGHER.

All this was well and good as a character reference, but it did nothing to broaden the field of suspects. It was true that over the course of a thirty-year career, Gallagher had made more enemies than the Rolling Stones had fans. But most of his stories were now as long in the tooth as the electric typewriter. It seemed unlikely that someone in the rogues gallery of Mafia thugs, crooked politicians, and pedophile priests would have waited so long to settle an old score, or that they would have latched onto a popular prescription drug as the means of getting even. And if the motive for the killing wasn't an ancient grudge, who else besides Jane could have had it in for Gallagher?

# FIFTEEN

Tom Klutsky had suggested the Billy Goat for our rendezvous, which suited me fine. I'd always wanted to visit the home of the "goat curse," which originated when the tavern's owner, a Greek immigrant named Bill Sianis, attempted to bring his pet goat onto Wrigley Field during the '45 World Series. The Cubs' owner had refused the goat entry, causing Sianis to swear, "Cubs, they not gonna win anymore." Sianis had proved to be a seer: the Cubs lost to Detroit and hadn't won a series since. Apart from the tavern's legendary associations, it seemed only fitting we should meet in the place where Gallagher had downed his last drop.

Klutsky met me on Upper Michigan Avenue and led me down the stairs to the street's lower level. Another set of stairs went down from the Goat's entrance to a low-ceilinged room overhung with smoke and the mingled odors of cooking grease and cleaning solvents. We squeezed into padded polyester chairs across a none-too-steady table. A waiter came and took our order—cheeseburgers, naturally—and bellowed "no fries, cheeps" on cue when prompted by Klutsky.

"How much do they pay them to do that?" I asked.

"Probably more than you and I make in a year."

Klutsky listened patiently while I told him what had happened and what I'd gleaned from my research. "So what else can you tell me about Gallagher?" I asked after finishing up.

Klutsky lowered his voice. "Well, this probably falls into the category of *de mortuis nil nisi bonum . . .*"

"Go on," I said.

"The guy was a total fraud. You've probably run across the type. They start out in life with more talent than they deserve and eventually fall under the spell of their own myth. Which isn't to say Gallagher wasn't a damn good reporter at one time. Some of the articles he wrote in his twenties and thirties, like the one that won him the Pulitzer, were brilliant. But instead of spurring him on to new heights, it made him lazy. Not to mention careless."

"I read about the lawsuits."

"Yeah, and that ought to tell you something. It's almost impossible for a reporter to get sued for libel under the First Amendment, but Gallagher managed to pull it off. Office rumor had it that Sam Welsh— that's my managing editor—was dying to get rid of him, but Gallagher was one of the few reporters around who still had a contract."

"What kind of contract?"

"Supposedly high-six figures with a multiyear guarantee, entered into some time back when Gallagher was still a big fish and could name his price. That's a lot of dough to fork over to someone whose column is losing readership, especially when the paper is laying off other employees left and right. Didn't sit well with some of the other investigative reporters, who were told to take a pay cut or leave. Gallagher was becoming a liability in other ways, too. The paper got hit with an EEOC complaint last year after he pawed some gal from accounting at the Christmas bash."

I was surprised. "They couldn't even fire him for that?"

"Under the terms of the contract, not until it was proven in court. These EEOC suits can take years to resolve. Meanwhile, the paper was on the hook to pay Gallagher's legal fees, and the suit wasn't doing it any favors in the internal harmony department, either. A bunch of female reporters presented Sam with a petition demanding that Gallagher be put on administrative leave, but apparently his contract didn't allow for that, either. Last I heard, Sam offered him early retirement and a million-dollar severance package to get out of the old deal, but Gallagher just laughed in his face."

All of which would make him pretty unpopular in the executive suite. Klutsky had given me a lot of information to digest, but one thought stuck out. "The EEOC charge, was it made public?"

"You can't get the file from the Dirksen building, but the employer has to be notified. And the lady in accounting wasn't shy about spreading the story around. Why?"

"I was just wondering whether Jane had gotten wind of it. What I don't get is why a woman like her was involved with Gallagher in the first place, especially if she's as gorgeous as everyone says she is. It's obvious Gallagher was always playing around. Why didn't she dump him years ago?"

"Beats me," Klutsky said. "But if I had to guess, it was the usual story of outsized personalities feeding each other's egos. And don't forget, Rory was mighty amusing to be with. Always had some little nugget of dirt to share. It was part of his charm. Gallagher may have pissed off a lot of people, but his pals got on with him well enough."

Our burgers had arrived. Klutsky bit noisily into his, squirting juice onto my sleeve. "Eat something," he urged.

It smelled modestly appetizing, but my arteries had already taken enough of a beating for one day. "If it's all right with you, I'll just bring it home with me. Do you think you could get me in to see Welsh?"

"I should be able to manage that. Why don't you come around the paper tomorrow morning and I'll get us an audience."

When I bid good-bye to Klutsky, I was restless and out of ideas, so I decided to take the roundabout way home, heading south on Lower Michigan until it met up with the River Walk. After a form of aversion therapy the previous spring, I tended to shy away from that particular stretch of path, but I thought a spell in the outdoors might take my mind off the case and help me get some shut-eye later on. I followed my nose to the water's edge, locating the steel balustrade with a thwack of my cane and letting the handrail conduct me east to a wider section of the promenade where benches sat in the shifting gray tones of a group of trees.

I sat down on one of the steel seats, leaned the cane against my shoulder, and opened the wrapper holding my uneaten meal, picking off little bits and tossing them onto the pavement. Before long, I was sur-rounded by dueling factions of sparrows and squirrels, noisily clamoring for their fair share. Amid all the cheeping and twittering a tour boat moved by, bringing the hubbub of animated conversation and the clink of cock-tail glasses. The evening was almost perfectly still, and the sounds coming from the boat, amplified by the water, carried clearly to where I was sitting. "Look, isn't that wonderful—he's feeding the birds!" a woman remarked. "Ssshh, not so loud!" a male companion warned. "He might hear you." I smiled ruefully and waved a hand in their direction, feeling like the subject of a cute animal video: "Blind Man Shares Supper with Wildlife."

The boat's passage reminded me of the hour, which was close to sunset. I recalled with sadness how the evening sky once looked, and wished I could return to the days when it promised a night of untrou-bled rest. The memory provoked a sudden inspiration. I took out my phone and ran my finger over the screen until it spoke the name of the app I wanted, double-tapped to get it started, and pointed the camera west to where the sun still shone, a wavering bright patch in the dis-tance. Available for free, the app came with two settings: simple colors (red, blue, green) and what I thought of as the Fruit Loops version, which I liked better because of its livelier descriptions. I moved the phone around to vary the camera's focal point and listened to the colors it read out to me—Pink Carnation, Ripe Cantaloupe, Persimmon Red, Violet Dusk—until night fell and the streetlights flickered on.

And then I went home and did what everyone had been urging me to do for days: I crawled between the sheets and slept.

The next morning I was feeling mildly human again, and even more so after I'd checked in with Hallie's surgeon. She was making good progress; the intracranial swelling was going down. He cautioned me once more that she probably wouldn't remember anything, and there was no way to predict how long her recovery would take, but so far the signs were encouraging. Her family was with her round-the-clock, another reason for me to keep my distance.

With that news to ease my mind some, I went about rectifying my dietary lapses of the last forty-eight hours. My pantry was never a model of good housekeeping, but a strip search of my fridge revealed the basics of a hearty meal: two eggs, a slice of bacon, and half a loaf of bread. I put the bacon in the microwave between paper towels, and two slices of bread in the toaster. I set a frying pan on the burner and kicked the stove to get the ignition to flare—like everything else in the apartment, the appliance was prematurely decrepit—and scrambled the eggs in a mea-suring cup. When heat waves began rising from the pan, I dropped a pat of butter in and waited for the sound of its sizzle before adding the eggs, stirring them with a fork and periodically testing their consistency with a finger. With a little more finesse I'd be ready for *Iron Chef*.

When the food was ready, I wolfed it down at the counter with a glass of orange juice and my pill for the morning before heading off to shower, shave, and dress. I put on khakis, a white shirt, and a blue blazer, and used my phone to select a matching tie. I combed my hair as best I could with the bandage still in place, took a swipe at my shoes with the kitchen sponge, and squared my Mets cap on my head. I then headed downstairs and over to the *Sun-Times*.

At one time, you couldn't miss the paper's headquarters, which occu-pied a commanding site on the banks of the Chicago River. When it was built in the 1950s, the gigantic glass box with the paper's name festooned in ten-foot-high letters on the roof was the very epitome of modern "Chicago" style. But as the decades wore on, the building began to seem like so many other featureless relics of the Cold War, so that not even the preservationists protested when a certain real estate mogul knocked it down to make way for a hotel-residential tower topped by a $32 million penthouse. The newspaper now resided less grandly in an annex of the massive Merchandise Mart next door.

Klutsky came to fetch me at the entrance on Kinzie, and we went up to Welsh's office in a glass-partitioned corner of the newsroom that did little to mute the cacophony of telephones ringing in the background.

"Fucking printers' union," Walsh bellowed as we came in. "I've got creditors salivating to get their hands on the paper's assets and legal bills piled higher than the Hancock Building, and all they can think about is how they're going to get their next COLA. Not to mention all the fine folks who think their newspaper should be delivered to their doorstep every morning for free. What I need is a time machine so I can go back and strangle Steve Jobs and all the other assholes who invented the Internet."

I pictured Ed Asner dressed in today's business-casual attire. He had the gravel-pit voice to go with it.

"Did I tell you that our ad revenues are down another five percent? It'll serve 'em all right when the only news they can get is from some two-bit blogger reporting on UFO sightings in New Mexico."

"Wait," Klutsky said archly. "Didn't we run a story just like that the other day?"

"Wiseacre. You know I didn't have a choice. It came over the wire from AP, and there would have been hell to pay if the *Tribune* picked it up and we didn't. Nation's a trillion dollars in debt, the politicos are in total gridlock, and the Corn Belt hasn't seen a drop of rain since last July, and what do they want to read about? Space aliens and celebrity fetuses. Christ, am I ready for retirement. So what have we got here?"

Welsh got up out of his chair, and Klutsky introduced us.

"I remember you," Welsh said immediately, shaking my hand. "From that feature Tom wrote. Aren't you the doctor who went back to seeing his patients literally the day after he went blind? I gotta tell you how much I admire that. If it was me the lights went out on, I wouldn't have left the house for a year."

"Yeah, well, don't believe everything you read in the papers," I said, sending a disgruntled look in Tom's direction.

"So, how do you manage it? It must be hell getting around. And not following sports events. I go crazy missing a single period of the Blackhawks."

Apparently someone else who had never heard of radio. "It's given me more time to catch up on my knitting," I said, smiling and taking the chair he pushed toward me.

"See, that's what I mean," Welsh said to Klutsky. "On top of everything, a helluva sense of humor."

"Laughter is what keeps me going," I agreed.

"So how can I help you?" Welsh returned to the seat behind his desk and squeaked heavily down, while Klutsky took the one to my left.

"I was hoping you might answer some questions about Rory Gallagher."

"OK. But what's your interest? Unless he was your patient. In which case, I'd sure like to get your story."

"Sorry, I didn't know anything about the man until two weeks ago." I described my involvement in the case, the attack on Hallie and me, and the note left at my office. I slid the copy over his desk. Welsh picked it up and read.

"This is great," he said happily. "Just great. I'll have it on the front page tomorrow."

"Not so fast," I said. "First, there's something you can do for me."

"I'm all ears," Welsh said. Then: "Sorry, I should have phrased that differently."

"I'll try not to let it depress me. How much looking into Gallagher's death has your paper done?"

"Pretty much none," Welsh conceded. "I mean, once the police arrested Barrett, there wasn't much to follow up on. The story was already out of the can. All we had to do was report it and shed some crocodile tears over the loss of our dear, departed colleague. Why? You think there's a question about whether she did it?"

"Could be. For starters, the motive the police pinned on her is a little thin."

"Not as far as I'm concerned. In my business you see it all the time. Middle-aged woman attached to a guy with a wandering eye discovers he's getting it on with a younger broad. She can't stand being replaced, so she does him in. Hell, it's just like the Scarsdale Diet doctor and that woman—what was her name? Plenty of dough, high-profile career, but all it took was being passed over by a seventy-year-old for her to go off the deep end. Like they say, 'hell hath no fury.' And I'm not even going to bring up change of life."

Klutsky, by my side, chuckled. "Good choice, Sam. Your wife might get wind of it."

Welsh said, "Here's one for you: how does a man know when his wife is in a bad mood?" He paused before delivering the punch line. "If she's in menopause, whenever she's awake."

Klutsky and Welsh laughed uproariously.

"OK, fellas, that's hilarious," I said. "But just for the sake of argument, let's say it wasn't Barrett. How many other people might have welcomed seeing Gallagher dead?"

"How high can you count?" Welsh replied. "Klutsky here must have told you his fan club didn't extend very far around here. But hating a bastard is a far cry from killing him. And I doubt you'll find many among the folks he put away who aren't still in prison or whiling away their remaining hours in a nursing home."

"I don't suppose you'd admit to wanting him out of the way yourself?"

Welsh didn't pull any punches. "The company lawyers aren't here to put a gag order on me, so I'll be candid with you. Damn right I wanted him off my payroll, if only to get the feminist office squad off my tail. But kill him? Sorry, I have too much to look forward to when I'm outta here."

It sounded sincere, but I wasn't sure I believed him. "OK," I said. "But how about stories he was working on? Wouldn't it be a motive for murder if Gallagher was about to blow the lid off something?"

Welsh discounted this. "Maybe when he was younger, but Gallagher hadn't come up with a credible scoop in years. I stopped paying attention to his column long ago, except to hand it over to the aforesaid lawyers every week to make sure it wasn't going to land us in another stink."

"Can you try to find out? There must be something in his files to indicate what he was working on."

"Can't help you in that department, either," Welsh said matter-of-factly. "The police went through Gallagher's office and walked off with everything that wasn't bolted down, including his computer. I doubt there's so much as a paper clip left in there."

For a newspaperman he was mighty uninquisitive. "How about your servers?" I said impatiently. "The police didn't walk off with them, too. Can't you look there?"

"I could, but I doubt it would turn up what you're looking for. After the last bill for e-discovery, Gallagher was under strict orders to keep anything sensitive on his machine at home. I could have one of my IT people go through the backup tapes, but it's going to take time—and money. What's in it for me?"

"A story, if I find one. And if I don't, I'll give you permission to print that note in your hand."

Welsh said, "Let me think about this for a minute or two."

I listened while he breathed heavily, no doubt weighing my request against his budget woes.

"OK," Welsh said finally. "I'm in. If there's something there, where do you want it sent?"

I gave him my and Bjorn's addresses.

"Don't mention it," Welsh said, as I was thanking him and getting ready to leave. "Just remember to reward me properly if anything comes of it. And what would you say to me hanging onto this little piece of paper here as security?"

I grinned broadly at him. "You must think I'm blind."

# SIXTEEN

Back on the street again, I was pondering what to do next when my phone rang. It was Rusty Halloran.

"Are you somewhere where you can talk privately?" he asked.

"At the moment, I happen to be standing on a corner outside the Merchandise Mart, so no. But I could come over."

"Please do. There's been another development concerning our friend Levin." He sounded unhappy.

"I'll be there ASAP," I said.

Even when I was sighted I always found the streets around River North confusing, so I used my phone to plot a course from the Mart to Rusty's offices, first heading two blocks east on Kinzie until it met up with LaSalle. I turned left at the corner and threaded my way through the clinking cutlery and grilled-steak aroma of an outdoor café before continuing up the block into a stiff wind. The sun was searingly bright, but it was easy to tell that fall wasn't far off, and I shivered each time I passed through a shadow, as much from the sudden drop in temperature as from the thought of the raw, monotonous winter to come. Another three hundred feet brought me to Hubbard, where I waited for the whoosh of south-flowing traffic on LaSalle to subside before crossing over. Remarkably, the ten-minute trip did not yield a single offer of assistance. I would have congratulated myself on another successful passage through the Twilight Zone if I hadn't been preoccupied with what Rusty had to tell me—and fearing the worst.

When I heard what it was, I was only partially relieved. "A second suicide?" I said from one of the cigar-smoke-infused leather chairs in his office.

"Unfortunately, yes. Just the other day. Another New Trier student he was treating for depression," Rusty said grimly.

"How?"

"Overdose of alcohol and mommy's painkillers. The young lady's parents were away for the weekend in Door County and found her when they got home. She was seventeen."

"Jesus. How's Levin taking it?"

"How do you think?"

I shook my head in worry. "He needs to be seeing another shrink. Have you had any luck convincing him?"

"No, but I've started a rearguard action through Betsy. She was going to stop by the home today. Nobody is as persuasive as my wife when she's got a campaign to sink her teeth into, so keep your fingers crossed."

"I will, but maybe I should talk to Levin, too."

"That would be ideal if we didn't have a court date coming up. We need to keep your knowledge of the second death to a minimum."

"Won't the fact come in anyway?"

Rusty gave out a long sigh. "It shouldn't. Usually evidence of so-called 'other bad acts' can't be introduced to prove that a person acted similarly in the case at hand, the rationale being that it's highly preju-dicial to the defendant and nearly impossible to contradict. But there are exceptions to the rule. I'll fight like hell to keep the girl's suicide out of it, but with two dead kids in the mix, I don't know of many judges who'll go along."

Poor Levin. And with two adolescent suicides on his track record, it wouldn't be long before the state board was breathing down his neck—whether he deserved it or not. I tried to think of something that might help.

"I wonder if it could be the beginning of a cluster," I said. "They're unfortunately common in people under the age of twenty-five. Was Danny Carpenter's death the subject of a lot of attention?"

"It was all over the North Shore papers for a week, in addition to the candlelight vigil his parents' neighbors staged at their church. And

I'm not including all the flowers and signs left at the place where he smashed up his car. For weeks you couldn't go up or down that part of Sheridan Road without seeing it."

It was frustrating, but such community outpourings of grief often made the situation worse, leading other vulnerable teenagers to follow in their peers' footsteps. That plus the wrong kind of media coverage—too much focus on the method and place of death—only increased the risk of further suicides.

"That might be an avenue of inquiry, then," I said. "Find out whether the girl knew Danny and how she reacted to his death. She may or may not have mentioned it to Levin, especially if she was trying to hide suicidal ideation, but her friends might be able to say. And keep your ears open for other similar cases. God forbid another kid should go off and kill themselves, but it would take some of the heat off your client. Three or more suicides over a short period of time is enough to get the health department to step in."

"I won't wish for that, but I'll keep it in mind. And now perhaps you'd be willing to share what happened to you? Somehow I don't think you cut yourself shaving," Rusty said, referring to the bandage still stuck to the side of my head.

I was glad he brought it up. There were a few things I wanted to ask him.

"So Hallie was concerned from the start that Jane was keeping something from her," Rusty said after I'd given him the whole story, including the events of the bond hearing, the attack on us, and the provocative, pasted-together note.

"Can you think of a reason for that, besides her being guilty?"

He thought about this for a few minutes. "Hmmm . . . guilt is certainly one possibility, but not the only one. When was the last time you partook of the sacrament of confession?"

I groaned. "You should know better than to ask a lapsed Catholic that. There aren't enough mea culpas in the world to cover all the years I've gone unabsolved of my sins. What about you?"

"I still go weekly. Not because I'm a believer in the man upstairs, but as a cheap form of therapy. It's the one place I can go to unburden my conscience with absolute certainty that nothing I say will ever be known to anyone besides myself and the good father. Can you say the same about your business?"

"Not a hundred percent, but pretty close. Patient confidentiality is one of the core ethical values of the profession."

"And one that you would go to great lengths to preserve?"

"Absolutely. The only reason I can think of for breaching it would be to save another person from serious harm, or to defend myself in a malpractice suit."

"Well," Rusty said, "The same, or a similar thing applies to lawyers. A lawyer can't disclose a client's secrets—even to another lawyer—except in rigorously defined circumstances. And while those circumstances include the malpractice situation you refer to, they don't include defending oneself against a murder charge."

I was beginning to catch on. "So you're saying that the information Jane was withholding from Hallie might have had something to do with one of her clients?"

"If you're looking for an explanation besides her being guilty of the crime, it's something to consider. Perhaps instead of a lover's quarrel, she and Gallagher were fighting over privileged information that somehow ended up in Gallagher's hands. The fellow was an investigative reporter, wasn't he? And in a downward spiral according to the news reports I read. Perhaps he abused her trust to lay his hands on something he wasn't entitled to."

I thought back to the bond hearing, the testimony of the witnesses who had overheard Jane and Gallagher arguing. What was it Jane had said? "You won't get away with it!" Could she have meant something entirely different than what the police imagined? It certainly fit into my theory that Jane had nothing to fear from Gallagher's attentions to Lucy Sparks. And it would explain what Jane had gone looking for in Gallagher's place afterward.

"All right," I said to Rusty. "I'm following you. But I find it hard to believe that faced with a choice between going to prison and damaging her client, she'd choose the former. Nobody's dedication to ethics runs that deep."

Rusty chuckled. "Just as nobody would ever accuse you of being cynical. But while I agree with you about human nature, Jane may have been biding her time, waiting to see how the case developed before she told Hallie. Or she decided that revealing the true reason for their quarrel would only hand the prosecution another motive for poisoning Gallagher. And don't forget, if my theory's right, disclosing whatever she knew would in all likelihood have cost Jane her license."

I thought about this, too. "Tell me something else. Under your rules, what would happen to Jane if the hypothetical information we've been discussing came to light on its own—I mean, without her being the disclosing party?"

"It depends on how you define your terms. A lawyer who sets in motion a chain of events that is sure to result in disclosure of a confidence—for example, tipping the police to where their client buried a murder victim—is as guilty of an ethical lapse as someone who simply fails to guard their tongue in an elevator. Of course, you'd have to be able to prove it."

"But if you couldn't prove it," I pressed. "If our theoretical lawyer were clever enough to tip a third party in a way that could never be tied back to them, what then?"

"I'd say our hypothetical tippee should be worried about who he's dealing with."

Over a corned beef sandwich at a nearby deli, I considered my next steps. My conversation with Rusty had given me the first plausible explanation for Jane's mysterious behavior but still left me tantalizingly in the dark. Clearly, I was supposed to find out something she was not permitted to tell me outright. What other reason could there be for a message that couldn't be linked to her through state-of-the-art forensic techniques? Given all the tools at the cops' disposal, I was sure they could identify the brand of paper and paste used to compose the note, but I had little doubt they were of a type that could be picked up in any drugstore. And with Jane's intimate knowledge of police methods, it was a safe bet that whatever materials she used had long since vanished. Come to think of it, I had probably smelled them going up in smoke when I was sitting in her penthouse. It brought home once again my limitations as a detective. I couldn't simply stroll over to see what was smoldering in her fireplace in the middle of a summer day, or draw any conclusions about the woman—except that she had expensive taste in sofas—from the items on display in her home. The only thing I could do was listen.

I caught myself and shook my head. Self-pity wasn't going to get me anywhere. I needed to come up with a plan. It was still a safe assumption that Gallagher's death was related to the story he was working on, but following up on that angle would have to await whatever further information Welsh could dig up for me—if indeed any still existed. Discovering the identity of the client Jane had been arguing about with Gallagher that night was similarly impractical at this juncture. I could look up all the companies she represented, but even with Bjorn's help I couldn't very well go knocking on the doors of executive suites across the city, much less expect anyone to disclose what secrets they had imparted to their trusted trial counsel. I could only hope that continuing to investigate would eventually lead me to some answers. In the meantime, there was another gap in my knowledge that needed filling, and I thought I knew just the person who could do it.

A short while later I was passing under the shadow of the Joan Miró sculpture on my way into the County Building. Originally called *The Sun, the Moon and One Star*, its title was later changed to *Chicago*. I didn't understand either name, since the only thing the artwork brought to mind was a huge table fork. It stood directly across from the even larger Chicago Picasso, which journalist Mike Royko once famously said looked like a giant insect about to eat a much smaller, weaker one. Another wag had proposed replacing it with a statue of

Ernie Banks. My own take was that Picasso had simply liked a good joke.

As luck would have it, the man I had come to see was in, awaiting the jury's return in the latest murder case involving a schoolchild mowed down by gang crossfire—Assistant State's Attorney Tony Di Marco. A thirty-year veteran of the department, Di Marco was often called "a lawyer's lawyer," though in my opinion he was more aptly described as "a shark's shark." Di Marco had conducted my first, eminently forgettable cross-examination, and while his tactics cut more corners than an upholsterer, I respected his ability. In his hands a hostile witness's smirking confidence was quickly reduced to pitiable insecurity and an urgent desire to flee the witness stand as quickly as their legs would carry them. I knew this because I'd been there. Beyond that, although we shared the same ethnicity, we got along together about as well as Frazier and Ali.

"*Dottore*," he exclaimed as I was being shown into his office. "So nice of you to drop by. To what do I owe the pleasure?" He came over and pumped my arm in a fake show of hospitality. "Oh, dear, look at you. Did you fall down? You really ought to think about getting a dog one of these days."

"I'd like to, but it might mistake you for a rodent. And stop pretending you didn't hear."

"About the mugging, you mean?" he said, returning to his seat and leaving me standing. "Yeah, what a shame. I haven't been able to get over to the hospital because of this trial, but I'm planning on it as soon as the jury comes back. How's Hallie doing?"

"She's making progress," I said, acutely aware of my own absence from her side.

"There's one thing that's got us all puzzled, though," Di Marco said.

"Like who went after her?"

"No, like why she hangs out with you in the first place. I mean, a beautiful girl like that. A lot of the guys here think it must be a mothering instinct. Me, I have a different theory."

"Go ahead. I know you won't be able to keep it to yourself."

"She's a sucker for men in black." He laughed himself silly over that one while I groped around for a chair. I realized I hadn't removed my sunglasses as I usually did when I came indoors, but decided to leave them on as a gesture of hostility.

"So what can I do for you?" Di Marco asked. "Besides refer you to Human Services?"

"Gee, Tony, I hate it when you get all mushy on me like that. I was hoping you might be willing to share some information."

"About what?"

"About another former colleague."

"Depends on what you want to know."

I figured I had no choice but to level with him, explaining everything that had happened since Hallie and I were attacked. When I was through, Di Marco's attitude had undergone what for him was a sea change.

"OK," he said. "I've heard enough. You've been square with me, so I'll return the courtesy. Normally, my lips would be sealed tight. There's an unwritten code here—what goes on in the office stays in the office. But I don't like it that some *cazzone* went after an ex-prosecutor, or that the prick took advantage of your situation to pull it off. Jokes are one thing, but beating up a blind man is going too far."

I wasn't enamored of his reasoning but bit back a retort in the interest of learning what he could tell me.

Di Marco went on. "I'm not saying I feel sorry for you—you're too much like me to earn anyone's sympathy—and I doubt we're ever going to be friends, but I'm going to put aside our differences for the time being. Here's the deal, though. You can't say a word of this to anyone—and I do mean anyone. That woman is poison, and I can't be taking the chance she'll find out it was me who squawked. So if I tell you what you want to know, you have to make like Deep Throat and not repeat it to a soul. *Capisci?*"

"I understand," I said. "The penalty for violating *omertà* is death."

Di Marco chuckled evilly. "You've got that right. OK, it all goes back to when we were starting out in '95 . . ."

He proceeded to tell me the story of how he, Jane, and another junior assistant, James O'Hara, were thrown together in a shared office and became comrades of a sort. "I'm not using the word 'friends'—at least not where Jane was concerned. She was always stuck up, didn't like to consort with the mere mortals among us, and was always critical of colleagues who didn't meet her exalted standards. But when you're spending all hours of the day and night in a twelve-by-twelve office space, you get to know people. Jimmy was a different story. A great guy, always willing to help out. Everyone in the place liked him."

The office pairing was fortuitous in another way. All three of the young lawyers proved well suited to their jobs and were promoted virtually in lockstep for the next several years, each of them eventually landing in the felony-crimes division. "From a raw-talent standpoint, Jane was undeniably the best, and I'm not saying that with any false modesty," Di Marco said. "I probably came next, and Jimmy . . . well, he was one of those guys who could have outshined us both if he hadn't been so nice. His trouble was not being able to turn anyone down. The supervisors love a guy like that, and he was always up to his eyeballs in files. When that happens, you can't help getting a little sloppy. There were a couple of complaints, defense lawyers claiming that he didn't turn over exculpatory material on time, but they always bitch about that and nobody could ever find proof that it was deliberate—just a busy guy falling behind on his paperwork.

"Fast-forward ten years to '05 when the then First Assistant was about to retire and the chief was looking for a replacement. All three of us put our names in, but I had to withdraw because my wife got sick. Jane should have been the front-runner based on her record, but you know how office politics are: nobody ever votes for the person they think is the best for the job, just who they think will go easiest on them. For the reasons I've mentioned, Jane was never very popular among the staff attorneys, especially the ones who punched the clock every day at five, and everyone figured there'd be hell to pay if she landed the job. Meanwhile, there was Jimmy, always a good sport and never a harsh word to say about anyone. When the tide started to turn in his favor, you could tell Jane was furious, though she kept a tight smile on her face the whole time. That's when the shit hit the fan."

I had a bad feeling I knew where this was going. "What shit?"

"That reporter pal of Jane's—Gallagher. Got his hands on some old dirt about an informant whose priors—convictions, that is—weren't disclosed to defense counsel in a capital case. A very big no-no under the discovery rules. If it hadn't been for the moratorium on the death penalty signed by the governor, the defendant would have bought the ranch on death row."

I remembered the story now from my Internet research. It was one of Gallagher's last big breaks, leading to reversal of the conviction and calls for disciplinary action against the prosecutor responsible for not coming forth with the information.

"You can guess who the ASA on the case was," Di Marco said.

"Your friend Jimmy."

"Uh-huh. Ruined his chances for the promotion and almost got him fired. That didn't clear the way for Jane, though. Nobody would say it—and I'm not claiming it now, you understand—but everyone assumed they knew who Gallagher got his information from. Folks started thinking back and remembered a few other times when Gallagher seemed to have the inside track on departmental matters. After that, no one would have anything to do with Jane. My boss realized he had a problem and hired someone from the outside. Jane quit and we all said good riddance."

"And Jimmy, what happened to him?"

"That's the worst part of the story. The stress of the investigation and all the haranguing in the press were too much for him."

"Was he forced to quit, too?"

"I wish. Poor bastard had a congenital heart condition. Nothing too serious so long as he remembered to take his medication."

I had another ugly premonition about where this was headed.

"He missed a couple of his pills and had a massive coronary right at his desk."

# SEVENTEEN

I had barely begun to digest this new piece of information when my phone starting ringing.

"Excuse me," I told Di Marco.

The caller was a clearly worked-up Bjorn. "You won't believe what I've got to tell you. I think I've cracked the case," he said over what sounded like a car phone, the posh accent for once abandoned or forgotten. "Where are you?"

"At the County Building, talking to my new *amico*," I said, lowering my sunglasses and winking over at Di Marco.

"Good. Pick you up in five at the southeast corner of Washington and Clark," he barked, ringing off before I could say another word.

"I've got to go," I said to Di Marco. "But one last question. Was your friend Jimmy's body autopsied?"

"Of course. That's how they knew he'd stopped taking his heart pills. ME could tell from the relative absence of the stuff in his bloodstream. And the standard tox screen didn't turn up anything else."

That didn't rule out all poisonous substances. A "standard" tox screen mainly looks for evidence of opiates. But given the findings, the ME's conclusion seemed solid enough. I thanked Di Marco and told him I owed him one.

"Damn straight you do. And don't forget—*stai zitto*."

We said our *ciaos*, and a few minutes later I was standing on the street downstairs, guarding my perimeter and daring anyone to lay a hand on me with a stony glare. Bjorn pulled up and tooted the horn—shave and a haircut, two bits (or maybe I should say, two bob)—and pushed open the passenger door, sending out a whiff of his exuberant aftershave. I climbed what seemed like a small cliff into the Land Rover, which idled like a restlessly slumbering elephant. Waylon Jennings pumped from the speaker system.

We swung south and then west in the direction of the Kennedy Expressway.

"Is now an opportune time to tell me where we're going?" I asked.

"I thought we might do a little electronics shopping," Bjorn said.

He turned down the music and proceeded to tell me what he had found out in the last twenty-four hours. The miles sped by quickly as he filled me in.

"You wanted to find out who was behind that motion for exhumation of the body. I was thinking about where to start when I remembered that big dispute at O'Hare last year. You hear tell of it?"

I shook my head no.

"Well, the city's been trying to expand the airport for some time and figured they had a way to do it. Only problem was the plans for a new runway ran right through a hundred-year-old cemetery, which didn't go over well with the families of the folks buried there. They said no to disinterring their loved ones, so the city politely condemned the land. The families fought back with a lawsuit that went all the way to the Illinois Supreme Court."

I was glad I'd missed that cheery item. "Who won?"

"I'm surprised you have to ask. They just finished shipping off the last of the remains last week. Anyway, it got me thinking about Gallagher—wouldn't they have had to notify his next of kin or something before digging him up? So I went back to the probate-court records and looked up the name of Gallagher's executor, an attorney named Gene Polanski. The name rang a bell, so I did some further checking and guess what? Polanski is the same guy Gallagher's nephew used when he was trying to shut down that Best Buy."

"Go on," I said impatiently.

"I figured it couldn't hurt to have a chat with him, so I popped by his office on Wells—seedy little space right by the 'L' tracks—and tried to get an audience. He was there—I could hear him yammering on the phone inside—but his secretary pretended he'd just left for lunch. I thought that was odd, and she was a nice-looking bird, so I invited her out to drinks after work. I give her points for not spilling the beans until we got back to my place that night."

"You can spare me the details of the conquest," I said, not wanting to imagine similar romantic adventures with Hallie. "What'd she have to say?"

"Polanski engineered the whole thing. He called on an old pal of his, a guy in the State's Attorney's office, and got him to initiate the exhumation request just so Polanski could show up and acquiesce in it."

"That seems like a rather roundabout way of going at it."

"Exactly. You see what it means?"

I admit that at this point I was utterly baffled. "No, but I'm looking forward to your penetrating analysis."

"Let's say Urquhart wants to knock off his uncle for the insurance money. Being Gallagher's only heir, he'd have to know how quickly suspicion would fall on him. So he decides to make it look like a heart attack. But it can't stay a heart attack forever if Urquhart is to collect under the double-indemnity clause. Eventually it has to be discovered to be a homicide."

"OK," I said, still at sea.

"He doesn't demand an autopsy right away because that would look too obvious. Instead, he waits until after the funeral, and then engineers it so that the exhumation request looks like it's coming from a state official. The beauty of it is that by the time the ME gets around to autopsying the corpse, the stomach contents have decomposed enough that no one can say exactly when Gallagher was poisoned. And, to be sure no one pins the murder on him, Urquhart uses a substance that will quickly lead the police to his uncle's lover."

I thought it sounded too convoluted but went along with his reasoning. "So you're saying Urquhart framed Jane for the murder?"

"Bingo!" Bjorn said in triumph.

"I don't know," I said. "Wouldn't the plan depend on his knowing about Lucitrol and its health hazards for someone like his uncle?"

"That's easy. Jane's victory in the Atria lawsuit was all over the news, and anyone who watches ten minutes of television would have seen the drug advertised multiple times with all of its warnings. They're very direct about saying someone with heart disease—not to mention a dozen or so other conditions—should not take Lucitrol."

He had a point. In fact, I thought wryly, given the amount of dire information about designer drugs circulating on the airwaves, it was surprising more people didn't think of bumping off their loved ones in a like fashion. "All right, but if it was a frame job, how did Urquhart know that Jane and Gallagher would be together that night?"

"That's easy," Bjorn said. "I saved the best bit of information for last."

I gave him an inquisitive look.

"You can't just show up and ask the Circuit Court to exhume a body—there has to be a reason. In this case, the ASA had an affidavit, conveniently signed by a close associate of Gallagher's."

"OK, you're killing me," I said.

"It was Sparks—Lucy Sparks—Gallagher's fiancée."

We passed the rest of the forty-five-minute drive in near silence, while Bjorn zipped in and out of truck traffic to the beat of Rockin' Country Rebels and I fidgeted in my seat. What he'd told me made sense in an Occam's Razor sort of way—wasn't the simplest answer usually the right one?—but Urquhart as his uncle's killer didn't begin to explain all the other strange doings in the case, beginning with Jane and Gallagher's quarrel on the night he died. I was sure their argument had something to do with his death, along with whatever information Jane had wiped from Gallagher's computer. And then, of course, there was the attack on Hallie and me and the anonymous note. If Bjorn's theory was correct, Urquhart would have had to be behind both, but to what end? Once the police had fingered Jane for the poisoning, his best course was to lie low and wait, not attract possible attention to himself by stalking and then setting upon two strangers. Even if Urquhart and the Luvabull were somehow in cahoots, there were too many loose ends involved in Bjorn's theory.

Urquhart's main store was situated in Orland Park, a community emblematic of the haphazard planning of many Chicago suburbs. Once covered with working farmland, it now consisted of miles of strip malls and housing developments, with nothing so petroleum-unfriendly as a sidewalk connecting them. According to Bjorn, the current cash crop was foreclosures; nearly every gated community we passed had a sign up. E-Z Electronics stood a mile from what passed as the town center at the back of an empty parking lot. Bjorn told me that Urquhart spent most of his days there, hunched over his sales reports and brooding over the Mom and Pop store Armageddon that was online retailing.

We stepped out of the Land Rover into a strong southwest wind that coughed up dust in our faces and traversed a pitted asphalt surface to the storefront, which Bjorn told me was dominated by offers of heavy discounts on everything from laptops to toasters. A bell jingled over our heads as we crossed the threshold.

I took Bjorn's elbow and followed him over to the sales counter.

"What can I do for you fellows?" came the thin, sour voice I recognized from the hearing as Urquhart's. Otherwise the store sounded empty.

"My cousin here is interested in buying a camera," Bjorn said, indicating me by his side.

Urquhart paused as though not sure whether he was being made fun of. "Is that some kind of joke?" he demanded of Bjorn.

"Which part—the camera or the fact we're cousins?"

"Both is what I meant," Urquhart said. "What business would he have with a camera?"

I always loved it when people referred to me in the third person. "Are you sure this is a good idea?" I said, turning toward Bjorn. "I mean, I can probably get a better deal on Amazon and I won't have to put up with any insults."

"Very funny," Urquhart said. "And I don't believe for a minute you two are cousins."

"I suppose he's never heard of albinism," Bjorn said to me.

"Sure I have," Urquhart said. "My mother's father was Albanian. Hey, wait a minute. I know who you are. You're the blind sonofabitch who testified at the hearing."

I was amazed at how long it took him to catch on.

"I don't have anything to say to you. Or to him," Urquhart said, obviously meaning Bjorn. "My lawyer told me not to."

"Your lawyer is why we're here," Bjorn said coolly. "We know he engineered the order seeking exhumation of your uncle's body."

"So?" Urquhart said.

"So how did he know that the autopsy would turn up evidence of poisoning? Unless someone told him."

"Like I said," Urquhart replied. "I'm not talking to you."

Bjorn pressed on while I stood by, eager to learn how a pro would handle the situation.

"Come now, Mr. Urquhart. Let's not play around. I'll tell you what I think. I think you knew ahead of time exactly what the autopsy would show."

Urquhart didn't flinch a bit. "That's crazy. And I've got work to do."

"That's funny," Bjorn replied. "I don't see any customers in here." He nudged my arm. "You, Mark?"

"Not a one," I deadpanned.

"Yeah, well," Urquhart said. "Business has been a little down lately."

"So I gathered from your credit reports. You're behind on your bank payments. And this store and everything in it are mortgaged to the rooftop."

"Again, so what?" Urquhart said, seeming not in the least perturbed. "I've got more bills than I've got money to pay them, like everyone else in this stinking economy."

"Bills that you'll be able to pay off quite easily with your uncle's insurance money," Bjorn said. "You don't really expect us to believe you were torn up over his death."

"Believe what you like," Urquhart said in the same flippant manner. "And now, unless you're planning on shopping for a camera for your pale-faced cousin, you can just take yourself off the premises. Or do I have to call the cops?"

I figured it was time for the amateur to get involved. "Good idea. Bjorn, why don't you go back out to the car and get the video. I'm sure the police will find it fascinating, along with all the other evidence you've collected."

"Wha—" Bjorn began. I stepped on his shoe as a signal. "Of course," he recovered quickly. "The video. Right, it's in the boot."

"What video?" Urquhart snarled. "What other evidence?"

"The evidence that you and your uncle's so-called fiancée were involved. You didn't think anyone would find out? Bjorn here snapped some very interesting footage of the two of you. That plus the insurance money and the two of you conspiring to have his body dug up should make for a very interesting tale."

"I didn't have anything to do with him getting killed. It was that bitch of a lawyer," Urquhart protested, finally starting to sound worried.

"Sure it was. Except that the bitch, as you call her, didn't go asking anyone to have your uncle's body exhumed. You did. How else would you know what the ME would find unless you put it there yourself? Though I'll allow it could have been Ms. Sparks who slipped him the pill."

"I . . . I can produce an alibi," Urquhart bleated.

I shook my head. "That's not going to help you get around a charge of accessory to murder. See, the way I figure it is this: you and Ms. Sparks have been an item for some time. Maybe your uncle introduced you, or maybe Lucy cozied up to him after the two of you hatched your little plan. There was never any engagement to Gallagher, and I'll bet when the police go looking for the receipt for that engagement ring, they'll find your name on it. Which means Ms. Sparks was lying when the prosecution put her on the stand, and not just about the wedding bells. She testified that she made Gallagher breakfast that morning and didn't eat any of it herself. It's as good an inference as any that she poisoned him, and no one is going to believe she acted alone—especially with a million and a half in insurance money going to you when he died. You see how it all looks, don't you? Once the police find out about you two, they'll draw the only sensible conclusion. What do you say we go over and tell them right now, Bjorn?"

"I'm for it," Bjorn said, pulling his car keys from his pocket and giving them a shake. We turned in unison as if to go.

"Wait, wait—you've got it all wrong!" Urquhart nearly shouted.

"Which part in particular?" I said over my shoulder. "That you murdered your uncle or that you were having it on with his girl behind his back?"

"She wasn't his girl," Urquhart said shakily. "Oh, all right, she slept with him from time to time after we got together, but it was just an act. We didn't want him to find out about us. I was afraid he'd get pissed off and write me out of his will. We met at a barbecue at his place last fall. And yeah, it was me she was going to marry. But we never tried to kill my uncle, I swear."

I turned to face him again: "I'm having a hard time believing that after Sparks perjured herself."

"That was just to shore up the homicide claim. Gene Polanski explained it to me. I'd get double if my uncle was murdered, and it was in our interest to point the finger at another suspect. I always hated Barrett, so it was an easy decision to try to pin the blame on her. Stuck-up piece of pussy. I never understood what Rory wanted with her, but she had him twirled around her little finger. I thought it would kill two birds with one stone to get her in trouble, so we had Lucy go to the police with that made-up story. Lucy wasn't even with Rory that morning. She was with me. We didn't know for sure he'd been poisoned until after the body was exhumed."

"Uh-huh," I said skeptically. "But then what made you think about digging it up in the first place? Or did a little bird just happen to come along and whisper in your ear?"

"In a manner of speaking," Urquhart said. He opened a drawer behind the counter. "I got this."

# EIGHTEEN

"Two anonymous notes in one case," Bjorn was saying on the ride back. "It's like a Halloween prank."

"Or an Edgar Allan Poe story," I said.

What Urquhart had pulled from the drawer had knocked the wind out of both our sails: another note, identical in appearance to the one left for me:

> TSK, TSK YOU'VE BEEN A BAD BOY.
> AREN'T YOU CURIOUS ABOUT
> WHAT REALLY KILLED YOUR UNCLE?
> DO A LITTLE SPADE WORK AND FIND OUT.
> BUT DON'T TELL THE POLICE OR
> THERE COULD BE GRAVE CONSEQUENCES.

According to Urquhart the note had arrived in his mailbox the day of Gallagher's funeral, sealed but without a stamp or a postmark. After contacting his lawyer, he and Polanski had determined not to show it to the police, since the opening line "You've been a bad boy" could easily be misinterpreted to suggest Urquhart had a hand in his uncle's death. Polanski had put on his thinking cap and come up with the way to keep Urquhart's name out of it by having Sparks sign an affidavit "on information and belief" that Gallagher was the victim of foul play, which Polanski then passed on to his ASA friend. In their haste to pin the murder on Jane, the police didn't look past Sparks's explanation that she "just had a feeling about Gallagher's death," and Urquhart begged us not to tell them the true story now. "It will just look like we did it," he moaned abjectly. I almost felt sorry for him.

"By the way, that was nice work you did back there," Bjorn remarked from the driver's seat. "How did you know Urquhart and the Luvabull were hot and heavy?"

"I didn't. But I thought her outpouring of grief at the hearing was bogus, and I figured if she was going out of her way to help Urquhart with an affidavit, they had to be more than just casual acquaintances."

"Do you think Urquhart was telling us the truth about Sparks being with him the morning Gallagher died?"

"No. I think he was scrambling to construct an alibi for both of them. I'd bet my last dollar she and Gallagher were together, just the way she testified. And I think Gallagher knew about her affair with his nephew."

"What makes you say that?"

"Go back to her testimony at the hearing. His remark to her— 'Lucy, I think it's time you got everything you deserve'—sounds like he knew something was off. If so, I wonder what he was planning for her?"

"The trouble with this latest development is that it puts a major dent in my theory," Bjorn said morosely. "I mean, if Urquhart didn't know about the poisoning ahead of time, he's probably innocent."

It also punched a gaping hole in my surmise that Jane was the author of the note left for me. Both the tone—and, according to Bjorn, the appearance—of the two missives were identical, implying common authorship. But I couldn't fathom why Jane would have pushed to get Gallagher's body exhumed, especially if—as was looking increasingly likely—she had something to hide.

"Do you think we should go to the police with what we have?" Bjorn asked.

"Not yet. As you say, it's sounding less and less like Urquhart was the killer, and if we go to them now it will just look like we're spinning our wheels. It won't help us later if we ever do find out who murdered Gallagher. I'd rather stay mum until we have proof of something concrete to show them."

Bjorn dropped me off at my home at 6:00 p.m. with promises to attack with renewed vigor the subject of Gallagher's whereabouts after

leaving Gene & Georgetti's that night, and to see what further information he could coax out of Gallagher's cardiologist—or her staff—
concerning who else may have known of the journalist's heart condition.
I could have taken that job myself but figured Bjorn's methods were
better suited to the task.

I arrived upstairs at my apartment feeling antsy and without any
plans for the night except fretting over Hallie and Mike. Marta, my
housekeeper, had been in that day and left a place setting out on the
table as a signal that she'd cooked a meal, though I could have guessed it
from the garlicky bouquet emanating from the oven. At least it meant
I wouldn't go hungry. I kicked off my shoes and trotted over to the
kitchen, stuck on a pair of cooking mitts—oversized ones that went up
over my elbows—and was gingerly maneuvering the casserole out and
onto the stovetop when my landline began ringing. It was my building
superintendent, telling me he had accepted delivery of an envelope for
me that afternoon and asking when I'd like to come down to get it. *Not
another one*, I thought pessimistically.

It turned out to be from Klutsky, as I found out when I got back
upstairs and put the first of five sheets on the scanner in the spare
bedroom I used as an office. "Nothing on the server front yet," he
informed me in a thoughtfully typed note. "But I thought you might
find these of interest." I fed the rest of the sheets into the machine and
went back to the kitchen to suss out what Marta had left for me, lifting a
corner of aluminum foil from the casserole dish and sniffing. It was one
of her specialties, a Venezuelan *pasticho* bubbling with tomatoes and
cheese. I cracked open a bottle of beer and wolfed down half the pasta
straight from the pan while the scanner did its *wheeze-click, wheeze-
click* in the next room. When I was done with the meal, I decided it
was high time I gave Marta another raise. I downed another of my pills,
scraped the leftover food into a refrigerator dish, and put the pan in
the sink to soak. Then I went to listen to the scanned report of what
Klutsky had sent me.

It wasn't much, but it was something: Gallagher's cell-phone
records for the last month of his life. I guessed that Gallagher's phone

had been paid for by the *Sun-Times* and congratulated Klutsky on having thought of that angle while I considered what to do with the information. Bjorn could probably engineer a reverse lookup of the numbers, but that would have to wait until morning and would in all likelihood yield nothing but a list of names. In the meantime, I could get a head start on things. The list of outgoing calls was as long as my arm, but it was better than moping or trying to find something to distract me on TV. I took a swipe at my watch face. It was a little after 7:00 p.m. With most Midwesterners turning off their lights around eleven, I had a window of about four hours.

The first thing I needed was an accessible list. I sent the scanned records to my Braille printer while I changed into a sweatshirt and jeans. I returned to the kitchen for another beer (for courage) and checked my phone to make sure its caller-ID function was disabled. When I returned to my printer it had obligingly produced a half-inch stack of pages with Gallagher's outgoing calls arranged in a single column from top to bottom in order of recency. I cleared the surface of my desk of clutter and got out a Braille eraser—a wooden device shaped like a golf tee but slightly larger and sturdier—and a 3-D marker, another handy tool with ink that dried to leave tactile markings on paper.

If you've ever wondered how it works, the Braille alphabet is based upon a "cell" consisting of six dots arranged in two side-by-side columns. The uppermost dot in the left column is numbered 1, the next one down 2, and the one farthest down, 3. The same pattern is repeated in descending order—4, 5, and 6—in the column on the right:

1 4

2 5

3 6

Not all the dots within a cell are raised. The ones that are identify a letter. For example, a raised dot at 1 is an *a*, raised dots at 1 and 2 are a *b*, and at 1 and 4 a *c*. And so on. The first ten letters of the Latin alphabet, *a* to *j*, use only the top four positions. The next ten are identical except for the addition of a raised dot at 3, and the letters after that pick up another raised dot at 6. The numerals one through ten are also identical to *a* through *j* except that they are preceded by a symbol shaped like a left-facing capital L, indicated by raised dots at 3, 4, 5, and 6.

As you might imagine, the dots have to be very small to allow as many words as possible to fit on a page. Space considerations also dictate that the area between lines be kept to a minimum, making one of the principal challenges not getting lost in a field of text. I usually solved this problem by reading two-handed, deciphering letters with my right hand while using my left as a guide to the next line. But with such a long list of numbers, I couldn't count on keeping track of my place. Hence, the eraser and marker.

I started on the most recent calls first. I got no answer to the first two numbers I called, so I erased the backward L in front of them by flattening the dots as a signal to return to them later. The third number put me through to the answering machine of Gallagher's dentist, so I drew a line through it using the marker. My fourth and fifth calls likewise produced no answers, so I checked them off with the eraser, too. On the sixth call, I got a human being.

"Yeah?" said a curt male voice coming on the line.

I launched into the speech I'd prepared.

"Hi, my name is Mark Halliday. I'm a paid canvasser for the Industrial Wellness Association. We're doing a survey of workplace satisfaction, and I was wondering if I could take a few short minutes of your time . . ."

Click.

A few more clicks made me think I ought to sweeten the pot, so the next time someone answered—a tired-sounding woman with a child screaming in the background—I modified my approach.

"Hi, my name is Mark Halliday. I'm a paid canvasser for the Industrial Wellness Association, and we're offering a chance to win an all-expenses-paid cruise to the Bahamas to anyone willing to answer a few brief questions. The entire survey will only take five minutes of your time—"

"What line?" the woman asked.

"Excuse me?" I said in confusion.

"I'm asking what cruise line. If this isn't some kind of scam, you oughta be able to tell me."

I improvised. "Royal Starfish."

"Never heard of them," she said, hanging up.

Before the next call, I went on the Internet and selected the name of a popular cruise-ship company to use in my spiel if questioned. This time it worked, and I got to ask my questions:

"On a scale from one to ten, with one being completely unsatisfied and ten being extremely satisfied, how would you rate your experience with your current employer?"

"I dunno," said the male voice on the other end of the line. His speech was slurred like he'd knocked back a few. "A four, maybe?"

I continued in this way, asking after his satisfaction level with his workplace conditions, supervisor, employee benefits, and salary, before getting to the information I was really after.

"And just to complete the survey, would you mind telling me your name and the name of your employer? I'll need that information to enroll you in the cruise ship drawing. You can be sure that the answers you gave me earlier will be held in the strictest confidence."

I held my breath while I waited to see if it would work.

"Sure," the man answered after a short pause. He gave me his first and last names. "I'm a baggage handler at O'Hare. When will I find out about the cruise?"

Thirty or so phone numbers later I was thoroughly impressed by the behavioral effect of free offers.

And getting nowhere.

I could well understand why Gallagher's reporting had fallen off. The majority of his calls were to businesses that served his personal needs—Sam's Liquors, a dry cleaner, the Men's Shop at Mark Shale, a barbershop, his local Jewel/Osco—and none of the others sounded like a serious lead. I got through to two city employees, a marine biologist at the Shedd Aquarium, a building supplier, an IDOT worker, a teaching assistant at Loyola, an insurance adjuster, and half a dozen personal assistants (all apparently as unhappy with their jobs as Yelena) before concluding I was wasting my time. If there was a connection to be found among these contacts, I couldn't see it. Trading places with Sisyphus would be as least as productive.

I got up and paced around my apartment, thought about having another beer and decided against it, paced some more until I had covered the same ground a dozen or so times, and finally tossed myself in frustration on my living-room couch. A Scrabble game I'd been playing against myself sat unused on the coffee table next to it. I picked up the tiles I'd last been working with—which were oversized and (obviously) embossed with Braille—and began idly moving them around, searching for a word with the highest numerical value and playing with various patterns.

And that's when it hit me. A pattern.

I'd been looking in the wrong place for one.

At one time, my photographic memory would have easily alerted me to what I now wanted to know, but except for things I'd seen before I lost my sight, it had regrettably been deactivated. Fortunately, there were ways to get around that. I went back to my office and dumped the scanned contents of Gallagher's phone records into a spreadsheet program on my computer. I then sorted the numbers in four ways: date, time, area code, and number. Once again, I turned to my Braille printer to create tactile lists with the results. I was most interested in the numbers, so I turned to those first.

I moved slowly down the list with my fingers, taking my time and looking for groupings with the same prefix. I found several of them: three numbers with a 744 prefix, six with a 507 prefix, and five with an 832 prefix. I selected one at random from the last grouping and called. It was now nearing midnight, so I was surprised when a live voice answered.

"Murphy here."

This time, I decided not to beat about the bush.

"Hello, Mr. Murphy? My name is Mark Halliday. I'm an associate of Rory Gallagher at the *Sun-Times*. You may have heard that Mr. Gallagher passed away recently. We've been trying to get a lead on the story he was working on when he died, and his phone records indicate that he spoke to you on . . ." I checked the date. "On August 22."

I heard a quick intake of breath followed by an epithet. "What the fuck?" He hurriedly lowered his voice and said, "I told him never to call me here."

"Right. Sorry about that. But you see, we've lost Mr. Gallagher's notes. If there's another number where I could reach you—"

"*Please*," he said, sounding genuinely frightened. "Please don't call me anymore. There's nothing I can do to help you. My wife just had a baby and the heat's turned way up on the investigation. I can't risk losing my job!"

"What investigation?" I asked sharply.

"Go to hell," he said and hung up.

I sat back and thought for a bit. Then I dialed the same area code and prefix—832—followed by the number 1000. A dulcet-toned recording came over the line: "Hello. You have reached the offices of Atria Laboratories. Our normal business hours are eight to five, Monday through Friday . . ."

# NINETEEN

"So this is what a shrink's office looks like," Bjorn said the following morning after Yelena had shown him in.

He stood just inside the doorway, presumably surveying the modest furniture, the shelves crammed every which way with books and papers, the collection of sixties memorabilia on the credenza behind my desk—including my prized King Zor and my *Man from U.N.C.L.E.* THRUSH gun—and the Grateful Dead dancing bears poster hanging above them. The office standards committee—headed by Jonathan, of course—was always on my case about adopting a more polished appearance, but so far I had managed to fend them off with the claim that the blind were in special need of familiar surroundings.

"Who's this?" Bjorn asked, walking over and picking up the framed photograph of Louis I kept on my desk.

"A nephew," I lied.

"I should have guessed. He resembles you."

Another thing Louis wouldn't have to thank me for. "What do you make of the stuff I e-mailed you?" I asked, anxious to get to the topic at hand.

Bjorn replaced the photo and settled himself into one of the chairs opposite my desk, putting a foot up against the top. "To tell the truth, I feel like a right idiot."

He and I both.

The night before, I'd lain awake again for hours excoriating myself for not making the Atria connection sooner. As soon as I'd hung up the phone, it had hit me like a lightning bolt what the Dwyers—the couple who had witnessed Jane and Gallagher's argument at Gene & Georgetti's that night—had overheard Jane repeating several times. It wasn't the name Lucy. It was Lucitrol. I remembered what Rusty had speculated, that instead of a lover's quarrel, Jane and Gallagher had been arguing over confidential information that Gallagher had somehow latched onto. The new information I'd wrested from Mr. Murphy confirmed that Gallagher had been talking to someone at Atria, and that Atria was under some kind of investigation, probably involving the same drug. But what kind of investigation? And what had Gallagher found that was enough of a threat to a person or persons to get him killed?

"In our mutual defense, we were led astray by the girl's name," I pointed out, feeling no less stupid.

"True," Bjorn conceded. "But that doesn't excuse us being such dunderheads. Not when Hallie's still lying in hospital. I went to see her last night, you know."

"How was she?" I asked, reminded once again how I'd abandoned her.

"Pale as a sheet, but breathing steadily. I met some of the members of the clan. Nice folks. Why haven't you gone, too? It might do you some good to see her."

"Well, that *is* part of the problem," I said, wishing it didn't sound so puerile.

"You know," Bjorn said, "If I didn't think . . ." He stopped himself. "Oh, never mind. It's none of my business."

I hastened to change the subject. "So can you get the names of the other people at Atria Gallagher was in contact with?"

"Already on it. And I'll be chatting with each personally as soon as I can track them down. The problem will be getting them to talk. If that fellow Murphy was as worried as you say he was, chances are the others will be as well. I'm not the coppers. I can't force anyone to tell me what they don't want to. By the way, we did get a lead on Gallagher's other whereabouts that night."

"And?" I asked hopefully, thinking this might be another break.

"Seems he spent an hour or so in a booth with another gentleman at a tavern on Rush. But it was dark and nobody could give us much of a description. Big guy, Caucasian with dark hair. A drink apiece and Gallagher paid the bill in cash."

"Time?"

"Just before Gallagher toddled off to the Billy Goat. I gave the bartender an incentive to call me if the fellow showed up again, but if it's our murderer he'll be smart enough to steer well clear of the place."

So Gallagher *had* met with someone else that night. But who? The only way to find out, it seemed, was to chase down whatever was going on at Atria.

After Bjorn had taken himself off, I ambled over to the office coffee room, taking the back way so that I wouldn't risk being seen by Sep, whose office was located just across the hall. Since I was supposed to be home resting, I didn't want to run into him by accident. I almost never used a cane in our suite, whose warren of corridors and felt-covered cubicles was as familiar to me as a rat's maze, and I was going at my usual fast clip, grazing the wall with my knuckles to stay on course, when I collided with a stack of boxes that someone had thoughtlessly left standing outside the file room. The stack went over and I went with it, ending up sprawled on the floor and swearing, with the change from my pockets rolling in several different directions. Fortunately, no one was around to witness the high comedy. I hurriedly gathered up what I could find of the money, shoved the boxes to one side, and continued on, making a mental note to ask Yelena to be sure everything was put back in order later.

When I arrived at the coffee room, the 10:30 a.m. klatch was in full swing, with a dozen or so colleagues companionably chitchatting around a table. Predictably, Graham Young was entrenched in the group's center, identifiable by his loud guffawing. I went over to the single-brew machine and pretended to be occupied with selecting a tea brand while I eavesdropped on the conversation. Alison was passing around photos of her partner's baby bump to collective expressions of admiration while Graham was giving Josh advice on his daughter's college applications. That was another thing that bugged me about Graham: he appeared to have a dossier on every doctor in our group, with information about spouses, children, recreational preferences— the names of pets, even—that he used to engage his sales marks while he was making his daily rounds.

I filled my cup and went over to join them. Josh spotted me coming and gave a swat to the empty chair seat next to him so I would know it was free.

"Dr. Angelotti," Graham sang out as I was getting seated. "How nice of you to join us. Here, have a sweet roll." He pushed a box of them across the table toward me. "I picked them up on Lincoln on my way down here this morning."

Normally, I would have declined on principle, free food being another arrow in the big drug companies' quiver of bribes. Today, however, I thanked him and stuck my hand in the box, locating a sugary *drozdzowki* and pulling it out.

"How 'bout a napkin to go with?" Graham asked, sliding one of those over, too.

"Better give him more than one," Jonathan said from his position at the head of the table. "He'll need it."

"Yes," I agreed. "Jonathan will have to have his SSRI refilled if there's so much as a crumb left on the table." I gave the pastry a vigorous shake before biting into it.

"I wish you two would try to get along," said Emily Weintraub, the office peacemaker, who was seated across from me.

"That would be like asking the British to embrace their similarities to the French," Alison remarked to my left. She turned to me. "By the way, how are you feeling? I heard what happened, but none of the details."

Everyone stopped talking then and plied me with questions about the attack. Between bites, I explained what happened.

"That's a shame," Jonathan said when I was through. "To think we came this close to losing you."

"I know," I said. "Imagine all those insanely funny jokes going to waste."

Jonathan said, "Speaking of which, did I tell you the one about Helen Keller and the Rorschach test?"

"Let me guess," I said, rubbing my chin thoughtfully. "She tried to drink the inkwell?"

Everyone laughed except Emily, who pushed back her chair in disgust. "That's it. I'm out of here."

"I am, too," Jonathan huffed, rising after her. "Someone around here needs to be attending to their patients."

"He's just pissed that you beat him to his punch line," Josh said after Jonathan had sulked off.

"I'm so sorry," Alison said, putting her hand on my arm in sympathy. "That must have been a horrible experience—for you and your friend. I'll send flowers."

"Better yet," Graham piped in, "we'll all send them. I'll get a collection going this afternoon."

The idle chatter resumed, turning eventually—as I'd hoped—to the subject of the Atria conference Graham had mentioned to me some time back, which was scheduled to begin the next day. Graham was enthusiastically describing the resort where it was to take place, which occupied twenty-one acres amid the rolling hills northwest of the city. In addition to jogging paths along the Fox River, it sported an Olympic-size indoor pool, a fully equipped gym, tennis courts, a discotheque, and, naturally, a championship golf course. "You're gonna just love the food," he was telling his eager audience. "The head chef trained at the Culinary Institute. And don't forget to stop by the hospitality desk when you arrive to pick up your complimentary spa pass, good for at least one massage after you've wrapped up your eighteen holes." There were general murmurs of satisfaction.

"Can you believe how they're lapping this up?" Alison whispered conspiratorially to me. "Whoever said loyalty can't be bought?" Like me, Alison was a critic of drug-company events such as Atria's, which allowed doctors to meet their annual certification requirements at a significantly reduced cost. Under a new industry-ethics code, the companies couldn't pay for the doctors' attendance directly, but that didn't stop them from underwriting the expenses of the supposedly independent programs. And it was more than just coincidence that the speakers at these events tended to be those who'd accepted fees—sometimes upward of six figures annually—for touting the sponsoring company's products.

"I have a few spots still open for anyone who hasn't rsvp'd yet," Graham was now saying. "How about it, Alison? I'm sure you and your partner could use a weekend away before the new arrival."

"Thanks, but no," Alison said tartly. "We'll be painting the nursery."

"Anyone else?" Graham persisted. "I know better than to ask Dr. Angelotti. Not if I want to walk out of here with my head still attached to my shoulders. Ha, ha, ha."

I raised my hand. "Actually, Graham, I was thinking I might take you up on the offer. If it wouldn't be too much trouble to get me in at this late date."

"Really?" Graham exclaimed, like he wasn't sure I was pulling his leg.

"Really?" Alison and Josh said in unison along with him.

"Why not?" I continued, trying to sound genuine. "I could use the relaxation, and it sounds like it will be highly ... informative." I could feel Alison and Josh staring at me in shock. "Also, to tell the truth, I'm behind on my CME hours," I finished with a flourish.

"Why, that's—" Graham began, still flabbergasted. "Why, that's absolutely wonderful! I'll get on your reservation right away. Will you be staying the whole weekend or just Saturday night? Do you want to be signed up for a foursome? Or tennis? I'm sure I can get you a special room if you need one. And you'll need to tell me whether you want the filet or the chicken at the opening banquet ..."

After he'd left to sign me up and the place had cleared out except for Josh and me—Alison's parting comment being *Et tu, Brute?*—Josh demanded to know what in the hell was going on. "I'm beginning to think that blow to the head really did knock the senses out of you."

"Why? You think I'm faking wanting to go?"

"Maybe it has something to do with the fact that the smirk on your face is as wide as my waistband."

"Do you think Graham noticed anything," I asked, worried.

"Relax. He looked like you'd just offered him an all-expenses-paid cruise to the Bahamas. Now tell me, what gives?"

I filled him in on the events of the last two days, including my conversation with Rusty about Jane's possible motive for secrecy, the visit to Gallagher's nephew, my feigned telephone survey, and the Atria employee who'd hung up on me.

When I was done, Josh said, "Well, I'll give you the Energizer Bunny award for staying busy. And I'm glad you've finally bowed to the advisability of getting a real investigator to help you. But what is this crap about attending the Atria event?"

"I thought it was something I could do that wouldn't attract attention."

"Oh, sure. I bet there'll be dozens of attendees sporting white canes at the conference. You'll blend in with no trouble. Besides, what do you think you're going to accomplish up there?"

"I know inconspicuousness isn't exactly my forte these days. But no one there except Graham will know who I am, and most strangers treat me like I don't exist. I figured I'd just hang out and listen—something I still happen to be competent at. You know how these events are— the hotel will be swarming with drug reps and they'll all be drinking like there's no tomorrow. Maybe I can pick up some hints about what's going on at Atria. If not, it'll just be a wasted forty-eight hours, but at least I won't be treading a hole in the carpet doing nothing but flagellating myself over Hallie."

"OK, but how're you going to find your way around? The place sounds huge and you've never been there before."

"If I let that deter me, I might as well sign up for Social Security right now. There are ways. I'll manage."

"I could come with," Josh offered helpfully.

"After that show of distaste you and Alison just put on for Graham? Forget it. He'd catch on right away that there was something going on. Even he isn't that dense."

"OK, but what can I do to help?"

"Stay in touch with Hallie's doctor. I'll feel a lot better knowing you're standing by while I'm miles away feasting on pretzels and cheese cubes."

I arrived back at my office close to noon, with plans on spending the rest of the day engaged in advance planning. With any luck, the resort would have an accessible website with plenty of maps. First, though, I needed lunch. I collected my cane from the hook on the door for a trip down to the cafeteria, absentmindedly patting my pants pocket to be sure I had my pills with me. I stopped and frowned. Other than the change I'd scooped up after my hallway spill, the pocket was empty. I checked the one on the other side. Also empty except for my handkerchief. No problem there. I'd probably left the pills in my jacket, which was hanging on the back of the door.

I took the jacket off the hook by its collar and shook it one-handed without hearing the familiar rattle of the pills in their bottle. I leaned my cane against the wall to free up the other hand and rifled through the pockets. Nothing. I went back to my desk and patted all over its surface, over and under papers and around empty cups and napkins, pens, pencils, and various Braille devices. The bottle wasn't there or in any of the desk drawers in or around my computer. With mounting concern I turned to my credenza, hurriedly groping through my toys and knocking my Magic Brain Calculator to the floor in the process. Maybe Jonathan had a point: my office was two steps away from being condemned. I was sure Melissa would be able to supply me with a refill, but it was embarrassing to have misplaced the pills, and I might not be able to get a substitute supply before the conference. I didn't want to think about what else I could lose if there was a several-day gap in my treatment. What in Christ's name had I done with them?

I stopped then and thought back over the morning. I had a firm memory of retrieving the bottle from its place next to the kitchen sink just after breakfast that morning. I'd tilted the plastic cylinder back and shook out one of the pills before washing it down with a glass of water and setting the bottle down on the counter—right next to my phone, Mets cap, and sunglasses so I wouldn't forget it. Then what? I mentally retraced my steps back to my bedroom area where I'd gone to the bathroom to brush my teeth before putting on a tie. Then it was back to the kitchen to collect my gear before heading out the door. The cap went on my head, the phone went into the holder attached to my belt, and the pills went into my trouser pocket. I was sure of it.

Then where had they gone to?

It was moments like this that made me reconsider my commitment to clean living.

I went back over all the places I'd searched before, this time adding a hands and knees sweep of the carpet around my desk and the area near the door. Since going blind I'd been known to drop things and not realize it unless there was a corresponding clatter. No dice. I went over all my shelves, collecting enough dust along the way to earn the admiration of Pig Pen and there was still no sign of them. I looted my desk drawers once more and succeeded only in stabbing my thumb with a loose pushpin. I had just wrapped the finger in my handkerchief and was considering what nearby object I could pick up and hurl against the wall when a knock came at the door.

"Dr. Angelotti?"

"Oh, hey, Graham," I said, trying to appear perfectly composed.

"Sorry to interrupt you, but I was coming by to give you some materials for the conference and I saw this in the hall."

"This?" I queried without a clue as to what he was talking about.

"Oh, sorry. I should have been more specific. It's a medication bottle with your name on it. I found it lying on the floor near the file room."

Relief flooded over me as he put the bottle in my hand.

"I hope it doesn't mean you're ill," Graham said, sounding genuinely concerned. "I've never heard of this drug before."

"You wouldn't have. It's uh ... experimental. Something for my sciatica."

"Sciatica? Well, now, if I'd known you had that problem, I could have helped you out long ago. We have a terrific new pain product. It's only been on the market two months, and the orders are literally pouring in. I can get you a few samples. People are saying they feel relief only minutes after taking it and . . ."

For once, I let him rattle on for as long as he wanted to.

# TWENTY

The string of fine fall days was still in place the following morning when Boris pulled up in front of my building shortly before 9:00 a.m. He got out of the driver's seat and took my overnight bag, giving me his usual terse greeting. As always, the town car was piled high with beverages, snacks, and magazines, along with a television set blaring the *Today* show. "I turn that off," Boris said as I climbed in, expecting I might want to follow our progress on my phone as I sometimes did during long car rides. "It's OK," I told him. "Leave it on if you want to." The resort was a good hour away even barring traffic delays, and I figured the mindless chatter would keep me from brooding.

We headed west to the Kennedy and then north toward Milwaukee, exiting the Tri-State near Libertyville and turning west again into McHenry County. Once we were off the highway and onto the back roads, I rolled the window halfway down so I could take in the country air, breathing in the fragrance of prairie grasses and freshly plowed earth. My first year in Chicago I'd done a century—a hundred-mile bike course—not far from the area we were in, and the memory allowed me to give free rein to my imagination as we motored past farms and orchards and fields dotted with livestock. I tried not to think about what it would be like to ride a bike outdoors again.

We arrived at the resort two hours before the start of the conference and pulled into a valet area bustling with what Boris informed me were late-model Mercedes, Lexus SUVs, and BMWs. During the ride, Boris was unusually quiet, even for him, so I asked him if anything was the matter.

"You will see," was all he said, resignedly. I wondered whether I should press him, but figured he'd tell me in his own good time.

Boris parked the car and walked me through a revolving door toward the commotion of the registration desk, teeming with newly arriving guests. He wanted to wait with me on line, but I told him I could handle it from there. We made arrangements for him to pick me up again on Sunday—early, so I wouldn't miss my Skype session with Louis—and Boris departed. It took a good twenty minutes to get to the head of the queue, where a hotel clerk greeted me questioningly.

"Are you sure you're in the right place?" he asked.

I put on a quizzical expression.

"The seeing eye dog school is a few miles down the road." He sounded embarrassed for me.

"I tried them first, but they were full," I said.

"As we are too, I'm afraid. I can help the next person in line," he said brusquely over my shoulder.

Evidently he'd been well trained at hospitality school.

"Pity," I said.

"Say what?" the clerk drawled.

"Pity when your manager finds out you've been ungracious to a paying customer." I removed a credit card from my wallet and slid it over the desk to him. "There should be a room waiting for me. If you don't mind taking my money."

"Why, no. Of course not," he said, just as dubiously. "Just let me have a look in our database." He began vigorously clacking keys on a keyboard. "Which conference are you here for?"

"I didn't realize there was more than one."

"Oh, yes. We're booked solid all weekend." He stopped in apparent surprise. "It appears we *do* have a guest room reserved for someone with your last name, but . . ."

I sighed.

It took another ten minutes to convince him that I wasn't a con artist posing as the MD listed in his records, that my credit was good, and that I could indeed handle a signature on the registration card if he'd just show me where to put it. I then had to cool my heels waiting for a bellhop to show me upstairs, having ascertained that the hotel's "commitment to meeting and exceeding all of the requirements of the ADA" did not extend to Braille signage on the doors of guest rooms.

"Sorry about that," the bellhop said as he was leading me over to the elevator. "We don't get many blind guests, and the powers that be didn't want to change all the signs. You probably know they don't have to unless it's new construction or they're making renovations."

He seemed unusually knowledgeable, and I soon found out why: he was completing a master's degree in rehabilitation counseling at ITT during the evenings.

"It's really cool you're a doctor," he said. "Most of the blind clients I've met at school can't get a job, even when they're fully qualified. It's like everyone's worried it will rub off on them. It's why so many of them end up helping other blind people."

"I was lucky I was already established in my profession," I said.

"RP?" he asked. It was a good guess. Apart from accidents, Retinitis Pigmentosa was the usual reason people my age lost their sight.

"Different pedigree, but similar effect." Normally, I liked talking about the subject about as much as I liked having a tooth filled, but he had such an open, honest manner it seemed churlish not to answer. "What's your name?"

"Nick."

"Mark," I said, extending my hand. "So what can you tell me about this place?" I'd pretty much struck out with the resort's website, which was no more accessible than the room signage.

Nick proceeded to give me a rough guide to the floor plan, which fit the blueprint of most hotel/conference centers I'd ever stayed at. There were two wings jutting out in the shape of a wide-angle V from the reception area, located in a multistory, south-facing atrium. The grand ballroom room, fitness area, and spa were on the ground floor behind reception, and the conference area was directly above them. "You'll mostly want to stay in the west wing, where your room is," Nick told me. "Just take the elevator down to the promenade level, where they'll be serving lunch. The CME will be taking place on the right side as you exit the elevator bank. The east wing on the left is for the company meeting that will be taking place at the same time."

"Company meeting?" I asked as the elevator let us off at what he told me was six.

"Yeah, Atria always buys out most of the resort this time of the year so they can get their sales staff rubbing shoulders with the doctors at the bar and on the course. The reps are always saying how good for business it is. While you're attending your lectures, they'll be next door plotting their marketing strategy for the year. I'd try not to wander over there, if I were you. They're pretty touchy about security. Even the hotel staff has to stay out of the room when they're meeting. I got my ass chewed off last time for not knowing about the spy stuff when I was tapped for coffee urn duty. I walked into one of their rooms with the refills and it was like everyone had a stroke."

"If I, uh . . . do get lost, how will I know which rooms to stay away from?"

"You're in luck there," Nick said. "They changed the meeting room names six months ago, so those signs do have Braille on them. The west wing rooms are all named after flowers—Rose, Tulip, Iris, and so forth. The east wing rooms are all named after trees—Oak, Maple, Elm, etcetera."

My curiosity got the better of me. "What were they named after before?"

"Foreign capitals. But someone in corporate decided it was un-American. So just remember to stick with the flowers and you'll be OK."

Nick showed me how to find my room, which required turning left off the elevator bank and continuing past six doors on the right side of the corridor. "I'll come back in a bit and stick a piece of electrical tape just under the number so you won't have to worry about making a mistake," he said. He opened the door and showed me in and took me all around the room, pointing out the location of phones, remotes, and climate controls. The room was regulation business hotel, right down to the king-sized bed with enough pillows in all shapes and sizes to supply a sultan's harem. Just before leaving, Nick took out a penknife and cut the corner off my key card adjacent to the magnetic stripe so I wouldn't have to try umpteen different ways of swiping it to unlock the door. I tipped him five dollars, and he was savvy enough not to refuse it.

"Call me if there's anything else I can help you with while you're here. Just press '0' on the room phone and ask for Nick. Turndown service with a complimentary water bottle is at eight o'clock."

"Thanks," I said, though I wasn't sure I'd be using the bed that night. A plan was beginning to form in my head that might require an early getaway.

In the movies, the blind man with his loyal German shepherd is as overdone as Italians in the mob. But the majority of blind people—even those more partial to dogs than I—get around using a stick. A lucky few develop "facial vision," a sensitivity to air pressure so acute that they can walk right up to walls and other obstructions without colliding with them. Possibly because I still relied on my eyes more than I should have, my attempts to develop this skill had been a bust, with little more to show for them than bruised shins and some near misses with gas-company excavation sites. After scaring myself this way a few times, I'd become resigned to hauling the cane around with me whenever I wasn't at home or at work. Nonetheless, a little while later found me exiting my room without it.

I planted one foot carefully before the other, wishing the carpet wasn't so thick. A better echo from my steps would have helped me stay in a straight line. Without the cane I felt exposed and unbalanced, and it was a struggle to keep my arms in a relaxed position by my sides as I made my way down the corridor, which was as dimly lit as a coal mine. It wasn't until I got to a turn that I could detect a diaphanous glow coming from an exterior window. I used that and the sound of the cars moving along their cables to ascertain the location of the elevator bank, set within a darker recess in the fog-filled landscape to my right. The scent of face powder and an impatient sigh told me I had company. I trained my eyes on what was surely a woman and smiled.

"Going down to the conference?" I asked brightly.

"Uh-huh. More damned CME. Are you a doctor, too?"

I shook my head. "No, just one of the salesmen. We're meeting at the same time."

"Too bad. I was hoping you could show me where I'm supposed to be."

"That's no problem. Just hit the button for the promenade level and turn right when you get downstairs," I said, enjoying the irony of being the one giving directions.

She thanked me just as the elevator chimed, announcing its arrival on our floor.

"After you," I said, always the gentleman. I followed the sound of her heels into the crowded car and managed to get over the threshold with only a minor stumble. Normally, I would have located a free space by feeling demurely forward with my cane, but all I had now was my toe. I inched it forward until it met with another person's shoe, grinning maniacally in the hope that no one would notice. "Floor?" asked a man to my right with a distinct tone of disapproval. "Promenade," I replied. I counted the chimes as the elevator stopped at four more floors, increasing its cargo each time until my back was pressed into the starched abdomen of the man behind me, who was breathing hot, foul air into my ear.

When the doors opened at the promenade level, the passengers streamed quickly out and I was pushed forward before I had a chance to gain my footing, nicking my shoulder as I passed through the door and staggering slightly. A woman to my rear stage-whispered, "Can you believe that? It's not even noon and he's already three sheets to the wind." I ignored her and extricated myself from the thick crowd moving toward the buffet area, whose location my nose left no doubt of. I found a wall and anchored myself there for a moment, sweating profusely. Once outside the swiftly moving posse of conference goers, the sunlight filling the atrium straight ahead was easier to detect. I gathered my courage and marched toward the glare until I met up with the railing overlooking the lobby below, where I stopped to rest and wipe a hand across my brow.

I flipped the crystal on my watch to check the time. It was then

11:45. Based on the scraping of cutlery and raucous conversation nearby, lunch hour was in full swing. The formal meetings wouldn't start for another forty-five minutes, which with luck would give me the time I needed. With my back turned to the rail, I was now facing north. To find the flower rooms I should have headed to my left. Instead, I took a deep breath and started out in the opposite direction.

After Nick left me I'd rung up reception from my cell phone—again with caller ID blocked—and explained that I was stuck in traffic and had misplaced my agenda for the Atria sales meeting. Could they remind me where the meeting would be taking place so I wouldn't have to waste time looking for it when I arrived? The clerk who answered told me I needed the Elm Room, just inside the entrance to the east wing. There would be an easel with a sign bearing the company logo beside the door. Unless I was blind I couldn't miss it.

As I crept forward the crowd thinned, and by the time I'd reached the entrance to the east wing, looming ahead of me like the maw of a huge black cavern, there were few footsteps around me. It appeared I was mostly alone. My next job was finding the Elm Room. The easel by the door would be of no help—unless I happened to walk into it—and massaging the walls with my fingers would have surely pegged me as your not-so-average salesperson, if not a bona fide nut. Fortunately, I was saved from blowing my cover by the sound of someone heaving boxes onto a table and swearing. I advanced toward the sound with my right hand held out a few inches in front of my thigh until it connected with a cloth-covered surface, and beamed in the general direction of whoever was standing behind it.

"Hi, there," came the candy-apple voice of a young woman. "Are you here for the sales meeting? You're early."

"I thought I'd get a head start on finding a seat."

"Smart idea. It'll be standing room only when the presentations get underway. I'm Gretchen, Mr. Henderson's assistant."

I stuck out my hand, introducing myself as Mark Halliday.

"Hmmm," she said quizzically as she took it. "I don't remember that name from the roster."

"I, uh . . . only got called to the meeting at the last minute. I flew in from the East Coast this morning."

"I wish somebody'd let me know. But the bosses are like that, aren't they? Always changing their minds at the last second and God help the poor slob who doesn't jump ten feet in the air to make it happen. If you're not on my list, I won't have a name tag for you. But I can make up a temporary. What did you say your name was again?"

I caught the whiff of a felt pen as she took down my alias.

"Office?" she asked.

"Westchester," I said with my fingers surreptitiously crossed. How many Fortune 500s didn't have at least one office in Westchester? She didn't object and took this down too.

"Here," she said, sliding something scratchy across the table. "You'll have to keep that around your neck so the security detail will know you're legit."

I located the plastic pouch attached to a length of string without too much difficulty and said, "Thanks. I hope I haven't put you to too much trouble."

"No trouble at all. Will you be around for the whole conference?" She stopped and added forwardly, "I wouldn't mind having a drink if you're free later on. You have nice eyes."

If only she knew. "Er, thanks, but I'm in a relationship." And even in my heyday I drew the line at robbing the cradle.

"Figures. The best ones are always taken. Here, you'll need this, too. But remember the rules: it goes right into the shredder after the meeting."

There was no other option but to swipe at the thing she was holding out to me. My fingers closed clumsily on a thick laminated folder.

Gretchen giggled. "Now I get it."

"Get what?" I asked, feeling myself start to color. Had I given myself away that easily?

"I was wondering why you looked so out of it. You had a few on the plane, didn't you?" she accused.

I breathed a sigh of relief and feigned embarrassment. "You won't tell anyone will you? I got upgraded to first class and it was hard to stop at just one mimosa."

"I'll bet. But you better let me walk you in. It's still dark in there. Come on."

I slid around the table and fell in behind her. Just inside the door, Gretchen flipped the switch on several lights, and the ballroom lit up like a baseball park. "Take any seat you like, but if I were you I'd stick to the back row," she said in amusement as she retreated from the room. I inched forward and found the last row of folding chairs without making too much of a commotion. I slid my hand along their backs until I came to the one farthest from the center aisle, sinking into the seat just as my knees were about to give out. I checked my pulse, which was racing like a Belmont thoroughbred, and vowed—unless fortune were ultimately to shine on me—never to leave my cane behind again. My hands were slick with perspiration, and I dried them on my trouser legs before opening the folder Gretchen had given me and spreading it on my lap. Much as I needed a breather, this was no time to relax. I could have company at any moment.

I got out my phone and began snapping pictures.

A short while later, I was lounging peacefully with the folder resting innocently on the floor underneath my chair as the first of the conferees started rolling in. What started as a drop here and there soon turned to a flood as bodies swelled to fill the warehouse-sized space. The salesmen laughed and cracked jokes and called out each other's names, their voices rising and falling like a hive of buzzing insects. All of the seats around me were soon taken, and before long there was also a phalanx of bodies pressed up against the back of my chair. Business meetings at my hospital were never this well attended. Or this lively. Based on the atmosphere, it could easily have been opening night at the Oscars. I soon figured out why by eavesdropping on the two fellows next to me: Atria's recently ended fiscal year had earned it record-breaking profits, and the salesmen were anticipating the announcement of whopping bonuses.

All at once music began to swell from loudspeakers placed in the four corners of the room, and the din of conversation receded. I recognized the opening bars of Wagner's *Ride of the Valkyries*, which drew loud laughter. While the music continued to mount, someone tested the microphone up front with a deafening screech and said, "Wait, wait, you guys. You're playing the wrong tune." The music abruptly stopped, to be replaced by the theme song from *Rocky*. Even more laughter broke out. Scratch the Oscars. It appeared we were in for vaudeville.

The music abruptly stopped again, and our MC said, "But seriously folks . . ." to further guffaws. "Our man of the hour, Rod Henderson, asked me to come out and keep everyone busy while he straightens his hairpiece . . . (pause for laugh track) and takes his Placeva . . . (more of the same). . . . So while we're waiting for him, I thought I'd tell you a joke. The devil visits an Atria rep's home office to make him an offer. He says, 'I'll increase your commissions by fifty percent, your doctors will respect you, you'll have four months' vacation a year, and you'll live to be a hundred. All I want in return is that your wife's soul, your children's souls, and all of their children's souls will rot in eternity forever.'"

He paused again before delivering the punch line: "The Atria rep thought for a moment and asked, 'What's the catch?'"

The room exploded into thunderous applause. If this is what passed for humor in corporate America, I decided, it was time to move to Canada.

It went on like this for another ten minutes during which I seriously considered the potential merits of deaf-blindness, when I felt a rough tap on my shoulder.

"This him?" a man asked in a distinctly hostile manner.

"That's right," I heard my friend Gretchen say. "He tricked me. He acted like he was drunk."

"Yes, ma'am" the man said. "Don't worry. We'll take it from here."

While he was picking me up by the shoulders, I heard another voice say, "Take him to the office behind reception and lock the door. He can stay there until the police arrive."

# TWENTY-ONE

Later that night, Josh was none too happy about having to come and bail me out.

"You did suggest I'd be better off without the cane," I observed from the passenger seat of his BMW. We were on the Kennedy, headed back toward the city.

"True. But if you'd asked, I also would have counseled against corporate espionage."

The weak link in my spy mission had proved to be Gretchen, who after relating the entertaining tale of the drunken salesman to several of her coworkers, was overheard by her supervisor and soon found herself being dressed down for a serious lapse in protocol. A quick check of the hotel's guest log—in addition to Atria's personnel records—revealed the alarming absence of a "Mark Halliday," whereupon a member of the muscle hired by Atria to watch over the conference had been summoned to fetch me. He and the head of house security had practically carried me out of the meeting and through the hotel to a closet-sized room, where I'd sweated under lock and key for hours.

"Besides," Josh said, "As I understood it, you were just going there to mingle."

"Which, as it happens, is the only thing I'm guilty of." I hadn't told Josh about the photos still safely hidden away in my phone. "It isn't my fault I wandered into the wrong room by mistake."

"I have a hard time believing you didn't know exactly where you were."

So did the security goon, who'd laughed out loud when I'd given him my excuse for crashing the sales meeting. "Sure you are," he said as he was confiscating my belongings. "And I'm the next Patrick Kane."

Happily, he and the house dick confined their search for stolen documents to the photo-taking application on my phone they were familiar with, overlooking the more blind-friendly program I'd used to capture the contents of the folder. With no proof that I'd been doing anything more felonious than trespassing, they'd finally given into my pleas to question the bellhop, Nick, who scolded me for forgetting his directions but corroborated my story. Still, it had taken a further phone call to Josh—and his promise to come and personally escort me from the premises—to finally spring me from captivity.

"You know you're lucky not to be spending the night in a real jail," Josh rebuked as he shifted into a lower gear next to me. His anger, so unlike his usual self, hung like a thick cloud between us. "What would you have done if they'd decided to press charges?"

The truth was, I didn't know. In trying to pass for normal earlier in the day, I had succeeded brilliantly, but at what risk? I shuddered to think of what it would have been like spending the night in a county lockup somewhere, in the company of Hells Angels, meth addicts, and carjackers. Without my cane I couldn't prove what I was, much less hold my own in a prison cell. I fingered the bottle of pills in my pocket, which seemed to have grown noticeably lighter in the last several days—still to no discernible effect.

Josh took my silence for an answer. "I know what you're doing," he said.

"Go ahead, analyze me. It's what everyone likes to do."

"You're acting crazy because you feel responsible for what happened to Hallie."

"Shouldn't I?" I asked bitterly.

"No, you should not. If you're right about the attack on her being intentional, it could have happened anywhere—with or without you in the vicinity. And do I really need to point out that you were hit from behind?"

"So?"

"So unless you had eyes in the back of your head, you still might not have seen him. You'd be just as in the dark as you are now."

"That's a gentle way of phrasing it."

Josh shifted to a more forgiving tone. "We're only a few blocks from the hospital. Why don't we go over there right now? Her surgeon said she could be coming out of it soon. She'll want to see you."

I wanted to, but I couldn't. Not when there was still work to be done. My George Smiley caper had turned up one solid fact: something *was* afoot at Atria. Something important enough to necessitate a search of my phone to be sure there was nothing in it I wasn't supposed to abscond with. Something that quite possibly had gotten Rory Gallagher killed. Which raised another disturbing fact: what would they have done to me if I'd been caught red-handed?

A thunderstorm was brewing when Josh dropped me off at my building, and I had to butt my way through a virtual wind tunnel to get to the lobby door. I yanked it open and took the elevator up, finding when I reached my apartment that the door there was also stuck. It was ten degrees cooler than usual when I stepped inside, and I soon figured out why. Somehow the door to my terrace had become unlatched during the day and was now banging back and forth, sending powerful gusts and the first drops of the storm into the room. I hurried over and forced it shut against the shrieking wind. It was a good thing I'd been booted out of the conference. I didn't think a burglar would climb nineteen stories to rob me of my pitiful collection of worldly goods, but coming home to a rain-soaked carpet and ruined furniture might have required that I finally do something to replace them.

I cranked up the thermostat and felt around to survey the damage, which seemed to consist only of a toppled floor lamp and some mail that I'd left on a side table, now scattered across the floor. I righted the lamp and switched on the light for comfort. The tempest outside was shaping up to be a late-season extravaganza. Thunderclaps were exploding directly overhead, and the rain was raking the windows like tossed gravel. If I stood still, I could feel the building swaying back and forth.

I poured myself a tumbler of bourbon and went to my office to start the download from my phone, hoping the power wouldn't go off before I had a chance to examine my booty. While I was connecting the cable I discovered that my computer was cold, which was odd because I almost always left it on. When it had heaved itself back to life and the download was underway, I went to my bedroom to find a wide-open window. This was becoming tedious. It was high time I got maintenance up there to check on all the latches. I changed into pajamas and a bathrobe, downed a container of cottage cheese over the kitchen sink, and popped my last pill for the day. I counted off another ten minutes before heading back to my desk and opening the file, anticipating a treasure trove.

It turned out to be anything but.

Most folks are better off not knowing about prescription data mining, the now-common practice in which pharmacies and benefit plans sell prescription information to third parties, who turn around and sell it to the big drug companies. Despite a barrage of criticism, it's a hugely successful business, with some estimates putting profits in the area of $10 billion annually. To ward off arguments about invasion of privacy, the data that gets sold is "de-identified"—that is, scrubbed of any information that could lead back to a particular patient—but it still supplies Big Pharma with the name of the drug in question, the prescribing doctor, and the dosage, all of which gets passed on to drug-company sales personnel. With the information instantly available on their smartphones and laptops, drug reps know exactly how much of their company's products a doctor ordinarily prescribes, and can tailor their sales pitches accordingly.

Like most doctors, I knew the practice existed, but I was unprepared to hear it laid out so graphically in a PowerPoint presentation, setting forth the previous year's sales results for specific regions, subregions, and practices. I learned that Atria divided my profession into ten "deciles" according to how much medication each doctor prescribed.

Compared to his peers, a decile 10 doctor was the highest-prescribing doctor; a decile 1 doctor prescribed on average very few medications. Decile 10 doctors, being the most potentially lucrative, were targeted by Atria for the biggest sales pushes, whereas decile 1 doctors were all but ignored.

I also learned that within deciles there were nicknames for various personalities based on their histories. A "spreader" was a doctor who generally did not favor one brand of drug over another but prescribed them equally across several name brands and/or generics. A "no see um" was someone like me who discouraged visits from drug company reps. A "sample grabber" was someone who couldn't get enough of the free drugs. Naturally, a "spreader" in decile 10 got the most attention, since it was there that Atria stood the best chance of capturing market share from its competitors. There were even several slides devoted to "superstar" representatives—Graham's name figuring prominently among them—and their most reliable prescribers of Placeva, Lucitrol, and other bestsellers in key geographic areas.

It was all as slimy as hell.

And perfectly legal.

A few years back no less an authority than the United States Supreme Court had overturned a Vermont law outlawing prescription data mining on First Amendment grounds. Since then, despite some grumbling in the profession, efforts to reform the system had focused on the creation of a program allowing doctors to opt out of sharing their information, which was currently subscribed to by less than 4 percent of the physician population. I wondered if the doctors who had turned down the program would appreciate seeing their names flashed on a screen in front of a thousand cheering salesmen.

I read late into the night while the storm thumped away—periodically jumping at the cracks reverberating through my building's Tinkertoy infrastructure—and in the end, the only thing I could do was shake my head. Was protecting this mountain of crap what had nearly gotten me jailed? To be sure, the bean counters must have worn out their eyeshades compiling the data, which ran to nearly twenty pages. After the PowerPoint there were charts of all sizes and descriptions and page upon page of figures comparing this, that, and the other thing to something else. There were enough acronyms—ROI, EBIDTA, R&D—to fill a dictionary, and more footnotes than I could count. You needed to be a CPA to figure out what most of it meant, but it sounded to me like all the other corporate Sanskrit regularly appearing in the *Wall Street Journal* and glossy annual reports, not the kind of deep, dark secret that would get someone like Rory Gallagher killed.

Toward two o'clock the next morning, I'd had enough. As if in sympathy for the punishment my ears had taken, my eyes were watery and aching when I turned out the last of the lights and folded myself unhappily into bed.

I tossed and turned most of that night, haunted by fantastic dreams. I was in a cavernous place lit by green light, surrounded by mountains of trash. Mike was there, cooking a rat on an open grate. He offered me a chunk on the tip of his knife, the gold in his chipped tooth gleaming. But I couldn't stay for dinner. I was already late for my appointment with Melissa. Then I was walking through endless tunnels limned with mold and dripping wet. I needed my cane, but it was back in my room. In the distance a single light burned, and I hurried toward it, finally becoming aware of the footsteps at my back. I quickened my pace, but the footsteps kept gaining. I reeled and turned to find the Red Queen leering at me with wide, toothless lips. Remember, she said, what the dormouse mouse said. Then her guards were upon me, and I was falling, falling...

I woke to find myself half out of bed in a tangle of sheets and breathing like an ultra-marathoner. I untwisted myself and got up, feeling forward with my toes. I went to the kitchen and poured myself another shot of bourbon, downing it in a single gulp and waiting for my pulse to subside before returning to bed.

When I woke again it was late morning and pale sunlight was

streaming through the window, the storm having finally taken itself off. In the bathroom I splashed water on my face and peered at my ghost-like reflection in the mirror. I went to the kitchen and put on a pot of tea and drank a big glass of water to ease the hangover. I took another pill and switched on the television, idly registering the white noise while I went back over the events since the previous Sunday. The attack on Hallie and me. The bizarre note left for me in reception. Jane's challenge—or was it?—to find out something she knew and wouldn't tell me. My trip with Bjorn to confront Gallagher's nephew and the discovery of the other note. My certainty, although I had nothing to prove it, that the thread running through it all was Atria and whatever had both terrified its employees into silence and come close to getting me arrested.

The exercise left me thoroughly depressed. I'd spent almost a week tracking down clues and was still no closer to understanding how or why Gallagher had died than when I'd started, all the while neglecting what should have been my first and only responsibility.

I'd long been aware of my tendency to wall myself off from others. Maybe it was a consequence of growing up the only child of a widowed, overbearing father. Maybe it was knowing that I never had—or ever would—live up to his impossible expectations. I'd stayed away from Louis for three long years, telling myself he was better off without me. Was I about to make the same mistake with Hallie? All my activity of the past week, senseless as it now appeared, was just a way of avoiding the dismal truth of my failure to protect her. I could pretend all I liked that it was about bringing her assailant to justice, but in reality I was simply running—from fear, from shame, from my own damnable help-lessness. It was time to stop. Let Bjorn—or Jane, if she ever decided to lift a finger in her own defense—figure it all out.

I spent the rest of the morning getting myself cleaned up and making plans: to make my long-overdue appearance at the hospital, to get a head start on the week's work, to see if Richard had made any headway about Mike. I had just picked up my phone to confirm the ICU's visiting hours when it began ringing of its own accord. It was Annie, calling to tell me that Louis was ill.

My blood pressure shot up like a Saturn V. "Does he have a fever? Have you taken him to the doctor?" I demanded in a cold sweat.

Annie let the irony of my asking sink in for a moment before replying. "My father came over early this morning. He'll be staying until Louis is better."

Which meant I wouldn't be Skyping with my son that day. My ex-father-in-law, Roger, despised me with a vitriol that exceeded even Annie's. So far, she and I had concealed from him the deviation from our custody agreement that enabled periodic contact with my son. It carried the bonus of not filling Roger in on what had happened to me since I'd left his employ. As far as Roger knew, I was still the same careless playboy who'd put his grandson in a grave, not the shambling mess I'd become. All things considered, I preferred to keep it that way.

"That's good, Annie," I said hoarsely. "What does your father think it is?"

"Just a bad cold. But we won't be taking any chances," she said, making no effort to keep the bile out of her tone. It sent a hot poker into my gut.

"Uh-huh." I fished about lamely for something to keep the conversation going. "What's Louis doing now?"

"Sleeping. He was up most of the night, but he's resting quietly at the moment. He was asking about you."

"While your father was there?" I said, panicking again.

"No, but that's another reason for my call." She lowered her voice. "I think we should tell him about our arrangement. I'm not comfortable with all the secrecy, and it's only a matter of time before Louis lets on he knows you."

"Won't your father try to shut it down?" It was what I feared more than anything else.

"Probably," Annie said, with a hard practicality that was new to her. "But I'm Louis's mother. And not such a daddy's girl anymore. That's one small thing you did for me. God knows I don't want you around us any more than he does, but we have to do what's best for Louis. I'd like you to come out to Greenwich as soon as you can. Then the three of us will sit down, reach some kind of understanding."

I was already imagining the scene: me entering with my cane, Roger wordlessly gloating, Annie off to the side with a brittle twist to her mouth. It sounded like being the butt of every joke in a full season of the *Three Stooges*. I swallowed hard and said, "I'll do whatever it takes to be a father to my son."

"Well, we'll see about that."

After she hung up, I abandoned the idea of accomplishing anything productive that day. My thoughts would all be with Louis in his sickbed. And with his brother, in whatever place babies went when their tiny, vulnerable hearts stopped beating. I said a fervent prayer for them both and wondered how anyone could put their trust in a deity that treated its creations so carelessly. If I were running the cosmos, there would be no sick children and especially no dead ones. Even mental illness wasn't reserved for the old. Hell, I knew of kids as young as ten being treated for serious depression . . .

And that's when the first piece clicked into place.

# TWENTY-TWO

"Explain this to me again," Bjorn was saying. "Shrinks can prescribe any drug they want, but the drug companies have to pretend they're not selling it to them? Sounds a little schizophrenic, if you'll excuse the pun."

We were again in my office, where I was taking the first steps toward a radical housecleaning, aided by Yelena, whose sunny mood was still holding, though she steadfastly refused to say why. I began to suspect that she had her sights on a more hospitable job placement—though it was hard to conceive of another institution that would pay her an hourly wage just for keeping up with the latest issue of *Glamour*—and was softening me up for a letter of recommendation. She tramped out of the office with another box of paper I'd decided I could live without while I continued with my explanation.

"It goes back to what I was telling you earlier. Compared to most other medical specialties, psychiatry is still almost as primitive as when doctors were leeching their patients. We know when people are suffering, and we can divide them into diagnostic categories based on their symptoms, but the brain is so complicated and difficult to study, we rarely know what's causing the underlying problem. Genes appear to play a part, but that doesn't explain why two people with the same genealogy can have radically different outcomes—for example, when one identical twin develops schizophrenia and the other doesn't."

"So you're basically in the dark when deciding what to do."

"That's right. Take antidepressants, for example. We know that they've been remarkably successful in reducing rates of depression and anxiety, and that they work by altering levels of neurotransmitters, the chemicals that cause brain cells to fire. The most common anti-

depressants are called SSRIs—or 'selective serotonin reuptake inhib-
itors'—because they disable the function in the brain that reabsorbs
the neurotransmitter serotonin, thereby maintaining a bigger supply.
What we don't have is any explanation for why SSRIs work. Study
after study has attempted to link depression to a serotonin deficiency
without turning up a shred of proof that it or some other chemical
imbalance is at the root of the problem. Same with other illnesses like
schizophrenia. It's clear that we're looking at a biological cause for most
of these problems, but we're still light-years away from understanding
what it might be."

"So how *do* you choose one drug over another?" Bjorn asked.

"Don't quote me on this, but it's mostly trial and error," I said.
"Oh, sure, there are studies showing that some drugs work better than
others—most of which, by the way, are paid for by the drug companies
themselves—but they're just as often contradicted by different studies.
Some drugs do seem to have fewer side effects, either alone or taken in
combination with other medicines, which can be an important reason
to choose them. But getting back to my depression example, when it
comes to picking which drug to prescribe to the average patient, it's
about as scientific as throwing darts. You try something and see if the
patient improves. If they don't, you try something else. Which is where
the antipsychotics, particularly the second-generation ones like Lucitrol, come into play."

"How? Aren't they only supposed to be for the real nutters?"

"In theory, yes, at least insofar as they were originally approved
by the FDA. But the number of people with schizophrenia or bipolar
disease is miniscule compared to the adult population with everyday
problems like anxiety, insomnia, and eating disorders—not to mention
adolescents presenting with those issues. The drug companies quickly
figured out that their profits from a drug like Lucitrol would increase
dramatically if doctors could be persuaded they were effective for a much
larger group. Since the FDA prohibits marketing for non-approved or
'off-label' uses—including, most notably, children—their dilemma was
getting the word out to psychiatrists without getting noticed."

"And you think that's what Atria's been doing?"

"Yes, if the documents you're holding in your hand are any indication. It's not immediately obvious and it took me a while to see it myself. But the list of 'top' Lucitrol prescribers in the Chicago area contains at least two child psychiatrists I know of and a few others with adult practices who wouldn't be caught dead in a psychiatric ward. Couple that with the astronomic growth in the company's sales revenue, and it's obvious what Atria's been up to. In fact, I blame myself now for not having put two and two together much earlier. The figures I gave Hallie to cross-examine that detective with also show revenue from Lucitrol sales well in excess of what you'd expect if it were just being used to treat serious mental illness."

"OK," Bjorn said. "But if I understand what you've already told me, the medicos are free to prescribe whatever they want to whomever they want. Where does it show that Atria is egging them on?"

"That's harder to spot, but I think it's reflected in some of the charts in the back, divvying up return on investment and comparing marketing expenses to sales of specific drugs. They're spending a huge chunk of change on Lucitrol, which wouldn't be reflected in the more generalized information they're putting in their public financial statements. I'm betting they've instructed their sales staff to cover their tracks by keeping mum about the promotional efforts with doctors and that Gallagher somehow caught wind of it. If you could prove it, it would mean billions in fines and legal fees. And it might tell us why someone was hell-bent on putting Gallagher out of commission."

Bjorn agreed. "It would also explain the cold shoulder I got from the Atria employees you put me onto. They were practically shitting their knickers when I tracked them down. I'm afraid we'll never get anything out of them."

I'd figured as much and was pondering various ways to break the logjam. But first I wanted to confirm a suspicion.

Getting into Jane's penthouse was much easier the second time around. Apparently she had instructed her watchdog that he was to roll out the red carpet the next time I was in the neighborhood, and he greeted me with only a half-suppressed snicker. Also departing from custom, Jane was waiting for me at her door.

"Doctor, how splendid. I was wondering when you'd return."

I leaned over the threshold and sniffed. "What? No evidence burning in the hearth today?"

She laughed. "What a suspicious mind you have. Come in," she said, moving aside to clear a path for me. Once again I breathed in her unusual scent, musky like incense but tinged with some type of solvent.

I remembered the way to the sofa and helped myself to a seat. The silk made a sliding sound as I settled in. I laid my cane on the floor and followed her with my ears as she took the seat opposite me.

"That's quite good," she remarked. "But I suppose you've learned to compensate."

"For bad manners, certainly. I try my utmost to overlook them. Aren't you going to offer me a refreshment?"

"I'm afraid we'll have to dispense with the social niceties on this occasion. You caught me in the middle of preparing for a deposition."

"For Atria?"

"Yes, they keep me very busy. But why don't we get on to why you're here. You look like a little boy just bursting at the seams with something to say."

"We'll get to that. But first, let's go back to the hearsay rules and admissions against interest. I checked with a friend of mine, another lawyer. It's not an admission of anything if I lay out a possible scenario and you simply listen. I can't see you, so no one can ask me if you looked guilty, though I imagine you're a genius at the art of the poker face. If I'm wrong, you can just tell me, since denials don't count as admissions either."

"I see you've done your homework. Proceed."

"So here's one theory of what happened on the night your boy-friend died. He came to you with a story he was planning to write, one that would have implicated Atria in something illegal. Maybe he threatened to name you as a source. Or maybe he didn't have to threaten, because you gave the story to him. That's what your pals back at the State's Attorney's office would have supposed. According to them, you'd been feeding Gallagher confidential information for years."

"My, my, you *have* been digging," was her only reaction.

"Even a rumor to that effect would have shut down your practice in a heartbeat. You couldn't allow that to happen. So after you dumped a quart of wine over Gallagher's head you went back to your office to consider your options, and there, sitting on your IT person's desk, was the solution. You knew Gallagher was under orders to stay off the servers at the *Sun-Times*, so any drafts would be on his computer at home, and you had a key to his townhouse. With me so far? You can just nod your head."

"Consider it done."

"I'm guessing Gallagher was only days away from publishing, so you had to act quickly. You knew his habits—that he'd be hitting the bars for hours that night—which gave you just the window you needed. You went to Gallagher's home, erased his hard drive with the disc-wiping software and took whatever else you could find, and *voilà*—problem solved."

I noted she hadn't denied anything so far. "Your only misfortune was that you were seen by our Mrs. Van Wagner while you were letting yourself in, and that someone else chose that exact night to slip Gallagher a Mickey Finn." I stopped and let this sink in. "Unless of course it was you who poisoned him."

"I prefer we stick to the first hypothesis."

"All right. Assuming there was another murderer, what was the motive? Gallagher had been washed up for years. If it was some enemy from his past, why wait until now to kill him? The better bet is that somebody connected to Atria found out about the story and murdered him to keep him from breaking it. That would also explain the way it was done—hoisting Gallagher on his own petard, so to speak."

"Clever. You're much better at this than I anticipated," Jane said.

"So now, let's fast-forward to when Gallagher's body had been dug up and you were arrested. You knew—or at least suspected—that he was killed to keep Atria's secret from the authorities. But you couldn't send the police in that direction without revealing what the company was up to. As I understand them, the rules governing attorney-client privilege are pretty strict. You could have asked your client for permission to spill the beans, but why would Atria give it to you, especially if the cover-up is what got Gallagher killed? And if you went ahead and disclosed a client confidence, you would have lost your license. Have I accurately summed up the situation?"

"Almost," Jane said, finally breaking her silence. "You've left out the most critical part: what I knew about Atria wouldn't have helped me defend the murder charge. It would only have given the police another motive—one, I might add, that was far more credible than the idea I killed Rory just to keep him from marrying that little tart. Under the circumstances, my best option was to keep the knowledge to myself."

"Is that a concession or are we still speaking hypothetically?" I asked.

Jane sighed. "That depends. Why don't you first tell me what you think Rory stumbled onto."

"Atria's been marketing drugs, Lucitrol prominent among them, for off-label use. It's clearly illegal, and the last company that got caught doing it was slapped with a billion-dollar fine. Not a bad reason for somebody at the company to want to bury him, and the story along with it. Again, assuming the murderer wasn't you."

"And you have proof of this?"

"Enough to take to the authorities."

Jane regarded me silently for a moment. "You're bluffing."

"Maybe. How far are you willing to trust your luck?"

She got up then and went to stand by the window in apparent meditation. I wondered how much of it was an act.

"All right," she said at long last. "I don't expect proving it will be as easy as you think. If Atria has followed my advice, any wrongdoing has long since ceased. But on the chance that you really do have something incriminating to share, I'll confide in you. It wasn't just that Rory threatened to name me as the source of his wretched news piece. I *was* the source."

For the next hour, and over the pot of tea Jane insisted on making for us, she told me the story of her tangled relationship with Gallagher.

"I first met Rory when I was starting out at the State's Attorney's office. He was a few years older than I, a media star, and devilishly handsome. Of course, I knew right from the start that he was a liar and a cheat where women were concerned, but then most men are."

I winced at this but couldn't disagree.

She continued: "But it didn't bother me because I wasn't looking for a commitment, or more significantly, marriage. I can't have children. There's a flaw in my makeup I'm not willing to pass on, and don't see any point in two adults promising themselves to each other for life unless they intend to raise a family. Besides, I always knew my true marriage would be to my career. It's the only thing that doesn't bore me. Rory fulfilled my physical needs and could be terribly amusing, and as the years went by, it was easier to stay involved with him than to go searching for partners in singles bars.

"A few months into our relationship were all it took to discover that his journalistic ethics were no more to be trusted than his steadfastness to me, which is to say that he bribed, paid for, or stole his way into every story he wrote. It put me on my guard, but not enough. In those days, I carried a lot of sensitive files home, long-term investigations I was working on at the State's Attorney's office or internal memoranda that would have made the headlines if they ever saw the light of day. One night, when Rory was sleeping over, I woke to find him reading through my papers, which he readily admitted he'd been doing for some time. I would have reported him, but as he explained to me, the damage was already done. By exposing him I would only have succeeded in exposing myself. At the time, I was still a mid-level assistant and hungry for advancement, so I let it slide on his promise it would never happen again."

"But you continued to see him," I pointed out, as I took a sip from a cup of her admittedly exquisite brew. It reminded me it was time for another of my pills. I opened the bottle without taking it from my pocket and downed the tablet as inconspicuously as I could.

"Yes. As I said, it was too much trouble to find another bedmate, and I was confident I could control the situation. Overconfident, as it turned out. He did it again, and at the worst possible moment. I suppose you've heard that I was in line to become First Assistant. Right around that time, we'd received complaints from several defense attorneys about prosecutors withholding exculpatory evidence in violation of the discovery rules, and I was appointed to an internal task force charged with looking into the matter. One evening, just before the two of us were to go out, I left some notes on that table right in front of you while I was showering. Rory came early and let himself in and must have read what was there because the next thing I knew, the name of one of my colleagues was splashed across the front page of the *Sun-Times*."

"Jimmy O'Hara," I said.

Jane didn't seem surprised that I knew. "Yes, poor man. A decent lawyer who'd made a mistake but didn't deserve the public flaying he was subsequently forced to endure. Of course, everyone at the office assumed I was responsible for the story. Jimmy was also being considered for First Assistant, and they decided I'd leaked the information intentionally—to rid myself of a rival. It didn't occur to them that I would never have acted so stupidly. I told Rory we were over and left the State's Attorney's office to start my own practice, which as you can surmise has been highly successful."

"And that was it between the two of you?" I asked.

"For a while. But it didn't take long for Rory to come crawling back to me, with renewed promises of reform."

"You let him back into your bed?" I exclaimed in frank surprise.

"As I said, he was good company. But not here, not in my bed. Only at his place."

"And you want me to believe you didn't hold a grudge?" I said.

"Believe what you like," Jane said, sighing and shifting in her seat. "But it's true. My philosophy has always been to make the best of a bad situation. Rory had harmed me, but it wasn't worth losing sleep over, and I soon found the challenges—and rewards—of private practice to be at least as satisfying as my former position. I had no reason to risk them—or deprive myself of a serviceable sexual partner—by getting even with him."

"Except that his filching from you didn't stop there."

"Apparently not, though I'm still at a loss to explain how he got his hands on the report. Naturally, I changed the locks to this apartment after he was no longer welcome, and the security here is state of the art. But I'm getting ahead of myself. Some months back, while I was defending Atria in the Lucitrol lawsuit, I came across information suggesting the company might be doing what you said—marketing the drug for off-label purposes. It wasn't pertinent to the case I was handling, but I did what any responsible lawyer faced with possible illegal activity by a client would have done: I took it to Atria's general counsel. Given the potential liability you mentioned, he was obviously concerned and asked me to investigate, which I did over the course of several weeks, interviewing dozens of salesmen and reviewing all of the company's internal marketing materials. I prepared a draft report and sent it off to my client. You can draw your own conclusions about what it said."

"And that's what Gallagher showed you when you were at Gene and Georgetti's that night?"

"Not showed me. He had the good sense to leave it at home. But he knew everything in it, and when I pressed him about how he'd gotten ahold of a copy, he wouldn't tell me. He merely laughed and said how much he was going to enjoy watching me fall from my high and mighty pedestal. I hadn't realized before just how vindictive he could be."

"That doesn't mean he got the report from you."

"True. But it didn't matter. Everyone would assume I'd either been careless or intentionally supplied him with the information, and I'd never be able to prove the contrary. My reputation would have been destroyed, and there almost certainly would have been bar proceedings. I couldn't risk that, so I had to act quickly."

"So it was you at his house that night?" I said.

"You insult us both by having to ask that. The point is, you wouldn't be helping me at all by disclosing what you suspect. It would only make the case against me stronger."

"And you're not at all concerned about finding Gallagher's killer?"

"Why should I be? Rory meant little to me, and my best chance of escaping conviction is to leave matters as they now stand, with a bumbling prosecutor and a wholly circumstantial case. I believe you're right—that what Rory found *is* what got him killed, whether or not someone from Atria was responsible. But I have no confidence that the authorities will find the murderer even if you go to them. The only thing I'm confident of is that it wasn't me."

I knew she was probably right, at least as far as the police were concerned. But I was still troubled by the implications of keeping what I knew to myself. "What about the matters discussed in your report? Don't you think they deserve to be made public? What Atria was doing is wrong."

"In a technical sense, yes. But as I said, I counseled them to stop. And even if the law was violated, who was harmed? Unless you'd like to make the case that scores of your brethren have acted irresponsibly by prescribing Lucitrol, or that the drug hasn't helped some of their patients."

She had me there. The blame lay just as much with the drug companies as with the doctors who repeatedly fell for their shenanigans, allowing themselves to be visited and flattered and even lied to in exchange for junkets and free samples. And as I'd explained to Bjorn, most psychiatric prescriptions were based on little more than guesswork anyway.

"All right," I said. "But there's still Hallie to think about. And identifying the person who attacked her. If, as we've been speculating, it wasn't you or someone at Atria who killed Gallagher, then who else might it be?"

"Once again, I'm afraid I can't help you with that question. But if you're still interested in finding out, I suggest you look to your own discipline."

I cocked my head in her direction. "What are you implying?"

"I'll let you think about that. And now, I really must be getting back to my work."

I was being dismissed. Again.

She rose to show me out. I collected my cane and followed her to the door. When we were only steps away she stopped abruptly and turned around, as though she had one last thing to say. "Forget something?" I said nastily. "Or did you finally decide to develop a conscience?"

Needless to say, I was completely unprepared for what happened next.

Before I knew what was happening she took two steps toward me.

And grasping me by the back of my neck sunk her lips harshly into mine.

# TWENTY-THREE

I don't know how I stumbled out of Jane's apartment with the taste of her tongue in my mouth and her laughter still echoing in my ears. Or how I got back downstairs. All I know is that my nerves were on fire. I barely gave a thought to Jane's receptionist as I careened past his guard station, nearly knocking over an elderly man in a tweed suit in my haste to escape. He shook his fist angrily at me as I lunged ahead. Beyond him the glass door to the street yawned, a portal of pure white light. I took the ten steps toward it in a bound, yanking the door handle open and nearly collapsing onto the street outside.

I found my way to an alley at the building's side, filled with broken glass and the stench of urine, and retched. All of my senses seemed to be stretched. What was wrong with me? I'd been kissed by a woman before, why was it having this effect on me? Thoughts of Hallie suddenly came over me. Hallie lying comatose in her hospital bed. Hallie calling to me. I needed to get to her right away. To apologize for what I had done—for what I so wanted to do—with Jane. I fished my handkerchief from my pocket and wiped the bile from my mouth, tossing it into a nearby Dumpster.

Outside the alley the sidewalks were teeming with people. I thrust my cane forward and struck up with the fast-moving crowd. The walking seemed to be doing me some good. My heart rate was slowing and the nausea was wearing off. Heads bobbed up and down in my path: male heads, female heads, heads with cell phones stuck to their ears. I was going faster now, almost gliding. Under the Metra tracks and up the small incline to the Randolph Street Bridge, sunlight glinting on the turgid water below. Past the fortress edifice of the Lyric Opera with its grinning bas-relief muses. Down another, steeper hill, moving even faster.

Was I going to make the light at Wacker? No, there wasn't time. Come up to the curb and halt, follow the progress of the cars rushing by.

An attractive woman in a plaid coat was stopped next to me. I tipped my Mets cap at her. "Beautiful day, isn't it?"

"Ye-es," she agreed, giving me a thoroughly puzzled glance. "But be careful. It's not safe to cross yet."

"I know that," I said.

Which is when I realized.

*I did know.*

And not just because I was hearing things.

I shut my eyes and squeezed them. Said a small prayer before opening them again. But it was true. Across the street, as clear as day, the pedestrian signal was blinking its orange "Don't Walk." Filled with encouragement, I stepped forward to get a better view.

The woman in the plaid coat didn't like this. "Didn't you hear me? Are you deaf, too?" Still standing by my side, she seized my arm. "Come on. You better let me help you."

I tore it away in annoyance. "I don't need your help."

"Fine," she said, with an acid expression. "Go ahead and get yourself killed."

The light changed and the foot traffic surged forward, the woman in the plaid coat going out of her way to leave me behind. I swung my cane out onto the asphalt before I remembered I didn't need it anymore. I looked down at my feet, still moving with a blind man's hesitant gait. I was out of practice, that much was apparent. All I needed to do was to look ahead, trust my peripheral vision to spot any obstacles in my path. I squared my shoulders and let the cane clatter to the ground, practically running onward.

At the far corner, I stopped once more, swirling in pleasure as I drank in the scene. The broad sweep of the Loop spread out before me, the 'L' trains making their slot-car journey around it, the afternoon sun reflected everywhere on canyons of granite and glass. It was all as I remembered it, and infinitely more beautiful. Even the trash in the gutters seemed shiny and new. I looked rapidly around and for the first time in two years found myself reading signs at a distance, hungrily exploring the faces of the people passing by. If I could, I would have canceled all my other senses just to savor the sensation of seeing—splendid, magnificent sense—this second time around.

How had the miracle happened? Then I remembered. Melissa. My Indian goddess. My savior from an otherwise cramped and hopeless existence. I couldn't wait to tell her how wrong she'd been. The pills *had* worked, and even better on me than anyone had predicted. I'd aced her precious study, proved myself the most worthy of test subjects. On my way back I'd stop and let her see for herself. But first I had a detour to make.

I hurried east, past the clownish facade of the State of Illinois Building—its pink and blue panels hadn't gotten any more dignified in the interim—the massive Corinthian columns of City Hall, the slate and steel expanse of Daley Plaza. Past the old Marshall Field's building and the stately Harold Washington Center. At Michigan, I had to sprint forward to beat the light before it changed, congratulating myself on my speed. I had a destination in mind and could hardly wait to get there. The daily party in Millennium Park was in full swing as I jogged up the shrub-lined steps to the Cloud Gate, easily bypassing the skateboarders clacking up and down in violation of several signed warnings. I thought about how long this brief journey would have taken me before, when I had to constantly stop and slow my step to listen for potential hazards. Now I was flying.

I won't say that my face shocked me, though it did seem older in the mirrored surface of the Bean, near where I'd sat waiting for Hallie—when was it?—only a week ago. There were more and deeper lines around my mouth than I recalled, and a tiredness that wasn't explained simply by my irregular sleep habits. My hair had receded another half inch or so, but there was still plenty of it to go around. I noted with satisfaction that I still had relatively few gray ones.

Then it was on to the big treat I'd been saving for myself. I mounted the hill next to the Pritzker Pavilion and caught my first clear glimpse of it, a crescent of pure ultramarine stretching as far as the eye could see. Viewing it once more in all its glory, I laughed out loud. A band of purple haze lay low over the horizon where the water met the sky, and small whitecaps danced across its surface under a frieze of rose-tinted clouds. Nearer to me, the elms, oaks, and maples of Grant Park were ablaze in fall color, all the more brilliant because of their proximity to the deep, blue, absurdly gorgeous Lake.

I ran from place to place, giddy with happiness. Each step seemed to bring me to a fresh rediscovery. The pink granite of Buckingham Fountain shimmering under its frothy cascade, the sailboats bobbing like corks in Monroe Harbor, the fall flowers planted in neat rows amid lawns of riotous green. I ate it all up like a starving man, marveling at the variety of the universe, its multiple sources of joy.

I must have wandered for hours, never tiring of what I was seeing, smiling madly at the amused passersby, who acted as though I was putting on a show for them. If they thought I was insane, let them. How many of them understood—could possibly understand—what it was like? I was liberated beyond my wildest imagining, freed at last from my dull prison. Everything suddenly seemed possible. No longer consigned to groping, my future had become immeasurably bright.

It was only toward dusk, just after I had clambered down a staircase south of the Art Institute, that I remembered Hallie again. I swore heartily at myself as I jumped a small ledge, regaining my footing on a rough gravel path. In all this time, I had forgotten the most important thing: seeing her for the very first time. And Louis. My treasured boy. How could I have forgotten about him, too? It was too late to catch a plane that night, but I had a recent photo of him in my wallet. It would take only seconds to pull it out. But it appeared I had misplaced it. In the spot where I usually kept his picture, there was only a blank square of paper. Where was it? I looked through everything again and couldn't find it. I began tearing through the wallet's contents, tossing credit cards and receipts and IDs over my shoulder in my frenzy to find the missing photograph. It was nowhere to be found. I went down on hands and knees to search again through the items I'd scattered on the ground, scrabbling in the dust and dirt between massive tree roots.

And that's when I noticed it: a slight tremor in the ground, coupled with the rumble of thunder. I looked up to see if a storm was forming, but there was no sign of one. The sky was as clear as liquid, without a disturbance in sight. The rumbling grew louder.

Just then, I also became aware of a man's voice shouting. "Are you crazy?! Get the hell out of there!"

I stood up and looked around, puzzled. What was he talking about? I didn't see anything alarming. Only the lovely twilight and the lights of the city beginning to wink on over the hilltop to my side. "There's nothing to worry about," I called back. "I'm OK."

"Like hell you are," came the voice again, closer than before. I heard the cranking of machinery and the sound of someone running rapidly toward me. "Didn't you hear me, you fucking fool? Get off the tracks!"

The earth beneath me was shaking harder now, and I wondered if we were having an earthquake on top of the thunderstorm. And a traffic jam. Someone was leaning on a horn. *Waaaaaaahhhhh! Waaaaaaahhhh!* I put my hands up to cover my ears.

Two searchlights appeared among the trees, along with another, smaller light at an angle. It was bouncing up and down, matching its rhythm to the footsteps that were now galloping toward me.

*Waaaaaaaahhhh!*

I smelled gas fumes and felt a violent onrush of air just as a rough hand seized me by the collar and jerked me out of the way.

The next thing I knew I was waking up with an itch in my arm. I rolled over to scratch it with my eyes still closed only to find that I was stuck. Something was holding me down. I tried to scratch the itch again and discovered that my wrists were bound. I opened my eyes a slit and saw that I was in a dark room. There was a sharp odor to the air, both sickly sweet and familiar, and the sound of trays being rattled in a corridor. I passed my tongue over my lips, which were parched and raw, and opened my eyes a bit more. A wavering oblong of light appeared to my right.

It took me a few more seconds to realize that the sounds I was hearing were hospital sounds.

The itch was becoming unbearable and I needed to pee, so I called out. "Hello? Is anyone there?"

A pair of rubber-soled shoes clicked up a few minutes later and a shape eclipsed the pale rectangle of the doorway. "Yes? Did you call?"

"Are you a nurse?"

"Oh, good. You're awake. Yes, I'm a nurse."

She switched on an overhead light. The sudden blaze sent drill bits into my eyes. I quickly shut them against the pain. She must have seen me cringe because she rushed to apologize. "I'm so sorry. They said you were blind."

"Can you . . . can you please shut that thing off?" I begged.

"Yes, yes of course." She flicked the switch, and the room became mercifully dim again. I relaxed back into the pillow. "I'm sorry," she repeated. "I didn't realize it would hurt you." She came over to my side and put a hand on my forehead. "Are you feeling any better?"

I looked up and realized with a crushing sensation that I couldn't see any of her features. I nodded and asked with apprehension, "What happened to me?"

"You went on a little sleepwalking expedition. Probably because of the concussion. No, don't try to sit up yet. I'll elevate the headrest for you. Can I get you some water to drink?"

"Yes, but you'll have to untie my hands first. And I have to urinate."

I felt her fingers slipping the knots on the restraints. "Don't mind these. We only did it to make sure you'd stay put. You were pretty disoriented when they dropped you off downstairs. Here now, you're free. But careful with the left arm. There's an IV line in it."

She placed a plastic bottle next to me on the bedclothes and went off to allow me some privacy, returning some moments later with a cup full of water and ice. I took it in both hands, found the straw with my mouth, and lapped at it greedily.

"That's good. From the look of things I'd say you're still dehydrated. Is it OK if I take your stats?"

I nodded. "What's your name?"

"Naomi."

While Naomi took my temperature I felt around my face. There was stubble on my cheek, but no cuts or bruises I could detect. I flexed my shoulders and wiggled my toes. I wasn't broken or sore. Other than being back in the gloom, I felt fine. Just to be sure of where things stood, I waved my hand back and forth in front of my face, sensing only the faintest of shadows.

"What time is it?" I croaked.

"Four in the morning. They brought you in around eight last night."

She slipped on a blood-pressure cuff and took my pulse. "You'll live. One thirty-two over a hundred. Pretty good for a guy who almost got flattened by a commuter train."

"What do you mean?"

Naomi readjusted my IV and went to stand at the foot of the bed. "Don't you remember? You were in the middle of the Illinois Central tracks, just south of the Van Buren Street station. God only knows what you thought you were doing. You were just lucky there was a South Shore employee checking the lines when you climbed down from the platform. They'd still be picking up the pieces if he hadn't pulled you out of the way in time."

So that explained all the lights and the noise.

"And my things?" I asked dully, remembering now how I had thrown away most of the contents of my wallet.

"Gone with the wind, as they say. Except for your clothes and the picture of the little boy. You were still clutching it in your hand when they put you on the stretcher. It's right here on the nightstand. What an adorable little face. Is he yours?"

I felt myself starting to shake.

"Oh, honey," Naomi said, returning to my side and putting a hand on my arm. "I'm sorry. What a big mouth I have. I shouldn't have told you all those things. Don't worry. You're going to be just fine. And I know one little fellow who's going to be very happy to see his father again. Speaking of which, do you want us to contact them for you?"

"Who?" I asked, wiping the back of my hand across my cheek.

"Why, your family. I'm sure they must be very worried. But until you woke up we didn't know who to call." She gave me a tissue.

I took it and blew. "No. I, uh . . . don't live with them. It's better that they don't find out."

"Are you sure? You look like you could really use somebody to hold you right now. Isn't there anyone I can call?"

There was. But she was somewhere far away where no phone could reach her.

Tim the resident came by to see me first thing in the morning. "I've got to hand it to you. You really know how to do concussion. Your pupils were as big as eight balls when they wheeled you in last night. And you were babbling away about some Indian chick and *Sleeping Beauty* and catching a rabbit before it escaped."

I was sitting up in bed with a breakfast tray over my lap. I forked a mouthful of powdered eggs into my mouth and made chewing motions. "Are you sure it was a concussion?"

"I'm still waiting on the results of another scan, but it's the most likely explanation. You took a helluva blow on the old noggin last week. Didn't I warn you about a delayed reaction?"

I replaced the fork on the tray. "True. But the scan you took then was clean, you said so. How much do you want to bet you won't find anything new?"

"How much money do you have? Oh, wait, I forgot. The switchman said you were merrily throwing away everything in your wallet when he spotted you."

I shot him an evil look and took a sip of something masquerading as orange juice. "With all due deference to your vast experience, I've treated people with concussions, and it wasn't anything like that."

"How so, ancient one?"

"I wasn't just confused or disoriented. I was seeing things. Things that weren't really there."

Lying in the darkened room for the last several hours, with nothing to do but replay the previous day's events, I'd come to several conclusions. First, that what had happened to me after leaving Jane's place didn't fit the symptoms of any concussion I'd ever heard of. Second, that I must have been walking around in a waking dream. I explained this to Tim.

"OK," Tim said. "But explain to me how a blind man 'sees' things in a dream. Sounds, smells, stuff like that I get. But you say you were literally experiencing visions."

"That's easy," I said. "The same thing happens to me when I go to sleep at night. My mind isn't blind. For that matter, technically speaking, neither are my eyes. The only thing that's missing is a working connection between the two. But in here"—I tapped my head—"I can still see things I remember from when I was sighted. The only thing I can't do is visualize someone or something I've never laid eyes on. You, for instance."

"I won't comment on everything you're missing," Tim said.

"And that's why I know I wasn't just confused." I took him through the old man in the lobby, the woman in the plaid coat, the street scenes, and the views of Lake Michigan and Grant Park. "Everything I saw—or thought I was seeing—was based on memory, probably dating from the year after I moved to Chicago. I did a lot of walking back then because I was dealing with something . . . something personal, and it seemed to help. In and around the Loop, up and down the lakefront, and when I had the time, farther afield. Those images, the places I went and the people I saw, are still sitting in my brain, and because of my photographic memory, just as clear today as when I first saw them. Yesterday, I wasn't really 'seeing' anything. I was remembering. Except for the one thing I couldn't remember."

"Which was?"

I handed him Louis's picture, which was tucked into the bed-clothes beside me.

"I won't ask whose kid this is," Tim said. "Though it doesn't take a Mendel to figure it out."

"I'll tell you about it over drinks sometime. The point is, I've never seen the face in that photograph. So I couldn't see it yesterday in my dream."

"I'm with you so far, but what do you think accounts for this extended dream state if not a concussion?"

"That's simple, too," I said. "I was drugged."

"Seriously?" Tim exclaimed. "That's what you think?"

I nodded.

"But who would have done that to you?"

There was only one person I could think of, and she was probably still enjoying the joke. But I didn't say anything about it to Tim, merely securing his promise to run some blood tests. If I was right, the tests would prove it, and I could decide what to do about the stunt then. In the meantime, I promised to be an obedient geezer and rest quietly in my hospital bed.

I spent a boring morning listening to daytime TV and was picking through a stew of questionable origin when Tim returned, bursting with youthful excitement.

"Holy shades of Timothy Leary, you were right!" he cried.

"What was it?" I asked, though I thought I already knew.

"I think I'm going to regret what I said to you about a concussion. It was LSD. Somebody slipped you acid."

"You're sure of it?"

"Absolutely. You'd metabolized most of it, but there were still enough traces in your bloodstream to make a positive identification. But what clued you in?"

"You don't really expect me to tell you that, do you? Let's just say I had a misspent youth."

"The thing I don't understand is, how did it get into your system?

Those little squares with the cartoon characters are hard to mistake, even for someone like you. You'd have to be tricked into licking it."

"Now who's setting himself up for criminal prosecution?" I asked dryly. "And it didn't have to be a tab. You can put LSD in a pill. In fact, it probably won't be long until it's approved once again for medical use. I was just reading about a Harvard study where it was being used as an experimental treatment for chronic headaches and—"

I stopped and sat straight up.

*Experimental treatment.*

*Pill.*

"What's the matter?" Tim asked. "You look like you just saw a ghost."

"Do you know where my clothes are?" I asked quickly, nearly knocking over the tray table with my lunch in my hurry to get up.

"Should be right over here," he said, going over to a door in the wall and opening it. "What do you want?"

I threw off the bedcovers and stood, hiking the hospital gown around my shoulders so it wouldn't fall off. "Whatever you can find that's still in my pockets."

"OK. Let's see. Phone. Change. Bottle of pills."

"The phone and the bottle, please."

He delivered them both to my trembling hands. I put the bottle on the bed and switched on my phone and swiped through the icons until I found the one I'd used to photograph the bottle the week before. The photo that I'd stored under the name White Rabbit.

"What are you doing?" Tim asked.

"Be patient. You'll see."

Double tapping to get in, I took another photo and asked Weary to find the same image among my saved results. "Searching . . ." she said. "This may take a few minutes."

It felt more like a century.

Finally Weary announced, "No results. Would you like me to search the Internet?"

"No. Try again," I said with mounting impatience.

A few minutes later, the same reply came back. "No results among saved images." I sat back down on the bed in shock.

"You want to tell me what's going on?" Tim said.

I blinked several times in disbelief. "It looks like that rabbit escaped after all," I said. "But maybe now I know where it disappeared to."

# TWENTY-FOUR

The next several days went by in a whirl of inactivity. For me, that is. At first, it was too early to call in the police—all I had was a hunch, after all—but I kept everyone else busy: Tim getting tests run on the bottle of pills that had been substituted for mine, Bjorn performing a thorough background check on the individual I now suspected of doping me, Josh making some discreet inquiries among our colleagues. When Bjorn's preliminary report came back, confirming some of my suspicions but adding a whole new layer of intrigue, I also put in calls to Tony Di Marco and Rusty Halloran, who were only too happy to help.

Other than that, there wasn't much I could contribute to the effort, so after going out and buying another cane—at the rate I was losing them, I ought to have been buying futures in fiberglass—I did what I ought to have done long before and went to visit Hallie. In the last several days, they'd transferred her from the ICU to a private room on the hospital's fifth floor, where most of the neurological patients were housed. I exited the elevator, asked at the nurses' station which room she was in, and didn't object when one of them offered to walk me over, leaving my cane against the wall just outside the door.

Upon entering, I was immediately attacked by a dog.

I may not have done enough before now to explain my aversion to the canine species, which probably has its roots in some long-forgotten childhood episode. The fact is that dogs and I have always gotten along like—well, dogs. I don't like them and they don't like me, a mutual antipathy that is usually expressed on the dog side by hysterical barking, jaw snapping, or aggressive exploration of my privates. Blindness only made matters worse, since I couldn't always be certain whether the beast baring its fangs to me was a five-pound Chihuahua or an eighty-pound Doberman. This one's size, however, was no mystery. It nearly knocked me down when it leaped up to prevent me from coming into the room, and was now emitting a menacing growl at my feet.

"Lola!" came a sharp command. "Bad girl. You know you're not supposed to do that. Get over here and lie down." Then to me: "I'm so sorry. She's been trained not to do that sort of thing, but she forgets sometimes."

Lola quieted and took herself off, toenails scratching on the floor, to where her owner seemed to be seated a few yards to my left. I took a step in that direction. "No need to apologize. I seem to have that effect on them. You must be Hallie's brother."

"That's me," he said, rising from his chair. "Gerry Sanchez."

I figured he was waiting for me to take his outstretched hand and said, "I'm sorry, but I've never really figured out how blind people do it."

"Are we talking about sex?" he said. "It's really not all that complicated."

I laughed. "I meant shake with each other."

Gerry laughed, too, a mirthful sound from deep in his belly. "So you're the mystery man we've all been wondering about. What took you so long? Here, try this. Come closer and wave it around. It's not pretty, but it gets the job done."

I did as he asked and felt my hand captured in a powerful grip.

"Mark Angelotti," I said.

"I know your name. Hallie talks about you all the time. I expect the first thing you'll want to do is see her."

He guided me over to her bedside and put my hand on hers. It was warm and pulsating with the slow rise and fall of her chest. I stayed there quietly for a while, breathing steadily in and out myself.

"She's gonna be all right, you know," Gerry said from beside me. "The doctor said so. He was in here half an hour ago, checking on her. They're going to start easing her out of her sleep tomorrow."

I nodded dumbly, then remembered he couldn't see it. "That's great," I said, reclaiming my vocal chords. "Are you the only one here?"

"At the moment, yes. My mom and sisters are downstairs grabbing lunch. The security guard, too. I told him I'd sic Lola on anyone who tried to get near Hallie. I guess she actually listened to me for a change."

I stood there awkwardly, not knowing what to say.

"Mind if I ask you a question?" Gerry said, filling the silence.

"So long as it's not how I use a knife and fork."

Gerry gave off another belly laugh and clapped me on the shoulder. "You're all right, man. Remind me to share some ways to answer questions like that. I've been doing it my whole life and know how to shut them down fast. No, what I wanted to know is why you waited all this time to come around? Were you afraid we'd bite your head off?"

"Something like that."

"Well, you shouldn't have worried."

"Why not? If it hadn't been for me . . ." I trailed off morosely.

Gerry sighed. "Look, I barely know you, but would you mind if I gave you a piece of advice?"

"Depends. Will there be a fee?"

"Uh-uh. That's your gig, not mine. But as one blind dude to another?"

"If it's the party line, don't bother. I've heard it all before and it hasn't made much of an impression."

"I'll bet it hasn't. But go lighter on the movement. More often than not, the organizations are headed by lifers like me, so they can't fully relate to what it's like to be a newbie. And with all the negative stereotypes out there, they have to spin it like it's no big deal. Me, I'm a realist. I've never known anything else, but it's gotta be a bitch getting used to."

"I've used heartier expletives than that. But if we're staying away from propaganda, what is it you wanted to say?"

"Just this. I don't know what Hallie's told you about us growing up, but my family went out of their way not to shelter me. You want to ride a bike? Great. Take the 'L' by yourself? No problem. The flip side of that is that when I got hurt—fell down and broke my arm, or came home with a black eye after some piece of *mierda* tried to mess with me—they didn't give me much sympathy either. If you're gonna live your life like anyone else, you've got to accept that shit happens."

"Even to your sister?"

"Even when it's my sister. That's what I've been trying to tell you. Nobody here blames you for being out late with Hallie, or even for where the two of you were when you were attacked. If we did, we'd all be big fat hypocrites."

Maybe he was just being generous, but it sounded sincere.

"Wanna know what else I think?" Gerry said.

"I have a feeling my wants are irrelevant to this discussion."

"I think you gotta give it more time. You've been at this what—two years? I've heard it takes a lot longer to get acclimated, to the point where you really start forgetting. But they say it happens—eventually."

I prayed he was right. "The problem is, will anyone else ever forget?"

"Yeah well, no sugar-coating on that score, either. Lots of 'em won't. You just gotta pick the right people to hang out with. Like my sister, since we're on that subject. And yeah, you can consider that a hint. Or, if you need more of my advice, a very strong push in that direction."

"Or you and your brothers will come after me with a baseball bat?" I said only half in jest.

"I think we've already seen enough of that action lately. And now, before I start preaching again, why don't I take myself off for a while? My mom and sisters haven't been getting much fresh air recently and Lola could use a potty break. I think I'll swing round to the cafeteria and we'll all go for a stroll so you can have some time alone with Hallie."

"Thanks, Gerry," I said, profoundly grateful for his forgiving attitude. Maybe it was time I stopped always anticipating the worst. And trusted that Hallie, when she knew everything, would forgive me too.

When we were finally ready to present our evidence to O'Leary, he was appropriately impressed.

"So you're saying he's been poisoning people for years?"

"That's one way of looking at it," I said. "Or you could call him the anti-poisoner."

We—Josh, Bjorn, O'Leary, and I—were gathered in a booth in the sticky recesses of the Double L, where I had just treated everyone to a round of drinks. I'd figured it was safer to meet there than in my office. If we were going to catch Gallagher's murderer, it was important that he be kept unawares, and though I had no idea what O'Leary actually looked like, he oozed cop like a squid oozes ink. When he wasn't needed at the bar, Jesus was also hovering in the background, hanging on our every word.

"And right under everyone's noses?"

I nodded a yes. I'd realized almost immediately how my pills had been switched but hadn't been prepared for the full truth. I let Bjorn explain.

"It all goes back to a murder trial you may remember. A geriatrics physician named Donald Tesma who was arrested and convicted for having engineered the deaths of scores of elderly patients in and around Chicago. The trial was sensational—front-page news here and nationally."

"I do remember this," O'Leary said. "Didn't they call him the 'Nursing Home Killer'?"

"That's right. His methods were ingenious and usually mimicked natural death in the old folks he preyed upon. Most often, he injected their IV bags with potassium chloride—salt, that is—but he sometimes used epinephrine and digitalis. In almost all cases, his victims were already frail, and it was just assumed they'd expired of previously existing conditions. He was only caught because a patient observed Tesma using a syringe on his IV bag and managed to press the call button before passing out. The authorities then began to look into other deaths at the facilities where Tesma had privileges and noticed a pattern. Eventually they exhumed the bodies of two dozen other patients whose deaths could be linked circumstantially to Tesma."

"But not directly?" O'Leary asked.

Bjorn said, "No, and that's an important point. In many cases the decomposed state of the bodies they dug up precluded saying exactly how they'd died, especially when Tesma used sodium, which is found naturally in body tissue. It was easier to identify the cause of death when he used other drugs, but the pathologists testifying for the state had to really push the science. The prosecution credited one in particular, whose name I'll save for later, as being instrumental in getting Tesma convicted."

"So he never confessed?" O'Leary again.

"No, and that's also important. Tesma insisted all along that he was innocent and kept on insisting even after his conviction was upheld on appeal. The families of the victims thought otherwise and successfully sued Tesma for all he was worth."

"Christ," O'Leary said. "And I thought doctors entered the profession to save people, not strangle them in their beds."

"Actually," Josh said through a mouthful of nuts, "it's thought that the health professions are riddled with serial killers who enter the field either because they have a pathological interest in life and death, or believe they're doing patients a favor by ending their suffering. The tragedy is these killers' crimes often get overlooked or can't be proved. Even when they leave one hospital under a cloud, with all the shortages in trained personnel it's easy for them to find work elsewhere. Sometimes they go on claiming victims for years."

"Which is another part of the story we'll get to," Bjorn said. "Anyway, you may not remember that Tesma had a son of the same name who was there for his father's entire trial and was said to be visibly distraught throughout the proceedings. The boy's mother had disappeared some years earlier—there was speculation that the father had poisoned her too—and Tesma senior was the only family he had. According to court watchers, it was the boy's testimony during the penalty phase of the case that saved his father's life. The jury wasn't prepared to orphan a child and spared Tesma the death sentence despite some serious outcry in the press. They could have spared themselves the criticism. After Tesma was sentenced to life in prison and his appeals were exhausted, he hanged himself. In the meantime, the boy had been sent to live with an aunt in St. Louis, where he finished high school. He was apparently a brilliant student and graduated first in his class, winning an academic scholarship to college. Just before he left home for his freshman year, the aunt passed away in her sleep of an apparent aneurism."

"Let me guess," Josh added, still chewing. "Her remains were cremated."

"Right-o," Bjorn answered. "From that point forward, our killer was on his own. One of the first things he did was get a legal name change, explaining to the judge who signed the order that he wanted to escape the stigma of his father's crimes and get a fresh start. After that, he completed college in three years, graduating *summa cum laude* with a degree in chemistry. Even got an award of some kind from the American Chemistry Association. From there he went on to medical school at Southern Illinois. It was around that time that he started exhibiting some troubling behavior—or at least the first time it got noticed."

"Troubling how?" O'Leary asked.

"Weird stuff, like spending extra hours cutting up cadavers in anatomy and hanging around the sickbeds of terminally ill patients. And cutting classes so that he could spend most of his time as a volunteer first responder. His grades fell off, and he began failing his courses. At the end of his second year, he was brought up on cheating charges and expelled. He never became a doctor. But as we now know, he eventually discovered an even better way to follow in his father's footsteps."

"I'll wait for that part of the story. So what first put you on to him?" O'Leary asked me.

I explained about my experimental eye treatment, my euphoric discovery that I could "see" again, and the hours I'd spent traipsing around the downtown in a walking dream, finishing up with my *Perils of Pauline* rescue from the South Shore Line. When I was through, everyone was quiet.

"I'm sorry," O'Leary said at last, breaking the silence. "I wish it had worked out for you—the drug, I mean. I'm also ready to kill the asshole who did it to you. It's amazing you weren't run over, and not just by that train."

I pretended not to notice the sympathy. "I think that's what he intended. We already know he has a good sense of humor. Take the new name he chose for himself—Graham Young. I looked it up online. The original Young was a notorious English serial killer who poisoned more than seventy victims before he was finally put away for life. Like our friend, he was a whiz at chemistry and could concoct almost any type of poison from commonly available substances. It's believed he poisoned his stepmother, although they were never able to prove it because her body was cremated. See the connection? At various times, the first Young also tried to poison his father, sister, and a school buddy, which earned him a stint in Broadmoor, the British hospital for the criminally insane. He was released as 'fully recovered' nine years later and went on to get a job at a chemical laboratory, where he proceeded to lace his coworkers' tea with thallium and antimony. During his trial, the British press dubbed him the Teacup Poisoner."

"Ugh," Bjorn shivered. "I'll remember that the next time I go for a cuppa."

I continued, "The original Graham Young was a diagnosed psychopath, and given all the evidence, I bet our Graham would fly off the scales, too. The fact that his father exhibited psychopathic tendencies lends even more support to the diagnosis. As I explained once to Hallie, the syndrome tends to run in families, with a heritability rate as high as eighty percent. There are also physiological effects associated with the condition. MRIs done on adult psychopaths have shown what appear to be significant anatomical abnormalities in the paralimbic system, the region of the brain associated with empathy and remorse. Oftentimes the trait shows up early, in childhood, in callous and unemotional behavior, and in extreme cases, in a fascination with inflicting pain. You've probably seen it on TV—the kid who pushes a sibling down the stairs or tries to skin the family cat."

O'Leary said, "You're giving me goose bumps, but I know what you're saying because I've run across the type. You can see it in their eyes—ice cold, no feeling whatsoever. I know cops who are afraid to be in the same room with them. But they can also be incredibly charming, which is what makes them so dangerous. So you think he was modeling himself on his father and this English guy?"

"Not only that, but had found a way to do them one better. After he was kicked out of medical school it was all too easy for him to get a job with Atria. The drug companies are always looking for recruits with that kind of background, and his college record was good enough that they were willing to overlook the cheating. It was the perfect cover for what he wanted to do, and his charm enabled him to shoot to the top of the company's sales force, probably gaining him access to all sorts of confidential information."

"OK," O'Leary said, "But how did you figure out that it was him who slipped you the acid?"

I took out my phone and showed everyone how the application worked. "It's a pretty sophisticated tool and picked up that both the color and the printing on the label were different from my 'White Rabbit.' There was only one time when that bottle wasn't in my possession." I told them about my fall in the corridor and Graham showing up a little later with the pills I'd lost. "He was smart enough to replace only a few of them so that no one would ever be the wiser. I had Tim get the rest of the contents tested. The other tablets were primarily . . . what they were supposed to be."

I wouldn't let Tim tell me what I'd been taking—drug versus placebo—since the knowledge might have gotten me kicked out of Melissa's study.

"Wouldn't it have been easier to keep the same bottle?" Josh said.

"I think that was also part of the joke. Not knowing about the technology on my phone, he wanted to lord it over me that I wouldn't be able to tell what he had done. He also wanted my hoped-for death to appear accidental, which is why he didn't try to poison me directly. I would just go walking out into traffic or do something else to get myself killed, and everyone would attribute it to the fact that I'm blind. The plan wasn't foolproof—I might have spent the whole time tripping more or less safely at home—but he'd still have had his fun. That's the way psychopaths' minds work. They view other people as test subjects to be manipulated like puppets. In his worst-case scenario I'd survive, but he'd still have had the pleasure of jerking me around."

"All right, I'm buying that he pulled the switcheroo on you," O'Leary said. "But how do you get from there to his being Gallagher's killer?"

"It goes back to the trial of his father. Jane was the lead prosecutor during the trial and, based on what Hallie told me, the main reason the state obtained a conviction in a case that could have gone either way. If I'm right, he was trying to frame her." I went back over the salient facts: Hallie's worry that Jane was withholding information from her, what Mrs. Van Wagner saw outside Gallagher's townhome—I was now thoroughly chagrined by my role in casting doubt on her statement—the erasure of Gallagher's records, my discovery of Atria's misdeeds, and Jane's belated admission that she was trying to shield both herself and her client from a public-relations disaster.

"It's too much of a coincidence that Gallagher was about to go public with some pretty damaging information about Atria just before he was killed. I'm guessing Young was the source of the leak. He must have helped himself to a copy of Jane's report at company headquarters and passed it on to Gallagher, knowing that Gallagher couldn't resist tipping his hand to Jane. Either she'd react in a way that would make her look guilty, or Young would make sure the police found out about the story Gallagher was planning to publish, thus supplying a motive. He then met with Gallagher himself, which is when he fed him the Lucitrol."

"Can you prove it?" O'Leary asked.

"Not to a fault, but the two of them were seen having drinks together later that night, after Gallagher left Gene and Georgetti's." Armed with a photograph of Young, Bjorn had gone back to the tavern where Gallagher had been spotted and gotten a positive ID on the salesman.

I went on, "Young used Lucitrol to poison Gallagher precisely so that the police would suspect Jane, whose victory for Atria was all over the news. He either surmised that Gallagher had a heart condition from what was widely known about the man's habits, or he wangled the information from Gallagher's cardiologist or someone on her staff while he was on his sales rounds. You wouldn't believe how good this guy is at sniffing out details about people."

"I can swear to that," Josh interjected. "He's like the CIA, the FBI, and the state troopers all rolled into one. I wouldn't be surprised if he knows which side of the bed I sleep on."

My mouth was getting dry from all the talking, so I took a sip from my drink. "Young was probably counting on an immediate autopsy, and when that didn't happen, he tipped Gallagher's nephew so that the body would be exhumed. Although I doubt he planned it that way initially, it had the bonus of making Jane look even guiltier."

"Still, a pretty elaborate plan," O'Leary observed.

"Again, that's how these people's minds work. Young is obviously highly intelligent. He'd probably score at genius level if you gave him an IQ test. If I had to guess, he's been stalking Jane for years, waiting for his moment. Killing her wouldn't have been good enough for him. He'd want her to suffer utter ruin and imprisonment—the same way his father did. And if he could manage it, on largely circumstantial evidence so that Jane would go on protesting her innocence to the bitter end. We know he was there throughout his father's trial. If he was already a budding psychopath, it would have been immensely galling to him that his father was being punished simply for knocking off a few geriatric patients. Getting back at the prosecutors who put his father away is probably an obsession for him."

"Was revenge also behind the attack on Hallie, then?" Josh asked.

"Maybe. She was a junior staffer during the trial and rarely in the courtroom. At the time, she may have escaped his notice. It's more likely he went after Hallie and me because he was enraged over the result of the hearing. But it would explain why Hallie knew her attacker. She told me how much sympathy she felt for the junior Tesma and how she'd never forget the look on his face while he was testifying for his father. When she shouted 'You!' at our attacker, I think it was him she recognized. And there's another thing you should know about."

I reported on my phone conversation with Di Marco, who supplied the fact that Jimmy O'Hara, the prosecutor who had dropped dead after "forgetting" to take his heart medication, was also at Tesma's trial, acting as Jane's second chair. "I doubt there's any way to prove it after all these years, but it wouldn't surprise me if Young got to him, too. Which brings us to the last piece of evidence. Bjorn, why don't you tell him the name of the pathologist who testified for the state at Tesma's trial?"

"Sidney Levin."

"Is that name supposed to mean something to me?" O'Leary said. "Though now that I think about it, I may have known him. Friend of my stepfather. Family lived down the block from us. But the old man must have died years ago. You're not saying Young had a hand in that as well?"

"Not him, but I think Young's been playing games with his son." I gave them a brief outline of the case Rusty had recruited me to help him with. "Remember how I said Young was the anti-poisoner? After we discovered his true identity, I became convinced he was using his position to make patients ill, and that the delivery mechanism was the free samples he gave out, which could end up in patient hands without going through a pharmacy. With his background in chemistry and access to the company's packaging, it would have been easy for him to doctor, so to speak, the samples. The trouble was, why hadn't anyone noticed? If he was substituting poison for the drugs, surely it would have aroused suspicion at some point, if not among the prescribing doctors, then among the families of the victims. Why hadn't any of them been autopsied before now? The deaths of Ira Levin's two young patients gave me the answer."

# TWENTY-FIVE

"**Y**ou mean he was supplying them with placebos?" Josh said excitedly, immediately grasping the implications.

It seemed like a long shot, but when I first learned about Levin's father providing crucial testimony during the Tesma case, it triggered a memory of something the psychiatrist had said back when Rusty and I were first interviewing him. The antidepressant Levin prescribed for Danny Carpenter was Atria's best-selling Placeva. And when Danny's parents stopped paying for the boy's treatment, Levin kept up his patient's supply by giving him free samples.

"I don't get it," O'Leary said. "If it's a placebo, it's harmless, right? So how can it hurt people?"

I allowed Josh to take over for me. "It wouldn't, unless it was substituted for something the patient couldn't live without—like a heart medication. Or, depending on various factors, an antidepressant. Scientists aren't exactly sure why some people are affected more severely than others, except that antidepressants enhance mood-regulating chemicals in the brain. It's theorized that an abrupt deprivation of those chemicals causes symptoms similar to an addict undergoing withdrawal, though the drugs aren't habit forming like heroin or cocaine. Whatever the reason, shutting off the supply can mean a rapid return to anxiety and depression."

I jumped back in. "It's often worse when the person has been taking the drug for some time, and when it's the kind that's easily cleared from the body. That's why psychiatrists don't advise quitting an antidepressant just like that," I said with a snap of my fingers. "The safer course is to taper off gradually. Danny Carpenter didn't have that opportunity. Or the other victim—the girl." I frowned, thinking of what it must have been like for the two of them. The sudden return to the depressed state that had brought them to Levin originally. Their conviction, perhaps, that they were doomed to spend the rest of their lives that way. Coupled with the usual impulsivity of teenagers and whatever other burdens were weighing them down, it was a potentially lethal combination.

"And you can prove he killed them, too?" O'Leary said.

I shook my head. "I can't say for sure what was going through their minds, or even if the sudden withdrawal of the medication 'caused' their suicides in a legal sense, but it can't have helped. The only thing we know for sure is the Placeva samples Young left at Levin's office weren't what they appeared to be. I had Rusty send them out to a private lab for testing. Over half were just sugar pills. Young was experimenting on Levin's patients, waiting to see what would happen—and hoping things would pan out so that Levin would get sued, just like Young's father."

"But why wait until now? You said Levin had a spotless record before the Carpenter kid died."

"Lack of opportunity. Levin was on a different salesman's beat. It wasn't until the other fellow's retirement six months ago that Young took over his accounts. I bet you'll find Young engineered it that way. You can ask Levin for the details. He's anxious to cooperate with the authorities to clear his name." If nothing else, I could rest happy that I'd helped him clear his conscience.

"And you think Young's been doing this for years?"

"Again, nothing that will be easy to prove," I said. "But giving a job like Young's to a psychopath is like putting a money launderer in charge of Fort Knox. I have a hard time believing he limited himself to just Levin's patients. And if I'm right that his *modus operandi* was surreptitiously removing his victims' life-saving medications, it was an ingenious scheme and one that was almost guaranteed to go undiscovered. In the worst case, where someone died and the absence of the drug was discovered on autopsy, the natural assumption would be that the deceased simply missed a dose. People forget to take their pills all the time. It would take a mighty paranoid coroner to look any further."

Josh said, "But just on the off chance we might find something, I went around yesterday collecting more free samples from our colleagues." He rattled a plastic bag. "They're all here waiting for you."

"All right," O'Leary said, grunting. "I'm sold. The question is whether it's enough to convince the boys up in Lake County. If it was a local prosecutor like Di Marco, I'd know how to get Young arrested fast, but it's in their hands for the time being. First thing we'll need is a warrant to search his place. You have any idea where he lives?"

Bjorn piped up with the address, in suburban Barrington.

O'Leary groaned. "Which means outside Cook County. I'll have to get the cooperation of the local cops, too. This is going to take a few days. In the meantime, Angelotti"—he poked me in the chest for emphasis—"you stay far out of his way. I don't want him catching on to anything and I sure as hell don't want the medics to be peeling you off a sidewalk somewhere—again."

"Don't worry," I assured him. "I promise to watch my back. And I don't plan on being anywhere but at home or in the hospital. I don't want to miss being there when Hallie wakes up." I thought of one more thing. "What about these?" I asked O'Leary, displaying the bottle with my pills. "Do you need them as evidence?"

"It's against protocol, but I think we can get by on the test of the contents your junior colleague performed. Unless Young is stupider than we think, he wouldn't have left any fingerprints on the bottle, and it's been tainted by you carrying it around all this time. Besides," he said, putting a hand on my shoulder, "I'd still like to think there's a happy outcome for you in all this."

"Thanks," I said, re-pocketing the bottle. "Just don't count on me becoming your star eyewitness."

As it turned out, I didn't have to wait long for word about Hallie. As I was downing the last of my drink, Jesus came over to announce that his cousin

Gerry'd just phoned. Hallie had started to stir and even opened her eyes several times. It appeared she was finally coming out of it. I did a quick pat-down of my appearance, deciding that my three-day-old beard probably made me look less like a leading man than a registered sex offender, and that my shirt could use changing too. I wanted to look my best when she first saw me, especially next to the competition presently seated at my table. The bar was only a ten-minute walk from my apartment. If I hustled I could be shaved, showered, and back at her bedside in no time.

Bjorn was also making preparations to leave, so I told him I'd see him over there.

"Uh . . . I don't think so," he said. "I've got somewhere else to toddle off to. Please give Hallie my apologies and tell her I'll be by soon." I wondered at this but was secretly pleased.

Josh gave me a hand to the door. "We'll talk some more later," he said sternly into my ear. "I didn't want to say anything in front of the others, but I could write a whole psychology textbook about what happened to you the other day."

"You're making some kind of point about subconscious desire?" I said.

"One, it's fair to say, the Freudians would have had a field day with. If you recall, I warned you about getting your hopes up."

"I'm fine. As they say, nothing ventured, nothing gained."

"Sure. And while you were telling us about your trip to Disney World, you didn't look like your whole world had just come crumbling down on you. Even O'Leary, hardened cop that he is, wanted to hug you. Do yourself a favor and tell Melissa you're finished."

I shook my head. "Out of the question."

"How did I know you'd remain stubborn?"

"It's not that," I protested. "I made a commitment. Even if the drug doesn't do me any good it might help somebody else with my disease to know why. That's what being an experimental subject is all about. I have to see it through to the end."

"Melissa would be the first person to tell you to quit if it was making you crazy."

"Which I swear it's not. On bibles, if necessary."

That at least produced a chuckle. "As your friend, I'll forgo that requirement. You're already treading on thin ice where perjury is concerned as it is. All right. I won't bring up the subject again. Just remember there's always a sleeve here if you need one. And an ample one at that. Go on. Get out of here. I can see you're anxious to get prettied up and back to Hallie."

After Josh released me I set out going the few blocks east, grateful to have finally made my escape. I couldn't admit it to him, but many of the same thoughts had been running through my own mind. I just couldn't decide what to do about them. Paradoxically, it wasn't the uncertainty that was killing me—since the episode in Grant Park I'd more or less given up on Melissa's treatment having any effect. But the limbo I was in had become a comfort zone, preventing me from dusting myself off and moving ahead. I thought back to the fortune-telling game Jane had played with me and for the first time understood why the hanged man she'd described was smiling. It was the grin of an imbecile who didn't yet grasp that his time was up.

So I took it as a further sign that, rounding the corner of my block, I heard loud hammering in the yard of one of the pricey townhomes across the street. I'd been moving along quickly and still had a little time to spare, so I swung by to investigate.

"Isn't it a little early for putting up Christmas lights," I said to the person standing there.

"You think so?" a man with a thin, reedy voice answered. "Wait until there's a foot of snow on the ground a month from now. It's a 'For Sale' sign," he explained, "since I'm guessing that stick you're carrying means something." He said it like it was nothing remarkable, and I wondered why it was so easy for some people to take it in stride.

"You a realtor?" I asked.

"No, I'm the owner. I just found out I'm being transferred—to Minneapolis, where it's even warmer, thank you very much—and I'm damned if I pay a commission to one of those sharks. Why? You in the market for a place to buy?"

"I might be. Right now I live over there." I pointed in the direction of my building. "But I wouldn't mind upgrading if I could find something else in this neighborhood."

"Well, you won't find much better around here," he said, putting the hard sell on me. "Three stories, two fireplaces, a rooftop sitting area, and the chef's kitchen my wife just put in that I'll never recover a dime of. Good views, too, if that's meaningful to you."

"I couldn't live without them. You mind telling me what you're asking?"

He named a figure I didn't think was too outrageous, so I asked him when it might be possible to see it.

"You can take a tour right now if it's convenient."

"I'm afraid I'm already late for an appointment," I said. "And I'd like to have a friend along so I wouldn't be taking the place sight unseen—so to speak."

He laughed. "I like you. And I like it even better that we might be able to do a deal without agents. Come by on Saturday then, if you're free, and I'll take you around."

We set a time and exchanged cards, and I walked off, feeling that I'd taken the first steps toward loosening the chains that were holding me in place.

When I arrived upstairs the apartment was frigid, and I realized with irritation that the latch on my terrace door had come undone again. It was a good thing I'd stopped to talk to my neighbor. I wasn't sure how much longer I could stand living in such squalor. I emptied the contents of my pockets in the bowl by the door, tossed my cane on the floor, and slipped out of my shoes before crossing the room to rectify the problem. Halfway there, I froze in the middle of my steps.

Someone was standing outside. Someone tall and smoking a cigarette.

"Bjorn?" I asked with only the faintest of hopes.

"'Fraid not. Try again."

"Graham," I said in resignation.

"Right as rain." Though the voice was the same, its tone had changed, from buffoonish affability to icy hauteur. It sent a ripple of dread down my spine.

"I don't suppose this is a social call?"

"That would be a fair assumption."

Let me pause here to give full scope to the peril I found myself in. Contrary to popular lore, most criminals who set out to dispose of blind people in their homes are clever enough not to do it after nightfall, when their physical superiority can (in theory) be neutralized by the simple expedient of turning off the lights. Nor has it ever been likely—except in the overheated imaginations of Hollywood screenwriters—that the blind person would emerge the victor in the ensuing struggle. For one thing, the criminal's pupils would soon adjust to the low lighting, leaving them no more helpless or confused than they were before. For another, not all of us can count on stumbling across large kitchen knives while our assailant is in hot pursuit.

Graham, of course, had shown up in the middle of the day. That, plus the fact I lived nineteen stories up, hadn't stocked my apartment with pepper spray, and did most of my wrestling with my conscience, all combined to suggest I was a goner.

I ran rapidly through my options. Turning and running for the door behind me was the first thing that came to mind.

"In case you were thinking of making a break for it, I have a gun."

"Naturally," I said, considering now whether there was any way I could get to my phone.

"And took the liberty of disconnecting your land line."

I nodded appreciatively. "Clever of you."

"Where's your cell phone?"

"Back there."

"Cross the room slowly and get it."

I did as I was told. "Aren't you going to tell me not to try any funny business while I'm at it?" I said over my shoulder, trying to think of something—anything—I could grab to defend myself with.

"Just bring it over here and put it on the floor."

I came back and placed the phone carefully on the carpet, lifting my hands in the air as I straightened.

"Very good," Graham said. "I always took you for a quick study."

"But I'm still waiting for you to sneer and tell me I'm not as smart as I think I am."

"In the present circumstances, I think that goes without saying." Graham came around behind me and stuck something hard in the small of my back. For all I knew, it could have been a broom handle. On the other hand, I wasn't about to test the theory. "Come. Let's go outside and talk."

He marched me over and through the door and pushed me down into one of the two lawn chairs. I shivered in the chilly wind coming off the Lake. "How did you know where to find me?"

"Yelena, of course."

I should have guessed.

"You really ought to have treated her better, you know. She responds very well to basic human courtesy. You could take a lesson from your fat friend. He never has to beg her to do her job. I doubt she's going to miss you very much. If you don't mind, I'm going to tie you up."

"You're the boss. But what will you use? I don't typically keep a supply of rope on hand for visiting psychopaths."

"No problem. I borrowed some of your sheets." He began fastening my wrists to the armrests with what felt like torn-off strips of my bed-clothes. I noticed he was wearing latex gloves.

"How did you know we were on to you?" I asked.

"Your pudgy friend again. In case you hadn't realized it, he's about as capable of keeping a secret as a teenage girl. I saw him running around collecting samples and figured it out. You should have gone to the police right away."

I took this to mean he didn't know about O'Leary, which might give me something to work with if only I could delay things. "You mind telling me how you got in?"

"You should have invested in better real estate. I sprang the lock with a credit card. It's a crime how flimsy most construction is these days. With the prices they charge you'd think folks would insist on something more solid. Take this railing for instance." He gave it a little knock. "I doubt it will hold even your weight for very long."

The realization of what he was talking about made me shiver again. How was I ever going to save my neck? My only recourse was to keep him talking. He seemed awfully familiar with the premises, prompting me to speculate this wasn't the first time he'd paid them a visit. "You've been here before," I said.

"Yes," he answered patiently, "While you were putting in that performance at the conference."

"What . . . what were you doing in my apartment?" I asked, remembering that night during the storm. For all I knew, he'd been in the same room with me the whole time.

"Getting to know you better. Oh, don't worry. I didn't tamper with much."

"So it was you who left the terrace door open. And the window in my bedroom."

"Mmm-hmm. I was hoping you might wander out of one of them under the influence of the little cocktail I prepared for you. By the way, I was impressed by all the bells and whistles on your computer. It took me a while to get the hang of the reading program, but once I turned down the speed I enjoyed the technology. I did consider wiping your hard drive clean like Gallagher's, but it was still useful to me and—"

I was caught totally by surprise. "Wait a minute," I broke in. "You're saying it was you who destroyed Gallagher's files?"

"Why? Did you think it was Jane? Of course, I'd always planned on Gallagher's records making an untimely disappearance. I had to be certain there was nothing in them to connect me to his silly story. It apparently never occurred to the police that there were two different visitors to his home, or that they came on separate occasions."

I nodded, cursing myself for not having thought of that possibility before now. Graham had finished tying my hands and sat down in the other lawn chair. I flexed my wrists and concluded I'd never be able to wiggle free. "You're saying she only took the hard copy of the report you passed to Gallagher?"

"Yes, because when I went looking for it, it was already gone and Jane was the only person who could have taken it. It's exactly what I would have done. She and I are alike in so many ways. I've been following her closely for years. You can imagine how pleased I was when she undertook that investigation for my employer."

It was as I'd suspected. Graham had set her up.

"Then you admit you tried to frame her?"

"Frame her? No, that would imply a more direct role in Gallagher's death. All I did was set in motion a series of events that I hoped would play out a certain way. It was only my good fortune that they did. Incidentally, I give her high marks for how it was done. Nearly flawless. Her only mistake was being seen by that schoolteacher. But then again, she's always been brilliant—"

"Wait," I said, floored even further by this new revelation. "It wasn't you who . . . ?"

"Fed him the Lucitrol? I'm sure that's what she'd like you to think. But no, it wasn't me." He said it calmly and almost sadly, as though he wished he'd come up with the idea himself.

My head was reeling, but I had to keep him talking. "Why should I believe you? There were witnesses who saw you with Gallagher at a bar the same night. Who's to say it wasn't you who slipped him the pill?"

"No one, unfortunately. That was *my* mistake. Agreeing to go over the facts of the story with him one last time. But when he bragged about how he'd put Jane in her place a little earlier and I saw all the signs— you couldn't mistake them; he was as pale as a corpse and sweating like a pig—I knew my girl had come through with flying colors. Unfortunately, the coroner neglected to perform an autopsy, so I had to intervene again."

"You sent that note to Gallagher's nephew. Why not to the police directly?"

"I knew they wouldn't pay any attention to it. The authorities are always getting letters like that from cranks and attention seekers. I thought I stood a better chance of getting the body exhumed if I sent it to someone with a financial stake in proving Gallagher didn't die from natural causes. Another correct assumption, as it turned out."

"And the second note? What was that all about?"

"Second note?" he said, sounding genuinely puzzled. "I'm sorry but you've lost me."

"The note you left in my office, after you attacked Hallie and me. You're not going to deny you were the one who came after us?"

"No. But I didn't send any letters. Why would I want to draw attention to myself? Going after you and your girlfriend was another mistake. I allowed my irritation over Jane's release to get the better of me." He stopped. "Is there anything else you want to know? It's getting late and I have a plane to catch."

I scrambled to come up with another line of conversation. "Why kill me? I had nothing to do with your father's death."

"The better question is why not? You're just like all the other imposters in your so-called profession. Calling yourselves healers when you have no more understanding of the potions you prescribe than the most primitive of witch doctors. My father always looked down on psychiatry, said it wasn't the true practice of medicine. And I proved it, didn't I? Nobody knows how the drugs work. They might just as well be the sugar pills I snuck into my samples. It's about time someone repaid your arrogance in kind."

It was time to play the O'Leary card. "You won't get away with it."

"That's also part of the standard script, isn't it?" Graham said coolly.

"Yes, but what you don't know is that I *did* go to the police. They'll be searching your place any minute now."

"And won't find a thing. Just as they won't find any evidence linking me to your apparent suicide. Of course, I'll have to relocate to a different country to avoid prosecution for whatever additional crimes they'll try to slander me with, but your death won't be one of them. It will be crystal clear to everyone why you chose to take your own life."

I fought to keep a cool head. "I've managed to stay alive all this time. Why would anyone think I suddenly decided to kill myself?"

"Why, the experimental study you were enrolled in. Everyone knows how you've pinned all your hopes on it. How sad for you that the miracle didn't happen, and how terribly depressed you became when you could no longer deny that your blindness was permanent. It doesn't matter anymore, but I'll let you in on a little secret: I tested the pills in that bottle you were stupid enough to lose in the hall. You were in the group getting the medication. So now you know: the treatment was a complete failure."

Somehow it paled in significance to getting out of there alive.

"My friends won't believe it," I insisted, without much conviction. If Graham succeeded in his plan, who would be able to swear I'd never considered it? Even Josh, if you put him under oath, would have to concede he'd been worried about me. And hadn't I impressed upon Rusty that most suicides were unpredictable? Nine-tenths of the population believed that blindness was a fate worse than death. When they found me hanging by a sheet from my terrace, why wouldn't everyone draw the simplest and least debatable conclusion?

"And then there's the e-mail you'll be sending," Graham added, almost casually.

"What e-mail?" I said, with rising panic.

"Haven't you been wondering all this time why I bothered to hack into your computer? It's already there, timed to go out just about now. The e-mail to your ex-wife and son, telling them about the treatment and apologizing for not having the courage to go on. Steady, now. I see that mentioning your little boy touches a nerve. What's his name again? Oh, yes, I remember. Louis. Well, it's a pity that Louis will have to grow up like I did. I always hated my father for leaving me like that—wasn't I a good enough reason for him to go on living? They say it's common for the offspring of suicides to experience such emotions. And now your son will come to despise you, too."

*NO*, I thought in near hysteria. Not that, too . . .

"HELP!" I screamed suddenly and at the top of my lungs while I jumped to my feet, thrusting myself and the lawn chair back and behind me with as much momentum as I could manage. If I couldn't save myself, the least I could do was create evidence of a struggle. "Help! I screamed again as the chair hit the plate glass behind me. There was a loud smack but no evidence of shattering. The chair toppled over from the force of the impact, sending me to the terrace floor in a fetal position with my wrists still attached to the armrests. I wasted no time kicking off the concrete with the sides of my feet and scuttling the chair backward against the glass again. This time I had the satisfaction of hearing a crunching sound upon impact. "Is anyone there? Call the police!" I continued to shout, still trying to make as much noise as possible. "There's a madman trying to kill me!!"

Graham came over and silenced me with a kick to my solar plexus. "That won't do you any good. By the time anyone gets here, you'll be twisting in the wind."

I lay there on the ground gasping for air while he slipped the homemade noose over my head and proceeded to detach my hands from the chair. As soon as my right had been freed and while I was still struggling to breathe, I reached into my pocket and pulled out all the detritus—loose change, cane tips, and whatever else I'd been able to scoop up while I was retrieving my cell phone from the bowl near the door. Before Graham could stop me, I flung them wildly at his face, still hoping to slow him down.

"My, my, we are full of tricks," Graham said. "That one will cost you, too." He hadn't been lying about the gun, which he now brought down butt first on the hand he'd been working on. I heard my radius crack and let out a shriek of pain. When he was finished, he pulled me up by the unbroken wrist and turned me out, facing the wind. "Take a last look," he said in my ear, pushing me forward until my feet were at the terrace's edge. "For whatever that's worth." He tugged on the noose to secure it and gathered me up in a bear hug while I struggled to wrest free. I felt my feet come off the ground and summoned the lungpower to scream once more. "Tell Louis it wasn't me!!"

Just then I heard a sound from behind us, like a playful little pop. And found myself sinking under Graham's considerable bulk.

# TWENTY-SIX

"Thank God she was able to stop him," Hallie said from her hospital bed. "But how did she happen to be there at just the right time?"

Jane's story, repeated many times to the police over the last twenty-four hours and with all-too-credible consistency, was as follows: that she'd been worried about me ever since I'd burst out of her penthouse several days ago in an apparently disoriented state. That after leaving several messages for me with my assistant—Yelena, reverting to her usual self, had neglected to pass any of them on—Jane became even more concerned about my welfare, resolving to come knock on my door as soon as her busy schedule permitted. That her receptionist, Gregory, had found my address in the online white pages and phoned ahead to make an appointment, only to discover that my phone line was disconnected. That she'd rushed over to the building, following one of my neighbors through the door and gone directly upstairs. That when she'd heard my screams from inside the apartment, she phoned 911 immediately—their records confirmed it—but thought the situation too dire to wait until the police arrived. That upon testing the door she discovered it to be unlocked and entered to see me struggling with a heavyset intruder on my terrace. That fortunately she always carried a semiautomatic pistol in her purse, having received several death threats during her tenure at the State's Attorney's. That when it appeared I was in imminent danger of being pitched over my balcony, she decided the use of deadly force was justified. That she did not consider herself a hero and was merely honored to have saved the life of the brave psychiatrist who had brought a dangerous psychopath to justice.

"I guess you could say I'm just a lucky guy," I replied.

I was holding Hallie's hand and she shuddered. "Luck doesn't begin to describe it. Oh, Mark . . ."

"No, don't start crying. I may feel compelled to join you."

I disengaged my hand and fumbled in my jacket pocket for a handkerchief. It required more maneuvering than usual because of the sling on my left arm. "Here," I said, shaking it out by the corner and handing it over. "It's probably against hospital regulations, but I don't want to go crashing around looking for a tissue."

She took it from me, sobbing in earnest now.

I moved in closer and patted her arm. "There, there. It's just the head injury. People are often emotional when they come out of it."

"It's not that," Hallie said, sniffling. "It's just that you . . . you were almost killed because of me."

I gave her a crooked grin. "And you were almost killed because of me. So we're even. Though I'm going to have to think long and hard before getting involved in your next case. This one nearly lost me my head. By the way, how is yours feeling?"

Miraculously, based on all the early tests, she appeared to have sustained no neurological damage apart from some weakness on her left side that could be cleared up with minor physical therapy. After I got the cast off, I'd be joining her.

Hallie blew into the handkerchief and said, "Like someone stuffed it full of mattresses and then stomped all over them. I'm just glad you can't see me. I look like Alvin the Chipmunk with a hangover. And I'm going to have to get a new hairdo when the dressings come off."

"I'm sure Bjorn won't mind," I said.

"Oh, him," she said dismissively. "Do you know he hasn't come to see me even once? Although he did send a nice flower arrangement."

"Men are so unreliable," I said.

Hallie laughed. "Of course, you know what that means."

"What?"

"You'll have to keep going to the theater with me."

"I think that can be arranged—unless the next one in your subscription is *Wait until Dark*. Can I ask you something?"

"If it avoids the subject of what I'm wearing."

"Are you sure it was Graham—I mean Donald Tesma Junior—who attacked us? It couldn't have been, say, a woman dressed up to look like a man?" Graham had admitted he was behind the attack, but I didn't know whom to believe anymore.

"Uh-uh. I'm positive it was him."

"You're really sure?"

"It's what I told you ages ago. I'd remember that face anywhere. If you don't believe me, ask the EMTs. I kept trying to tell them, but they wouldn't listen."

I smiled indulgently at her. "The only thing you said in the ambulance was that you were sick and needed to use a phone."

"Maybe that's what it sounded like, but I was actually giving them a clue. It just got lost in translation."

"Why, were you speaking Spanish?"

Hallie sighed. "OK, I know it wasn't the easiest message to follow. But if you recall, I wasn't exactly lucid at the time. I wasn't using the words 'sick' or 'phone.' I was saying 'ill' and 'app.'"

"Well, that certainly clears it up for me."

"If you don't shut up I'm going to throw this water jug at you. 'Ill.' and 'App.' are abbreviations—lawyer shorthand for the Illinois Appellate Reports, where all the opinions of the appeals courts are published. They're organized by volume and page number. I was telling them where to look for the decision affirming Tesma's conviction. For some reason it was the only thing I could come up with while I was sinking into oblivion."

I shook my head in amazement. "You mean it? That's what you were trying to say?"

"Yes, and if you or anyone else had bothered to tell Jane she would have caught on immediately. She would have led you to Tesma's son long before he tried to kill you."

Somehow I doubted it.

"Now it's my turn to ask a question," Hallie said. "What were you thinking of when . . . when he was about to push you off? It must have been terrifying."

"You mean, did my life flash before my eyes? Let's just say I was busy counting up all my sins. There's one in particular I need to tell you about. But later, when you're better. In the meantime, there's another misconception between us that needs clearing up."

"Like what?"

"Like this," I said.

I imagined her eyes opened wide in surprise as I leaned in to kiss her.

The next morning, while I was getting dressed for my two appointments, a knock came on my door. Since it was only 6:00 a.m., I hoped it didn't mean I'd been observed sneaking back from the men's room with my shaving gear. Following the episode with Graham I hadn't worked up the nerve to go back to my apartment—which in any case was now a cordoned-off crime scene—and had been camping out at my office, which had the dual virtues of proximity to Hallie and a twenty-four-hour security patrol. Just in case, I'd also had office management install new locks on the door, which was now double-bolted against intruders. "Just a sec," I said, while I finished buttoning my shirt and tucking it into my waistband. I opened the door to find—of all people—Yelena.

"'Hark, hark the lark at heaven's gate sings,'" I said. "What are you doing here so early?"

"I could ask you the same thing. I hope you're not planning on moving in here permanently. It's enough of a dump as it is."

"About that. Do you think you could come in this weekend and help me do some more straightening? I'm sure I could arrange for time and a half."

"I'd like to," Yelena said. "But I'll be busy."

I should have known our détente wouldn't last for long.

"But maybe another time," she added, surprising me. "When I get back."

"Get back from where?"

"The vacation I put in for. Two weeks ago. But I suppose you weren't paying attention."

Thinking back to the episode with Graham, I had to admit she was right. "I'm sorry," I said to her. "I've . . . I've had a lot on my mind lately. Was there something you wanted to tell me?"

"Just that you're invited to a party on Sunday. If you can make it. Boris won't be free to drive you, but Dr. Goldman said he'd be glad to pick you up."

I decided she must be talking about her birthday, the date of which I realized I'd never bothered to ask about. "Sure," I said. "I'd be glad to come. And I promise not to ask how old you are."

"It's not that kind of party," Yelena said in mock irritation. "Here's the invitation." She handed me a linen envelope about the size of a CD. "I can stay and read it to you if you want me to."

"Er, no thanks," I said, now filled with embarrassment. All the signs had been there. I just hadn't noticed them. "May I ask who the lucky fellow is?"

"For the answer to that, you'll have to go back to your favorite play."

"Huh?" I said as she turned to leave.

"'The instances that second marriage move . . .'" she quoted, making her exit while I stood there with my mouth stationed just above the floor.

"More tea?" Jane asked.

"Please," I said. "Provided that's all I'm drinking."

She laughed in merriment. "You should be more trusting. We're sharing the same pot, aren't we?"

"That's no guarantee I won't soon be writhing on the floor in convulsions. I brought you something you might want to take a look at some time." I removed some papers from the backpack I'd been wearing when I came in, which in combination with the sling and the cane no doubt made me look like some species of armored insect.

Jane took them and scanned rapidly. "You needn't have bothered. I'm already familiar with the questionnaire. I see you brought the long version."

I wasn't entirely surprised. "You know what it is?"

"Certainly. The Hare Psychopathology Checklist. A diagnostic tool developed by a Canadian psychologist based on his work with psychopaths in prison. It 'scores' an individual on twenty different items like boredom, shallow emotions, lack of empathy, and so forth, with the numbers zero, one, or two, depending on how pronounced the trait is. Shall I tell you what my score was?"

"In the mid-twenties, if I had to venture a guess."

She sounded delighted. "You *are* perceptive. Not as high as it might have been, but thanks to a good therapist I was able to shed many of the less socially desirable characteristics in my youth. As you can see, I work long hours and take my responsibilities seriously. Nor am I especially promiscuous. Of course, shading the truth comes easily, but that only helps me perform better in my profession. Did you know that some estimates place the incidence of psychopathy among lawyers and politicians at nearly twenty percent? It's one of my favorite statistics."

"So you were diagnosed early?"

"As a teenager. In those days you could have given me a starring role in *The Chalk Garden* and I wouldn't have had to act the part. Are you familiar with the play?"

"Sure. It was also a film, wasn't it?"

"Yes. I always found it amusing that the writer attributed Laurel's wildness to feelings of abandonment by her mother. She was a junior psychopath if ever there was one. My situation was quite different. I grew up in a loving home with every advantage, both material and emotional, though it wasn't sufficient to overcome the trait. Inflicting physical pain was never of much interest to me, but I found other ways to torture my siblings. Then, when I was fourteen I pushed a classmate down a flight of stairs at the Lab School. It should have gotten me expelled, but my parents were wealthy and influential enough to get the matter hushed up. They settled quietly with the girl's parents and enrolled me in an outpatient program at the university hospital with the threat of sending me to the Orthogenic School if I didn't cooperate."

I nodded. "And did you—cooperate?"

"I was fortunate to get the attention of a brilliant psychiatrist, a pioneer in the field, who recognized at once how intelligent I was. He put the issue to me very simply. I couldn't be cured in any real sense of the term, but I could learn self-control. If I did, my life could be as productive and happy—though that's not an emotion I ever really feel—as any normal person's. If I didn't, I would probably end up in prison. Being trapped like that was the worst fate I could imagine, so I went along with his behavior-modification program. Over time, I learned to take my pleasure, such as it is, from success. And from manipulating people into doing what I want."

"Like you manipulated me," I said.

"Perhaps. Why don't we play that version of blind man's bluff we played before? The one where I nod when you're on the right track but don't otherwise confirm it."

"All right," I said, drawing something else out of my backpack. "For starters I thought I'd ask if you recognized this. If I'm not mistaken, you left it for me right after Hallie and I were attacked." I tossed it onto her coffee table.

"I don't think I'll pick it up," Jane said. "Someone—I won't say who—must have gone to a great deal of trouble not to leave any fingerprints."

"And arranged it so that it couldn't be traced back to the sender in other ways. You, for instance."

She laughed again. "Now why would I do that?"

"You were trying to hit me over the head with it."

"That's a droll way of saying it. Surely you're not accusing me of being the one who attacked you?"

"I did wonder for a while. But after thinking it over I decided you wouldn't have stooped to anything so crude. And Hallie is very definite about it being Tesma's son. What I don't understand is how you knew he was our attacker."

"That isn't damaging to my interests, so I'll answer. You remember the investigation I undertook for Atria? One of the first things I did was commandeer a room at company headquarters so I could conduct private interviews of all its salesmen. I recognized him as soon as he walked through the door. He recognized me too, though we each pretended to be complete strangers."

"But you didn't do anything about it—like tell the authorities he'd taken on an alias?"

"Come, doctor. You're too intelligent for that. What would revealing his background have accomplished? The name change was perfectly legal and aboveboard. I would have done the same thing in his place. And nothing came out of our interview to suggest he was anything other than a successful, law-abiding citizen. I would have been laughed out of a job if I'd gone to Atria's management and told them they were harboring a murderous psychopath on their sales force."

"Fair enough. But what about later on? Why didn't you expose him after you'd been arrested?"

"Again, no one would have believed me. Accusing him of Rory's murder would only have made me appear desperate—not to mention guilty as charged."

"So you had to get someone else to pin it on him."

"Exactly. Originally, I had planned on it being Hallie. As good as she is in the courtroom, I didn't hire her solely for her skills as an advocate. Sooner or later she would have gone looking for old enemies and remembered the trial we worked on together. But after Donald Junior scuttled that plan, I had to settle for a different helper."

"So you played me." Like a piece on a chessboard, I thought.

"Yes, you were my white knight."

And she could read minds, too.

"I suppose he contacted you right afterward."

"Also correct. He copied me on the note he sent to Rory's nephew. That was also part of his plan—to make sure I knew who was behind it all. I expect you now understand why the two notes looked the same."

Of course she would have planned it that way.

"I don't suppose you'd ever admit to killing Gallagher yourself?"

"You may once more assume that I'm nodding my head. And you should know by now that it will be impossible to prove. I can only guess at what Donald Junior told you when he was slipping that noose around your neck, but they'll never let you on the stand to testify about it. And I almost forgot about this."

She handed me a stapled sheaf of paper.

"What is it?"

"An insurance policy, of sorts. I found it among Rory's papers when I went to his home to retrieve my report. It's a holographic will, canceling the bequests to his nephew and leaving all of his property to a fund fighting public corruption. I thought it might come in handy someday. If I have to, I'll make it public, and they'll try Urquhart and his mistress for Rory's murder. It's always been the likeliest scenario anyway."

I could only shake my head.

"Don't look so downcast," she said sympathetically. "After all, thanks to me you're still alive."

I got up to go.

"Two more things," I said. "The Tarot card—The Hanged Man. You weren't lying when you said I picked it out myself?"

"It leaped out of the deck like it was waiting for you."

"And that last time I was here. Did we . . . I mean, did you—"

She didn't let me finish. "I have no idea what you're talking about. But if things don't work out between you and Hallie . . . well, let's just say you'll know where to find me."

"I'm afraid I have to agree with her," Tony Di Marco said, after I'd told him the whole story.

"Go over this with me again," I said. "I'm a little slow."

"It goes back to the function of the jury in our system. Only the fact finder is allowed to decide who is telling the truth. And to do that, in most cases, they have to be able to physically observe the speaker. Except in a few narrowly defined situations, the rules don't allow a witness to swear to something he heard from somebody else."

It was exactly as Jane had explained the hearsay rules to me. "Which would include Young telling me that Jane was Gallagher's killer."

"That's right. In a homicide case it's the classic hearsay example—someone whose reliability the jury can't assess claiming to know who the murderer is. It's only when the surrounding circumstances strongly suggest that the declarant—that's the legal term—is trustworthy on the point that the statement comes in. Admissions against interest are one exception. Another are dying declarations, based on the idea that most people are inclined to tell the truth when they're about to meet their Maker. But that won't work here, either."

"Because Young didn't know he was about to die."

"That's right. And as you've described the situation to me I can't think of any other hearsay exception that would get your story in front of a jury. It's too bad. I did try to aid the cause, you know."

I'd figured as much. "You were the ASA who went to court with the exhumation request."

"Who else? I was on to Jane as the killer from the day Gallagher dropped dead, so I was all too happy to give Polanski a helping hand when he came to me with that trumped-up affidavit. The only trouble was my bosses wouldn't let me near the case, and it ended up with that preschooler from Lake County. If I'd been in charge Jane would still be in pretrial detention, and you would have been spared all the detective work. Thanks to you, we caught one monster, but at the cost of letting another one go free."

I frowned, knowing he was right. "There's really no way your colleagues would reopen the case?"

"It's a nonstarter. They already have egg all over their faces for going after Jane in the first place. And now that she's a hero for saving you no one will have the slightest appetite for it. No, take it from me, it'll never happen."

"Will you still follow up on the other thing—the Atria investigation?"

"The subpoenas to its sales personnel are being prepared as we speak."

"And you'll let the guys at the *Sun-Times* in on whatever you turn up? I promised them."

"Consider it another on the long list of favors you owe me. And now, if you'll take my good advice you'll go home and forget you ever met the lady. It's like I told you in the beginning. That *donna* is poison."

After I left him, there was one more stop I needed to make before heading back to my office. The weather had turned sharply colder, and I put up my collar against the wind at my back. I went east, more or less retracing the route I had taken some days earlier, deriving a fresh sense of pleasure from the sounds and smells of my adopted home. The cars stuck in traffic and blaring their horns, the sweet aroma of a pretzel stand on State, the 'L' trains chiming their synchronized stops overhead. I walked steadily but without hurry, through the Loop and across the park, barely conscious of the hard-earned technique that kept me moving on a straight path. I thought about how far I'd come and what the future might look like and all the important things I would tell Louis when he was older.

When I reached the harbor's edge, I stopped and shut my eyes, recalling the place as I'd last seen it, now almost two years ago. The crystalline water of the Lake with its flotilla of gently rocking boats, the fall leaves swinging cheerfully in the breeze, the soft palette of the distant horizon blending into the sky. I stood there quietly for a long time, awash in memory. When I opened my eyes again, it was time. I took the bottle with the last of the pills from my pocket and tested its weight with my good hand. Then I reached back and hurled it into the air as far as it would go.

Tomorrow I would call Melissa and explain.

Though I expected she already knew.

268 — DANTE'S POISON

Coming up on my office building a little while later, I thought I was hallucinating again.

Two figures were chatting by the guard station.

Richard and . . . *could it really be?*

I started running, sending off pops like a firecracker. "Mike! I shouted, as I reached their voices. I tossed my cane aside and gathered him up in an embrace, nearly weeping in relief. "Mike, you ugly bastard! Where the hell have you been?"

He peeled himself away embarrassedly. "I'm sorry, Mistuh Mark. Richard here was just sayin' how worried you were about me. I didn't mean to cause no alarm."

"Well, you scared the shit out of me. I was looking all over for you."

"I'm sorry again," Mike said. "My old cell mate called me from Rockford. Said he was sick from the drugs and about to die from the shakes."

"You didn't buy for him, I hope?"

"Naw. But I helped him get into a treatment program. Stayed on some days after to make sure he come through the bad part alright."

"Tell him your other news, Mike," Richard said, nudging me in the arm.

"Well, the folks in that program, they say I done a good thing by my friend, and seein' as how they knew some other folks down here in Chicago maybe they could get me a room in one of them gov'ment hotels. I been on the waitin' list close to two year, but they got me jumped ahead."

"I could have done that for you, too," I said. "If you'd given me the chance."

"Aw, you know how I don't like to be botherin' folks. Anyway, you got enough troubles on your own. I see you is all busted up again."

"Yeah," Richard said. "What on God's earth happened to you this time?"

I laughed and said, "Would you believe me if I told you I fell out of a tree?"

# ACKNOWLEDGMENTS

A great deal of research went into the writing of this book, but I am particularly indebted to Daniel J. Carlat, MD, for his book *Unhinged: The Trouble with Psychiatry—A Doctor's Revelations about a Profession in Crisis*, which opened my eyes, to abuse a pun, to the uneasy relationship between the medical profession and the pharmaceutical industry, and started me down the road of thinking "What if?"

While the majority of events described herein are made up, some of them, such as the practice of providing free samples and the clandestine marketing of drugs for "off-label" use, are not. In a welcome development, the drug company GlaxoSmithKline recently announced that it will no longer tie its sales personnel's compensation to prescription volume, or pay doctors to speak about its products. Hopefully, other major pharmaceutical companies will soon follow suit. That said, any and all factual mistakes are solely mine.

I am deeply appreciative of Dan Mayer, my editor, for bringing my work to light and for his continued support of the Mark Angelotti series. A special thanks also to Laura Carter, Mary Coasby, and Jim Ziskin for reading and commenting on earlier drafts, and to my friends Caryn Jacobs, Karen Behles, Paula Shapiro, and sisters Blair and Reid Wellensieck for cheering the book on. I am also indebted to my agent, Brooks Sherman, for his wise and continuing counsel. And last, but not least, a huge thank you goes out to my copyeditor, Julia DeGraf, my proofreader, Jade Zora Scibilia, and my cover designer, Jackie Cooke.

Of course, none of this would be possible without the support and encouragement of my husband, Stanley Parzen, who has acted as a one-man kickstarter campaign for my writing career and never fails to lift my spirits with a well-timed joke. Kendra, Jacob, and Tamsin, thank you for being who you are.

# ABOUT THE AUTHOR

LYNNE RAIMONDO is the author of *Dante's Wood*, a *Library Journal* Mystery Debut of the Month. Currently a full-time writer, she was formerly a partner in the Chicago law firm Mayer, Brown & Platt, the general counsel of Arthur Andersen LLP, and the general counsel of the Illinois Department of Revenue. To learn more about Lynne Raimondo, visit her website at http://www.lynneraimondo .com.

pitch ninja

# pitch ninja

Persuasive Pitching and Presenting

Mike Moyer

Lake
Shark

ISBN **978-0-692-20291-3**

This publication is designed to provide accurate and authoritative information in regard to the subject matter covered. It is sold with the understanding that the publisher is not engaged in rendering legal, accounting, or other professional service. If legal advice or other expert assistance is required, the services of a competent professional person should be sought.—*From a Declaration of Principles Jointly Adopted by a Committee of the American Bar Association and a Committee of Publishers and Associations*

All brand names and product names used in this book are trademarks, registered trademarks, or trade names of their respective holders.

Published by Lake Shark Ventures, LLC
Lake Forest, IL
www.LakeShark.com

To Mindy!

Thank you for being a
Pitch Ninja!

— Mihaly

3-16

To Anne, Anson, Merrily and Norvin

## My Promise

If, after reading this book, you don't feel that it contains not just good advice, but the greatest advice on the subject that you have ever received, I will happily refund your money and apologize for wasting your time.

**Mike@Pitch.Ninja**

## Virtual Dojo
www.pitch.ninja

To help you better understand the concepts in this book, I have created a series of video tutorials and posted them to Pitch.Ninja or PitchNinja.com in a members-only area called the Virtual Dojo. The Virtual Dojo has different levels of membership; the "book" level is the least expensive and you can access it for a month *for free* (maybe even longer!)

To access the Virtual Dojo, visit Pitch.Ninja/VirtualDojo and sign up for the "book" membership.

# Preface

I love presenting. It's fun, it's invigorating and there are few things I'd rather do. One of those few things I like to do *more* than presenting is *teaching* other people to present. There is hardly anything I find more satisfying than showing someone a few simple techniques that will change how they think about presenting and change the way they present for the rest of their lives.

For me it's a win-win-win. My clients get transformed into total *Pitch Ninjas*, their audiences are spared from painfully boring presentations, and I get paid. It's a wonderful thing with little to no bloodshed (Pitch Ninjas aren't violent).

The good news is that when it comes to giving presentations, the bar is set pretty low. Most people haven't had five minutes of presentation training. If they do get some training, most of it is focused on the *content* of their presentation. Hardly anybody provides training on the *style* of the presentation. The most you will get on style is a little feedback here and there during practice sessions.

This book, *Pitch Ninja*, provides *detailed* instructions on *exactly* how to create a winning presentation. Although I will touch upon content, the focus is on style and the specific things you can do to persuade your audience, including lots of non-verbal body language that will really make a difference.

These techniques work. In 2003 I used them to win a business plan competition at one of the top business schools in the country. Over the next ten years I coached and taught seven other teams. *All* of them won. Now I teach all my students these techniques, and all my students and clients become world-class presenters whether they like it or not!

I realize that there are lots of other places where people present and that winning business plan competitions isn't the same thing as giving other kinds of presentations. But business plan competitions do have judges who can react to the presentation itself rather than their personal need for the product or service being pitched. I think business plan competitions are a place where presentation skills can take you to the top even if your underlying concept isn't rock solid.

However, in order for presentation skills to matter, they have to advance a speaker and their audience forward in life or their career. When I touch base with my former students I see that they have used these skills to raise millions of dollars in startup capital and land millions of dollars in sales revenue. In fact, I have *personally* raised millions using these techniques and I'm happy to share them with you.

Be forewarned, however, that you will be pushed from your comfort zone and you will be asked to do things that might not come naturally. In the end I promise that if you follow the advice, the results will be nothing less than spectacular and your speaking life will be forever changed.

I hope someday I can work with you in person to help you hone your technique and become a speaking master. I want you to be *awesome*. Let's begin....

# Contents

# *Introduction*

This is a book about giving *formal* presentations. A formal presentation is planned, rehearsed and performed in front of a live audience.

Most of the presentations people give are *informal.* They are not planned or rehearsed and may or may not take place in front of a live audience. An informal presentation usually consists of a bunch of people sitting around a conference table or in a coffee shop talking about something. Sure, there may be an agenda or a report to go over, but the structure and flow of the presentation isn't really planned and rarely, if ever, do people rehearse what they are going to say or do during the meeting.

Formal presentations are important—very important. A formal presentation allows a relationship to move forward whereas an informal presentation may not. A formal meeting *redefines* a relationship. You can't more forward unless you occasionally redefine the relationship. Moving from prospect to customer, for instance, is a redefined business relationship.

Think about a couple dating. They may go on any number of informal dates. They go out, have fun and enjoy each other's company; all the while they are getting to know each other more deeply and intimately. Their relationship is *defined* as a "dating couple" and the content of that relationship is based on the nature of their activities together.

Eventually, one of them (usually the guy in our man/woman dating scenario) decides he wants to ask her to marry him. This means he must give a formal presentation. He will plan the interaction and rehearse what he will say. He will plan where the event will take place and even what his body will do. For instance, he may go down on one knee or he may stand up so he will appear on the megascreen at a sporting event. He may invite friends, buy a new shirt and plan a nice meal. This meeting is most likely going to happen in person. This formal meeting will, without a doubt, *redefine* the relationship.

If she says yes, they will cease being a dating couple and will now be an "engaged couple." If she says no, they will be forced to have a serious discussion about the future, which will also redefine the relationship. If she says, "Hell no," their relationship will be redefined as single again. Let's pretend she said yes.

Now the couple is engaged. Their

relationship moves from happy-go-lucky dating to being focused on the transition to being married. They become a unit and now must redefine their relationship with those around them, including friends, family and even the government. So, they will plan and rehearse yet another formal meeting that they will perform in front of a live audience. The wedding will redefine their relationship with the world and each other, no matter what the outcome.

This happens in business all time. Informal meetings *define* the business relationship whereas formal business meetings will *redefine* the business relationship. Consider an employee annual review. This is a formal meeting that must be planned and rehearsed—especially if the news is bad. After the meeting, the relationship will be redefined. This is a small example. The more formal the presentation, the more profound the redefinition of the relationship.

So, if you want to move your relationship to the next level, you have to redefine it under the terms of the new level. The problem is that most formal presentations suck.

## Bad Presentations

I've seen a lot of presentations in my career and most of them are pretty bad. In fact, most of them are completely horrible and outright embarrassing for the presenter. Just the other night I was an investor panelist at a business pitch night and all of the presenters looked more like they were delivering *eulogies* rather than business ideas.

Think about it: here were people who are on a journey to *fulfill their life's dream* and they showed *no passion whatsoever*. It's depressing. This kind of presentation is so common, however, that we may not even realize how bad it is. That is, until we see something better.

Companies spend thousands or millions of dollars on brand images, brochures, websites, trade shows and all sorts of other marketing tools. They pore over every word and detail of their marketing materials before sending them to legal for a stamp of approval. The time and money spent developing good marketing materials can be exhausting. In spite of this, little attention is paid to how people present the company and concepts to others. Don't get me wrong, most people spend *some* time on preparing and practicing presentations. Some even spend a lot of time, but all too often they are practicing the wrong things.

When I was a kid I wanted to be a skateboarder. I sucked at it. I didn't want my friends to see how bad I was so I practiced, by myself, all the time. I'd practice and practice and practice and practice and practice. I never got better because I was *practicing the wrong things*.

Years later I put my son in skateboard lessons. His teacher gave me a few pointers and I was *instantly* better than ever. If I had only known what I should be practicing, I wouldn't have wasted all that time never getting better!

Such is the way with giving presentations. People put together a PowerPoint deck and then go "practice the slides" over and over. So many people practice the wrong things, no matter how much they practice, their presentation will never get better. I'm going to tell you what to practice so that when you do practice, you will improve the chances of giving an awesome presentation.

The first step in the process is to understand why most presentations are as bad as they are.

Chapter One:

# *Magnetic South Pole*

Most people are familiar with the Magnetic *North* Pole. It's that special place in the Northern Hemisphere where the Earth's magnetic field points downward, allowing people to navigate with compasses. It gave mankind the ability to proceed with confidence in the right direction.

Magnetic *South* Pole is just the opposite and instead of attracting the needle of a compass, it only affects presenters. It appears, out of nowhere, right under a presenter's feet whenever he or she stands up to present. It pulls on the nails in their shoes so they can't move and draws their jowls down, forcing a frown. It's usually to the immediate right or left of the presentation screen and it ruins presentations.

It saps their energy and dampens their voice to a monotone drone. Seemingly unable to lift their feet, they stand in one place for the *entire* presentation using the occasional slight hand movement. Because they don't move, they have to say things like, "As you can see on this slide," (which, of course, nobody can see).

## *Weaving*

Because getting stuck on Magnetic South Pole is uncomfortable, some people sway their body side-to-side, shifting their weight from one foot to another in a tedious rhythm.

Horses do this. It's a "stable vice" known as "weaving" and their owners *hate* it because it's annoying—not because it's harmful (it's not). Horse owners will go to great lengths to prevent their horse from weaving, going so far as to stick a pig, goat or even a few random chickens in the stall in an effort to entertain, or at least distract, the horse so it won't weave. This kind of annoying presentation behavior is all because of Magnetic South Pole.

## *Pacing*

Sometimes a presenter will move from the spot they are standing and proceed to pace back and forth across the front of the room. This is just as tedious as standing in one place, except now the audience has to turn their head from side to side like they're watching a tennis match that never ends.

Yet another variation is stepping forward and backward over and over. Again, this is

Magnetic South Pole at work, causing people to act in a horribly boring fashion.

## *Swagger*

A swagger is worse than pacing. A swagger is an arrogant pace. When someone swaggers, he has a lazy stride and lazy movements that make him look like he thinks he is too good to be there.

In this case, Magnetic South Pole has taken the spring out of his step and caused him to replace energy and confidence with arrogance and overconfidence. When people are nervous, they try to correct by trying to relax. A swagger is evidence of overcorrection. You can use nervous energy to your advantage.

## *Podiums*

To make matters worse, the location of Magnetic South Pole is often marked on the floor with a podium. This way the presenter can actually *hide* from the audience instead of doing something interesting.

Podiums are presentation *killers* and you'll have to avoid them at all costs. Unlike real ninjas, Pitch Ninjas are anything but stealthy. They don't hide behind podiums.

## *Laser Pointers*

Magnetic South Pole is the reason there is a

market for laser pointers. If people realized they could simply *walk over to the screen and point* to it they would never even think of buying a laser pointer. Rarely, if ever, is a screen so high that a human being can't reach it. To make matters worse, your nervousness will cause the pointer to shake and the little red dot will move so much it will make you look like you are overdosing on Red Bull. If you own a laser pointer, go get it now and flush it down the toilet.

*The right place to put laser pointers*

In spite of fact that I hate laser pointers, I actually own several of them. That's because the manufacturers of presentation remotes actually *integrate* the foolish devices into the remote. Presentation remotes are great, laser pointers are not. More on this later.

*PowerPoint*

The last evidence of Magnetic South Pole is overcomplicated and over-written PowerPoint slides. PowerPoint is a great program, but overreliance on it is usually because someone is overcompensating for Magnetic South Pole.

I like the way my friend, David Fernandez, puts it: "PowerPoint is not the message nor the messenger." You are the messenger, and what comes out of your mouth is the message. PowerPoint is simply there to help.

A bad PowerPoint presentation consists mostly of content to help the *speaker*. A good presentation consists of mostly content to help the *audience*.

*Why Magnetic South Pole Exists*

Magnetic South Pole sounds silly, doesn't it? It's true. It's there. Watch for it when you see your next presentation. The influence of Magnetic South Pole is overwhelming, and for good reason—what else are you supposed to do?

There was a great scene in the movie *Talladega Nights* where the lead character, Ricky Bobby, is being interviewed for the first time on national television after doing well in his first race. As he speaks to the reporter in an overly soft tone of voice, his hands slowly rise up in front the camera for no apparent reason. He admits to the reporter, "I'm not sure what to do with my hands."

"If you could just hold them down by your side," the reporter responds. A minute later the hands slowly rise up again in front of the camera. Ricky has no idea what to do. It was hilarious (look it up).

Magnetic South Pole exists because most people have *no idea* what to do with their bodies during a presentation. There are two reasons for this. The first is that they are too worried about what they are going to say. The second is that nobody has ever told them what to do. For you, that's about to change.

## Virtual Dojo

### Magnetic South Pole

To see a video describing Magnetic South Pole, visit PitchNinja.com and click on the Virtual Dojo or scan the code.

Chapter Two:

# *Persuasive Choreography*

Magnetic South Pole exists because most people have *no clue* what they should be doing with their bodies. Almost the entire remainder of this book is going to cover just that—what you should do with your body, including where to stand, when to move, how to move your hands, how to make eye contact, and how to use your voice. I call it "Persuasive Choreography." It's the art of designing the sequence of movements that will inspire an audience to see things from your point of view.

Persuasive Choreography is putting on an *awesome* show for your audience with the specific intent to *persuade*, not just entertain. A little planning in this area will go a long way.

You can't *bore* people into buying from you. In most cases buyers buy *in spite* of your boring presentation, not because of it. This means they were predisposed to buying what you're selling and, luckily, your boring presentation didn't get in the way. They were able to get the gist of what you were offering before they nodded off to sleep.

What you want is for the opposite to happen. You want them to love your presentation so much that they buy *in spite* of your product or service. By this, I mean I want them to be so excited about you and your passion that they want what you are offering no matter what, but I don't mean you should try to con anyone by pretending. Persuasive Choreography is about communicating genuine emotion, not about pulling the wool over someone's eyes.

Let me say that again lest I'm misunderstood: *This is not about conning anyone into buying a substandard product or service.* It is possible to use Persuasive Choreography to con someone, but that goes for any selling skills.

*The Y Factor*

Think of it this way: your idea and the work you have done around your idea or what you are selling is "X." You and your presentation skills are "Y." When you present your idea to an audience, your outcome is a function of both those factors.

X *minus* Y (x-y) means you pretty much suck at presenting and your presentation made your idea look worse than it actually is. Most people fall into this category. If they still have a positive outcome, it means their idea was so great that it compensated for their poor presentation skills. This does happen and it lulls people into thinking they were successful.

X *plus* Y (x+y) means that you effectively communicated the idea and showed passion and excitement. This is less common, but pair a good idea and a good presenter and you have a slam dunk. If you don't have a slam dunk, it means your idea is so boring that even good presentation skills can't compensate.

X *times* Y (x*y) means that people *love* you so much they don't even care what your idea is— they just want in. People who can do this can change the world (but they still have to have good ideas).

For the best presenters in the world, Y is an exponent of X. Their presentation is X to the "Yth" power ($x^y$). This means the speaker added *exponential* value to the basic idea. Tony Robbins is a highly successful motivational speaker; look him up on YouTube.com and see how he moves and how he uses his voice and his hands and his face.

Persuasive Choreography is about ensuring your Y-factor has a positive or even exponentially positive impact on your ideas. In most cases people are X *minus* Y. A good speaker is hard to find!

## Caring

The purpose of your presentation is to persuade

someone to your point of view. If you believe in yourself and you believe in your product or service and you believe that you will be able to add value to your client in excess of what they are going to pay you, your presentation should make this clear. Most presentations fail to make this clear.

In order to be effective, the audience needs to know that you *care* about what you are talking about. Remember that people won't care what you know until they know that you care. In order to show them you care, you have to exude energy and excitement.

This is especially important for startup companies whose products or services are bound to have plenty of bugs to work out. If the audience believes in you and your vision and falls in love with you and your energy and passion, they will overlook potential flaws with what you are offering because they want to work with you. Investors in startup companies often invest with teams they love in spite of glaring holes in their business models. It happens all the time, and it should. Good teams are hard to find. If they have a vision they believe in, they can probably find a way to get there.

In fact, in most growth-oriented companies you will be pitching to clients that are out of their league. Most companies grow because they are consistently pushing the boundaries on what they are capable of doing. Few companies grow because they are playing it safe and fishing in tidal pools. In order to grow, you've got to venture out to the big, blue ocean.

Every time you present, you are selling yourself as much as you are selling your company. In many cases you are selling yourself more because your company may still be developing, growing and changing. The buyer has to believe you *and* believe *in* you. The buyer has to love you and you have to love your client. Business relationships are real relationships.

## Who Are You?

If you are still with me and I've been able to convince you that showing passion, energy and belief in yourself and your product is important, you have to ask yourself the following question: Who am I?

Are you someone who is passionate about what you are presenting? Do you actually believe in yourself and your team? Do you actually believe that you have something to offer of value in excess of what you are charging? Do you actually believe you can provide that something to your potential client? Are you worthy of being trusted by your client? *Are you worthy of being loved?*

If you do a little self-examination and realize that you don't believe in yourself and your team and your product and the value you offer and everything else I asked, you should probably find a different line of work.

Everybody has doubts and fears and

reservations, but if you genuinely care about what you are doing and you rise above these feelings and exude confidence, poise and bravery, you will be much more successful at presenting.

## Authenticity

What I'm going to ask of you in the following pages may feel very strange and awkward at first. I've had clients or students tell me that Persuasive Choreography doesn't feel natural. That's because it's not.

What's natural is to get overcome by Magnetic South Pole and let it sap your emotions and force you to give a boring presentation.

Dancing like Michael Jackson isn't natural either, but it's still awesome.

Just because something doesn't seem natural doesn't mean it's not authentic. Go find a guitar or other instrument that you have never played before and try to bang out a tune. Chances are that it will sound horrible. Playing an instrument is anything but natural, unless you know how. However, if you know how to play guitar, you can use it to express your authentic self in interesting ways.

If I teach you to paint, you can communicate your emotions through art. If I teach you how to write, you can communicate your emotions in stories. If I teach you how to sing or play music or any other form of communication, you can communicate your emotions using your new skills. I'm going to teach you the art of Persuasive Choreography so you will be able to communicate your authentic self to an audience.

These skills take practice, but even a little progress will go a long way. You don't have to be perfect. It's like a wedding dance. Seeing a newlywed couple try to pull off a dance with no prior practice or training is just plain embarrassing. A little effort turns the dance into a touching event. If the groom dips the bride at the end, the crowd goes wild! Yes, it may be a little corny, but it's the couple's willingness to push the limits of their own capabilities that touches us, not their perfection.

That being said, a wedding couple that puts some real effort and practice into their wedding dance winds up going viral on YouTube.com. Just because it is kick-ass doesn't mean it's not authentic.

If you get through this book and still don't think Persuasive Choreography is compatible with your personality, I recommend that you consider getting in touch with a good therapist who can help you "find yourself." If your personality is more closely aligned with Magnetic South Pole you are going to have life problems beyond your ability to present well.

I'm going to assume from here on out that you are someone who believes in yourself and you are someone who can show passion, excitement and energy for what you have to offer.

In order to persuade an audience, you are going to have to replace the boring style of Magnetic South Pole with a bold, exciting and passionate style. You have to have something, other than nothing, to do with your body.

## First, You Need the Right Pitch Ninja Moves

You can't choreograph anything unless you have a few dance moves. Michael Jackson had lots of moves. He had the Moonwalk, the hat tip and the wiggle-leg thing, along with many, many others.

Ballet dancers have lots of moves too, including plié, passé, jeté, fouetté, and other moves that are spelled with accent marks.

Ballet choreographers arrange ballet dance moves into a full dance that can be enjoyed by audiences, and the best performances communicate real emotions. The best performers and choreographers can make the audience feel any way they want. A sad dancer will make the audience cry, while a happy dancer will make the audience smile.

In the next chapter I'll go over a number of key moves that good presenters use to persuade an audience.

## The Stage

All presentations happen on a presentation stage. That stage might be a wide-open lecture hall appointed with the latest technology, or that stage might be a crowded Starbucks. It could even be an elevator. No matter what, you as the presenter have the right and the responsibility to set the stage however you want. This means you can move the chairs and furniture (if practical) and even assign seating to the audience members.

In Chapter 5 I'm going to introduce you to one of the most powerful concepts in this book. It's called the Super-Awesome Presentation Zone Program and it helps you understand how to coordinate your moves and your content for maximum impact.

In theater, "blocking" refers to the movement and position of actors on a stage. Just like in theater, you will be mindful of blocking when you present.

## Be a Silverback Gorilla

If you have something important to say, you need to *own* the room and command attention from the audience. You will use your body language and voice to command the audience and control the environment.

In the wild, the silverback gorilla is the center of his gorilla troop. Everything revolves around him. All decisions are made by him; he is the master of his universe. When you present, *be a silverback gorilla*. I said before that Pitch Ninjas aren't stealthy like real ninjas. Pitch Ninjas establish a presence.

To do this, you will have to stand up

straight, put your chin up, smile and show your armpits a lot. Silverback gorillas show their armpits when they want to take command. You will also have to square your body up with the audience. This, "silverback gorilla" stance should be your default. You won't use it all the time, but you will use it enough. When in doubt, act like a silverback.

This is important because as presenters, we are rarely in a power position. People in power positions usually don't have to do formal presentations if they don't want to. Have you ever heard of a venture capitalist making a presentation to an early-stage startup? If it happens, it's because the startup is so awesome that the VC feels the need to convince them to take their money.

When you present, you owe your audience. When the president of the United States speaks, he or she owes his or her audience an explanation of what's going on with the country. When the salesperson presents, she owes the audience a solution to their problems (if they have problems).

So, because the presenter is essentially liable to the audience, the best thing she can do to deliver is to become the center of the room long enough to make her point. Once the point is made, the audience can decide what they are going to do. If, however, the presenter *allows* the audience to take control, he may lose the opportunity to get the full message across and wind up following the audience's agenda and not his own.

I'm aware that many people are used to more conversational meetings with clients and potential clients and many times those types of meetings are appropriate. However, if you want to persuade someone, I *highly* recommend you take control of the room long enough to make your persuasive point. This means you'll have to get there early, set the stage and present from a *standing* position. Michael Jackson never entertained his audience from a seated position and neither should you.

Chapter Three:

# *Ninja Moves*

The first thing I'm going to do is teach you a few critical dance moves, then I'm going to provide an overview of the stage and finally, I'm going to tell you how to match the moves to the stage and your content so you can choreograph your presentation.

The top five *most important* moves in Persuasive Choreography are:

1. Smile
2. Smile
3. Smile
4. Smile
5. Move your body

Smiling is—by far—the most important thing you can do to win over an audience. If you don't smile, not much else matters. Think about it—if your own product or service isn't interesting enough to make *you* smile, why should

it be interesting enough for your prospect to buy
or otherwise be persuaded by your message?

## Smiling

If you learn *nothing else* from this book, please
learn the importance of smiling. Smiling is
everything. Magnetic South Pole is the enemy of
smiling. It draws the jowls down so the mouth
can't help but frown. You have to fight to smile.

When you smile, people like you. When
you present, it is *absolutely imperative* that the
audience likes you. They won't buy from you or
invest in you if they don't like you. There are no
ands, ifs or buts about it. No like = no sale.

Most people are at least a little nervous to
present in front of an audience and, therefore,
they don't smile.

There are two components of smiling. The
first is to know *how* to smile and the second is
*remembering* to smile.

### How to Smile

Most people know how to smile. People
smile everyday—even on bad days they
sometimes smile. A genuine smile is called a
*Duchenne* smile and it's the smile that creates
crow's feet around the eyes. When you give
someone a Duchenne smile you give them a
warm feeling inside. It conveys warmth, trust,
love, interest, excitement and a flood of emotions

that are important when you are trying to persuade someone.

A fake smile does not engage the eyes and, therefore, no crow's feet appear. This smile, also known as the "Pan Am" or "Botox" smile, is more of a polite smile and does not express the same level of intimacy.

It's important—critically important—that you understand that although a Duchenne smile is better than a Botox smile, *any* smile is better than no smile at all!

*Remembering to Smile*

The biggest problem with smiling is remembering to do it. So, I'm going to show you how. To remember to smile, do this:

1. Take out a piece of paper and tear off a piece about five inches long by five inches wide. Precision is not important.
2. Draw a smiley face on it.
3. Write "I [your name] promise to remember to smile during my presentation like a Pitch Ninja."
4. Wad it up into a little ball.
5. Stick the little ball in your shoe right under the arch of your foot.

Now every time you take a step, the sharp edges of that wadded-up little paper ball will jab into the bottom of your foot. It can be quite painful. If it hurts enough it will remind you to smile. Remember, any smile is better than no smile so a pained smile will have to do if you can't remember to use a Duchenne smile.

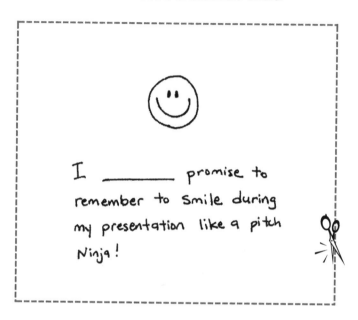

If you use this smile reminder trick, something very interesting will happen. Your pained smile will actually start making you happier and your smile will magically become less pained and more genuine. The edges on the little paper ball will get smashed down as you move and won't hurt as much, but its presence will continue to remind you to smile.

Of course, it's not always appropriate to smile. If your presentation is about saving the starving children in Africa, you probably don't want to smile while you describe their hardship, but it's certainly appropriate to smile when you describe how promising your proposed solution is and how excited you are to bring them nourishment.

If your presentation is on a somber subject, you should look for opportunities to work in positive messages during which it will be appropriate to smile. The more smiling that happens, the better your presentation will be.

At first, smiling may feel weird and unnatural. I warned you about this. Do it anyway. It's not weird and awkward to your audience. What *is* weird and awkward is to hear someone described their passion with a deadpan expression.

Newscasters are great at smiling all the time. Next time you watch the news, pay attention to how they smile. They smile at all sorts of things—even the weather!

## Eye Contact

The next super-powerful move presenters have is eye contact. Your eyes are one of the most communicative parts of your body. They can either help build trust or foster suspicion. There are lots of things that a person can do with their eyes, but for the purposes of presenting I want to focus on two: *gentle* eye contact and *steady* eye contact.

*Gentle Eye Contact*

A social, or professional, gaze is one where your eyes move within a small triangle formed by the other person's eyes and mouth. If your eyes wander outside this little triangle, the gaze becomes more intimate and, therefore, less comfortable in a professional setting.

In a professional setting it is polite to look at someone's face, but less polite to let your eyes wander to their hair, eyes and chest. Even if the person is super-hot, you don't want to undress them with your eyes while giving a professional presentation. It's not cool. Keep it professional.

*Steady Eye Contact*

The next type of eye contact I want to emphasize for presentation is *steady* eye contact. This means a steady stare at the other person's eyes. If you are standing far from them (which is likely) you will concentrate on the space below the other person's eyebrows and above their cheeks.

When you do this you are letting them know that what you are saying is important and that you need to know that they understand what you are saying.

When using steady eye contact it's important that your eyes continue to blink and that they move between the person's eyes. This can be tricky if they have one eye or a lazy eye, but do it anyway. Failure to blink and keep your eyes moving can be misinterpreted as aggression.

Staring without blinking at the space on the other person's forehead just above the bridge of their nose is called "power" eye contact and it expresses your intent to overpower the other person. It can be very off-putting to them. Steady eye contact shows concern for understanding. Power eye contact is threatening.

## Making Eye Contact

The way you make eye contact with audience members matters. Hold eye contact too long and you'll come across as creepy. Hold it too short and you'll appear shifty-eyed and untrustworthy. Luckily, there is a simple trick you can use to make sure your eye contact is just right.

As a rule of thumb, make eye contact with an individual long enough to complete one or two sentences or phrases and then move on to the next person. This allows you to finish a complete thought on one person, which is long enough to engage, but short enough to be natural. If you break eye contact *during* a sentence or phrase you will look shifty-eyed.

There are a number of exceptions to this rule that are worth mentioning. First, if you are answering someone's question, you can focus on that person while you answer her question.

Second, if you notice someone in the audience who isn't paying attention, you can hold a gaze on that person until your eyes connect. Then hold the gaze a little longer to bring them back into the presentation. When you have too many people not paying attention, you begin to lose the whole room.

Third, if you see someone who has their arms crossed, has a furrowed brow, or is otherwise indicating confusion, you can keep your eyes on that person until they loosen up a little. If there are a lot of people doing this, you might have to adjust your message a little. Crossed arms are an especially bad sign. It means people aren't receiving your message very well.

Like all the moves I'm going to cover in this chapter, I'll go into more detail about how and when to use eye contact later in the book. For now, I just want you to understand what the moves are.

## Voice

Magnetic South Pole turns people into drones who use a dull, monotone voice most of time. Your tone of voice is an important part of how you communicate energy and excitement. There are a number of components that matter here, including volume and melody.

Warning: I'm not a musician and I'm

going to use some musical terms in this section so I'm sure some *real* musicians are probably going to send me emails correcting me on my use of these words. This is fine; I welcome feedback. My email is Mike@Pitch.Ninja

*Volume*

Volume refers to how loud or soft your voice sounds to the audience and has to do with how much effort you are putting into it and the direction you are facing. If you are facing away from someone, your voice will sound softer. This may sound obvious, but I bring it up because when you address an audience this is always an issue and you may not be aware of the impact it has, especially in a large room. In some cases, you don't care if everybody in the room can hear you—more on this later.

*Front-of-the-Room Voice*

The voice you use when you are speaking to someone one-on-one or in a small group is your front-of-the-room voice. You will use this tone of voice, under certain circumstances, during your presentation. For the most part, if you are speaking clearly, even the people in the back of the room will hear you just fine.

*Back-of-the-Room Voice*

The back-of-the-room voice is loud enough so that the people in the back of the room can hear you just fine. It's not shouting. You should never have to shout. If the room is so big that the only way to hear someone is if they shout, then you should probably bring a PA system. ("PA" stands for "Public Address," in case you didn't know. I looked it up just now.)

*Crescendo and Decrescendo*

When your voice becomes louder it's called a crescendo. When it becomes softer it's called a decrescendo. Moving your voice from softer to louder and vice versa provides a number of cues to the audience with regard to what's going on in your presentation. For instance, crescendo often builds    excitement    and    energy,    whereas decrescendo often brings the room down into a more serious or personal mood.

Crescendo and decrescendo are especially important when you move around the room making transitions from one topic to another. It keeps your audience engaged and makes what you are saying much more interesting.

When people are nervous they tend to trail off at the end of sentences like this... This is another symptom of Magnetic South Pole and it's annoying. Decrescendo at the end of a sentence should only be used when you are ending a section or topic in the presentation. You may notice that many popular songs fade out at the end. This provides a natural transition to the end of the song or onto the next topic.

During your presentation you should maintain the volume of your sentences or even do a crescendo to maintain momentum in your presentation.

## Virtual Dojo

### Volume

To see a short video about volume, visit PitchNinja.com and click on the Virtual Dojo or scan the code.

## Melody

The melody of your voice refers to the notes of your voice. Most people use one note throughout their presentation, which is tedious for the audience. Imagine going to a Broadway show and hearing just one note. That would be horrible. The melody of your voice provides interest to what you are saying and helps you communicate more emotion. Try saying this:

*I'm really happy to be here*

Then try saying this:

*I'm really happy to be here*

The upper bar sounds insincere while the lower bar sounds sincere and energetic. Most people only use a couple of notes over and over and over and over and over.

When speaking you have to be mindful of the melody of what you are saying. My example above only includes three notes, mostly because there aren't that many words in the sentence (and I have no idea how to write music.) However, you should learn to move through a complete octave of notes or more to keep the presentation interesting.

The melody you use will help you communicate excitement and energy. A monotone voice sounds depressing. Worse yet, if you increase your volume while remaining monotone you will sound like you're mad at the audience.

A good melody can communicate upbeat confidence. Too much melody can make you sound condescending… so be careful!

To make melody work, you need to connect your words together so that they flow. You can stop at the end of a phrase or sentence (which is also a good time to move your eye contact). Doing this will help you avoid the ums, uhs and errs (more on this later).

Another thing I want you to keep in mind about melody is the *duration* of the words you use. By varying the duration of your words, you can improve the melody and provide important emphasis on the words that need emphasizing. Notice in my previous example there is a half note, instead of a quarter note, over the word "really". This means I'm saying, "I'm reeeally happy to be here." This little emphasis helps me sound more sincere about my message.

The last thing to know about melody is that your melody can include breaks and pauses. A properly timed pause can add dramatic emphasis to your points and, as a nice aside, give your audience a moment to think about what you said.

I realize that there is a lot to remember about the melody of your voice, but the main takeaway is to be mindful of how you come across to your audience based on how you are using your voice.

## *Virtual Dojo*

### *Melody*

To see a short video about melody, visit PitchNinja.com and click on the Virtual Dojo or scan the code.

## Unnecessary Words

One of the most common questions I get is how to stop saying "um." "Um" is an unnecessary word that can get really annoying and it is a symptom of Magnetic South Pole. If you are standing still, using scant few hand motions and talking in a monotone voice, your nervous energy needs an escape. So, it escapes through your mouth in the form of "um."

There are several ways to avoid this. The first is to project your voice. Projecting your voice not only makes it difficult to say the word "um," but also makes it painfully obvious when you are saying it. Try it now. Read the following sentence using a normal, monotone voice:

> *Four score and, um, seven years ago, um, our, um, forefathers brought forth on, um, this continent a new, um, nation.*

Now, go back and read it again, but this time project your voice as if you were speaking in a large room. I think you will find the "um's" are harder to say and they really stand out, which will remind you to drop them.

The next thing you can do to is connect the words together as though you were singing them. People do this all the time when they sing, but they pause between words when they talk and they fill the pause with an unnecessary word, like "um." When you connect the words there is no space for the unnecessary words:

> *Four-score-and-seven-years-ago.-Our-forefathers-brought-forth-on-this-continent-a-new-nation.*

Lastly, to keep from sounding like a boring robot, throw in a little melody and elongate the words a little:

> *Foour-score-and-ssseven-years-agooo-our-forefathers-brought-forth-on-this-continent-a-newww-nationnn.*

The key is to have an interesting-sounding voice and avoid boring monotone voices. "Um" isn't the only unnecessary word. People inject all kinds of irritating words into their speech.

I once had a professor who said "typically," "essentially," and "actually" at the end of nearly every sentence, so much so that the students would wager on how many times he would say one of those words.

Sometimes people add the word "OK" to the end of each sentence. Once in a while this is a good way to check comprehension with the audience, but use it too much and everything you say will sound like a question, making you look unsure of yourself or untrustworthy.

Record yourself speaking to see which repetitive, unnecessary words you use. It will, um, be enlightening I'm, um, sure, OK?

## Shutting Your Mouth

One of the most powerful things you can say is nothing at all. A long pause can add drama and intrigue to a presentation. People aren't expecting it and presenters are usually so nervous that they talk too fast (I do this all the time). However, a nice, long pause at the right time can make all the difference. Try saying this:

> *Four score and seven years ago our forefathers brought forth on this continent a new nation.*

Now say it again, but include some pauses:

> *Four score......and seven years ago.......our forefathers brought forth......on this continent......a new...nation.*

A few pauses, without unnecessary words, sound pretty cool. Whenever you want something to sound important or dramatic, try throwing in a few strategically-placed pauses and see what happens.......it will work......I promise...

## Hand and Arm Motions

Gesturing can be an important part of how people emphasize what they are saying. It can also be super annoying. When Magnetic South Pole sets in, most people use very small, repetitive hand motions that do not reflect what they are saying. It's not uncommon to see someone with "flapping" hands in front of their body.

Your hands are one of the most important parts of your body and one of the most critical components of what makes humans human. There are an endless number of things you can do with your hands but I want to break it down into some easy categories to help you remember.

Think of your hips and shoulders as making a box. There are three kinds of hand motions you can use: inside the box, outside the box and fully extended.

Whenever possible—and this applies to all types of hand gestures—keep your palms open and facing forward. Openness is a key Pitch Ninja style. It shows confidence and honesty. Not every hand gesture or arm movement will lend itself to an open palm, but it should be your default place to go. Open palms are like smiling—do it as much as you can.

*Inside the Box*

When you are close to another person, you need to keep your hands *inside* the box so you don't overwhelm them. Pitch Ninjas move a lot during a presentation and in some cases they get right up close to the audience. Inside-the-box hand gestures will allow you to emphasize points in a personal way.

Presenters who are overcome by Magnetic South Pole keep all their hand gestures inside the box. They appear small and weak. Remember, you are a *silverback gorilla*.

*Outside the Box*

Keep your hands *outside* the box as much as possible. This means your elbows are up and away from your body and your armpits are showing. If you are the kind of person who has sweaty armpits, do something about it. Use extra antiperspirant, wear a T-shirt under  your shirt or cover your armpits with sealing wax—whatever it takes. Pitch Ninjas show their armpits all the time so be sure they are presentable.

Outside-the-box arm movements and gestures are interesting and bold. They show passion and excitement that literally *can't be contained* inside the box. It's easy to forget to keep our hands outside the box and recoil them like a sickly little lamb baby (if it had hands).

You're a gorilla, show those armpits!

*Fully Extended*

When you need your hands to point to specific points of interest on your presentation, you will need them fully extended. When you extend your arm and lock your elbows, your arm becomes a pointer.

Remember what I said you could do with that silly laser pointer? Pitch Ninjas don't use laser pointers; they use their arms and fingers to point.

If you are too short to point to the areas of your presentation that need attention, grab a long stick or get a chair and stand on it. Al Gore used a scissor lift in his presentation "The Inconvenient Truth." If he can do it, you can do it. That being said, getting a scissor lift inside a lecture hall seems pretty inconvenient, to tell you the truth. Not to mention a waste of energy!

## Virtual Dojo

### Arm and Hand Motions

To see a short video about arm and hand motions, visit PitchNinja.com and click on the Virtual Dojo or scan the code.

## The Itsy-Bitsy Spider

*The itsy-bitsy spider went up the water spout*
*Down came the rain and washed the spider out*
*Out came the sun and dried up all the rain*
*And the itsy-bitsy spider went up the spout again*
*Nailed it!*

The itsy-bitsy spider is not kidding around. He is focused, determined and is Pitch Ninja material through and through. All we need to do is get him an audience and set of itsy-bitsy galoshes.

When you read the itsy-bitsy spider song, you were probably thinking about how, when you were a kid, you "did the motions" with the lyrics and made the spider crawl up the spout by pinching the fingers of both hands together in an alternating style. Next, you used your hands to recreate that horrible, spider-thwarting rainstorm—lowering your voice and grimacing to communicate the plight of the itsy-bitsy spider. Then, your hands shot upwards to the sky, fingers outstretched to represent the rays of the sun that come out to save the day. Lastly, the intrepid itsy-bitsy spider makes his way back up the spout, as boldly represented by your pinched fingers again. A big smile on your face ends the song on an upbeat, to be greeted by a standing ovation of parents and teachers.

This, my Pitch Ninja-to-be, is how you do hand motions. You had it right in kindergarten, but somewhere along the way you may have forgotten the awesome power of songs with motions. The *motions* are what make the itsy-bitsy spider memorable, not the song. The song itself is pretty boring. Think about it.

## Virtual Dojo

### Itsy-Bitsy Spider Sing-Along
To see a kid sing the song and do the motions, visit PitchNinja.com and click on the Virtual Dojo or scan the code.

There are an infinite number of hand and arm motions that you could use to emphasize the words coming out of your mouth. When I coach pitch teams, I work a lot with them on how they can create interesting gestures to accompany what they are saying.

The key thing is to create a gesture to accompany important words or concepts, especially if they express emotion.

Remember how I mentioned that you could extend the duration of certain words to create an emphasis? This is a good place to start:

create a gesture to accompany that word. Also, create gestures to help your audience organize their thoughts. For instance:

*Three Things*

On your PowerPoint or Prezi slides you will often have a handful of points you want to communicate. In fact, the default style of a PowerPoint slide is bullet points. When you reach a slide that has three points (or two or four or five or six, but no more than that), hold up three fingers (hands outside the box) and say, "There are *three* things I want to tell you about!" Next, hold up one finger and say, "The *fiiirst* thing I want to tell you about is blah, blah, blah." Then hold up two fingers and say, "The *sssseecond* thing I want to tell you about is yadda, yadda, yadda." Last, hold up three fingers and say, "The *thiiird* thing I want to tell you about is humina, humina, humina!" Do all of this while you're smiling, of course.

Use your fingers to count out the points on your slide for the audience and you will come across as organized and efficient. This is a Pitch Ninja itsy-bitsy spider move.

*Love*

Love is the most powerful of all human emotions so using it will bring out the passion you have for the business or the idea. Don't be afraid to tell them what you love and, when you do, emphasize it with an itsy-bitsy spider gesture. If you are a woman, put your hands flat over the middle of your chest on top of one another and say, "I *llooove*, nanotechnology!" If you are a guy, touch your fingertips to your chest and say, "I *llooove* big data!" Do this, and smile, to come across as sincere and passionate.

*Excitement*

Always be motivating the audience with energy and excitement. Telling them how excited you are will get them riled up. *Showing* them how excited you are will put them on the edge of their chair, hanging on every word you say. The itsy-bitsy spider motion for excitement is smile, arms outside the box, hands in front of you with two thumbs up as you say, "I couldn't be more *exciiiited* to be here today, your company is *grrreat* and I'm really *geeeked* about the possibility of working with you!"

*Pain*

In many cases your audience has a problem they need solved, which is why you were invited to present in the first place. If they have a problem, they are in some kind of pain. Show them that you can empathize with their pain by holding your arms and hands outside the box, fists clenched, scowl on your face, knees bent and say,

"It is so *iiirrritating* when you can't get access to enough qualified job candidates!" This "pain stance" reminds them how horrible their life is and how you surely do understand them, and if only there was a perfect solution to this problem....

*Fear*

Not all customers have problems. Sometimes things are just fine, but they may fear some future event. At the turn of the century there was a lot of fear about what would happen when computer systems moved from 1999 to 2000, known as Y2K. There is fear when a new president is elected. There is fear when a family is expecting a baby. There is fear when students go off to college. Impending change creates anxiety and fear. You need to let the audience understand that you understand the fear. You could just stand motionless and monotone over Magnetic South Pole and say, "Y2K has the potential to bring down corporate information systems...." Or, you could show real empathy with your audience by using a itsy-bitsy spider gesture.

Unlike pain, however, you have to be careful not to exaggerate fear because you will come across as condescending by mocking the audience's genuine feelings. In this case you could put your arms together in front of your body, inside the box, clench your fists and shrug a little and say, "The impending Y2K change has caused

a lot of *anxiiiety* across all business sectors
because of the unknown impact on information
systems." Use the itsy-bitsy spider gesture only
for a moment when you say, "*anxiiiety.*"

*Pleasure*

Sometimes the customer has neither fear nor
pain. Life is good. The only reason they are
speaking to you is because they think you might
be able to make life even better. Venture
capitalists seem to be a pretty happy lot from
what I can tell (from the outside). They look at
potential deals because they want to improve
their financial position. There might be fear or
pain, but the predominant feeling is the pleasure
of potential gain.

The pleasure of financial gain, for
instance, is exciting so the itsy-bitsy spider gesture
will be similar. In this case you'll use three
gestures: 1) the thumbs-up gesture, 2) the
international sign for cashola, which is rubbing
your thumbs against the tips of your fingers, and
3) the Cheshire Cat gesture, which means you
give a big grin and press your index fingers into
your cheeks.

It will play out like this: smile, put your
arms outside the box, hands in front of you and
say, "I couldn't be more *exciiiited* [thumbs-up] to
be here today. I'm going to present what I believe
to be a surefire way of participating in the very
*luuucrative* [cashola] cloud storage space that I

think will be very *saaatisfying* [Cheshire Cat].

This set of gestures, combined with the right melody and a nice smile will be very expressive and persuasive to the audience.

*Easy-Peasy*

Throughout your presentation you will want to communicate how you and your team can do whatever it is that you are promoting you can do. Your team, unlike the rest of the world, is so smart and clever and awesome that you can magically alleviate pain or fear and seamlessly deliver loads of profits. To communicate the feeling of "no problem," you could use the following itsy-bitsy spider gestures.

First, you will have to point to your team. When you point, don't use your index finger. This kind of pointing is confrontational. (Remember your parents teaching you that it's rude to point?) The right way to point is to make the "A-OK" hand gesture by touching your index finger tip to your thumb tip and extending your other three fingers straight. Use those fingers to point. I also like to call this the "Preacher Point" because priests and ministers use this when they make a cross in the air to bless the congregation.

Next, you'll need to make the "no problem" gesture, which is holding your hands flat and parallel to the ground and waving them back and forth a few times over one another like you're smoothing a sheet on a bed.

You say, "*Thhhis* technology team [Preacher Point, fully extend arm] is so good at Scrum they make it look *eeeeasy* [no problem hands]."

By the way, it's OK to brag about your team, but it's less OK to brag about yourself. I'll address this in more detail later.

*The Itsy-Bitsy Spider Is Huge*

There are lots and lots and lots of different gestures that you can do with your hands, arms and entire body. The key is to incorporate an itsy-bitsy spider gesture whenever you feel overcome by Magnetic South Pole. This will give you something to do with your body other than nothing.

Your teammates can help you here (if you have them). When you are practicing, they will see you getting sucked back to Magnetic South Pole and can stop you and help you come up with a plan for your hands.

**Body Movement**

Moving your entire body off Magnetic South Pole is an important part of making your presentation interesting. Standing in one place the whole time is boring, even if you are doing everything else right. There are two ways you can move your body: you can move front to back and you can move side to side.

*Side to Side*

Moving from one side of the room to the other is used to *emphasize* what you are saying. Say one point, move a few steps to the left. Say the next point, move a few steps to the left. Say the next point, and so on. If you run out of room, start moving back in the other direction.

Typically as you move from one side to the other, you will keep the same volume of your voice, hand movements and other nonverbal Pitch Ninja moves.

*Front to Back*

Moving frontwards and backwards is how you *relate* to the audience. Later, when we talk about zones, you will learn how moving from one zone to the other changes your relationship with the audience and even with individuals in the audience. Stepping towards an individual when they ask a question, for instance, will help you form a better relationship with them. When you step back you are able to address the larger group and raise the excitement level in the room.

I mentioned this before, but it's worth mentioning again: moving your body does not mean pacing back and forth. Pacing is annoying, moving is not. Pair your movements with what you are saying and be sure to stop moving once in a while to allow your message to sink in.

## Ninja Uniforms

When I was in high school I always wanted to wear my shirt untucked because I thought I was a cool skateboard-surfer dude and I thought that skateboard-surfer dudes were too cool to tuck their shirts in. So, I kept my shirts untucked and wrinkled. My audience, who were often teachers and other adults, interpreted my sloppy appearance as evidence of disrespect. I guess I cared more about what my peer group thought than my audience. I'm not sure that my peer group was even paying attention. I was not voted most fashionable. Perhaps I should have dressed for my audience, not my peers.

What you wear says a lot about who you are and your level of respect for the audience. In many cases those two messages are in conflict. In the high school example, I may have fit in well with my peers, but I wasn't showing respect for the audience.

The same concept applies to presentations. You need to dress in a way that shows respect for your audience. Sometimes this may run counter to your own personal style. So be it. Giving a good presentation is about your audience, not you. If the cast of *Cats* wanted to wear jeans and T-shirts instead of tights and face paint, the show wouldn't have been nearly as interesting.

When it comes to what to wear, there are

two rules to keep in mind:

1. Dress one notch better than your audience
2. Wear a white or light blue shirt

To adhere to rule number one, you will need to know what your audience is wearing.

| If they wear... | You wear... |
| --- | --- |
| Bermuda shorts and tank tops | jeans and a T-shirt |
| jeans and T-shirts | slacks and a golf shirt |
| slacks and a golf shirt | dress slacks and a dress shirt |
| dress slacks and a dress shirt | Slacks and a sport coat |
| Slacks and a sport coat | Suit and tie |
| Suit and tie | Suit and tie |

If you are a woman, wear the equivalent to what a woman would wear. I'm a guy, so I wrote about guy clothes here.

By the time you get to the "slacks and a dress shirt" category, your dress shirt should adhere to rule number two, which means it should be white or light blue. No grey shirts, French blue shirts, brown shirts, tan shirts, pink shirts, purple shirts, green shirts or black shirts. For some reason investors like to invest in people wearing white or blue shirts. If you don't believe me, do an image search for "business plan competition winners" on Google and look at what comes up. The majority of the winners are wearing light blue or white shirts (if they are dressed up). Yes, you will find people wearing grey shirts, French blue shirts, brown shirts, tan shirts, pink shirts, purple shirts, green shirts or black shirts. But most of them aren't. Stack the odds in your favor and wear a light blue or white shirt.

### Instant Google Search
Scan or click the code to launch a Google image search of "business plan competition winners."

*Bonus Points*

If you want an extra edge, find a way to coordinate everyone so you will look like a team. You can do this by wearing matching ties or shirts or something with your company logo on it. I know it might feel corny, but it works. We live in a world that likes corny.

Lots of teams wear matching T-shirts with their company logo. This is an acceptable exception to the attire rule.

*Extra Bonus Points*

For an even greater edge, find a way to coordinate with your audience. If you are giving a presentation to Nike, wear Nike shoes. If you are giving a presentation at a college, wear their school colors. Do whatever you can to establish a connection and build rapport with your audience.

## Presentation Remotes and Pointers

The presentation remote is the Pitch Ninja's ultimate weapon. Without it, you are doomed to tap the mouse or arrow keys on your computer each time you want to advance your slide, which will be a *major* cramp on your style. Even worse, you might have to ask someone to advance your slides for you, which is presentation suicide.

Don't rely on the venue to have a remote for you. Buy yourself a good presentation remote and a good old-fashioned telescoping pointer just in case you have to present in a room with an extra-tall screen. Whatever you spend will be well worth the investment.

You can buy a good presentation remote online for between $25 and $50. The key is to get a simple tool. You don't need a lot of bells and whistles. Avoid remotes with more than three or four buttons and make sure the buttons are nicely spaced. If they are too close together, you will inadvertently click the wrong button. All you really need is a front and back button and, if you want, a blackout button that will turn the presentation on and off. You don't need mouse control, volume or (gasp) a laser pointer built in.

The Kensington (K33373US) is a great option. It has a little weight so it feels good to hold. I recommend you buy one now:

### Presentation Remote
Scan or click the code to buy a Kensington Presentation Remote.

I mentioned this before, but remember that the other item that you'll want to pick up, if you want to be prepared for anything, is a telescoping presentation pointer. It's like a pen that expands to a pointer so you can reach the tops of large screens. You can also stand on chairs or a scissor lift.

You may wonder why you can't use a laser pointer instead. Laser pointers don't require you to move your body. Being a Pitch Ninja is about getting *off* of Magnetic South Pole and doing something interesting. Hardly anybody uses a telescoping presentation pointer, so you will stand out when you do it. Besides, by now you've already tossed your laser pointer in the toilet.

I just gave you the Pitch Ninja brain dump. By now you might feel pretty overwhelmed with all the things to remember. It is a lot, but much of it will start coming naturally after a little practice.

Remember, Pitch Ninja moves are designed to give you something to do with your body *other than nothing*. Without making a conscious effort to move your body in interesting ways, you will fall into the clutches of Magnetic South Pole.

Here is a little recap to help you remember:

- Smile, smile, smile
- Make gentle or steady eye contact, hold for one or two sentences or phrases and move on to the next person
- Vary the volume and melody of your voice to add interest
- Extend the duration of words to emphasize them
- Keep your arms inside the box when close to people, outside the box to generate excitement and fully extended to convey information
- Use itsy-bitsy spider gestures to emphasize important words and emotions
- Move your body side to side to emphasize points and front to back to relate to the audience

Pitch Ninjas, just like real ninjas, have a lot of moves to choose from. At any given time they are using a combination of the moves to perform.

In your case the performance will be a persuasive pitch or presentation. The real ninja's performance will be to kick someone's butt.

Chapter Four:

# Ninja Slides

There was a time in my life where I was committed to having *no words whatsoever* on my slide deck. I gave some cool presentations, but it was extremely difficult to pull off and these days I do include words, but I use them as sparingly as possible. Mostly they just help me remember what I wanted to say. Even a Pitch Ninja needs a little help once in a while. Sometimes the amount of rehearsal necessary to remember every word of your presentation just isn't practical. The lectures I give in the classes I teach, for instance, sometimes change at the last minute so I have to bring notes and use my slides to help me stay on track.

Still, you don't really *need* a slide deck to be persuasive and there are presentation coaches who will try to talk you out of them altogether. I'm on board with this approach, but I don't really mind if you do use them. It's pretty difficult to present financial projections without a slide—

not impossible—but the necessary preparation would be impractical and the incremental value would be minimal.

The problem with slide decks is that people try to pack every single point they want to make on the slide and cover every single important aspect of their business. This leads to content-heavy slides with lots of small type that can hardly be seen.

To make matters worse, teams email their decks back and forth to review them and people keep adding content because they want the slide to be understandable even without a presenter. Simple slides require a presenter to understand.

Sometimes people want to provide details because they want their slide deck to serve as a leave-behind and are afraid that the recipient won't understand the slides without the details. This is true. But it's also true that your deck is much more likely to be tossed in the trash than it is to actually be looked at by someone who matters—even if the presentation was good.

To be a Pitch Ninja you have to keep your slides simple, clean and crisp without a lot of detail. You are the messenger here, not your slide deck.

A Pitch Ninja uses *only* three kinds of slides in her deck: 1) a backdrop, 2) visual aids and, 3) information. If a slide does not fit into one of these categories, the Pitch Ninja changes it until it does or she discards it altogether. Having slides that do not fit into one of these categories is problematic for reasons that I'll go into later.

## Backdrop Slides

A backdrop slide is there to make you look good. Ideally, it is a large photograph or other image that helps set a mood for the presentation or makes a personal connection with the audience. Backdrop slides are used in the beginning of a presentation and throughout as sort of a way to center the presentation on an overall theme of excitement and passion. The more personal your backdrop slide, the better.

*Selfies*

One of the best backdrop slides you can have is a shot of the presenter, or presenters, engaged in something relevant to the audience. This is a way to immediately establish you and/or your team as human and build a personal rapport with the audience.

When visiting a client in Minneapolis I used this horrible selfie of me at the Mall of America:

While the slide was up I told a personal story of my quest to purchase a presentation remote for them at the Mall of America. The image is not high quality, but it allowed me to easily break the ice and build a more genuine connection with the audience.

Most of the time presenters show a picture of their logo at the beginning of presentations. This is far less meaningful than an emotionally charged or personal image. With backdrop slides, it's the thought that counts. Rough and candid images will make you look even more genuine.

*Photos of Others*

If you don't have a picture of yourself, you can use another image that helps you convey your message. If you want to establish yourself as an advocate for education, for instance, you might use an image like this:

Perhaps you are doing a presentation about community involvement. Your backdrop slide could look like this:

The important thing is that the image helps set the tone for your presentation, makes a personal connection and adds interest. For instance, this image of the beach:

Sets a different tone than this image of the beach:

The first photo better captures the beauty of the beach, the second better captures recreation at the beach. Make sure the image properly reflects the tone you want to convey. Worry less about the quality of the image itself.

*Photos of Places and Things*

In some cases you can build a connection with the audience using images of places and things. If you are giving a presentation about national monuments, you might use a backdrop slide that looks like this:

Perhaps you are giving a presentation about how to deliver great customer service. You could use a stock image like this to help set the tone:

These aren't breathtaking images, and they don't have to be. The key is to provide a visually stimulating slide that will just be there while you are talking. When backdrop slides are up, you are probably not referring to the slide itself. You are probably telling a story as part of your introduction or at some other point during the presentation.

## Visual Aids

A visual aid slide helps clarify and reiterate what you are saying. It is used to describe business process or abstract concepts. Keep the slide simple, bold and clear with an obvious flow. Your visual aid does not have to tell the whole story; that's what you are for. The visual aid has to help the audience keep track of where you are in the story.

Here is a slide that I use from a presentation called "Guts, Brains and Balls" that describes the importance of emotional branding.

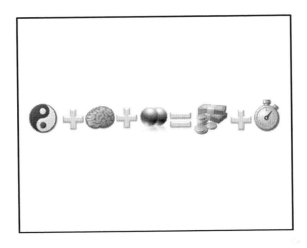

I tell the audience that making an emotional appeal (yin-yang), then a logical appeal (brain) and having the balls (green balls) to follow that order will result in stronger financials (money) and time to react to competitive threats (clock).

This slide does a nice job of making my point. I then follow up with another slide that helps me tell the flip side of the story:

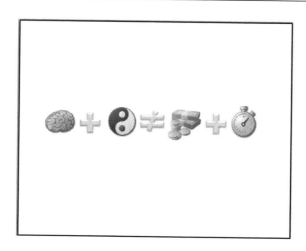

This slide shows that if you attempt to make a logical (brain) connection with your customer before making an emotional connection (yin-yang) you will not enjoy stronger financials (money) and you will not have time (clock) to react to competitive threats.

The point of the visual aid is just to help you tell your story.

## *Virtual Dojo*

### *Visual Aids*

To see a more examples of good and bad visual aids, visit PitchNinja.com and click on the Virtual Dojo or scan the code.

### Information Slides

The last kind of slide is the slide that contains more detailed information about your business or concept. These are the facts and figures that back up your claims, without which there would be major holes in your story. If you're pitching a business concept and claim that you will make millions, most people are going to want to see at least a high-level explanation of how you are going to get there.

Here is a sample slide from a business plan presentation showing a high-level breakdown of the financial projections:

| Financials – Veterinary Industry | | | |
|---|---|---|---|
| | 2015 | 2016 | 2017 |
| Revenue | $1,750,140 | $6,030,000 | $12,285,950 |
| COGS | $1,154,628 | $3,779,442 | $7,957,619 |
| **Gross Margin** | **$596,112** | **$2,250,558** | **$4,328,332** |
| Operating Costs | $1,063,127 | $2,340,842 | $3,089,430 |
| **Net Income** | **$(467,015)** | **$(90,284)** | **$1,238,902** |
| Offices | 332 | 902 | 1,567 |
| Mail/Client | 1.8 | 2.2 | 2.6 |
| Margin/Office | $1,796 | $2,495 | $2,762 |

Notice that is doesn't contain a lot of detail, just enough to convey the important parts. The actual financial model behind this slide is huge and far too complex to be presented in a meaniful way. Getting rid of the detail is one of the biggest challenges you have as a presenter.

Even better than a spreadsheet layout is to use graphs and charts to convey trends over time. This slide is great for highlighting specific areas of concern:

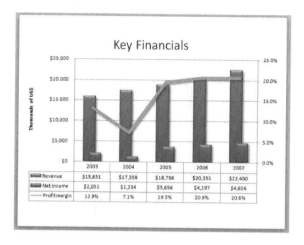

This slide will allow the Pitch Ninja to easily address the elephant in the room (profit dip) without getting distracted by details.

All of this is not to say that the details aren't important—they are. But too much detail during your presentation will suck the life out of it. There is no reason why you can't have a handout set aside with more detail for those who want it.

## Builds and Animation

In general, I tell my clients to avoid too many complex builds and animations on their slides. They have a tendancy to not work the way they were intended and can be a distraction to the presentation itself. When I do builds I usually create each build on a separate slide.

This causes problems when printing the slides, but I rarely, if ever, print my slides. If you need a leave-behind, create a separate file.

The point of the builds and animations in a slide deck is to bring a little sizzle to the show for people who are stuck on Magnetic South Pole. You bring the energy and excitement to your presentation by being a Pitch Ninja.

**Crossover Slides**

Avoid slides that fit into more than one category. It is extremely common for a visual aid to contain detailed information and vice versa. Don't let this happen if you can avoid it. I call this a crossover slide and it means that you will have a physically challenging presentation to deliver. You'll be hopping back and forth between zones. This will make more sense when you read about the zones. Sometimes the extra physical activity works, but in the beginning it's best to stick with the program.

Chapter Five:

# *The Zone Program*

I like to refer to this as the Super-Awesome Presentation Zone Program because it is the *backbone* of a super-awesome presentation. However, that name would have messed up the table of contents so I'll just go with Zone Program. The Zone Program is one of the key concepts that makes a Pitch Ninja a Pitch Ninja. It provides a structure for how to move around the room so that movements aren't random and repetitive. This is where you bring everything together. You have the moves, you have the content, now you get the structure.

With the Zone Program you divide the area in which you will be presenting into three distinct zones. In each zone you will have a specific set of moves and a specific type of slide content.

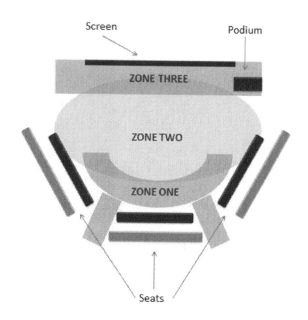

Zone 1 is as close to the audience members as you can get. It's right up front, up the aisles or anywhere else that will get you close to the members of the audience.

Zone 2 is any space that you can move around in and wave your arms. It is in this space that you will use big arm movements and let your inner gorilla come to life.

Zone 3 is right up next to the presentation screen. You will be standing so close that you can easily touch the screen. It is from this zone that you will be conveying the details of your presentation. When you are in this zone, pretend you are the weatherman (or woman) reporting the weather on the news. Your arms will be outstretched and you'll be referring to data points on the screen. You will be *physically* touching the screen so make sure you are close.

*The "Weatherman" Position*

I mentioned before that you can and should take control of how the room is arranged to maximize the impact you are able to have. I don't care if it's a university lecture hall, a venture capitalist boardroom, or a local coffee shop—you have to *own* that space for the duration of your presentation.

Make sure there aren't chairs or tables in the way of your ability to easily move through the zones. Make sure the important people are accessible in Zone 1. You can even tell people where to sit. They may not always do what you say, but ask anyway. You *own* the room.

Different spaces have different layouts, but no matter what the space, it can always be divided into the three zones.

In a conference room, Zone 1 is all the way around the table and so is Zone 2, but the zones are relative. When you are addressing an individual from right next to them, you are addressing them from Zone 1; when you are talking to them across the table, you are addressing them from Zone 2. Zone 3 is right in front of the presentation screen.

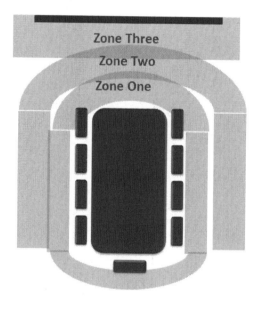

*The Zones in a Conference Room*

In a public space like a coffee shop, your zones are smaller and you may not be able to stand up when you present. Pitch Ninjas stand up whenever possible. *It is virtually impossible to give a good presentation from a seated position.* Think about it. Nobody ever applauds for a seated speaker. Nevertheless, if you are meeting at a coffee shop, the table space can be broken into zones.

Make sure the most important person you are addressing is sitting next to you, not across from you. Squaring your shoulders with someone is confrontational. I know that earlier I said to square off like a silverback gorilla, but when you are seated it doesn't work as well. You want to come across as collaborative, not confrontational.

If there are two important people attending, you can ask the second most important person to sit across from you while the most important person sits next to you. The third most important person, or your partner, would sit on your other side. This way, you can not only avoid the confrontational stance, but also the "tennis match" movement of your head from side to side as you talk to your audience.

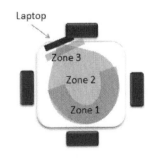

*The Zones at a Coffee Shop*

If you are meeting with more than one or two people, push for meeting in a more private setting where you can stand up and give a more formal presentation.

I recently coached a client who told me that he had never once presented standing up. I walked him through the moves and the zones. He was nervous about it, but he did a spectacular job. The structure of the zone program will help you overcome some of the nervousness because it gives you the right moves.

## Zones Are Everywhere

Any place you make your in-person pitch can be divided into zones. If you are selling a car or a blender or a facelift, the space between you and the prospect can be used according to the zone program to instantly improve your ability to connect with them in a meaningful way.

## Zone 1 – Intimacy

Zone 1 is the *intimacy* zone. It is in this zone where you will form intimate bonds with your audience. Fair warning here: there is a lot of touchy-feely stuff going on in Zone 1, so brace yourself!

Your goal in this zone is for them to love you and for you to love them. Yes, I said *love*. You want them to see you for the real, actual person you are: a person who has passion, a person whose life has meaning, a person worth loving and capable of being loved.

Similarly, your job in this zone is to reach out emotionally to your audience and see them for who they are: people who have passion, people who lead meaningful lives, people who are worthy of your love and capable of being loved. Your job is to apply love as a verb. To *love* these people is to care for them and take their needs seriously. This is heavy stuff, but it will set you free!

Most people have trouble with this level of intimacy with people they actually love, let alone a room full of strangers. This is completely understandable. I sometimes do the "I love you" exercise with my students and clients by asking them to stand up and find a partner, preferably someone they don't know that well. I ask them to look into each other's eyes and say "I love you" to them in their most sincere tone. The only rule is that they can only say those words, nothing else.

The reaction is usually giggles and eyes rolling and extreme discomfort. One student almost broke into tears when faced with the prospect of telling a guy she hardly knew that she loved him. "What if he thinks I really love him?" she asked me. Just because you express love to someone doesn't mean you have to *marry* them. You can just love them and leave it at that.

People often add words onto the phrase like, "I love you, man," or, "I love you, you're the best." Or they change the phrase to "Love ya!" They do this to protect themselves from the emotional discomfort. For some reason, people find it hard to say a simple "I love you" to another person.

I tell my students and clients to pay special attention to how they are *feeling* when they say it. They feel afraid, uncomfortable and nervous. These are the emotions that are *getting in the way* of their ability to connect with an audience in a genuine way. This is the feeling that they must understand in order to move past it. If they can get control of these emotions, they will be set free and truly become a Pitch Ninja. This, my dear reader, is the Pitch Ninja's source of true power on the stage: his or her ability to overcome the discomfort and allow him or herself to love the audience and be loved by them. *This is power.*

In most business settings we guard our true selves and we don't show vulnerabilities. On the stage, however, it is your command of emotion that will allow you to truly connect with your audience on more than just a superficial level. The focus of the audience's love that you want to cultivate is on your passion for the subject matter about which you speak.

I've mentioned passion throughout this book and it's a word that gets used a lot in business, but I want to take a moment to define what it means so that it will make sense in the context of the intimacy zone.

Passion is a combination of two things (in

my opinion). The first element is an intense *emotional* desire or compulsion for just about anything. (Contrast this with a *physical* desire or compulsion for just about anything. If you have a physical desire or compulsion, you may have an addiction.)

The second element of passion is an accompanying sense of pride for being associated with the thing you feel strongly about.

So, someone who is passionate about sports is not only emotionally compelled to do sports, but also is proud to be known as someone who does sports. Likewise, someone who is passionate about math is not only emotionally compelled to calculate, but also is proud to be known as a math person.

Bottom line: if you want someone to believe in you, you will have to get them to understand your passion and love you for it. To do this, you must be willing to love them back.

*Sharing Your Passion in the Intimacy Zone*

Nearly every presentation you do should start out in the intimacy zone. You should move directly into the intimacy zone without hesitation, and tell your personal story of why you are excited to be addressing the audience and individuals in the audience. Your personal story is one about emotions and passion, and less about facts and credentials. Here you will set the tone for the presentation and establish yourself as someone who speaks from the heart. By entering right into the intimacy zone you are doing something called "breaking the plane," which is an invisible wall that divides the speaker from the audience. Most speakers never break the plane physically or emotionally—you will do both.

You break the physical plane by getting close to the audience. Moving your body forward will allow you to relate to individuals. Go right up to them and speak to them in your front-of-the-room voice. This is the voice that you would use if you were addressing them personally, which, of course, you are, because the intimacy zone is about personal relationship building.

You will make gentle eye contact and your arm movements as gestures will be inside the box. If they are *outside* the box you will come across as overly aggressive. You are too close to people in the intimacy zone to use outside-the-box gestures and steady eye contact. Don't worry, you are still a gorilla because you are standing up and your audience is sitting down.

You break the emotional plane by telling your personal story. Tell them why you are excited to be speaking to them about the subject at hand. For this you may have to dig deep within yourself to find out exactly what is motivating you to do what you are doing.

Most people's instinct is to provide their *credentials* to the audience. The rationale is that people will be impressed with your experience and trust what you have to say. There is a time and place for credentials because it is important that you *know* what you are talking about, but it's more important that you *believe* in what you are talking about.

For example, let's say Norvin is a salesperson giving a presentation to sell a customer relationship management (CRM) application. He could say, as he stands in front of a slide with the company logo:

> *Hello, thank you for having me today and hearing my presentation. My name is Norvin and I have over 20 years of experience in sales technology with the last 10 years as head of CRM development at Super CRM Company. I was named employee of the year three years in a row and I got my MBA at Top MBA University. Today I'm going to talk to you about why you should buy Super CRM to streamline your company's sales efforts. It's the best CRM package on the market and we have the most impressive client list of any company in the market.*

This is a perfectly polite, logical introduction to a sales pitch that you might hear from anyone—other than a Pitch Ninja. It *does* establish Norvin as an experienced person, but it also sounds a little boastful. When you are talking about your own credentials you are much more likely to sound boastful than passionate. He also made the mistake of passing judgment on his own company. "It's the best CRM package on the market," and, "We have the most impressive client list of any company in the market," are two statements that will leave the audience scratching their heads trying to figure out if they agree. Both statements can be argued. Clearly, Norvin *knows* what he is talking about, but does he *believe* in what he is talking about?

If Norvin was a Pitch Ninja he would have said something like this as he stands in front of a picture of him and his sales team with their arms around each other's shoulders in front of the prospective client's office:

> *My name is Norvin and this is a picture of me and my team getting ready for today's presentation. We are all smiling because we* couldn't be more exciiiited *to tell you about Super CRM and how it will change the way you do business forever. For the past 20 years I have had the* priiivilege *of working with these people in this industry and I love it because I get to see how it impacts people's lives every day. When I first got started in sales at XYZ company right out of college I loved sales, but I was frrrustrated with how hard it was to keep everything straight like names, numbers, meetings, appointments, customer service issues and all kinds of things that* sloooowed *the process down. I was first introduced to Super CRM as a customer and instantly* fell *in love with how much easier* my life was. *With Super CRM I could concentrate on providing* reeeeal value *to my*

*customers without getting bogged down in administrative details.* I jumped *at the chance to join them and* I looove *going to work every day because I know I'm changing people's lives, just like my life was changed so many years ago. Today I'm going to show you how Super CRM will change your life just like it changed mine.*

This personal story is filled with emotion and passion. Norvin delivers this from the intimacy zone where he walks right up next to the people he is addressing. He speaks to them directly, uses gentle eye contact and smiles to show his excitement. The backdrop slide helps establish himself and the others in his company as passionate people full of life.

He changes the melody of his voice to communicate emotion and emphasizes important words and phrases by extending the duration of words and using itsy-bitsy spider gestures. For instance, he gives two thumbs up when he says he's excited and he touches his fingertips to his chest over his heart when he says, "I love sales."

Norvin does cite a few credentials, but they come across as less boastful and more as evidence of his undying passion for helping others. Nothing he said can be argued by the audience because he is not making blanket statements like "we are the best"; instead he is making statements about what he feels. Which Norvin are you more likely to believe in?

Done right, the connection you will make

in the intimacy zone is profound. It will touch people and make them fall in love with you in the way you want to be loved at that moment. In order to pull it off, you will also have to love them.

You can visit the intimacy zone whenever you need to make personal connections with the audience. This will be especially true during the questions and answers at the end where you will walk right up to the person asking the question and address the person personally.

I know that the intimacy zone can be kind of intense and certainly out of your comfort zone, especially if you are someone who has traditionally given presentations from a seated position or from Magnetic South Pole. But this, more than anything else you do, will establish the kind of rapport you need with your audience if you are going to persuade them to your point of view. Once you have them on the hook, you will need to pump them up in Zone 2.

## Virtual Dojo

**Intimacy Zone**
To see me do an overview of the intimacy zone, visit PitchNinja.com and click on the Virtual Dojo or scan the code.

## Zone 2 – Excitement

Zone 2 is the *excitement* zone. This is where you

get the entire audience on board with what you have to say. If you're starting from the intimacy zone, you will move your body backwards into the excitement zone. Moving backward makes you visible to more people and allows you to relate to more people. Remember that moving frontwards and backwards is how you relate to people. Moving frontwards allows you to get closer to individuals in the intimacy zone, while moving backward allows you to relate to the larger audience in the excitement zone.

Your arms move outside the box, your armpits should be showing. Your smile is big and you use your back-of-the-room voice. Energy and excitement are the name of the game. You have established yourself as a passionate authority on the subject, now channel the passion like lightning to everyone in the room. Keep gentle eye contact but move around the room, paying special attention to people who seem to be showing signs of disinterest or disagreement.

If you see someone dozing off, hold eye contact long enough to connect with them and bring them back into the room. If you see someone with a scowl or crossed arms, slow down a little, and take a few more pauses to give that person time to catch up.

In the excitement zone you should be using visual aid slides. As you go through your key points, you can emphasize them with your body by moving from side to side. Here is how you would present this solution from a company called FixedRatePower.com:

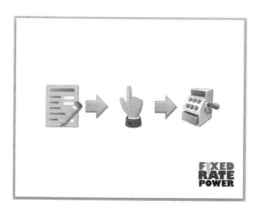

*If you're a small business* [Preacher point to the audience] *that wants to saaave money* [arms outside the box, "money-rub" your thumb and fingertips] *then Fixed Rate Power can help. First,* [start stage left, put your hand in the air with one finger up] *enter a few details about your business and some numbers from your monthly bill. Second,* [move one step to the right, put your hand in the air with two fingers up] *choose from a variety of electricity providers who waaant yooour buuusiness* [two-handed Preacher Point waving from side to side]. *Third,* [move one more step to the right, put your hand in the air with three fingers up] *each month you will save a bundle and have prediiictable* [point "knowing" finger to your head, armpit showing] *savings over the looong term* [hands apart like you're showing how big that fish you caught last week was].

Say it this way, with a big smile, and people will be sitting on the edge of their chair waiting to see what you're going to say next. The slide acted as a visual aid to support what you said, but the slide alone didn't tell the story—you did.

The excitement zone is where most of your presentation should take place. It's the excitement zone and if what you are presenting isn't exciting, you probably shouldn't be presenting it at all. Topics you will cover in the excitement zone include:

- Problem definition: present the problem your company solves or the problem your prospective client has. Be sure to outline the problem in a way that you can solve.

- Solution: present your incredible solution to the problem in such a way that the prospect can't help but want it.

- Business process: explain the unique business process that makes your company special and capable.

- Maps: show maps of sales territories or coverage areas or real estate deals.

- Team: *brag* about how great your team is. While it's not cool to brag about yourself and your own credentials, there is nothing to stop you from bragging about your team and their awesome credentials.

There is really no limit to what you can present in the excitement zone. In the intimacy zone you will establish yourself as a passionate person. In the excitement zone you will show the extent of that passion through energetic expression of the core concepts behind your position on whatever it is that you are presenting.

Smile as much as possible, use your back-of-the-room voice, show your armpits and be a gorilla!

## *Virtual Dojo*

### *Excitement Zone*
To see me do an overview of the excitement zone, visit PitchNinja.com and click on the Virtual Dojo or scan the code.

## Zone 3 – Information

The last zone is the *information* zone. It is here that you will stand right up next to the presentation screen, fully extend your arms to point to important information, and use your back-of-the-room voice. When you make eye contact with audience members, use steady eye contact to keep them engaged and allow you to look for confusion or disagreement.

As you might imagine, using this kind of body language in the intimacy zone would be overwhelming and aggressive for an audience member, but in the information zone it is totally appropriate.

Smiling is still important, especially if the message is about how much money you are going to make or key statistics that help build your case.

Touch your finger to where you want the audience to look. Never say, "As you can see…" without pointing to *exactly* what you want them to see. Stand in front of anything you don't want them to be looking at and move only when you are ready for them to see what is behind you.

You will be using an information slide which has numbers, tables, graphs and diagrams on it. Only about 10-20 percent of your slides should be information slides. You want to spend most of your time in the excitement zone. If you have an information-heavy presentation to pull off it's not impossible, but expect it to be a little exhausting for you and for the audience. It's more bearable if you're a Pitch Ninja, however.

# *Virtual Dojo*

### *Information Zone*
To see me do an overview of the information zone, visit PitchNinja.com and click on the Virtual Dojo or scan the code.

*Types of Information*

In the information zone you will be presenting complicated information. Unlike the visual aid slides in the excitement zone, it would be difficult, if not impossible, to convey the right information without the information on the slide. For example, it would be nearly impossible to explain a pro-forma income statement without showing the actual numbers. As I mentioned above, there is a limit to how much detail you can provide so long as your slide is still legible. Simpler is always better. Financial slides are classic information zone slides.

Research results and statistics are also information zone-type slides. So are detailed schematics, flowcharts and other types of detailed information. However, if it is possible to simplify the information enough to make it an excitement zone slide, do it. The fewer information zone slides there are in your presentation, the better.

*Software Demos*

Software demos are also information zone types of information. However, avoid giving live software demos at all costs. I have never, ever seen a live software demo go off without a hitch. Even if the stars are in alignment and there are no computer or web connectivity problems (which are *extremely* common) you are going to force the audience to sit through the painful experience of watching your mouse cursor fly all over the screen as you nervously click buttons, and God help you if you have to enter information. They will sit and watch you type and misspell things and delete characters or even worse is, "sdfaerh argar sdljf sd," which is the gibberish you bang out on the keyboard just to get through a form.

The fundamental problem with live software demos, however, is that they are virtually impossible to do while presenting from the information zone. You have to stand in front of your computer so you can use the mouse and keyboard. In short, don't do live software demos.

Instead of live, take screenshots of every screen after each step. This way you will have no bug problems, no computer problems, no connectivity problems, no typing problems and no other problems that will impede your ability to give a good demo.

The key is to create a screenshot of every step and click through the slides *as if it were live*. Instead of clicking the mouse cursor on buttons you will simply tap the button on the screen with your finger and, at the same time, click your presentation remote, which will advance the slide to the next screenshot, giving the audience the impression that you actually clicked a button that made something happen. Of course, the audience is probably smart enough to figure out what you're doing, but that doesn't matter. You aren't trying to show your software, you are trying to show how your software works.

Similarly, if your software requires that you fill out a form, you can show a screenshot of the blank form then do "air keyboard" with your hands on the screen and click the presentation remote to show the next slide, which is a screenshot of the same page with the form completed.

# Virtual Dojo

**Software Demo**
To see me do a software demo, visit PitchNinja.com and click on the Virtual Dojo or scan the code.

*Magic Hands*

The software demo incorporates a special technique that is bound to amaze and delight your audience called "Magic Hands." Magic Hands is when you touch the screen and something on the screen changes because you are also clicking the advance button on the presentation remote. It looks like magic (hence the name). In the software demo you can use Magic Hands to pretend you are clicking buttons or "air typing."

You can also use Magic Hands to make highlights appear on the screen, or even swipe the slide to the next slide. Any slide animation or build you create can be accompanied by Magic Hands to add interest to your presentation. They take a little practice sometimes, but the work is well worth it.

If you think this sounds corny, think again. Magic Hands show a level of polish and flair that tells your audience that you really care about doing a good job. Caring this much about communicating helps build a powerful connection with the audience. Pitch Ninjas use Magic Hands in Zone 3.

## Virtual Dojo

### Magic Hands

To see Magic Hands in action, visit PitchNinja.com and click on the Virtual Dojo or scan the code.

## Summary

The Super-Awesome Zone Program gives you a basic structure within which you can move your body without coming across as repetitive and random. Put the Ninja Moves from Chapter 3 and the Ninja Slides from Chapter 4 in the right zones and you have everything you need to choreograph an exciting, energetic and interesting presentation that shows your passion for the subject and will persuade an audience to your point of view.

**Zone 1**, the intimacy zone, forces you to break the plane and make personal connections with audience members. The goal is to make them fall in love with you.

**Zone 2**, the excitement zone, helps keep your presentation upbeat and engaging by allowing you to dominate the room like a silverback gorilla and connect with the entire audience.

**Zone 3**, the information zone, gives you the ability to clearly communicate more complex concepts and important details to your audience in a way that is engaging and captivating. Never before has a financial statement been so interesting!

As you plan and practice your presentation, always consider the appropriate zone and what type of body language is appropriate. Match the zone to the content of your slide and *you will not fail* to give a great presentation.

You might hear someone say that the zone program is too structured and not natural. Give them a Ninja wag of the finger. *This is the whole point.* The *point* of the program is to provide a structure *because* these skills aren't natural. The natural instinct is to hover over Magnetic South Pole and give a crappy presentation.

If you apply the zone program to your future presentations, the skills will *become* natural and you won't even have to think about them anymore.

However, just because you have the skills and the moves of the Pitch Ninja, you may not be a Pitch Ninja. You need to have a presentation that has the right *flow*. Disorganized presentations don't work, no matter how well they are presented.

Chapter Six:

# *The Flow*

Even if you are doing everything right, your presentation won't be very impactful unless you have it organized in a way that makes sense. When it comes to presentation content, I can't tell you how often the main hindrance to the message is the overall *organization* of the information, *not* the information itself.

Most people giving formal presentations have at least a little expertise on the topic that they are presenting. Nobody would ask me to give a presentation on pediatric neurosurgery, nor would I offer; I don't know anything about the subject except that it has something to do with poking a kid in the brain with a sharp knife (not my cup of tea). There are lots of other subjects, however, that I would be *happy* to talk about because I know them well. If I'm doing a presentation on a subject I know well *and* I'm using Pitch Ninja presentation style *and* I'm *still* not persuasive, it's because I have a problem with the *flow* of information, not the information itself. If I'm doing a presentation on something I don't know anything about and I'm not persuasive, it's because I shouldn't be giving a presentation in the first place.

In fact, if you are giving a presentation on any subject, your expertise in the subject matter (or at least your knowledge) is *implied*.

The main reason people struggle with flow is because most people watch too many television shows. In order to make a television show work, you have to create suspense throughout the show and then wrap it all up at the end. This formula is important on TV because the producer has to hold people's attention long enough to get plenty of ads in front of them. Producers think that if the audience knows the outcome of the story too early they will turn off the TV and go exercise or eat a healthy snack or study math or do something other than watch more TV. This would be unfortunate for the producer; luckily, she has a formula that works!

Of course, this is not entirely true. In many cases knowing the punch line in advance doesn't ruin the story because the story is so great. TV shows about true events can be very interesting. Most presentations are about true events and real things. They are nonfiction works.

A good presentation will not wait until the end of the presentation to tell you what happens. A good presentation will tell you the main points and then it will tell the story behind the main points and then it will tell you the main points again.

Journalists have a saying: "Don't bury the lede." This means, don't hide the main point. A good presentation should flow like a good piece of journalism. The lede, a concise summary of the main points, should be one of the first things out of your mouth. Not necessarily *the* first thing, but close.

With that in mind, *every* presentation you give for the rest of your life should open something like this:

1. A personal story
2. Summary of the main point(s)

The *nature* of the main point will vary based on the goal of the presentation, but you will still want to provide this summary. For instance, if you are doing a sales presentation, your main point will be a summary of the solution that you provide to solve their problem (if they have one). If you are presenting a scientific research paper, your main point would be your hypothesis and what your research revealed about your hypothesis. With the main point out of the way, you can get to the details to explain why your main point is what it is.

For purposes of Pitch Ninja, I'm going to provide a basic overview of how a business plan presentation might be presented to communicate the basic structure of a Pitch Ninja presentation.

Then I'll provide a few notes to help you understand variations.

## Basic Structure

The basic presentation format is an individual or team of individuals presenting in front of an audience. The audience might be coworkers or potential customers or potential investors or judges (in the case of a business pitch competition). You should get a handle on who your audience is beforehand so you can hone your message to fit the audience. If you're presenting to customers, for instance, your message will be different than if you're presenting to investors. In this example I'm going to show you how a presentation might be delivered to investors.

There are exceptions to every rule, but in general, a business plan presentation should be no more than 15 to 20 minutes, leaving plenty of time for discussion at the end. In a competition format you might have about five minutes for discussion; in an investor presentation you could have much more time depending on the interest level of the investor and their personal time restrictions. Most professional investor meetings will last about an hour. A business plan flow should look similar to this:

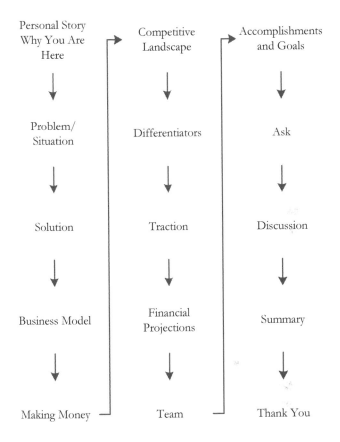

By the way, this does not imply a separate slide in your presentation for each topic. You can have as many slides as you need to tell your story, but make sure it flows. This is intended to map out the flow of your story and avoid common mistakes.

For instance, a common mistake in business plan presentations is the explanation of team bios early on in the presentation. If you present the team too early, the audience won't understand why the people who are on your team are on your team. If you present the team after you have explained the business, the audience will understand what needs to be done and can relate the talents of the team to the needs of the business. It's OK to introduce you team by name and title early on, but don't go into too much detail until the gist of the business has been communicated.

Another common problem is to present accomplishments and goals *before* the team. If you can wait until after you present the team, you can use these important bragging points to show how awesome your team is.

There is also a physical flow to your presentation. Matching the content of your story to the right zone will help your story flow.

In many cases you will have more than one team member presenting. In these cases you will have to be mindful of transitions and each speaker will have to make a personal connection with the audience. Team dynamics during the discussion are especially important. More on this later, but keep in mind that the way your team handles questions will provide insight into whether or not you are a team at all. Your presentation should unfold like this:

*Personal Story*

To open the presentation, step forward into the intimacy zone, close to the audience members. Smile and say how happy/honored/excited you are to have the opportunity to present.

Tell your personal story on why you care about the topic about which you are going to discuss.

> My *name is Norvin Moyer and I couldn't be haaappier to have this great opportunity to talk about how technology can make our lives easier.*
>
> *I remember my first exposure to computer programming. I was still in middle school and had an early computer with the Basic computer programming language. I would spend all day writing programs that I found in computer magazines. I loved every second of it, even though the programs were simple and didn't do much. I wrote simple games and created graphics. Once I spent the entire day programming a graphic of a Christmas tree with Christmas music in the background. By the time I was ready to show my parents it was very late. My parents thought it was great, but told me I had to go to bed. So, I turned off the computer,* erasing *all my work.* [pause] *It didn't bother me a bit because it never* occurrrrred *to me that I could* ssaaave *my work. I didn't even know what a disc drive was! I've come a long way, but I still love the process of developing computer programs.*

> *Today I'm going to show you how I used this love of programming to create a team that has built a very useful software application to solve a simple problem. This application gets used over 3,500 times per day, allowing us to generate over 10,000 marketing emails a day.*

This story establishes the speaker as 1) someone who can program a computer, 2) someone who has a lot of experience programming computers and 3) someone who loves it and shows passion for the subject matter. It's a great opener. Note that it hits upon some important metrics of users and emails. This story, along with the metrics, really builds credibility. The audience assumes the speaker has decent credentials.

If you are presenting as a team, each person (during their turn to speak) should enter into the intimacy and tell their personal story before they do anything else.

## Problem/Situation

Next, it's important to frame the issue in a way that sets it up for being addressed by the business solution. The speaker now *steps backward* into the excitement zone so he can address the entire audience and start building excitement. His arms move to outside the box with armpits showing:

> *Today I love creating technologies that help make*

*life easier. One of the frustrations I experience on a regular basis in business, and specifically sales, is sending information to prospects, but not knowing when to follow up. I'll send an email with a link or two and then call them and say, "Have you had a chance to take a look at the information I sent?" If I call too early, they haven't seen it yet, and I don't know how often I should call back before I become a pest. If I call too late, the person may have forgotten what the information was about. This drives me crazy! Turns out I'm not the only salesperson that has this problem. We found that 97 percent of salespeople struggle with not knowing when to follow up with prospects. I guess the other 3 percent are clairvoyant or just don't care!*

Now the speaker has framed the problem in a way that expresses emotion and his ability to relate to a common problem. Plus, he has set himself up to tell the rest of the story—guess who can solve this problem perfectly?

*Solution*

Now he can hit them with the solution:

*BlipNut.com was created to solve this problem by allowing users to create links to content that provide alerts—or blips—when content is accessed. This way I know* exaaactly *when my prospect checks out what I sent them. Let me show you how it works....* [Ninja software demo with Magic Hands]

Once he has set up the solution, he has to let them know how it makes money.

*Business Model/Making Money*

How a business makes money is important and should not be left to the end. It's not uncommon for a business plan presentation to wait until the financial section of the presentation before the business model is really addressed. The business model is a description of the main components of your business with extra emphasis on important revenue drivers. In the case of BlipNut, the speaker would stay in the excitement zone (to continue building excitement for the product) and describe the revenue model and key cost drivers. He doesn't need to get into too much detail; he just needs to touch on them.

> *Unlike other URL shortners, BlipNut.com is an email marketing company. We make money by embedding relevant advertising in the body of the email. Ads are based on the target URL to increase relevance. Every time the link is clicked there is a new revenue opportunity for BlipNut.com.*
> *We will supplement the email marketing with on-page advertising. Initially we will simply integrate Google AdSense to keep costs low.*

*BlipNut.com is a highly automated site.*

*Competition*

After the business model, you have to address the elephant in the room, which is who else is doing it. All businesses have competition and investors will balk at anyone who says there is no competition. Competition is a good thing because it, more than just about anything, validates the existence of the market. It's good to talk about your competition in the context of market validation. For instance:

> *We are confident that there is strong demand for BlipNut.com given the current players in the market, which fall into two main categories. The first category is URL shorteners like Bit.ly, TinyURL and a number of brand-specific shorteners offerred by Google, Twitter, and WordPress.*
>
> *The second category is companies who offer link-tracking like Yesware and Toutapp. These are all great companies with a solid offering. However, we think that BlipNut offers some key differences that will allow us to attract a loyal customer base.*

When talking about the competition you need to be careful not to badmouth what they are doing. If you are mentioning them at all it's because they are probably successful and there is no reason to think you are better than them. In fact, trying to position yourself as *better* than the competition is a bad idea. "Better" is a *highly* subjective term and depends heavily on the audience's personal experiences and biases. The critical message you want to get across when discussing the competition is how you are *different*.

*Differentiation*

Differentiation is *critical*. In fact, in order to be better, you have to be different first. If you're not different, you can't be better. It's a simple fact of life. If you focus your message on how you are different, you won't come across as boastful, arrogant or presumptuous. Don't worry, there will be a time and place to toot your own horn— just make sure it's not at the expense of others.

It's not uncommon to see a business plan presentation use "Harvey Balls" to compare the company to the competition. This is how a slide might look:

|  | Bells | Whistles | Small Bells | Loud Whistle |
|---|---|---|---|---|
| My Company | ● | ● | ● | ● |
| Their Company | ○ | ◔ | ◑ | ● |
| That Other Company | ◑ | ◕ | ◔ | ○ |

This can be a great way to show how you

are different. But, be careful. Notice that in the example above, "My Company" does everything while the competition falls short. This indicates that the management team either doesn't really understand the competition, doesn't have the ability to focus or is just plain delusional. In a startup company, you can't do everything and do it well. Focus is critical. Use diagrams like Harvey Balls to show how you are different, not how you are delusional.

> *There are several key differences between BlipNut.com and the competition. The first* [holding up one finger] *is that we allow the user to post a trackable link anywhere a link can be posted. Email productivity apps only track links within emails, for instance. The second key difference* [holding up two fingers] *is the real-time alerts though email Blips. It's true that other services do track links, but the user must set up an account, login, and find the report. BlipNut tells you what's going on in real time.*
>
> *As I mentioned before, email marketing is a key revenue driver for BlipNut.com. When someone shortens a link, they are giving us permission to email them with a welcomed message.* No other *service gets this kind of access to the end user with such simplicity. This makes BlipNut.com an aaawesome money-making machiiiine* [Arms spread wide, thumbs up, big smile].

I told you there would be a time to toot your own horn. You can brag about your differences because you aren't stepping on anyone's toes. The speaker can use opportunities like this to show how excited he or she is about the product.

*Market and Marketing*

Once you establish that there *is* a market for your product or service, it's time to talk about the nature of the market and how big it is and how you will get people from the target market to become customers. You will need to focus on the segment of the market that you can actually address. Entrepreneurs consistently get this wrong. Most of the time entrepreneurs talk about huge markets, with little attention paid to how you are going to access them. For the speaker to say that the market for BlipNut.com is anyone who has a computer may be right, but how will the people who work for BlipNut.com reach billions of people on a bootstrapped budget? In order to be believable, the team has to focus on a market they can actually reach.

In the market section you will need to describe the market you are going after. The more detail, the better, within the time limits of your presentation.

*As with any online application, BlipNut.com is available to anyone with an Internet connection. More narrowly defined, however, we think our product is most useful in a business environment, yet we are aware of social applications as well. We estimate a total market for this product in the U.S. at well over 75 million people.*

*That being said, our initial focus will be on U.S.-based salespeople that focus on B2B technology sales. These people can be reached through a variety of direct means, both online with email and social media marketing, as well as offline at trade shows and events. This gives us an initial market of over 200,000 individuals.*

To be convincing, your market needs to be big in terms of dollars or numbers of potential customers, preferably both. Niche products are great, but they don't always attract real investment dollars like more mass-market products.

In addition to showing how big your market is, you will have to show how you plan to reach your market. The more specific you can be, the more credible you will sound. Get into tactics. Lots of people claim that they will establish a social media presence, but very few explain how they are going to translate that into sales. Lots of people want to create viral videos, but very few explain how they are going to make sure it goes viral. Be specific about the tactics and techniques you are going to use.

*BlipNut.com has been building a three-tiered SEO program over the past six months that has allowed us to rank on the first page of Google, Bing, Yahoo and*

*YouTube for eight of our top ten keywords. First,* [finger in the air] *we have had a high level of interaction on sales forums, guest posting at high* PR *sites and partnerships with several sales training companies. Second,* [step left, two fingers in the air] *our software has widgets that can be embedded on websites who want to publically show their statistics. This initiates visits from curious web browsers. And third, users can add other people's email addresses to receive blips. On average, each link has 2.3 email addresses associated with it when it's created and over 75 percent of the owners of the additional email addresses use BlipNut.com at least once. This creates more links.*

In this case the speaker provided enough detail on the SEO strategy to be believable and touched on some evidence that it's working. This evidence, called traction, is hands down, far and away the most important part of your presentation. It's so important that you could stick it earlier in the flow and it wouldn't be out of place. In fact, you could open with a few traction proof-points if you wanted. You still have to tell your personal story and everything else, but don't overlook the importance of traction.

## Traction

Traction is any evidence that your business model is working. The best evidence is paying customers—the more customers, the better.

If you don't have *paying* customers, then customers who promise to pay you when you are able to deliver can be evidence of traction. Sometimes a letter-of-intent can show that what you are proposing has value.

Beta customers who are trying the product or service for free can show traction. This isn't nearly as good as paying customers, but you have to tout what you have. Website visits, survey results or other kinds of proof that what you are proposing has a chance to turn into the business that you envision can serve as evidence of traction.

Investors want to invest in a business model that they know will work. No matter how good your presentation is, the proof is in the pudding. Show investors concrete evidence that value exists and you will have a much better chance of getting them to invest, or in the case of a competition, pick you as the best one.

The best possible scenario is a keen understanding of customer lifetime value and the cost of acquiring a customer. If you have these two bits of information, investors will see a money machine. They put $X in the machine and get $Y back. This is awesome.

*BlipNut.com's marketing model is becoming very predictable. In the past six months we have grown from less than 10 new URLs shortened per day to over 3,500. With click activity we are sending out over*

*10,000 emails per day. More importantly, the click-through rate on email advertising has also been climbing, with an average rate of 67 clicks per thousand. Our revenue per click is 85 cents, giving us daily revenue of between $500 and $600 per day, which is over $200,000 annualized.*

With these kinds of numbers, investors are going to take real interest. The company has proven beyond a reasonable doubt that they can do the following:

1. Attract new users
2. Retain users
3. Stimulate the desired action (clicking ads)
4. Make money

With this evidence on the table, the investors are going to want to know what the financial picture looks like and what the future holds.

*Financial Projections*

A typical business plan's financial projections will project three to five years in the future. This is information zone content so the slide is more detailed than an excitement zone slide. You should have a basic spreadsheet showing sources of revenue, direct costs (such as cost of goods sold), major cost drivers for operations and, of course, net earnings before income tax, depreciation and amortization (EBITDA).

In some cases you may want to describe a

"unit model," which is a description of a single building block of your financial picture. For instance, if you are running a chain of ice cream shops, a single shop would be one unit. Your financial projections would depend heavily on the number of units you have in place. Similarly, if you had an event company, a single event would be a unit and you would want to show the costs associated with marketing and hosting the event.

It's worth noting that you should present your best guess of the future. Say what you really think is going to happen. Do not be conservative and never, ever actually use the word "conservative." Saying, "Our numbers are conservative," is the same thing as saying, "Our numbers are wrong." There are few words that make an investor cringe more than the word "conservative."

*Here is our three-year pro forma income statement showing actual numbers for the first six months. Here* [point to number] *you can see the $550-per-day number I mentioned earlier.*

*Our main cost drivers are salaries and servers. We would like to add a full-time outreach person who will do online marketing and public relations. Accelerating trial is a critical part of our growth strategy.*

*We have already reached cash flow breakeven* [show graph with breakeven], *but we think that in order to scale we will need to invest in a more scalable architecture and new dedicated servers in addition to the new full-time staff.*

*By year three we expect to be at a daily rate of over $10,000 per day, at which point we would consider ourselves a good acquisition target for a competitor or a company in the sales software or CRM space.*

This explanation covers all the important facts and tells an exciting story. My story about BlipNut.com is made up (even though it's a real thing). Your company may not have money coming in or real users. That would be unfortunate, but build upon what traction you do have to make your financial story believable.

*Team*

Now that you have told this wonderful, exciting story using good choreography and the right Ninja moves, your audience will be on the edge of their seat. "Who *are* these people?" they will want to know. Now you can tell them.

I mentioned earlier that if you present the details of your team in the beginning of the presentation, the audience won't know their purpose. Now that they know what you are doing, the composition of the team makes more sense.

I also mentioned before that as an individual you establish credibility through the telling of a personal story that shows your commitment and passion. Bragging about your credentials and qualifications is less impactful and makes you sound arrogant. However, you *can* brag about your team. In fact, you *should* brag about your team. If you're not excited about them, why should the investor be excited?

> *The most exciiiting* [two thumbs up] *part about BlipNut.com is the team. I've never worked with a more qualified team with better chemistry than this one. Anson is our lead developer and he is a coding ROCK STAR* [air guitar]. *He can write code that will make you weep with joy* [rubbing the corners of eyes]. *He graduated at the top of his class at Harvard where he won every development award possible before they had to invent new ones for him. He is one of those rare individuals who has high technical skills, but also high interpersonal skills. It has been an honor to work with him.*
>
> *Merrily has been working part-time with us as our marketing person. She is the one that we hope to bring on full-time. She....is.....awesome* [arms in the air]. *She has an uncanny ability to meet the right people at the right time and say just the right thing. People love her and she loves them. There is no other person I would rather have representing my company.*
>
> *I'm just a guy who loves solving everyday problems with technology. I am humbled every day that I go to work with these guys and I look forward to every minute I spend in the office.*

It's virtually impossible to lay it on too thick when it comes to your team. Think about it. Did you hire a bunch of losers to be on your team? If not, why not take some pride? The assembly of your team is probably the most important thing you have done!

*Accomplishments and Goals*

To keep up the momentum, tell the audience, with great excitement, what this great team has accomplished. Investors want to see that the company is moving forward and they want to see how well you share the credit with your team.

> *In the past six months this fantastic team has accomplished a lot. We have built out a platform with core functionality; we have implemented our advertising model; we have attracted a healthy user base that is steadily growing; we have created and refined a marketing model that allows us to attract users for a low variable cost; and we have demonstrated our ability to build a profitable business.*
>
> *In the next year we will build upon that success by redeploying our program on a more scalable architecture with a broader range of functionality and a more sophisticated marketing engine. Anson is up for the challenge and ready to go. I'll do what I can to help, but he is really the brains behind the operation.*

*This slide* [an information zone slide, step back to Zone 3] *shows our projected user growth over the next three years. These spikes represent the implementation of new marketing features to help accelerate growth. We expect this growth to be consistent with other programs we have implemented so far. For instance,* [point to actual numbers spike] *this spike occurred right after we launched the ability to add others to the Blip distribution list. With Merrily on board I am totally confident in our ability to hit these goals spot-on.*

By now you have told your whole story. The audience is left with a concrete understanding of what you have actually done to get where you are and what you need to do to get to the next level. They are excited about the business and are asking themselves, "How can I be part of this exciting new business and this great team?" You can provide the answer.

*Ask*

Every business plan presentation should ask for something. You aren't presenting for your health or to hear yourself talk. You are presenting because you want something. It could be money, advice, connections, ideas or anything else that people in the room could do to accelerate your plans. Be specific about what you want.

Most of the time you will be asking for

money, so you will have to say how much you want and give a breakdown of how you will spend the money. Additionally, you will want to give them an idea as to the terms of the deal.

In many cases an early-stage investment from friends and family or non-professional investors will be a convertible note. Angel investors and high-net-worth individuals may also take a convertible note or convertible equity. Later stages of investment with larger amounts of money—over $1 million—will want equity and a variety of investment terms that will be negotiated.

> *BlipNut.com is raising $250,000 to move the company to the next level. Of this, $50,000 is needed to build a more scalable technology platform, $75,000 is needed to add additional staffing and $125,000 is needed to accelerate our acquisition efforts.*
>
> *Based on the traction we have had so far, we expect that we can acquire over half a million new users and reach cash-flow breakeven in less than six months. We are hoping to secure a convertible loan on the entire amount.*
>
> *How much of the $250,000 do you think you would like to invest?*

Note the ask at the end of the above sample. It takes guts to lay it out there like that, but it is important that you make sure you ask for what you want.

Before we move on, I do want to take the opportunity to plug one of my other books: *Slicing Pie*. If you are a bootstrapped startup company and you haven't read *Slicing Pie,* you should. The book provides detailed instructions for dividing up equity in your startup among founders, employees, advisors, partners and investors.

**Slicing Pie**
To learn more about Slicing Pie, visit SlicingPie.com or scan the code.

*Discussion*

Once you have made your ask, it's time to talk about the deal and answer questions. A typical, non-Pitch Ninja presenter would show a slide with the word "Questions" on it. A Pitch Ninja has a final slide that summarizes the most important aspects of the presentation. For BlipNut.com the slide would say something like this:

BlipNut.com

- Simple, yet powerful value proposition
- 3,500 new URLs per day
- 10,000 emails per day
- Predictable revenue stream
- Asking for $250,000 for development, staffing and marketing

This slide provides a nice summary for the audience. In this example the speaker asked for all or a part of $250,000 from the audience. If the investors say they are interested, you can end like this:

*Great, I look forward to working out the details. How would you like to proceed?*

Professional investors will want to put together a terms sheet or may have follow-up questions. I've had this happen to me before, but it's more common for people to want more information before they invest. In this case, you would say something like:

*Thank you for giving me the opportunity to share with you what I believe to be an extreeeemly exciting new technology. The team has built an application that works and delivers real value to users. Our path to growth is clear and we would like nothing more than to talk to you about how you can get involved as an investor.*

At this point you will experience an awkward silence. This is the dead pause that occurs after the presentation is over, but before people begin to ask questions. There are several ways to overcome this.

The first way is to just wait. Wait until they begin to ask questions or they tell you to leave. It's not a good sign if they don't ask any questions.

The other thing you can do is pose a question of your own. You can ask just about any question except, "Are there any questions?" A good question to ask would be, "What can I tell you about BlipNut.com that would make you more comfortable with an investment?" Or, "Is this the kind of company your firm considers?" Either of these questions will get the ball rolling.

The last thing you can do, if possible, is *plant* someone in the audience with a question. Tell them, in advance, what question to ask and tell them to ask it only if there are no other questions right away. It may feel a little sneaky, but it's a great technique for presentations to a large audience, such as a keynote address. It gets the ball rolling and avoids the awkward moments.

In most cases, discussions will consist of back-and-forth Q&A. This is a critical time for your presentation that I'll cover in more detail later.

*Ending*

At the end of your scheduled time, you should end the discussion and the presentation. If the hosts want to keep talking, that's OK, but you want be sure to give them an out so they can get back to whatever else they need to do that day. When your time is up, say something like this:

> *As much as I'd looove* [hands over your heart] *to talk about BlipNut.com all day, you mentioned you only had until 2:00 and I want to be respectful of your time.*
>
> *I think the next step is to make sure you have the opportunity to use BlipNut.com yourselves. I'll be sure to get you the links to get started and I'll include you on some shared Blips so you can see what that experience is like. I'd also like to set up a meeting next week to talk about moving forward.*

Always mention the next step so you can continue the new, redefined relationship. Remember that a formal meeting will redefine your relationship. It's a good idea to make sure you know what the new relationship is, and only additional interactions will let you know. Unless, of course, you blow it and the new relationship is no relationship. But this rarely happens to Pitch Ninjas!

If you are participating in a business plan competition and the buzzer goes off, you could say something like this:

> *It pains* [grimace] *me to have to stop talking about BlipNut! I sincerely hope that when you deliberate the outcome of this competition that you will remember not only the great traction that BlipNut has achieved, but also the dedication and passion of the team. Thank you very much for your consideration!*

Keep it short, but remind them of a few key details, and wrap it up. Be sure to keep smiling and end on a positive note.

Hopefully, from the above example, you were able to understand some of the key movements and patterns that help keep the presentation impactful. Don't get too bogged down in the content of the above example; the important lesson is how the presentation flows together in a logical direction. As the content is delivered, it is important to be mindful of what your body and face are doing while you talk. In fact, it is absolutely critical.

It's easy to get so wrapped up in what you are saying that you succumb to Magnetic South Pole and come across as if you're some kind of mindless drone. Always remember, if you aren't able to communicate your passion and excitement to your audience, they will probably not feel any excitement or develop any interest in what you are saying.

Chapter Seven:

# *Variations*

The basic structure in Chapter 6 applies to any presentation you do. What changes will be how much content you can include, what you choose to focus on and any situation-specific specialized content you include.

For *all* presentations, you should start with your personal story and make sure the audience understands your personal passion and commitment to the topic being discussed. Work the intimacy zone and make a positive impression. From there, the flow depends on what kind of presentation you are doing. Below are a few examples:

## The Elevator Pitch

An elevator pitch is the Pitch Ninja equivalent of a roundhouse kick to the throat. It takes a little practice and some skill, but it's extremely effective once mastered. A good Pitch Ninja will have a good elevator pitch prepared for every occasion so that he can deliver in a moment's notice. In my other book, *Trade Show Samurai: The Four Core Arts for Capturing Leads*, I'll teach you to create extremely short pitches, called "trailers," for each type of attendee at a trade show.

**Trade Show Samurai**
Buy a copy of *Trade Show Samurai* by scanning or clicking the code.

The first time I participated in an elevator pitch competition, I bombed. It was embarrassing. I thought an elevator pitch was like a little business plan pitch and that you had to talk really fast to get it all in. It's not. Since then I've learned how to do it and given a lot of real elevator pitches with great success. I've even delivered them in actual elevators. The elevator to the twelfth floor of the Chicago Merchandise Mart is especially good for pitching.

Unlike a business plan presentation or a sales presentation, the elevator pitch strips out everything except for the core elements. The goal is to get the person on the hook long enough for them to get their appointment book out and set some time to talk in more detail. Rarely does the elevator pitch seal the deal—but I never say never! An elevator pitch flows more like this:

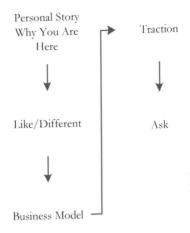

You still need to make a personal connection right away, but you may want to use a "Like/Different" summary. This means you compare your business to a similar business and then say why it's different:

> *BlipNut.com is* like *Bit.ly, but* different *because BlipNut.com sends you real-time email alerts.*

Many entrepreneurs want people to think their idea is totally unique and nobody on earth is doing it. They loathe the idea of comparing their concepts to someone else. I understand this, but in the absence of time, a Like/Different statement will help you help your audience get a concrete understanding of your idea very quickly.

Once your audience has a clear understanding of what you are or aren't, you can tell them how you make money and tell them about the market and your traction. Then, of course, you ask for the money.

After that, you're done. If they want to know more about the team or the details of the marketing plan, they can set up a time to talk in more detail where you'll have the chance to give them the complete pitch. The elevator pitch should provide just enough information to make them want more.

## The Sales Presentation

A good sales presentation has similar elements to a business plan presentation but with a few key differences. The main one is that the client or prospect is going to be interested in addressing a specific issue and hopes that you can bring a way to address the issue. Also, you can probably streamline a little because the prospect is less likely to want to know about your company's business model, financials and other business-related topics.

The key in sales presentations is to first sell them what *they* want and then to sell them what *you* want. By this, I mean be sure to address the issue you were brought into address, then you can show them what else you do. So, if the prospect wants a minivan, but you think they would be better off in an SUV, you will first have to show them the minivan option. Once you've done that, you can tell them about your SUV options.

If you don't know what they want, you have probably missed a few steps in the sales process and may not be ready for a formal presentation. You need to make sure you have asked the right questions before you stand up and give your pitch. This isn't a book about *selling* per se; it's a book about pitching and presenting. Your pitch isn't your sale—it's just a part of it.

Below is an example flow diagram for a sales presentation.

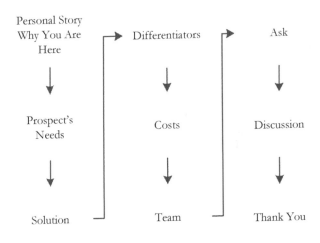

As always, you will want to start with a personal story, then provide an overview of what the client needs or what they have asked for. Talk about your solution in the excitement zone, to get them excited. In the information zone you will cover key differentiators and costs. You'll go back to the excitement zone to talk about your team and then move into the intimacy zone to ask for the sale. Don't forget to ask for the sale! Most people don't. Here are some ways to ask for the sale:

- ✓ Do we have a deal?
- ✓ Can we move forward?
- ✓ Have you heard enough to want to move to the next step?
- ✓ Is there anything else you need to feel comfortable with this, or can we move forward?
- ✓ Does what I've outlined meet your needs?

Before you give your sales pitch, you should have a good idea what you hope to accomplish. Sometimes you want the actual sale, sometimes you want to get the next meeting. Like I mentioned before, this isn't a book about sales strategy; it's a book about pitching. If you can't find a good book about sales strategy and would like me to write one, let me know at Mike@Pitch.Ninja.

## Demos and Props

Sometimes you will have a message that will be enhanced through the use of physical items. If you are selling hand tools with super-comfort grips, it might be helpful to have some products on hand.

Similarly, handouts can be used to provide information that doesn't show well on a screen. A detailed financial statement, for instance, would be an example.

## The *Infomacy* Zone

When you hand something to an audience member, there is a profound shift in the space-time continuum. What was once the Intimacy Zone has just become the Information Zone. I'll bet you didn't see *that* coming!

Actually, it's become a hybrid—the *infomacy zone*. In the infomacy zone you will use techniques from both the information zone and the intimacy zone. Specifically, you will need to point at the document or object in front of people to show them what you are talking about instead of at the presentation screen (you can even turn off the presentation if your remote has that feature). Use direct eye contact rather than the more natural gentle eye contact. This sends the message that you are the one they should concentrate on, not the object or document.

When you hand someone something, they will turn their attention away from you and onto the thing you just gave them. It is important to command their undivided attention so that you can continue with your message. Interacting physically with whatever you just gave them is one way to do this.

Try to minimize the distraction. If you are

demonstrating the hand grip on a power tool, consider just bringing the grip and not the tool. They may be too captivated by the shiny bolts and sharp blade that they forget you're even in the room!

The infomacy zone, used properly, will add another layer of interest to your presentation. Without the infomacy zone and the related techniques, your handouts and samples will be distractions from your presentation. It's OK to use them, but you have to manage them properly.

I often see presenters pass out their slides before a presentation. Then I see the audience members flipping through it to see what comes next instead of waiting for the presenter to present the material. If you've done your slides right, they won't be self-explanatory anyway, so what good will it do to pass them out?

Chapter Eight:

# Q&A Pitch Killers

The best presentation in the world can be *killed* during the question-and-answer period and discussion. The discussion can often last as long as or *even longer* than the presentation itself, yet people do little to plan for it and even less to practice for it. In fact, the whole idea of practicing your answers to questions might seem strange or even ridiculous. It's not ridiculous—it's *critical*.

I was once in a presentation where the presenter was asked the following question by a potential investor: "You mentioned your family was in the same business as you, but how come they haven't invested in your company?"

The presenter responded, "They don't want to take the risk." Bad answer—game over! If the presenter had *practiced* for this question, he might have given a much better answer, like this:

> *"My family is behind me 100 percent. They have taught me a lot about the business, made introductions to important vendors, given me access to intellectual property and provided their full support. They are heavily invested in their own infrastructure right now, but are interested in investing as soon as they are able."*

An answer like that would have kept the conversation moving in the right direction. But how, you might ask, could he have anticipated this question, in advance, without some kind of psychic abilities? An apt question, the answer to which is "50/50."

## 50/50

The best way to prepare for the discussion is to do what I call "50/50." First, sit down with your team and create a list of 50 questions that might get asked. Brainstorm the possibilities. Nothing is off-limits. Put yourself in the audience's seat and figure out what they are going to ask. Below are some brainstorming prompts (in no particular order) to help you:

- ✓ Customers
- ✓ Relationships
- ✓ Family background
- ✓ Value proposition
- ✓ Sources of revenue
- ✓ Pricing model

- ✓ Differentiation
- ✓ Partnerships
- ✓ Investors
- ✓ Financing
- ✓ Marketing and sales channels
- ✓ Primary activities
- ✓ Key hires
- ✓ Team
- ✓ Cost structures
- ✓ Unit model
- ✓ Personal work situation

This isn't an exhaustive list, but it will help you get your first 50 questions. Once you get your 50 questions, write out responses that cast your company in a positive light. This may take a little thought.

## Virtual Dojo

### Investor Questions
To see a list of possible investor questions, visit PitchNinja.com and click on the Virtual Dojo or scan the code.

Remember the BlipNut.com application I mentioned earlier? A question I might get from investors is, "Why can't Bit.ly just start sending out emails when someone clicks on their links?" This is a classic question. Investors always want to know why your competitor can't just implement your idea. This question throws a lot of entrepreneurs who might be tempted to answer something like this:

> *Bit.ly is a slow-moving company with a lot of bureaucracy and an arrogant management team. We aren't afraid of them.*

Or...

> *Our market is too small; they are looking at a larger market.*

Or...

> *By the time they realize what hit them, we will be buying them!*

All of these answers are horrible, but they are all similar to answers I have heard in real life. It's important to *not* show arrogance and/or ignorance during the Q&A and instead show humility and respect for those before you. This doesn't mean you don't have to show confidence, but recognize that you probably aren't the only person in the world who can accomplish something. A better answer would sound like this:

> *They can. Bit.ly is a dominant player in this market and they could certainly implement an alert system like BlipNut.com, and we are certainly keeping an eye on them. However, BlipNut.com is different than them in that the email alerts are a main focus of our service. If*

*Bit.ly added email alerts, they probably wouldn't make it the focus of their service; it would probably be an option the user could set. Otherwise they would have to revamp their message and make a major change to their homepage. We don't think this is likely; URL shortners have come and gone and Bit.ly does not appear to have changed their strategy with each new competitor. More than anything, we look at Bit.ly as validation of the market. There is clearly demand for URL shortners and we are confident that the simplicity of our service and the branding focused on Blips will allow us to get a foothold in the market.*

An answer like this is thoughtful and respectful of competitors, yet it lays out the main differentiators between the two services. By planning an answer like this in advance, the speaker can be prepared to address it professionally.

For each question on your list, you should designate one person on your team to answer it. It's poor form for multiple team members to jump in on a question during a Q&A session. If you are all having a discussion it might be OK, but if it's a formal Q&A, stick to one person per question.

When multiple people from your team answer the same question, you stop looking like a team. If your answers contradict one another, you look like idiots. Pick the most logical person on the team to answer the question and assign it to him or her. Also, don't let your CEO do all the talking during Q&A; mix it up to keep it interesting.

I call this exercise "50/50" because once you get the 50 questions and answers outlined, you should sit down and do 50 more. It can be a lot of work, but nothing will prepare you better for the post-presentation discussion. Much of what you develop can be reused for future presentations and even other marketing efforts, so it's time well spent.

## Answer the Question

One of the most common mistakes people make when handling questions is not answering the question. In fact, it is extremely common for the presenter to provide an answer that has virtually nothing to do with the question. For instance, let's say the prospect asks, "How much does it cost?" A presenter might answer:

> *Our product is well worth the investment. In studies we see a tenfold increase in speed and accuracy of our product in a variety of application across a range of environments. We provide a number of low-cost financing options and have an extremely high customer satisfaction rate.*

This is the answer to another question. We still don't know how much it costs. I see this problem all the time. It's quite surprising. By coming up with questions and preparing answers in advance, you mitigate the chances this will happen.

The correct answer to this question is something like, "$38.50." Of course, you might not want to be so specific:

> *Our pricing depends on volume; the base price is $38.50, but that's without any plan. If you cap your use to three times per month you can lower the price to $28.50. Some enterprise customers pay as much as $500 per month or more.*

You might not want to answer this question at all, in which case you might say:

> *The price you pay depends on your volume, frequency and length of your contract. I would be happy to provide a complete assessment of your needs and provide a detailed estimate.*

If they press for an answer, you can say:

> *The price goes from $28.50 at the low end to over $500 for enterprise customers. In order to get the right pricing for you I'd have to take a closer look at your X's, Y's and Z's.*

Being prepared for your Q&A means you are prepared to answer the question being asked. I think this might be a function of not listening and maybe nervousness; I'm not sure. I do it myself sometimes. It's a weird phenomenon.

Pitch Ninjas answer the question.

## Rabbit Holes

Similar to not answering the question is not shutting up when the question is answered. This means the speaker answers the question and then keeps talking and talking and talking. They are going off on tangents that are rarely productive. For instance, when asked, "How much does it cost?" a rabbit-hole answer might look like this:

*The service is $28.50 for the basic program and $38.50 for the deluxe service, which includes a variety of additional features including our XML API, which will allow you to integrate with most major manufacturing options. We don't currently integrate with company X, but we are working hard. Our development team is based in India and we are in the process of looking for someone with expertise in company X. We have one candidate, but he hasn't returned our calls. We are confident, however, that we will find someone within the next month. The good news is that we have a workaround for customers who require interfacing with Company X. It's a little complicated, but we do most of the work. All that's required is that you output your reports using a PDF creator. There are a number on the market that will work. Adobe Acrobat is a good option, but there are some free versions that work just as well. Windows 7 comes with a built-in*

*PDF creator. You can download a printer driver that looks like a printer, but actually prints out a PDF...*

Ugh. This is a horrible rabbit hole that is going nowhere. Rabbit holes come in all forms. They are a result of too much information in the mind of the speaker and an inability to control nervous energy. The speaker has so much they want to say and never enough time to say it all, so they start presenting again during the Q&A. It's a problem. Again, planning the Q&A in advance will help eliminate rabbit holes.

The main problem with rabbit holes is that they rarely, if ever, improve your story. In the example above, the presenter raised several issues that could potentially *derail* a sale and may have nothing to do with the question being asked.

## Good Questions vs. Bad Questions

The difference between a good question and a bad question is important. A good question is one that makes you and your team and your idea and your company look good. A good question strengthens the argument you are trying to make. For BlipNut.com, a good question might be, "Can job seekers use BlipNut.com so they know when employers are looking at their application?"

A bad question, on the other hand, is one that makes you and your company look bad. For

BlipNut.com, a bad question might be, "Don't most URL shortners go out of business because the cost of server space far outpaces the potential for revenue?" See the difference?

The reason I point this out is because it's not uncommon to hear an inexperienced presenter say, "Good question!" every time a question is asked. When you say, "Good question!" you are rewarding the person who asked it. Don't *reward* people who are making you look bad! You should answer their question, but you should not go out of your way to make them feel good about asking it! This is a subtle point, but discussions can become hostile when the wrong people are encouraged to participate.

## Hostility

In some cases an audience member might be downright hostile. This is more common than you might think. It seems that some people have their guard up when someone else is trying to persuade them. They may be confrontational as a defense mechanism, or sometimes they just like to tear others down. They may preface their question with, "I'm just playing the devil's advocate…." If they say this, you are probably dealing with a hostile individual.

I once heard about a pitch for a chain of beauty stores in Russia. An audience member said, "Aren't most women in Russia fat and homely? Why would they care about a cosmetics store?" This kind of question can spark rage in a presenter. I wasn't there when that question was asked, but later the presenter and I came up with this answer to add to her list of 50/50:

> *During the Cold War, most images coming out of Russia were drab and depressing. This has created an international perception that people in Russia don't care how they look. However, nothing could be further from the truth. Russian women take great pride in their appearance. In fact, because of this perception, the market is wide open for a chain of stores.*

This is a good answer to a hostile question.

It's easy for a question like this to trigger an emotional response from the presenter. I was once pitching a marketing technology service for the veterinary market when an attorney in the audience pooh-poohed the whole idea, saying that it was too complicated to work. My blood boiled. Who did she think she was? I invested over a year of my life in the project and the bulk of my life savings. I had spoken to hundreds of vets about the product. Did she really think she was so much smarter than me that she could just dump on my idea?

The only way to move forward is to bury your emotions deep down, keep smiling and address the question or comment in the best light.

In hindsight I should have been more open to her message—she was right, my program *was* too complicated!

## Get Out of Jail Free Card

No matter what the question is, you can always play your Get Out of Jail Free card. To do this, simply say, "I don't know, but I can get back to you with the answer."

By saying this, you free yourself from the responsibility of answering the question and can avoid a bad scene. It's a great way to cut off a hostile audience member or discourage a line of bad questions. It's a wonderful thing.

However, be smart about how you use the Get Out of Jail Free card. Using it once is OK, use it twice and you're probably fine, but use it too much and you start to look like you have no clue what you are even talking about. The Get Out of Jail Free card is more about dealing with people and less about getting out of tough questions, but use it as you see fit. It is my gift to you.

## Awkward Silences

Sometimes there is a weird silence after your presentation is done and before people start asking questions. If this goes on too long, someone might break into applause, which normally signifies the end of the presentation.

This will kill your chances of neatly launching into a meaningful Q&A.

As I mentioned before, you can avoid this by finding a friendly audience member and planting them with a question that makes you look good. Tell them to ask the question if nobody else asks a question within 10-20 seconds after the end of the presentation.

For BlipNut.com I might plant someone to ask, "Can you set up a Blip with multiple email addresses at one time?" This softball question breaks the ice and gives me the opportunity to expound upon a nice feature that I may not have covered during the presentation. I've used this technique many times with great success. It doesn't even matter if the audience knows the question was a plant; it's not meant to be deceitful, it's meant to get the conversation started on the right tone.

Similarly, you can use your audience plant to clap or laugh at certain times during the presentation. For instance, you might mention that one of your team members recently won an award for some great thing. Your audience may not know if they should clap. In fact, they may be wondering to themselves if clapping is appropriate. If you tell your plant to be sure to clap when you say something, the rest of the audience will join in. This will raise the energy level in the room and make your presentation more exciting.

Plants aren't usually members of your

team. They are usually friends, existing customers or other allies. I recently did a presentation for a large audience at one of my client companies; I asked one of them to be sure to clap when I showed a certain photo. He did, everyone clapped and it was very natural. It would have been awkward to ask someone I didn't know, but he and I had the kind of relationship where I didn't mind asking and he knew it would improve the reception of the message.

Pitch Ninjas are aware that the post-presentation discussion is just as important as the presentation itself and deserves the same level of attention. A little planning and discussion goes a long way toward avoiding the landmines that could hurt your chances of persuading the audience to do what you want them to do.

Chapter Nine:

# Zones During Discussion

During the Q&A and discussion you should still stick to the Zone Program. Remember, the zones provide something to do besides getting sucked in by Magnetic South Pole. Responding to questions from Magnetic South Pole is just as bad as doing your presentation from there.

You will likely end your presentation in the excitement zone; stay here when the Q&A starts. If you ended in the intimacy zone, take a step back into the excitement zone. Your team should join you here.

You and your team should stand together ready to answer questions. Make sure you are still smiling as much as possible; you don't want to look like deer in the headlights.

## Intimacy Zone

When someone asks your team a question, the team leader should immediately step towards them into the intimacy zone. This is one of your best opportunities to make a personal connection, so make it count!

Make gentle eye contact and listen intently to what they are saying. Do not interrupt! It is extremely common for presenters to hear a little piece of a question or comment and think they know the rest and interrupt the person talking. This is rude and you will appear to be a rude person if you interrupt. In fact, before you answer you should take a moment to ponder what they asked. A five-second pause should suffice.

If the question is complicated, it is OK to repeat it back to them to make sure you know what they are saying. At this point you will have to decide who on the team is going to answer. Your entire team should know this because they have planned in advance. The right person to answer the question should step forward. Let's pretend it's you.

If they are asking a bad question or making a hostile comment, you can address them directly. Remember, do not say, "Thank you," or, "Good question." Just answer their question in your normal, front-of-the-room voice the best you can (hopefully from a premeditated answer). When you are done answering, back up into the excitement zone and wait for the next question.

## Excitement Zone

You will stay in the intimacy zone to answer bad questions, but good questions—those that make you look good—you will want to answer in the excitement zone. When the person asking finishes talking and you have clarified the question if necessary, take a few steps back into the excitement zone and *repeat the question* in your back-of-the-room voice and be sure to smile.

Now that the whole room is engaged, you can say, "Good question!" and proceed with your answer. You want to make a little fanfare to amp up the room.

The key difference is the nonverbal feedback you are giving the person asking the question. You want to *reward* people who ask questions that forward your agenda and you do not want to reward those people who don't. You're not *punishing* people who as bad questions, you're just not *rewarding* them.

Good questions are springboards for you and your team to continue the momentum you have built in the room and keep the energy levels high. If you get a string of bad questions, your energy level will drop in the room. During your 50/50 planning you should brainstorm ways to "spin" your tough questions to your benefit. If you can find an angle, you can present this answer as you back into the excitement zone.

## Information Zone

Occasionally you will get a question that requires you to go back to a slide or pull up a slide from an appendix material you brought. When this happens, you will have to bring up the slide and present it in the information zone.

If you are responding to a good question, you should *spring back* into the information zone and enthusiastically go over the material. However, if it's not a good question, *do not* use the information zone. Stay in the intimacy zone and present from there.

Presenting a complicated slide from the intimacy zone is nearly impossible to do well. This is OK; remember, you are not trying to encourage the asker to ask any more tough questions, so make the answer tough to digest. Not pointing out critical information will confuse the asker and make him feel bad about asking.

You are still being polite and direct, but by not presenting from the information zone you are engaging *Pitch Ninja Super Powers.*

Your super power is the subtle application of pressure on the asker. Nobody will know what you are doing, but it will feel uncomfortable for the asker. Don't worry, you will not alienate them; as long as you give a logical answer, they will be satisfied. You can get them excited again when you get some good questions. They might even ask one!

Stick to the Zone Program for every phase of the presentation. It will make sure that you are always maximizing your impact on the audience.

Chapter Ten:

# Nailing It

Practice makes perfect and presentations are no exception. Practicing and rehearsing are essential. The Zone Program will make sure you are practicing the right things.

To get the most from your practice sessions, try to recreate the actual room layout you will be using for your actual presentation. It's OK to ask the client or prospect about the room. If possible, you can go visit to make sure you understand everything.

It's important to get the entire team together for a least a few practice runs of your presentation. You can always practice on your own, and you should, but the teamwork is much more productive. You can also take the opportunity to snap a couple of team photos for your introduction slides.

Make sure that you make time during your practice sessions to actually practice. It's really easy to get sidetracked by the slides themselves and spend the whole time nitpicking about words and images.

## What to Practice

Your team should be helping to make sure that you are all applying the Zone Program to your presentation. This means they need to watch for body movement through the zones, arm movements and gestures, facial expressions (especially smiling) and itsy-bitsy spider motions.

Be *hardcore* about the application of Pitch Ninja techniques. If your presentation doesn't pop during rehearsal, it certainly won't pop in front of a live audience.

Over-emphasize *everything* during practice. When people are nervous, they tend to dampen their enthusiasm when they talk. This is why Magnetic South Pole exists in the first place.

## Pitch Gems

One trick to getting the right elements into the pitch is to be on the lookout for gems. A gem is something that you do during practice that is initially intended as a joke or even outright *mockery* of the process. Yes, you may find yourself openly mocking the Zone Program because of its structure or other deep-set emotional issues that you formed as a child. Whatever the cause, my instinct is to rejoice in the creativity rather than curse the creator.

I was once coaching a client on a pitch and one of the slides was about data analysis features of the software that allow the user to "drill down" into the information. As a joke, he pretended to be twisting a giant drill into the floor. Everyone laughed at the Pitch Ninja's expense. "Yes!" I shouted, "That is great!" This motion, as corny as it sounds, was a *fantastic* way to emphasize the drill-down message. He was embarrassed at the prospect of doing it live, but did so at the encouragement of his teammates and it went over well with the client. A joke like this is always appropriate, and laughing ups the energy level in the room. These guys pitch multimillion-dollar deals; sometimes the deals are over a billion dollars. Everything goes—don't hold back. Remember, you can't *bore* them into buying.

You and your team should keep an eye out for gems like this and find a way to incorporate them into your presentation. You won't regret it.

## Not Your Personality

Sometimes a client or a student will come up to me and tell me that the Pitch Ninja skills don't feel right. They tell me that the skills may be fine for someone with an outgoing, gregarious personality, but they are reserved introverts that aren't comfortable in front of a crowd. To them I say this: *so am I.*

I'm not a naturally outgoing person. I tend

to keep to myself and don't always know what to say. I knew, however, that these personality traits were going to get in the way of my success in business so I created the Zone Program to help me overcome my own shyness and nervousness when it came to presenting.

By having something to do while you present other than standing in one place, I think you will find, like I did, that you can channel your nervous energy into a presentation that is exciting and engaging.

Above all, I hope the Pitch Ninja skills will give you confidence and poise at your next presentation.

## Getting Help from Mike

I've tried to provide a complete description of how to be a Pitch Ninja in this book. That being said, I can help you and your company by being your personal Pitch Ninja coach. I love doing it and want you to be my client.

Normally what I do with clients is provide coaching in day-long chunks. The first thing I like to do is a live Pitch Ninja-style presentation that covers the main concepts in this book. This lays the foundation for the rest of the sessions and lets people see real-life examples of the concepts. I go over the zones and the non-verbal aspects and all that stuff.

Next, I coach individuals and teams for their presentations. During these sessions we break down their actual presentations and rehearse everything from what to say and where to stand to the subtleties of itsy-bitsy spider motions.

I've coached lots of people to become Pitch Ninjas, ranging from student companies pitching investors to huge companies trying to cinch multimillion-dollar deals. I've had people tell me time and time again that my coaching was the best sales training experience they ever had—which is nothing short of my goal.

One of the most common things my clients tell me is that they get great feedback on the presentations they do. *Their* clients tell them how great their presentations are. When you're a Pitch Ninja, people notice.

Please don't hesitate to contact me at Mike@Pitch.Ninja, and I will do *whatever* I can to make sure you and your team become the best Pitch Ninjas possible. I wish you nothing but the best in your pitching and your career!

### Hire Mike

To learn more about hiring me to help coach you, visit PitchNinja.com or scan the code.

## Talk to Mike

Please feel free to reach out to me with any questions, comments or concerns. Or, as I promised before, if this wasn't the best pitching advice you have ever received, I will happily refund your money.

| | |
|---|---|
| Email: | Mike@Pitch.Ninja |
| Phone: | (773) 426-6353 |
| Twitter: | @MikeMoyer |
| Facebook: | facebook.com/mikedmoyer |
| LinkedIn: | linkedin.com/in/mikemoyer/ |
| Website: | Pitch.Ninja or PitchNinja.com |
| | MikeMoyer.com |

## Free Upgrades

From time to time I may release updated versions of Pitch Ninja that incorporate new ideas and feedback from my readers. As a purchaser of this book, you are eligible for free PDF upgrades when they are available.

### *Free E-Upgrades for Life*
To register for free upgrades of Pitch Ninja for life, visit **Pitch.Ninja/free-upgrades** or scan the code.

*Enter the code "ipitchem"*

# Leave a Review

***Pitch Ninja on Amazon.com***
If you liked Pitch Ninja, please leave a review on Amazon.com. I would really appreciate it! Scan the code to link to the review page.

*The End*

**Special thanks** to the individuals who provided important, early feedback that helped make me make *Pitch Ninja* better!

Bob Brutvan
Derick Chen
Ian Langman
Jackee Schwartz

# About the Author

**Mike Moyer** discovered he was a Pitch Ninja when the teams he coached for business plan competitions seemed to always win and his clients closed bigger and bigger deals.

A professional entrepreneur, he has started companies from scratch, joined startup companies, helped others start companies, raised millions of dollars of startup capital and helped sell startup companies.

He has worked in a variety of industries ranging from vacuum cleaners to motorhome chassis to fine wine.

Mike has an Master of Science in Integrated Marketing Communications from Northwestern University and an Master of Business Administration from the University of Chicago. He teaches entrepreneurship at both universities.

He lives in Lake Forest, Illinois, with his wife, three kids and the Lizard of Oz.

## Other Books by Mike Moyer

Now that you are finished with this book, you might want to take a look at some of Mike's other books, including:

## The Virtual Dojo Series

Pitch Ninja is part of a series of three books that helps people master environment-specific communication scenarios that are outside the normal situations we find ourselves in every day. The three unique scenarios covered in the series are presentations (this book), trade shows and job searches. The other two books are:

- *Trade Show Samurai: The Four Core Arts for Capturing Leads*
- *Job Jitsu: An Employment Guide for the New Reality*

## Slicing Pie Series

Entrepreneurs all over the world have discovered the benefits of Grunt Funds, a perfectly fair way of dividing up equity in early-stage companies. Slicing Pie provides detailed instructions on how to make sure each person in a startup company gets what they deserve—no more and no less.

Books include:

- *Slicing Pie: Funding Your Company Without Funds*
- *Get Them Gators: A Primer on the Power of Dynamic Equity Splits for Potential Investors, Partners and Employees*
- *Pie Slicer Handbook*

## Other Books

Mike has also written books for high school and college students, including:

- *How to Make Colleges Want You: Insider Secrets for Tipping the Admissions Odds in Your Favor*
- *Business Basics*
- *ACI: Career Basics: the Insurance Industry*

## Buy Mike's Books

To access Mike's books, visit PitchNinja.com and click on Books or scan the code.

Made in the USA
San Bernardino, CA
25 February 2016